THE
BARRIER
BETWEEN

THE COLLECTOR SERIES BOOK 2

STACEY MARIE BROWN

Stacey Marie Brown

ALSO BY STACEY MARIE BROWN

Contemporary Romance

Buried Alive

Blinded Love Series
Shattered Love (#1)
Pezzi di me (Shattered Love)—Italian
Broken Love (#2)
Twisted Love (#3)

The Unlucky Ones
(Má Sorte—Portuguese)

Royal Watch Series
Royal Watch (#1)
Royal Command (#2)

Smug Bastard

Paranormal Romance

Darkness Series
Darkness of Light (#1)
(L'oscurita Della Luce—Italian)
Fire in the Darkness (#2)
Beast in the Darkness (An Elighan Dragen Novelette)
Dwellers of Darkness (#3)
Blood Beyond Darkness (#4)
West (A Darkness Series Novel)

Collector Series
City in Embers (#1)
The Barrier Between (#2)
Across the Divide (#3)
From Burning Ashes (#4)

Lightness Saga
The Crown of Light (#1)
Lightness Falling (#2)
The Fall of the King (#3)
Rise from the Embers (#4)

A Winterland Tale
Descending into Madness (#1)
Ascending from Madness (#2)
Beauty in Her Madness (#3)
Beast in His Madness (#4)

Savage Lands Series
Savage Lands (#1)
Wild Lands (#2)
Dead Lands (#3)
Bad Lands (#4)

To a monkey-sprite and his goat.

Stacey Marie Brown

ONE

Run.

Sweat dripped down my spine, soaking my top. Adrenaline pumped through my veins, escalating the panic already contracting my heart. My lungs ached as I desperately sucked in the thin air spinning around my head. The high altitude altered my equilibrium, and I stumbled.

A large hand shot out and caught me, keeping me from plummeting to the ground. The six-foot-three male Viking next to me seemed immune to the vertigo which twisted my head and stomach. But I had no time to be sick. "I'm okay."

Ryker looked skeptically at me before letting go and increasing the pace. Our boots hit the unevenly paved road in tempo, tearing through the streets packed with tourists. It felt like we were in an old game of pinball, bouncing from body to body. The bag against my hip thumped in rhythm with my steps. Sharp chirps told me Sprig was awake and not having a good time in there. I was pretty sure I heard him swear when he crashed into the video camera and my *Art of War* book with which he also shared his space.

"You now stopping..." a policeman cried out in broken English. After eight times in Spanish, he was trying to see if we would respond to what he thought was our native language. He could have screamed out in Swahili; it wasn't going to stop us. No matter what country I was in, running for my life and freedom was becoming my norm and priority.

"This way." Ryker grabbed my elbow and yanked me down a narrow lane. Colorful woolen bags, blankets, and ponchos hung from racks lining the merchants' row. It didn't take me long to figure out where we were in Peru, South America. Images of Machu Picchu covered every T-shirt, postcard, and coffee cup with nauseating abundance. And Aguas Calientes was the village nearest the ancient ruins. It was an area I dreamed about visiting for a long time but not running from the local police.

With another jerk on my elbow, Ryker swerved us around a group with precision, pushing past the sightseers enjoying their day shopping for trinkets. The late afternoon sun exacerbated the moisture clinging to the steep rainforest mountain ravine surrounding the village. Humidity soaked beneath my jacket, leggings, and heavy boots. Less than an hour ago it had been morning and cold.

In Seattle.

Only this morning we had been in the Pacific Northwest, and I had been a normal girl. Okay, not normal, but now I was some freak science experiment running around in South America.

And how did we find ourselves in a remote village in Peru?

Me.

Because an extreme fae-caused electrical storm last month transferred Ryker's powers to me, I now had the ability to jump wherever I wanted in a split second. The problem was I didn't have the *whenever* down and not the precise wherever. None of it worked at my beck and call, which would really be handy right now.

"Fucking bartender," Ryker grumbled. "He had to call the cops on us."

Not sure I blamed him. We magically appeared out of thin air and crashed into his pool table. Think I would have freaked out too.

I was curious what claims he would make against us. We didn't break anything, except for the case of beer he had dropped when he saw us appear. We weren't going to stop and ask the cops.

"*Alto*," another policeman shouted out. I glanced over my shoulder. Four of them trailed close behind us, working their way through the crowds.

Shit.

Warmth buzzed through my muscles, an odd feeling I had begun to experience recently. My body wanted to jump.

"Ryker." I wrapped my fingers around his hand. He looked over his shoulder and saw something in my expression.

Pressing his lips together, he gave a quick nod. "Think of somewhere safe."

I relaxed into the humming sensation, trying to think of a sheltered location. Funny when I needed to think of one, nothing came. It wasn't like I had a ton of places I considered safe. Seattle was the only home I ever knew, and it certainly didn't make me feel secure.

Jump, Zoey! I yelled at myself. Nothing happened.

"Dammit," I swore under my breath.

The cop yelled at us again, progressing closer.

A growl came from Ryker, frustration clenching his mouth. A nerve danced along the edge. He ducked into a backstreet, pulling me with him, and slipped us through a maze of alleyways. Clothes hung from webs of cords tied across the back alleys.

"In there!" He pointed at a tall woven basket holding laundry, tucked inside an open entrance to someone's house.

"Are you kidding?"

The nerve along his jawline twitched again. Without ceremony he picked me up and shoved me down in the container, slamming the lid over me.

"Feeling very Indiana Jones right now." I curled down at the bottom.

"Stay there and be quiet," he grumbled, and then I heard his footsteps retreat.

"You okay, Sprig?" I whispered, moving the bag so I didn't squash him.

"Not talking to you right now," the little monkey mumbled through my bag. I patted it in response.

The sound of feet clomping down the cobblestone froze me in place.

"*A dónde fueron?*" One of the men asked where we had gone. His feet moved closer to the basket.

Keep going. Move along. Nobody here. I felt like I was trying to perform a Jedi mind trick on them. If I could ever get the damn fae powers to work, now would be a good time.

"Check every basket, bin, or corner," another cop ordered in Spanish. The accent was different here than the Spanish I had studied, but I could grasp the basic meaning.

I felt a hand hit the top of my hamper. My stomach sank. They would find me in a matter of seconds. Light came into the space as the top lifted up.

Don't see me. You don't see me, I repeated over and over in my head.

A dark-haired, older, heavyset man peered down, his dark eyes rolling over the insides of the basket. Our eyes connected. Sweat prickled down my spine and air halted in my lungs.

His mouth dipped open to speak, his brows furrowed. The lid crashed back down on me. "Nothing in there," he stated and moved away.

A river of relief rushed through me. My head fell back, and my eyes closed as I took a deep breath of air.

Holy shit! It worked.

This was a good and a bad thing. The stronger Ryker's powers became in me, the more they might not revert to him. His chances of getting them back were getting slimmer and slimmer. If we didn't find someone soon who could help us, Ryker would lose them forever.

In the last month, my life had turned a complete one-eighty. I'd been a Collector, hunting and capturing fae. I had a sister, a home, and a man I loved. I had also despised fae, but now?

The top of the basket came up, the rays of light blinding me to everything except two electric white-blue eyes staring at me.

Ryker...

His solid hands came down, curling under my arms, helping me stand. He was gasp worthy, either out of fear or attraction. I still hadn't decided. His face was striking and distinct, with defined cheekbones and a strong jawline. A dark blond scruffy beard covered his lower face, highlighting his full lips. A few scars ran through both eyebrows, setting off his white unnerving eyes. Tight braids lined either side of his head, his hair left loose on top, almost like a Mohawk. He was in jeans, a T-shirt, and heavy combat boots. With a battle axe strapped to his back, he seemed to have stepped off a Viking movie set.

He was sexy, commanding, and dangerous. I bit down on my bottom lip, uneasy with his close proximity. We both had started out despising the other. Slowly over the month, it grew into tolerance, then to understanding, now to respect. I glanced away as he helped me out of the basket.

A line dented the space between his eyebrows. "You used glamour?"

I nodded, straightening out my clothes, peeling off the jacket and hoodie, and tying them around my waist. The tank top underneath was soaked with sweat, but the slight breeze felt good as it brushed my damp skin. "I didn't think it would work, but I kept repeating, *Don't see me,* in my head."

"Is this the first time you've done that?"

Yes was on my lips, but something triggered a memory of trying to escape Garrett and his men one night at the Red Cross shelter. He was Vadik's leader and muscle and wanted nothing more than to catch us and take the Stone of Destiny back to Vadik, an extremely powerful, dangerous, and wealthy man. That night one of the fae walked right by me and asked another man if he had seen me. At the time I chalked it up to luck and ran for it. Looking back I could see there was only one way I could have gotten out of the situation. I wouldn't have gotten away so easily if it hadn't been for glamour. I shook my head, my loose ponytail flicking over my bare shoulders.

Ryker nodded, seeming to know the answer. "It was far too commanding for it to be your first time. The cop was intent on seeing you, but you still blocked him. Not newbie stuff." He frowned again.

"I'm sorry."

He jerked his head over to me. "Why are you apologizing?"

"Because I know what it means." I placed my hands on my hips, glancing at the ground.

"We don't have time for this. We need to get out of here." He spun around, heading back the way we came. "Don't apologize for something you can't control." He was angry. I could see the muscles in his shoulders drawn close to his ears. The frustration wasn't at me but the situation. Still, I felt awful. If I could open my chest, take his powers out, and hand them over to him, I would. I didn't want them. And it was even worse knowing at any moment I could die, and I would take them from him for good. We were working against an invisible clock.

As I tracked Ryker's figure down the path, Sprig's voice rose out of my bag.

"Please, no more running. You're lucky we haven't eaten in a while or your bag would smell really different right now. And why the hell is it so hot?"

His head popped up and took in the scene around him. "What in sprite-nuggets? Where are we now?"

TWO

Life in Seattle was uncertain after the electrical storm, but it had been easy finding a place to stay as so many left the city to escape. Death and destruction made it a free-for-all, and squatters right became law.

Aguas Calientes was a town near Machu Picchu. I had investigated this area, being strangely drawn to the mystery and beauty of the "Lost City of the Incas." South America had always been at the top of my list to visit, and Machu Picchu was the place I wanted to see the most.

The small town was full of tourists taking up the limited hostels, B&Bs, and hotels. The locals fed off sightseers by selling trinkets, offering "authentic" guided tours, lodging, and food. The town was financed from the tourism industry, and the persistence of the residents wanting to make a living off it was only intensified by the remote location. The town lay in a deep gorge below the ruins. It was fundamentally an island, cut off from all roads and fenced by stone cliffs, a towering cloud forest, and two rushing rivers.

My dream for a long time had involved moving to South America with Daniel and Lexie to open a day camp for orphans and disabled kids. Now I was here, but neither Lexie nor Daniel would ever be.

We crossed over a bridge to the other side of town where we found more local inhabitants, though even here you couldn't get away from the infestation of B&Bs and rooms for rent to vacationers.

It was one of these places where Ryker stopped when he spotted a room-for-rent sign. We had no money, but with two thieves who held glamour, we easily persuaded the clerk into giving us the room. He was short and on the skinny side with the dark hair, eyes, and deep tanned skin of a local.

"We will pay him when we get money," I whispered to Ryker as we walked up the two flights of stairs.

He sighed but nodded. "Let's deal with one thing at a time."

I was a survivor, always had been. I used to steal, fight, and cheat to get what I needed. Growing up in foster care could take away the right and wrong of things. When you had no consistent home and little food, you did what you needed to survive. Most people would stick their noses up at me, but they had no idea what it was like. To imagine it was far different from living it. But being a part of the Department of Molecular Genetics, DMG, and having Daniel and Lexie in my life changed me a lot.

I tried to put my dark past behind me and become a new person, a respectful person. But when so many of us ended back on the streets after the destruction of Seattle, I realized the girl I had once been was not as hidden as I thought. She came out with a roar, almost killing another girl in a street fight. It terrified me.

Ryker was the one who said I had to learn to accept all sides of myself, even the dark twisted parts. I learned early to play a part, be what people wanted, to keep myself in compartments, even with Daniel. I didn't want him to know much about the "real" me, but in the short time I'd known Ryker, he had seen it all.

Still, I didn't like stealing from people who were doing their best to get by. If I were going to rob or not pay, it would be from the uber-wealthy.

"*Aquí lo tienes.*" *Here it is.* The landlord unlocked the room and moved to the side so we could step in. "I rent it by the week or month. Whatever you decide, I need the money up front."

It was a compact room, with worn, creaky floors. A small, pointless rug sat at the foot of the bed too dingy to see its original colors. The walls were painted in a cream, chipping and peeling in the corners. Sheer white curtains covered two large windows which looked onto the street below. A wooden table and two chairs were stationed in front of them. One tall dresser sat between the bathroom door and a closet. A miniature refrigerator stood next to the table, an old TV sat on top of it, with a desk fan set on the TV. The center of the room was filled with a queen-size bed.

One bed.

I ignored the thought and walked over to the restroom. We had shared a bed many nights, but the last time was different. It was uncomfortable and tense, and it took me a long time to fall asleep. I peered into the bathroom. It had an old claw tub with a clear plastic hanging curtain, a pedestal sink, and toilet. Simple, but efficient.

"We'll take it," Ryker spoke in Spanish to the clerk.

He nodded. "There is also a community bathroom at the end of the hall. No kitchen, but there is a hotplate in your closet."

Of course. Where else would you keep a hotplate?

"I'm Diego, and I live in the first apartment on the main level if you need me," he said to us in Spanish, dropping the keys on the table before shutting the door. I hadn't seen Ryker glamour him, but I knew Diego wouldn't have left without payment.

We both stood in silence for a moment. We were finally safe. For the moment anyway. Exhaustion pressed down on my shoulders, lowering me into the chair at the table. Everything I discovered in the past few hours crept into my head.

"Soooo, what's for lunch?" Sprig jutted his head out of my bag.

"It's past lunch here." I unlooped the bag from my neck and set him on the table.

He crawled out, squatting back on his hindquarters and looked at me with his huge brown eyes. "Then dinner?" His little face tilted to the side as he clasped his hands together in a hopeful plea. His long tail curled around his feet.

"Sprig," Ryker warned, crossing his arms.

"What? I am hungry. You know how cranky I get if I don't eat."

I put my head in my hands. The video of Daniel came flooding back in my head.

Experiment.

Dying.

"Sprig, shut up." Ryker lowered himself on the bed, lying back.

"But it smells like churros." He sniffed the air. "I loooovvee churros."

Tears filled my eyes, and I quickly looked at the floor.

"Sprig!" Ryker bellowed from the bed.

"What?"

"I said shut up," he growled.

Sprig huffed and was about to turn his back to the Viking when he saw my face. "Wait. You cry?"

I had been crying a lot lately... for me, but only one person so far had seen me do it. The man across from me.

"What don't you understand about shutting up?" Ryker sat up, glaring at Sprig. Ryker's face was so severe even I scooted back in my chair. He never stopped being intimidating, but I could see past it—most of the time. Right now he was back to being terrifying. He could make a sumo wrestler cower in the corner with one look.

"I was merely asking." Sprig crossed his arms in a huff, twisting away from Ryker. "Asshat," he mumbled under his breath.

I swiveled in my seat to address Sprig. "Let's say you are not the only experiment in this room."

"What? They dissected you too?"

"Not exactly. They created me. From scratch," I explained. "Unfortunately, I came with a defect. One that will kill me."

It was strange to say it out loud, but it was true. At

any moment my mind and body could decide it had enough. It had been only hours earlier I learned Daniel Holt Senior, under Dr. Rapava's orders, created me in a lab.

"A seer egg and sperm from a donor were cooked in a tube and then mixed in a dish to produce stronger seer babies. But then something went wrong and the babies were born with a fault in their makeup. My makeup." I swallowed, feeling the truth swell my tongue.

Daniel said most of the babies died right away, but a handful who did survive past their teens, including me, were slowly dying from this flaw. DMG had known about it and ignored the results and Dr. Holt's objections. Dr. Rapava, who ran the DMG, would stop at nothing to produce a massive seer army to combat the threat of fae. Seers could see fae aura and were not fooled by their glamour, making them the perfect defense against a fae attack.

Like true experiments, the DMG sent the survivors out to be raised in different conditions to see the diverse effects on the subjects. Some were raised by families, some grew up knowing what they were, and some were tossed in an orphanage to deal with a harder life. I was the latter. Then I was bounced from foster home to foster home in some of the most sickening situations and conditions. I grew up hard, cold, and fucked up. Lexie, my foster sister, was the only one to save me from turning into a full-blown criminal.

Sprig stared at me, his mouth hanging open.

"Sprig?"

"Holyy buunnyy faarrttss!" He stretched out each syllable in utter shock. "Turtle dumplings! Are you kidding me right now, *Bhean*?" He plopped back again on his legs. "Sprite crumpets. I thought they messed me up."

The reason Spriggan-Galchobhar looked like a cute little monkey was also thanks to DMG. He was once a sprite living in the Otherworld till one of my kind caught him and took their collection back to the lab. There Dr. Rapava dissected and experimented on him, creating the specimen in front of me: a sprite who would never be accepted by his kind again, and a monkey who could never fit in with other primates.

An outsider.

Like me. Like Ryker.

Ryker was one of the few Wanderers known to exist. A novelty. This made me wonder why Dr. Rapava had been willing to kill him earlier in the morning. Not that he's easy to kill. Not with manmade weapons. But Collectors carry fae-designed guns. When we did need to shoot and not merely stun, it was to kill.

"Why didn't you tell me? Now I feel awful." Sprig flung his arms dramatically.

"Yeah, because this is all about you, furball." Ryker snorted.

"Funny you bring it up."

"Bring what up?" Ryker shifted and rolled over on his side.

"Me," Sprig chirped, pointing to himself. "Because *I am* really hungry."

If the little guy did it on purpose or not, it was the exact thing I needed—to smile.

"Come on." I waved to Sprig, stretching my legs. "My stomach is requiring churros now."

"No." Ryker shook his head, standing. "We need to keep under the radar for a day or two. At least in the daytime."

"I doubt they're still looking for us." I waved him off. "Plus, I can glamour them again."

It was like watching a tiger prepare to strike. Muscles along his shoulders, neck, and jaw coiled, convulsing under his skin. "I don't want you to use *my* powers." His words came out low and forced. "The more you use them, the more they will adapt to you."

I shifted back, leaning against the table. "Right," I whispered.

"I'll get us basics. Water, food." He rubbed at the top of his head, his hair glistening with sweat. "When I return, we can come up with a game plan on what to do from here. But I think it will be a good idea to stay put for a while."

I agreed.

"Seattle is far too dangerous. You are not only being hunted by DMG. If Marcello lived and you step foot back there, his gang wants you dead also. And we don't need to mention the people after me."

The gang, particularly Marcello himself, if he survived after Ryker bashed him in the head, would be pursuing Ryker more ruthlessly than me. Garrett was also out searching for Ryker. The list of people who wanted us dead or at least semi-alive was getting longer and longer.

"You want anything else?"

"Clothes." I pulled at the thick, dirty leggings I was wearing. From my reading, I remembered the rainy season was just ending here, but the fresh rain from earlier hung in the air, holding in the humidity. The cotton contained my body heat, torturing the already suffocating skin. "Toothbrush. And batteries."

I touched my bag; the video camera still lay snugly at the bottom. It was my last link to Daniel, to my origins, and the insane truth of my existence.

Ryker nodded and walked to the door.

"Wait!" Sprig leaped off the table toward Ryker.

"No. No way." Ryker shook his head.

Sprig tugged on the bottom of his jeans. "Come on, Viking man. Let me come. My tummy can't wait till you come back. If I don't eat now, I swear I will keel over and die."

Ryker tilted his head as if to say, *hopefully.*

I snorted. "Ryker, please take him. Otherwise he's going to drive me insane. Right now I need five minutes in a bath. Alone."

I never had a mother, but damn if I didn't sound like one.

Ryker glanced at the ceiling and blinked several times. "Fine. You can come, but you have to stay quiet. And follow the roof lines."

Sprig twittered excitedly, scaled Ryker's body, and plunked himself on his shoulder. "Why would I need to follow you on the roofs when I got the tallest perch here? You tower over everyone in this village."

Ryker's gaze met mine; his face contorted with murderous rage.

"Come on, it's not like having a monkey on your shoulder is strange here." I shrugged, not hiding the smile on my face. Most people here probably wouldn't notice the tiny monkey sitting on the large Viking's shoulder. Sprig was no more than five inches tall. Five inches of soft dark brown fur, a sweet, little, round face, and huge brown eyes.

The Wanderer grumbled to himself and grabbed for the doorknob. "Lock this after me." He slipped through and shut it behind him.

Stillness in the vacated room filled my ears, rubbing at my nerves. The distant activity from the streets below echoed up. I let out a heavy sigh. I thought I wanted peace and quiet and a moment to myself, but it was when my nightmares came to torment me. Day or night, it didn't matter. Alone meant time with my thoughts, with cruel memories.

THREE

I tugged the stretchy cotton off each leg. Sweat, blood, and dirt compelled them to stick to my legs with an adhesive grip.

The hot water was heaven on my skin. Even though cool water would have felt good, it had been too long since I had an actual hot shower. Even at the Red Cross, it had been no more than lukewarm. A month of grime washed down the drain and pooled around my feet before draining slowly out the bathtub.

There was no shampoo or conditioner, but I could wash my hair later. I needed to get the first layer of filth off me. A bar of soap sat on the side of the tub, and I tore into it, scrubbing fiercely at my skin. Bruises still coated my ribs, and cuts and scars glared at me in reminders of what I had been through. Only last night I had still been held captive by Marcello's gang and forced to be in a street fight against another gang in a battle for dominance and territory.

Ryker had saved me, from the gang and from myself.

Dried blood I hadn't cleaned off the night before

stained my skin. Was it my blood or the girl's I almost killed? With one more strike to her face I could have made her choke on her own blood. Suddenly my mind morphed the girl's face into Lexie's. My legs gave out, and I hit the bottom of the tub with a thud.

"Zoey, stop." Lexie coughed, blood gurgling out of her mouth. "Don't let me die."

Razors slashed inside my gut. Lexie, my light, was gone. Burned to death in a house fire as a result of the electrical storm caused by fae more than a month ago. This lightning storm destroyed Seattle, taking it to its knees, and turning it to embers. Electricity destroyed the area for a hundred-mile radius surrounding the Emerald City. Thousands were killed, among them my former caretaker Joanna and... Lexie. I wasn't there to save her. The outline of her wheelchair engulfed in flames haunted my every thought. I often woke screaming.

Lexie came into my life when I was thirteen. She was only four. A tiny thing, whose legs would never be able to hold her. From the moment she entered the house, I knew my life would never be the same. I was her mother, friend, and protector. I was the one who took her to school, doctors' appointments, got her lunch and dinner, paid for her special shower equipment, and held her when she had a nightmare. I learned early she watched what I did more than listened to me. So, if I wanted her to get out of the hellhole we were living in, I had to be better. I stopped hanging out with my so-called friends, stopped drinking and having random sex with guys for affection. I studied hard and got into college. The only thing I didn't give up was my street fighting. It brought in too much money. And to be honest, I loved it. It was my release for all the pent-up anger and resentment I felt. The years of abuse and struggle disappeared for the one night. I could be this other person, the Avenging Angel. People respected and feared her. Like an actor on stage, I could let go of me and lose myself in a character.

I tilted my head back and let the water run down my face. My muscles unknotted, and my arms drooped. It took me a while to finish the shower, but I finally climbed out. The heat of the room dried my skin almost instantly. I grabbed a towel and wrapped it around me, glancing at the lump of cloth on the floor. "Right." I had nothing to get into, and there was no way my clean body was going to put those hot grubby items back on. "Towel it is."

I glanced in the mirror. My heart-shaped face was bruised and cut. Long tangles of wet chestnut brown hair hung past my breasts. My green eyes held too much sadness and anger for someone my age. I ran my fingers through my snarls. My cheeks were flushed from the shower. I didn't look like a girl who was dying.

Dying...

A speck of an idea slowly began to form, then with a whoosh it flourished, crashing into my mind.

"Of course. Why didn't I think of this before?" I expressed to the image in the mirror.

The reason I worked at DMG was to collect fae so the doctors could experiment on them. We were trying to save and cure humans of cancer and other defects with fae blood. I carried Ryker's powers. They were adapting to me. Why wouldn't it work on my defect?

For the first time since learning the news of my possible demise, optimism ballooned in my heart. Spinning around I reached excitedly for the door and yanked it open.

A large mass stood on the other side, filling the doorframe. His fist in the air.

"Ahhhhh!" A scream tore from my throat as I jumped back. My towel slipped from my clasp and dropped to the floor. "Shit!"

Ryker stood frozen in place. His eyes taking me in.

"Shit," I repeated again and scrambled to grab my towel. My hands fumbled, and it took me several tries to successfully clutch the towel and draw it in front of me.

Ryker never broke eye contact with my figure, causing my cheeks to flush hotter.

"What the hell, Ryker?" I wrapped the towel back around me, tucking it tightly in front. "Warn a girl."

"I was about to knock."

"You might be the size of Goliath, but, damn, you sneak up like a ninja."

He leaned against the doorjamb, his eyes wandering brazenly down my form again. It stirred every nerve in my body. I glanced away, nibbling on my bottom lip.

"Fae aren't embarrassed of the naked form."

My eyes narrowed and flashed to him. "And how would you know? You were raised by humans."

He smiled, and half his lip hitched up on one side. "Instinct, I guess. It's in my nature."

"Is it in your nature to ogle?" I marched to him, meaning it as a challenge, but the moment I moved—

mistake. I went into the "danger" zone between people, where it was no longer a safe conversational space, but intimate.

He kept his casual pose, but I saw him tense. His eyes went across the edge of my towel, and my skin prickled along my uncovered shoulders. Even being covered with a towel, he made me feel completely exposed.

His teeth tugged at his bottom lip, dampening it as he continued to watch me. Air departed from the room, forcing my lungs to work harder for air. Heat, not caused by the temperature outside, ignited my veins.

Neither of us moved, though somehow we were getting closer and closer.

Was this really going to happen? Was he going to kiss me?

I could feel his breath flutter, skating down my neck and tickling the space between my breasts. *Oh, Jesus...*

"Churros!" A cry came from the window. Ryker and I jerked back. "We have churros, *Bhean*." Sprig bounced in the window and onto the table. "So good. I've already had two."

A low growl arose from Ryker. "I am going to kill him," he mumbled under his breath and turned, walking away.

Me too.

"Thank you." I smiled tightly at Sprig.

His mouth was already full of the pastry, and sugar clung to his fur and nose. He shook the paper bag at me while reaching for another piece. An automatic smile lit up my face. It was impossible to be upset with him. I went over and rubbed his head, his huge eyes peered at me with adoration. Being petted while eating a sugary pastry equaled a happy monkey.

I reached into the bag and pulled out a warm doughy concoction. The sweet bread melted on my tongue. "Oh my God, it's good." My lids closed.

"I know. Right, *Bhean*?" Sprig garbled over the huge bite in his mouth. I was convinced he first started calling me Bhean, *woman* in Gaelic, because he couldn't remember my name. Now I couldn't imagine him calling me anything else—a term of endearment.

Ryker tipped over a shopping bag onto the bed. "I got some clothes for you, some shampoo, and a toothbrush." A tank top, shirt, pair of flip-flops, shorts, pants, toothpaste and brush, water, juice, and other items lay on the bed, even underwear and a sports bra lay in the pile.

"Wow." I picked up the shorts. Damn! He even got my size right. "How did you know?"

He frowned, ignoring my question. "I figured anything else you need you can get yourself later."

I put the shorts back down. "We need to figure out how we can repay these people. Obviously, I'm not above stealing, but not here." I did have a moral code. Deep down, but it was there.

"I agree."

My eyebrows hit my hairline.

"What?" Ryker slanted his head. "Yes, even this deplorable fae has standards."

"You are not deplorable."

He looked over at me. "Really? And when did your opinion change?"

I couldn't recall the moment when it changed, but it

had.

"If you're terrible, then I'm even worse." I swallowed. "Have you beaten someone almost to death for the sheer pleasure of it?"

His gaze fixed on me for a long time. "Yes."

For some reason his declaration rushed relief into my sour stomach. I wasn't alone. Letting out a strangled laugh, I said, "We both are really fucked up."

He snorted. "Yeah, *we* are."

My heart noticed the way he said "we."

A snore came from the table. I glanced over at Sprig, who was sprawled on the table, covered in sugar. He hugged an uneaten churro to his chest.

Another freak in our messed-up family.

Ryker took a shower while I changed into the clothes he bought: cotton army green shorts and a black tank top. While I waited for him, I stuffed myself with churros and orange juice. I tried to ignore when he came out in only a towel, grabbing his clothes before heading back in. I shoved my head into a pillow and groaned. A man's body should not look like his.

I teased him by calling him a Viking, but there had to be some truth to it. Dark blond hair, white-blue eyes, broad shoulders, and toned arms only magnified his massive frame, creating an image of a Norse god coming to life. His fair skin was covered with tattoos, rolling down his arms, back, and ass. The man's rear end was a godsend itself. And I couldn't deny my fingers wanting to trail down the ripples of his abs.

Ryker's presence demanded impure thoughts to

enter my brain. This was typical fae—their appearance was the perfect bait to lure in humans. Fae were the perfect hunters, and humans would willingly take the bait. They used humans and consumed us for our life essence, whether it was through dreams, sins, or sex. For me, it was different.

I knew what they were and how they used us. I appreciated their amazing physiques and faces but never saw past the true form or the fae killer inside.

Until now.

"Are you all right?" Ryker's voice came from behind me.

No. "Yes." I turned over and leaned against the headboard.

He moved toward the bed and changed his mind halfway, grabbing a chair. He turned it backward and sat, folding his arms over the top. He wore army green pants with a bunch of loops and pockets down the sides and a navy blue T-shirt. He definitely bought our stuff at the same store. It was odd picturing him leafing through the women's department, picking out my clothes.

His hair was wet and slicked back. The braids on the side of his head glistened with water. His beard was trimmed to a sexy scruff. He naturally had an enticing scent, but now it mixed with fresh soap. I took in a deep breath, almost tasting the stormy sweet fae smell on my tongue.

"We need a game plan," he said.

Right. Business. I sat straighter, folding my legs.

"A lot has happened the last couple of days..."

"Yeah. You could say that." I nodded. I sensed him

waiting for me to continue.

"Zoey..."

"Wait." I held up my hand. "I had a thought earlier."

"Uh-oh."

"Funny." I rolled my eyes and continued. "I know you don't want to hear this, but your fae powers might be the one thing keeping me alive."

"What do you mean?" Ryker shifted on the chair.

"DMG's first notion wasn't all bad. Fae DNA saves human lives from diseases and the flaws in our own genetic material. I don't know for sure, but what if your powers have corrected my defect?"

He leaned back, pondering the idea. "You think it's possible?"

"Yeah, maybe. It's a stretch, but I've stopped getting headaches since I acquired your magic."

Ryker's head went back as he looked at the ceiling, his hand scratching at his scruff. "What about the nosebleeds?"

"Yeah." My shoulders sank. "I didn't say it was definite. Merely a possibility."

"Let's hope there is a reason for all this." Skepticism sounded in his voice, but a glint of hope hinted in his expression. We stayed quiet. Confidence in my theory dwindled from when I first thought of it. I wanted to believe I was right, but many things were telling me not to grip too hard.

Ryker cleared his throat. "Our game plan... what do you first want to deal with?"

"No matter what, you need to get your powers back. That is first... finding someone who can transfer your magic to you."

"Not merely someone. A man named Regnus."

"Regnus?"

"He's someone I met through Amara. He is an extremely powerful shaman, the head of the shaman leaders. If there is a person who could help us, it would be him."

Amara's name always drove daggers of reality back into my heart. Reminding me our little bubble here was temporary.

"He won't be easy to find. He's a major recluse and uses spells to hide from people."

"But we'll do it." I nodded. "We will track down this Regnus, get your powers back, and then I will go after DMG. Even if it's my last act, I will take them—"

"Zoey." He tried again to cut me off.

"I need to try and stop DMG from creating more like me. More babies who will die because the one thing Daniel begged I keep from them, those files with the information needed to take DMG down, are now in *their* hands. I failed him."

Ryker scrubbed roughly at his chin.

"He has done so much for me. He risked his life for me and for what?" I shook my head, my teeth scraped over my bottom lip. "Without him in my life, I am not sure what would have happened to me. He saved me from myself. Brought me out of the gutter."

"No." Ryker shifted in his chair, irritation twisting the tendons in his jaw and neck. "*You* saved yourself."

"You don't understand. Daniel—"

Ryker slammed his hand into the chair. "Daniel,

Daniel, Daniel... he's not a fucking saint, Zoey."

Warmth pooled in my chest like gasoline. A single spark would ignite the rage building.

"Yes," I seethed through my teeth. "I know he's not. But Daniel asked two things of me, and I botched one of them. What he's done for me... I can't... I won't let him down again."

"Jesus! Shut up about Daniel." Ryker pushed out of the chair, his head rolling back in annoyance. "Daniel is dead. You can't disappoint him or please him. He's gone, Zoey. You need to deal with it."

Spark. Flame.

Fury zapped through me and stood me on my feet. "Excuse me?"

"Daniel. Is. *Dead*."

"Fuck you!"

A strange emotion twitched over Ryker's features but disappeared too quickly for me to comprehend it.

"How dare you? You have no right to tell me what to do or how to feel," I spat. "You know nothing about him or *me*." I stabbed at my chest.

"I don't know you? Are you kidding me?" Ryker's mocking laugh chafed my nerves, pushing my head up higher in annoyance. "I'm probably the *only* one who does."

Stormy rage thundered in my chest. A part of me knew he was speaking the truth, but it only drove my fury higher.

"You think Daniel knew the *real* you?" He pushed the chair out of his way, moving closer to me. "Did you ever tell him how you enjoyed the taste of blood? Or you liked fighting because it made you feel alive? It was the only time you finally felt you were living your own life. Not for Lexie. Not for Daniel. But for yourself." He loomed over me, his eyes growing iridescent. I wanted to retreat, to hide in the corner—away from the truth. But I held my ground, looking up as he towered over me. "Did he know stealing gives you a high? It's your way of saying fuck you to all the people who have better lives than you? And when you fight, deep down you feel you are getting back at the man who raped and abused you?" Breath caught in my throat. "It's your way to control. Of taking back the times you couldn't protect yourself. You still don't think I know you? I can go on." He threw up his arms. "Let's start with your abandonment issu—"

"Stop!" I put my hands over my ears, fighting back the rage billowing inside. Ryker saw every one of my deepest fears I thought I kept tightly tucked away from view.

It pissed me off.

I dropped my arms, stepping up closer to him. "Like you should talk? You hate humans because the only family you ever loved, and who probably ever loved you, died. And you couldn't save them. Instead of 'dealing with it' you turned your anger around on them. Blamed them! When in actuality you hate yourself for not being able to protect them. Your family, your little sister burned to death in a fire, and you couldn't help them. They *died*. Why don't *you* deal with it?" I leaned forward, my hands on my hips.

His mouth clenched so hard, muscles along his jaw jumped and twitched.

"Do you want me to start on *your* abandonment issues? What about Amara?" I jabbed my fingers into his chest. It rose and fell deeply, pushing back into my fingers. I knew I was going too far, but I couldn't seem to stop myself. "If you *really* loved someone, there is nothing you wouldn't do to get them back. *Nothing.* Even give up the stone. But I don't think you actually love her. She's easy and convenient. You can't love anyone. You won't let yourself."

Even I cringed at my words. Way, way too far. Ryker's face turned a deep purple, and he took a step back. I waited for the tornado of fury to erupt my way. Instead, he turned away from me and went back to the table. He leaned over it and took in a heavy gulp of air.

"So, we're agreed. We start searching for the shaman tomorrow?" he said evenly.

I blinked several times before responding. The switch in emotion and subject unnerved me. "Yes."

"Great." He picked up the chair and slammed it in its place at the table, waking Sprig.

"Is the leprechaun dancing on the bar again?" Sprig mumbled, raising his head. "Huh? What?"

Ryker stomped toward the door.

"Where are you going?" I suddenly didn't want him to go. How could we fight so horribly, and I still wanted him to stay next to me?

"Out."

"Okay. Where?"

He yanked open the door. "I don't have to answer to you, *human.*" He slammed the door, shaking the room.

"Is Daddy mad again?" Sprig sat up, already munching on a cold churro.

I stared at the door. "Looks like it."

"Do we know why this time?"

Yes. "Nope," I answered instead.

"Okay, so normal."

"Yep."

FOUR

After a while, I couldn't handle sitting another moment in a room dripping with angry words, throttling me. Sprig and I departed the cramped space. I needed to get my mind off Ryker and our fight. I also wanted to do a little more "shopping" for some clothes and personal items guys didn't think about.

Walking through the village at a slower pace, tourists seeped into the already clogged streets of people and stands. Lines of cramped stalls carried duplicates of heavy llama wool blankets and trinkets at exorbitant prices. I read that despite its magnificent setting, surrounded by tall peaks and magical dense forest, Aguas Calientes was not the most pleasant town. The influx of tourism caused the settlement to grow fast and callous. Maybe it was why I was attracted to it, why I felt a connection to the place. It was a lot like me. But the thing I didn't like was the locals looked at the tourists only as dollar signs, shoving knickknacks in their faces as they walked by.

A train whistle blew, and the rumble of a departing train permeated the air, signaling the last train to Machu Picchu for the day. I wandered along the main square, finding a tiny store with the items I needed. There were few places to shop not filled with tourist crap. I focused hard as I gathered the items I needed and watched the storekeeper place them in a bag.

"You know me well, so put it on my tab, under Ms. Daniels," I stated, keeping my eyes locked on his. The merchant put my stuff in the bag and waved to me as I left. Another place on our list to repay. We needed to get money. In Seattle, not paying for things had been a matter of survival. Here it felt wrong.

Sprig stayed on my shoulder and no one batted an eye. I didn't want to use my glamour unless I had to. Then Sprig forced my hand into the "had to" category.

"Mango chips!" Sprig pointed, bouncing up and down on my arm. "They're dipped in honey. Look!"

"Shhh!" I held my finger over my lips.

"*Bhean*, they are dipped. In. Honey."

"Shush!"

A guy about my age stood near with a group of students. "Dude... her monkey *talked*. I swear to God."

"Sure, Brandon." A blond-haired guy smacked his friend's shoulder. "How many tequila shots did you have?" He stumbled into a group of girls, his attention going to them.

"No, seriously." Brandon pointed at me. "Your monkey fucking talked. I heard it." Fear was laced so deep in Brandon's eyes I could see him sobering up right in front of me.

Hell.

Pulling from deep down and striking at the power inside me, I felt it warm my insides. I caught his eyes and focused hard. *You did not see or hear anything. You will not remember me or the monkey,* I said in my head, filled with determination. The magic wrapped around my bones, pumping adrenaline higher. It felt good.

The kid blinked, shook his head, and ran past me, catching up with his friend, who had attached himself to the girls. "Thanks for ditching me," Brandon called after him.

"You're the drunk ass claiming to hear talking monkeys." The blond-haired guy draped his arm around his buddy's shoulder.

"What the hell are you talking about?" Brandon's voice tapered off as the crowd engulfed them.

My gaze darted angrily to Sprig.

"Sorry," he whispered in my ear.

"Do not do it again."

"Okay, but can we still get the mangos? Pleeeeaaasse?" His soft voice tickled my ear.

I laughed, rubbing my temples. "Yeah."

When we got back, Ryker was still gone. The sun dipped below the steep mountains, illuminating the window in rich reds, deep purples, and vibrant oranges, which exploded across the room.

I placed Sprig's sleeping form in the top chest drawer on a hand towel for cushion. I plucked Pam, Sprig's stuffed goat/friend, from my bag and laid her next to him. He'd wake up later for dinner, then dessert, then a late snack before actually going down for the night. Seriously, I was caring for an infant... or a hobbit. Could be either.

With a mango chip between my lips, I settled on the

bed with Daniel's *Art of War* book and the video camera. It was going to be difficult to watch again, but I needed to know every single detail Daniel laid out for me. It would help me with the DMG since they now possessed the actual files. But honestly, I was watching it for me. To see Daniel again, to feel the comfort he always provided me. I also wanted to see if he left me any more clues in the book. Starting off easy, I opened it. I needed to build up before seeing Daniel. Scouring each page, I searched for any code I hadn't seen before, but nothing new emerged on the pages. On my third time through, I realized I was avoiding watching the video.

"Come on, Zoey. It's not going to get any easier," I muttered, drawing my knees to my chest and grabbing the video camera. My finger hovered over the play button about to push down.

Bam!

A loud crack hit the door, causing me to jump. The fear was immediate and tapped straight into my adrenaline. *Did DMG find us? Did Garrett?*

Thump.

Another crash banged at the door. I leaped off the bed, my gaze searching for a knife or weapon. Dammit. Ryker had them all. Trained to work in unforeseen conditions, I assessed the room quickly. My heart thumped as the handle of the door twisted. It was locked, but if someone wanted in, they would find a way.

My eyes landed on my choice of weapon. I ripped the cord from the wall, plucking off the lampshade. It was heavy and made of a cheap metal. It wasn't the best, but it would have to do.

Thud.

I tiptoed toward the door, the lamp in one hand. Rising up on my toes, I peered through the peephole. An eyeball stared back into mine. A garbled cry broke from my mouth, and I scrambled away from the door, tripping over myself.

"Leeett mee inn," a voice slurred out. "Soey... lettt mmmee inn." A knock rattled the door, then the sound of fabric sliding against the wood frame.

"Ryker?" I inched back toward the door.

"Swoey?" A childlike chuckle followed my distorted name.

My hand went to my chest, feeling the panic ebb from my muscles. "Fuck, Ryker." I plopped the lamp on the table and went over and unlocked the door. "You scared me."

As the door swung open, half of Ryker's body fell into the room. He lay on the floor, giggling. I gaped at him. Normally, I would never put giggling and Ryker in the same sentence.

"Wow. You are drunk."

A huge smile engulfed his face, making him appear younger. "I. Am."

I couldn't stop the amused smile tugging at my own lips. Red nosed and cheeked, chuckling like a schoolboy, he was adorable. And he made it impossible to be mad at him. I wanted to crawl on him and curl up on his chest like a kitten.

"Come on, let's get you to bed." I squatted, grabbing his arms.

"Will you be there?" he slurred.

"Since it's where I sleep, I'm going to go with yes."

"Then we should have sex," Ryker mumbled as I helped him sit up.

"What?"

He blinked. "What?"

"What did you say?"

"Huh?" His attention already on something else. I sighed and pulled on his arms, trying to get him to his feet.

"Come on." I draped his arm over my shoulder.

He stopped and turned to me, grabbing my arms. "I was mad, b-but you were right." He licked his lips, focusing on staying vertical. "I tell you something..." He stumbled over to the table, holding himself up.

"What?" I encouraged.

"It hit me..." But his attention fluttered away, his thought drifting off.

"What?" I was going to strangle him.

"I need sleep." Ryker moved past me and crashed onto the bed fully clothed. It was only a moment before his snores matched Sprig's.

Awesome.

His face turned toward me, his cheeks ruddy with drink. His large muscular arms grabbed for a pillow, tucking it under his head. The fabric strained against the bulging masses. His tall body stretched on the comforter, his feet slightly hanging over the end of the bed. His pert ass, which taunted me from day one, curved so shapely under his pants it was hard not to pet it.

Damn you, Wanderer, and your perky behind.

Shaking my head, I walked to the end of the bed, unlacing his boots. After several times trying to remove them, I finally straddled his leg and yanked. The first boot slipped off, and I braced for the smell of stinky feet, but only a sweet, woodsy smell wafted up my nose.

"Seriously?" I stuck the boot to my face. "You fae don't even have the decency to have smelly feet? Come on, there's got to be something wrong with you." This was bordering on insult. I knew after a month of running, sweating, and continual wear, my boots reeked. But not Ryker; his smelled like Keebler cookies.

I stepped over his other leg. This boot took more effort, but finally it began to slide off. My finger fumbled with the weight of the shoe, and it fell to the floor. A muted thud reverberated off the rug. The boot was a lot heavier than the other.

"What the hell?" I bent, my knees hitting the small rug. I picked up the boot, feeling its mass.

The boot looked like an ordinary biker boot, but something niggled at my intuition, suggesting there might be more to this shoe. I pressed at the sides and yanked on the heel, but nothing gave. The heel was usually where spies kept things. My nails crawled at the edge of the heel padding inside. It lifted up like it had done it many times.

I glanced over my shoulder at the man on the bed. Confirming he was asleep, I continued with my task. My heart accelerated, sensing I was going to find something under the insole. The liner peeled away.

"Oh hell."

Inside the cavern of the heel, I found a smooth stone, the size of a toddler's fist. It appeared unassuming, like an ordinary rock you'd collect on a beach in the northwest.

I knew better. The night Ryker told me about it came flooding back.

"Have you ever heard of the Stone of Destiny? In fae mythology there are four magical artifacts: a sword, spear, cauldron, and the stone. Lia Fáil, Stone of Destiny. Most think they are merely legends because no one has seen any of these objects for centuries. Legends stem from truth. These items are so powerful, they can destroy the world if put in the wrong hands."

The Stone of Destiny. This was the most powerful chunk of rock in the Otherworld.

And the fucker had it with him the whole time.

Ryker stirred, hitching up one of his legs. My focus was glued to him with painful anxiety until I saw his breath even out in a measured cadence. I exhaled and turned back to the boot. Tipping it, the stone rolled out into my palm.

The moment it touched my skin, energy slammed into me, throwing me back onto the wooden floor. Images of fae kings and gods winning every battle and ruling vast lands passed through my mind. Then the stone was lost and found its way into the human world. Here men and women came into contact with it, changing their destinies by receiving their every whim and desire. Happiness, success, dreams were granted. Generations and generations of the stone's life passed through my head like flashes of light. The power of the stone pulsed and throbbed in my hand, telling me it could give me everything I'd ever wanted. The potential appeared unfathomable.

"Like what?" a curious voice asked. It was my voice, from deep inside. In my vision I saw myself freeing all the test subjects in DMG before it blew up. Behind me cops were arresting Dr. Rapava.

"You can stop it, Zoey. Honor Daniel's *dying* wish," the stone spoke, deep and smooth, every word soaked with ancient knowledge. "I can take all your pain away. No one will ever be able to hurt you again. I can help you show them the errors of their ways."

Another image flashed in my head: The feel of a cold steel weapon weighing heavy in my hand. On his knees before me was the man who raped me. His face contorted in terror as tears spilled down his face. "Please, no," he cried. Vehemence, rage, and disgust shook my body seeing his face, those hands and lips that had touched my skin many nights. But this time I was in control. He was at my mercy now. I had shot him before, but only in the leg. This time it was straight in the heart.

"I am sorry. Please forgive me," he begged, holding his arms by his ears in surrender.

"Fuck you." My finger pulled back and the gun boomed.

The moment the bullet left the weapon, the scene around me vanished. The man who had hurt me for so long evaporated into nothing.

"We can help others. Together." A picture of me opening the doors to a research hospital for kids born with disabilities. A different flash showed orphaned kids running to me at a center where they could find safety, acceptance, and love.

"And you will never experience hunger or loneliness again."

More visions of me, wealthy, in my backyard, with a large pool and patio. Me, draped in a long black silky off-the-shoulder wrap, with huge Armani sunglasses. A group of friends surrounding me at a table, food and cocktails lavishly adorning the tabletop in fancy china bowls. Kids running all over in the background, splashing in the pool—mine. Ones I've adopted.

"Zoey, where are the buns? Your father is about to barbeque the hamburgers." A beautiful older woman resembling me stood on the steps, her hand shading her eyes. A large breathtaking colonial-style ranch house stretched behind her. A handsome gray-haired man joined her on the step, holding a tray of burgers. His green eyes, the exact same as mine, twinkle in the daylight. My parents.

Arms came around my waist. "Hey." Daniel's voice emerged from behind me. His lips skated over my shoulder. "Missed you."

"Zoey, watch this." Lexie waved at me from the diving board, her long, lean legs strong and defined, as she did a cannonball into the pool.

My heart exploded with happiness. Yes. This is what I want. What I've dreamed for years. She was the reason I made it out of my teens and got into college. Without Lexie I probably would have dissolved into the street life, quit school, and got money by stealing and street fighting till I was caught. I wanted more for her than the life we had lived. To get out of the mobile home park and far away from Joanna.

I looked over my shoulder at the man I loved. Daniel's image wavered. "Every day your feelings grow more uncertain. Your heart is divided. Perhaps this is what you truly want." The stone's alluring words spoke into my head. Daniel faded out, and the man behind me turned into Ryker. His white eyes flashed as he grinned mischievously at me. He kissed the curve of my neck. "I can see your true most desires... even if you don't want to see them," the stone spoke again.

No. I love Daniel.

Ryker's image dissolved back into Daniel.

"I love you," Daniel mumbled into my ear.

"Good thing." My hands go to my belly, feeling the small bump. *Our* baby. When I look back, Daniel's eyes are white. A few scars run through his eyebrows.

"Don't tell me this is not what you always dreamed of, Zoey," the stone whispered.

Family, love, security, and a home—this is everything I've always wanted but never had. The stone tapped those secret desires. Dreams I'd never told anyone.

"And it is only the beginning. You can have so much more, Zoey. All you have to say is yes," the stone murmured, enticing me to see and want more. "Say yes."

"Ye—"

"Zoey!" My name sounded from far away. I looked around for the owner of the voice. "Zoey, let go!"

"No, Zoey. All you have to do is say you want this and all your pain and loss will be forgotten. You can have them back. Your sister. Daniel," the stone cajoled.

"Say it. Yes."

"Y—"

A sharp sting sliced across my face, snapping me out of the dream.

The stone didn't say anything, but I could feel it trying to hold me there, flashing more images of Lexie, of parents I never had. Of Daniel and me making love before the figure above me shifted to Ryker. Rocking deep into me, producing a moan to burst from my mouth. Intense desire gripping me, making me tremble.

"Zoey, wake up." My body shook, breaking me of the stone's hold. "Open your hand."

My lids fluttered open. Ryker stood over me. His hands clasped my arms, shaking me.

"Drop it," he demanded. His face contorted with wrath.

It took all my strength to uncurl my hand. Finally, the stone slipped from my grip and landed on the rug.

Air shot back into my chest, and I bolted into a sitting position with the need to fill my lungs. Ryker bent down, his arm sliding around my back and helping me stay upright.

"You all right?"

"Holy shit," I mumbled, glancing at the innocent-looking stone on the floor.

Ryker's brows furrowed, and the crease between his eyes deepened. He sat back on his butt, rubbing his forehead. "What were you doing, Zoey?"

"I was being nice and pulling off your boots so you could sleep."

His frown inched down farther.

"Soooo." I pulled my knees to me. "That's the Stone of Destiny."

"Yeah."

"You've had it this whole time?"

He nodded. "Though I lead people to believe I hid it; I didn't trust it wouldn't be discovered by some spell or something. At least if I have it, I can protect it."

"Is that what it does? Show people their deepest desires?"

"The stone is alive and extremely smart. It is quick to figure out what makes you tick, finds your weakness, and controls you that way. It is exceptionally powerful and can give you what you want, but it comes at a cost. Eventually, the stone will overpower you and drain you into a shell, before it moves on to someone else and consumes their life essence." He scowled at the rock. "It's hard to resist. Most can't fight it, and once you accept its offer, there's no way out. It binds you."

"What?" I cried out. "I was a breath away from saying yes to it."

Ryker leaned back on his arms. "What did it show you?"

The vision of his chin on my shoulder, him kissing my neck, flashed back. His form over me, our bodies intertwined, rocking with passion.

The blush to my cheeks was automatic, and I glanced down into my lap. "I can't tell you."

"You can see why it is so dangerous... if it falls into the wrong hands."

"You lied to me," I said quietly, looking at him. "It was never about the right price or money. You were never going to sell it. You are protecting it from others."

Ryker turned away, licking his bottom lip.

"You're a good guy," I said.

Ryker smirked, his eyes serious as they found mine. "Don't tell anyone."

We matched each other's smile, our eyes locking. I dropped my gaze and focused on my feet. We were quiet for a few moments.

"Now you know my secret. The one thing Vadik will torture and kill you for."

I set my chin on my knees. "He'll have to get in line."

Ryker snorted, his fingers playing with the fringe on the rug.

"I'm sorry. Curiosity killed the cat and all that," I uttered, shifting uncomfortably. "But thank you for saving me. You were out cold. I'm surprised you even got to me in time."

"Thank my bladder."

I motioned to his lower stomach area. "Thank you."

Ryker climbed back on his feet, holding out his hand he helped me up. He stepped back and peeled off his T-shirt.

Uh. My eyes didn't know where to look. In the dream I could feel everything like it was really happening. The feel of his hands, of him inside me, seared my skin and mind.

He leaned down and wrapped the stone with the fabric and dropped it back in his boot.

"It doesn't affect you having it close all the time?" I

questioned.

"No. It's when you touch it, then it will stick its claws in you and pull you in." He tucked the insole of his boot back in tightly. "If there is ever a reason you have to retrieve it again, make sure you have gloves or some kind of barrier. If it even gets a wisp of bare skin, it will take hold of you."

I nodded.

He lined his boots up and pushed them under the bed, then stretched to his full height.

"It feels strange knowing it's there. Like it is goading me to touch it again. What if I can't resist it?" The thought made me nervous.

"It feels like you won't be able to withstand it now because it still has a piece of you. The stone has gotten into your psyche, but after a while it will lessen."

"Speaking from experience?" I turned my head to look at him.

"Yeah." He scratched his chin. "You're the only one who knows its location. I can't express enough the need to keep this secret."

"Amara doesn't know?"

Ryker shook his head. "No. I told her I buried it deep in the wilderness of Mongolia near the China border."

He didn't have much of a choice in telling me, but I felt honored. Even Amara didn't get the truth. My gaze caught his. "I promise your secret is safe with me. You can trust me."

"I do," he said quietly before he strolled around me and disappeared into the bathroom.

FIVE

"What is wrong with you?" Ryker folded his arms, leaning back in the diner chair, staring at me critically.

It's funny... after your brain has images of you having sex with someone, real or not, you can't help but look at them different. For the entire morning I could not look Ryker in the eye. It pissed me off because we were hardly friends, yet this nervousness stirred me, making it hard for me to sit still—like I had restless ass syndrome. Yes, recently there had been a few strange moments between us, but after they passed, we both pretended they never happened. I liked it that way. Now I felt like I was sliding down a steep mountain not able to stop the momentum.

What bothered me most was how all this reminded me of when I first starting falling for Daniel. The giddy torture of my chest clenching and stomach twisting into knots when I saw him. To feel it again, so soon after Daniel's death, made me disgusted with myself and angry at Ryker. It felt like a betrayal to Daniel, especially because Ryker was fae. He and Sprig were shifting my feelings on fae, but it didn't mean my emotions would change overnight.

The images relentlessly played in my mind when he brushed by me this morning getting dressed, sending a flutter of drunken bats through my stomach. Now the sensations wouldn't go away. His naked body on top of mine, feeling his hand slither up my thigh, his lips consuming mine.

"Nothing." I shifted in my chair, staring at the menu in my hand. We had stopped for breakfast at a café called Izel's so Sprig didn't turn into a cannibal and start eating his own arm.

"That. One," a voice whispered from the bag on my lap, before a long finger came up, tapping on the laminated menu.

"Yes. I got it the first ten times you told me."

His finger kept poking at the picture of the crepes drizzled with honey and butter. I knew what I was going to order the first minute we sat down and I spotted the word honey, but the menu was a great distraction.

Ryker's stare still burned into me from across the table. I sighed and set down my menu. "What?"

Ryker sat forward, his elbows on the table. "You're being weird today."

"Weird?" I laughed. "I am a lab experiment. This might be my normal."

"You know what I mean."

I tilted forward, mimicking his posture, placing my elbows on the table. "My weirdness also could be contributed to being taken hostage by a rock last night."

His lids narrowed. "And whose fault was that?"

Mine. "Carrying one of the most powerful objects in

the Otherworld in your boot is *such* a great plan."

"It was until you found it."

"*Bhean?*"

"It's stupid."

"Are you really in a place to judge me?" Ryker leaned farther toward me.

"The only thing I was stupid enough to do was get caught by you," I seethed, irrational anger squeezing my shoulders to my ears.

A nerve jumped along Ryker's jaw. It was his telltale sign he was angry.

Rage boiled between us.

"*Bhean*," Sprig said a little louder.

"What?" I growled at my bag.

Sprig kept his eyes on me as he tapped the menu.

"I. Get. It. Sprig! You want the *fucking* pancakes," I yelled. Silence filled the café, eyes turned to me.

Ryker jumped out of his chair, grabbed me by the arm, and wrenched me to my feet. "I think we need a little time-out," he grumbled and hustled me out the door.

When we stepped outside, I yanked my arm from his hand.

"Fuck, Zoey. You want to completely expose us?" Ryker threw out his arms, stepping into my personal space.

"They'll merely think I'm some crazy kook, talking to my bag. Really not far from the truth." I pressed forward, his face only an inch away from mine. His nostrils flared, neither one of us willing to back down. We stood there, panting with heavy emotion.

His gaze dropped, landing on my mouth. Then he shifted back on his heels, licking his lips, and turned away from me. "Let's start toward the Mandor Waterfalls and work back. There are a lot of fae in the area who might help us find the shaman, Dark and Light. But they will not be easy to find." He cleared his throat. "We need to be on alert. Most won't come out, and if they do, they probably won't be nice."

Ryker turned and stalked off. My feet clung to the ground, not moving.

"I don't get my pancakes this morning, huh?" Sprig stuck his head out of my bag, a huge sigh lowering his shoulders.

I rubbed the top of his head. "Sorry. I'll get you some churros on the way."

He exhaled dramatically again. "Okay, but they aren't the same as honey pancakes."

"I know, buddy." I scratched behind his ear. "And I'm sorry for yelling at you."

Huge dark eyes turned to me, his hand patting mine. "I understand. You're sexually frustrated."

I choked. "What?"

"Do you still have those condoms I gave you?"

"Sprig!"

"I'm a sprite. We sense these things." He shook his finger at me. "It's either you two need to have sex or you're hungry. Lack of food makes me grumpy too... speaking of..."

"Yes, I will get you food." I increased my pace, heading after Ryker. Embarrassment at the truth of his words flushed my entire body.

Please let it be hunger... please.

Sprig slept at the bottom of my bag, stuffed full of churros, papaya, and Inca Kola. The drink was way too sweet for me, but he had downed it, hopped out of my bag, and went crazy with the zoomies, until he passed out mid-climb up a tree, and fell asleep. He was narcoleptic, but sugar triggered episodes faster. Getting a sprite to stop eating sugar was like asking him not to breathe.

Venturing out of town, we followed the train tracks through a valley of trees and flowers that looked like they had been dipped in green, orange, and purple dyes. I had studied and looked on the Internet at pictures of this area, but nothing could describe actually being here. A café, Mama Angelica, across from the entrance of Mandor Gardens, was almost too quaint to be real. Plants wrapped up posts, draping their arbor in vivid blue and purple blooms, and shading patrons from the sun. It was almost too idyllic to eat there.

"Anything?" Ryker scanned the groups of people around.

The entire way I kept a sharp eye out for fae who thrived in gardens and nature, but my seer sight never found an aura to clasp onto. I shook my head.

"Maybe by the water." Ryker headed inside the entrance of the garden.

The ground was wet from the rain overnight, slicking the trail. It was another mile hike to the waterfall, and I got lost in the smells and beauty of the rainforest. Dense green vegetation cascaded down the mountains, carpeting every inch of space. Strange plants sprouted bigger than my head, finding their way to the sun through the thick foliage. Huge banana leaf trees lined the trek, making me feel like I stepped into a prehistoric land.

Ryker noticed I was more into investigating the pretty scenery than searching for fae, but he didn't say anything.

When we reached the waterfall, I couldn't help but sigh. Everything about this place was beautiful. Except the crowd. Several groups of tourists hung around the cascade. Ryker immediately locked up, folding his arms, his expression growing dark. Like me in reverse, his dislike of humans didn't disappear because he could tolerate me.

"Come on." I nodded to a trail leading away from the waterfall. We followed it to an isolated part of the river.

Seeing a perfect spot to sit and relax, I stepped on a stone, glossy with water. My feet slipped from underneath me. "Whoa." Hands came down on my hips, holding me in place. His warm fingers gripped at the bare skin between my pants and top.

I straightened up, regaining my footing, and glanced over my shoulder. "Thank you."

He nodded and let go. I climbed a bigger rock, settled myself down, and placed my bag next to me. Sprig's snores were drowned out by the river, but the bag pulsed with his breathing. I inhaled a deep breath, the soft rush of water flowing down the river, soothing me. The heavy, sweet smells of flowers, fruits, and plants growing around filled my nose. Sunshine trickled through the leaves. A ray fell across my face, and I turned to its warmth. It was cooler by the water, but higher in the forest moisture clung to the earth, heating it.

Feeling a body settled next to me, I opened one lid and looked over at the Viking next to me. He kept his attention on the river, but he knew I was watching him. We sat in silence, listening to the sounds of water and forest.

"I'm sorry about earlier." I hugged my knees to my chest. Ryker ran a hand over the top of his head then rubbed at his beard, not able to settle down. "What's up with you?" He still didn't look over at me when I spoke. "You're the one acting odd now."

A long exhale of air blew from his lips, and he stretched his legs out, leaning back on his elbows. It was still a full minute before he finally spoke. "As you probably know, fae aren't big talkers... at least about feelings or anything." *No shit, really?* "It's seen as a weakness, guaranteeing it will be used against you."

"Doesn't sound much different from how I grew up." I let my folded legs drop, my knee hitting his thigh. Neither of us moved away from the contact.

A slight grin tilted his mouth. "Yeah, strange how different our worlds and experiences are, but we still have a lot in common."

"Unfeeling criminals who like to rob and beat the crap out of people." I smiled, stealing a glance at him. His eyes flickered over me, watching me. My stomach clenched.

When did this happen? When did his gaze start knotting my stomach and halting the air in my lungs? My focus went back to the water.

"You've been through a lot lately." He stared out at

the forest across the way. "If... if you need to talk about it or anythi—"

"No." I cut him off, detaching myself from Sprig's carrier. I rubbed at my shoulder where his weight sat, then let my arms fall to my lap.

Ryker gave a quick nod. "All right."

I watched as my fingers coiled around themselves. I sucked at talking to people, letting them in. The DMG therapist told me it was the way I protected myself from being hurt. If I didn't let anyone in, no one could hurt me. The problem was the two people I actually did let in were dead. My heart was already broken. But not even Lexie or Daniel knew all of my past. Ryker did. At the time I felt secure talking to him. Almost like speaking to a pet. Someone who wouldn't judge or care about what happened to me. Simply listen. Now his presence looped around me like rope. He no longer seemed safe.

We stayed quiet for a long time, but Ryker's shoulders never relaxed. Then his deep voice broke the silence.

"I didn't tell you the complete truth about the day I lost my family. The fire. I didn't go and save my family first like I told you."

"What?" I jerked my head toward him.

"That day... I also lost the woman I was going to marry."

My mouth fell open.

Ryker pulled his knees up; his hand clasped the other wrist, locking his arms around his legs. "Even though the village knew I was different, I'd grown up among humans, and I naïvely thought I could have a normal life. A human one." He stared down at his hands. "Her name was Tanvi. We were quite young and thought ourselves in love. Her father did not approve of our relationship, already seeing what I didn't want to— my life and world was never meant for her. But try telling that to young lovers.

"Her father and mine banned us from seeing each other, but of course this made us even more anxious and careless. She became pregnant..." His Adam's apple bobbed as he swallowed. "This was back in a time when shame in a family would get you killed, but she would not get rid of the baby. She hoped it would get her father to relent and let us marry. It did not." Ryker closed his eyes briefly before continuing. "On the day of the fire, I was out hunting. She was supposed to meet me in the woods. We were going to talk about running away together. But she never came."

"What happened?" I twisted to face Ryker, feeling the dread of where his story was going.

"When I saw the fire and ran back to the village, it was her house I went to first. Her father was standing in front, watching it burn. He turned to me and said, 'She brought shame on this family. I no longer have a daughter because you took something which never was supposed to be yours. You do not belong to this world, Wanderer, and nothing in it belongs to you.'"

"He let his daughter burn to death?"

"Yes." Ryker nodded. "In some cultures, shame is the worst sin. Death is the only way to redeem yourself or your family."

I laid my hand on his arm, understanding his sadness. His eyes darted to my touch, but I didn't pull away. His stare lingered on my hand then slowly rose to my face, causing heat to flush my cheeks. The intensity of his gaze was like a boom in my chest. I quickly pulled my hand away, breaking the contact.

I heard him clear his throat, his focus shifting to the water. "I heard later he had caught her trying to sneak out and locked her in her room. He set the fire."

"What? He started the fire? He wanted his own daughter to burn to death?"

Ryker nodded. "It was only meant to kill her, but he lost control of it. It took the whole village." He rubbed a hand over his face. "Trying to save her was the reason I didn't get to my family in time and why my little sister died. In the end I lost them all."

Including his unborn child. My heart ached for him. Even if it wasn't his fault, he felt every death as though it was. I understood his resistance to humans even more. "I'm sorry."

Ryker's lips pressed together, then he slid off the rock, his feet hitting the riverbank. "Since then, I've lived away from humans. Grown to hate them. I accepted I'm fae and believed humans should not coexist with fae beyond being their energy and food. Even if none of the villagers died that day, they would have eventually. If the baby took after Tanvi, and was human, it would be dead now too."

The thought of Ryker having a child did something inside me. I felt torn between empathy for Ryker's loss and a strange sense of jealousy that he would have had a baby with someone else. This notion didn't sit right with me.

I scooted to the edge of the boulder. I knew human

lives were a blink compared to a fae's, but I wanted nothing more than to change his mind. To show him caring for a human was still worth it.

His demeanor changed. Ryker picked up a rock and threw it into the riverbed. It bounced off another rock and burst into pieces, shattering into dust and coating the top of the water before it washed away. Anger rose off his skin, coiling the muscles in his back. "I was happy with hating humans. Content," Ryker yelled, spinning around to face me. His eyes were full of fury.

I blinked and slid from the rock. "Wait. Why are you mad at me?"

"Because." He shook his head, forcing his heated gaze from me, his voice low. "You changed *everything*." He turned away from me, my hand automatically grabbed his. He stopped but didn't look at me, keeping his head down.

My body felt out of my control as I moved in front of him and reached for his face. He tensed as my fingers slid along his jawline and cupped his cheeks. "Look at me," I whispered. When he did this to me, it centered me.

He resisted, but I didn't move, nor did I ask again. I stood there waiting for him. Finally, his lids flickered up. Our gazes latched on to each other's. There wasn't much I could say. It would not change the past or the fact I was human and would eventually die. Actually, now that I had his attention, I felt at a total loss. I wanted to comfort him, ease his pain, thank him for revealing something so private from his past. Most of all I wanted to kiss him. This impulse was as strong as my fear to do it.

His brow cinched, his hand came up, tucking a strand of hair behind my ear. "Fuck you for screwing everything up," he whispered hoarsely, letting his hand glide down my face.

"And fuck you, Wanderer, for wreaking havoc in mine," I responded in the same breathy tone.

He pulled me in, and my heart dropped to my knees. He tipped his forehead against mine.

"What am I going to do with you?"

Only one response came to my lips, and I swallowed it back. *When the hell did this happen?* It was so gradual I could not really pinpoint a moment, but they were there... feelings.

Dammit. I wanted them to go away.

No, that was the problem; I didn't want them to go away, which made me wish they would.

Emotions between us, or even purely on my side, were pointless and stupid. They could lead nowhere. I didn't want them to. Deep down, we both knew fae and humans didn't belong together. And when I thought about the fact I wanted a *fae* to kiss me... Except he wasn't only fae.

Ryker was the man who put a candle in a bread roll a couple nights ago to celebrate my birthday. Who came back from the dead, fighting everyone in his path to get to me. Who held me when my dreams turned to nightmares.

I stepped away from him, staring at the water trailing between the rocks I was standing on. "Maybe we'll find fae on the way back." So far the day had been a bust.

He cleared his throat and placed his hands on his hips, peering back at the trail. "Yeah, we should get back before it gets dark. The fae who come out at night in these forests are *not* ones we want to run into."

I grabbed Sprig and was up the path before Ryker could even take a step. I was hoping the faster I walked, the quicker I would leave those newfound emotions behind, drowning them in the rushing water.

I should have known once you open a sealed jar, it can never be truly closed again. Feelings and thoughts bled into the cracks and seeped in. Modifying, changing, corroding what had worked perfectly before.

SIX

During the next couple of days Ryker, Sprig, and I went out searching for fae. Ryker said Regnus was not going to be an easy man to find, but finding fae who could help us was also becoming a challenge. After the first day of nothing, I spotted a lot of fae around the area, but mostly mountain trolls, river fairies, and various small shape-shifters. Ryker felt they wouldn't know anything.

On the fourth morning of searching, Ryker was hitting the end of his patience. "Mountain trolls literally live under a rock. Stupid fuckers. But the water fairies *might* be useful."

A laugh burst from my mouth. Of course, Ryker would be interested in talking to them. In my Collector days I had dealt with quite a few of them.

Seattle was almost surrounded by inlets and rivers. Water fairies were the tramps of the fae world. Always horny. They got their energy from the power of the water and the life in it. They were charged and naked all the time, sex was their release. From what I studied, they had to have sex. It took the edge off the enormous amount of magic flooding them daily. They'd go insane if they didn't, and they weren't particular if they did it with humans or fae, though they definitely preferred strong, gorgeous males.

Understandable.

Humans often confused water fairies with succubi or sirens. Succubi needed to live off the energy produced by sex, and from what I read, sirens didn't actually have sex with any of their victims. Their beauty itself would make any man or woman plunge to the bottom of the sea. The sirens lived off the energy of sacrifice, which came from the person's willingness to die.

As we traveled to the upper part of the Rio Aguas Calientes, the water fairies were not hard to find, especially when they caught sight of Ryker. From a distance and with a normal human eye, the water fairies appeared to be locals—men, women, and children—fishing or playing in the water and mixing in seamlessly with the true residents among them. Unless they wanted you to see them in their other form, wanting to ensnare a male traveler passing by.

What I saw were sexy, partially clothed women splashing around in the water. Four women danced around in thigh-deep water, the cream cotton blouses they wore were so tattered and see-through they barely covered their voluptuous breasts, which bobbed around like small toddlers in a bouncy house. Their long brown skirts were thin and slit up the sides, letting you see the outline of their shapely legs. Each one had hair past her waist, full lips, and bright blue-green eyes.

No guy, straight anyway, could resist them. They were a typical cliché for a reason. Perfect bait to lure in their next sex victim, though their victims probably wouldn't consider themselves too much of a victim.

"Gee, I wonder why you were eager to talk to them," I grumbled.

Ryker grinned. "You'd be surprised by what they see and know."

"Amazed." I rolled my eyes.

Ryker and I walked over to them. The women stopped, turning to us. Their eyes went straight to Ryker like he was a deity rising from the water.

"I was hoping you ladies could assist me," Ryker said, low and commanding. He was naturally carnal and imposing, but he was upping the charm.

A tall brunette, legs up to her ears, stepped from the water. She pulled up her skirt to her knees as she stepped onto the bank. "I will assist in anything you want."

"I am hoping you can help me locate a shaman or someone who might know of one." Ryker's eyes trailed over the woman. She brazenly walked right to him, pushing her chest into his. Her hand met his torso and slithered around him as she circled him.

"You are so masculine and virile. Sexy." She purred into his ear. "And primal."

"Thank you." Ryker smiled, making no move to prevent her fingers from exploring his chest and arms. "But I really need information."

The brunette's hand curved over his ass.

A snarl raged in my chest, but I swallowed it back. *Where the hell did that come from? Am I jealous? Oh no... nononono.* I didn't do jealousy. For one thing, I was terrible at it, with a tendency to hit or take the item causing the green-eyed monster to emerge.

"So... do you know of any healers in the area? An

elder, perhaps?" Ryker's voice sounded low and sexier than normal. Besides Amara, Ryker felt the only people who might know of Regnus' whereabouts would be another high-ranking shaman. Or at least someone who could get word to him.

Another water fairy came to his other side, this one had long red wavy hair. Her smooth porcelain skin stood out next to the brunette's olive complexion. "No, but I can help tend to your needs."

I rolled my eyes. *Could they be more of a cliché?*

Ryker glanced over at me, then cleared his throat and stepped away from them. "Thanks anyway."

"Wait. Don't go." Two more dark-haired girls ran to him from the water. "You are far too magnificent to let go. A mind-blowing specimen."

"Seriously?" I threw up my hands.

Ryker's gaze drifted to me, a smirk flickering on his mouth. He was enjoying this. "Just looking for a shaman, ladies. A particular one named Regnus." He took a few steps toward me when all four girls encircled and trapped him.

"I might know of someone," a woman's strong voice rose from the middle of the waterway. A blonde goddess of a woman stepped onto the bank. I almost wanted to cry. *Where the hell did she come from?* It was as if she rose from the depth of the river.

She stood over six feet tall, long, lean giraffe legs hooked out from the slits in her skirt. Her golden locks tumbled down her waist in glistening waves. Her face was so perfectly proportionate, it was almost doll-like. But it was the way she held herself that seized your attention. She embraced a confidence and a cleverness even more than the other girls.

I couldn't have felt tinier, more boring, or more insubstantial, which only made me want to fight her.

"You know where he is?" Ryker pushed through the girls surrounding him. They stepped back, sending Ryker longing stares. The way the blonde woman moved and the response of the other girls to her told me she was their leader.

"I did not say that. I said I *might* know of someone."

"Either you do or you don't. Damn, you fairies love to play games."

"Oh, I think you do, too, Wanderer. Kinky ones. I can feel it in you. I can guarantee you will love playing them with me." She looked him up and down, her eyes undressing him. "Yes, we know who you are. You are a legend among us fae." Other than Amara, this gorgeous, confident woman was one I could picture with Ryker. "Maybe we can work out a deal."

One of his eyebrows went up. "A deal?"

"We help you, and you help us. Scratch each other's backs... and I've got an itch needing attention. If the gossip is true, you are exceptional in that area." She pressed closer to him. She revealed not one ounce of shyness or doubt he would say no to her proposition.

"You've got to be kidding me," I mumbled, my nails digging trenches into my palms.

"What do you say, Wanderer?"

Ryker slid his hand down her face and pulled her body in line with his. His other hand pushed her ass into him so she could feel every part of him. The woman's knees buckled; her eyes widening with desire.

Anger bristled up my neck till I thought my hair was

standing straight.

He grasped her hair and yanked her head back. "I don't make deals." Then he turned away, moving toward me.

"Wait," the blonde yelled. "I can't give you a name, but you need to meet back here at sundown. I know someone you can talk to."

A smile spread over Ryker's face, his eyes on me.

"Tonight then." He didn't even look back as he grabbed my arm and tugged me back on the path.

"Bye," a girl's singsong voice rang out after us.

I yanked out of his grip, adjusting my bag on my hip. Sprig's weight lopsided one end of the carrier.

"What's wrong?" he asked.

"Nothing."

"Really?" One eyebrow cocked up.

"Yes." I flicked my eyes to the side in annoyance. "But I mean, was that necessary?"

"What?"

I crossed my arms and tilted my head back to the women.

"Are you jealous?" Ryker snorted.

"Jealous of gorgeous women with Jessica Rabbit bodies and legs up to their temples? Please..." I kept moving forward, quickly.

"Jessica Rabbit?"

I waved it off. "I guess if you like them dumb as shit." And beautiful and willing to do anything in bed.

Fuck.

I rubbed at my forehead. What man wouldn't prefer a bunch of stunning, eager-to-please vixens?

Double fuck.

"You *are* jealous." He slowed so much I had to stop walking and turn my body to look back.

"No, I am not." The words rushed out of my mouth with force. *I'm not.* But whatever I felt, I did not like it.

"Really? So, you wouldn't care if I took one of them up on their offer? Or maybe all of them at once."

I whirled around, picking up my stride. "Do what you want."

"Zoey."

I ignored him.

I heard his shoes crunch in the dirt as he jogged to me. "Zoey, you know I was only playing them to get what I wanted. I knew they wanted me, and I worked it."

"Jeez. Ego big enough?"

"It's a fact. Water fairies are not the brightest of fae and only want one thing."

"Sounds like a man."

He grasped my arm and stopped me. "Look at me." I turned my head to his. "I don't want any of them. I like women with a bit more depth and stubbornness to them."

So many emotions exploded in my chest, and I glanced away. "Good thing for Amara then," I mumbled.

He didn't respond for a breath before replying, "Yeah."

A deep plum color coated the steep peaks and valleys as we made our way back to the river later that evening.

I was glad Sprig stayed back in the room. The TV worked, although it only showed three channels. One of them was a Spanish soap opera channel.

We handed him a bag of honey roasted cashews, and he didn't even look up when we said goodbye.

Yes, I was using TV as a babysitter. A sitter for my narcoleptic, monkey-sprite who was ADD and had a honey addiction.

I was all right with that.

Ryker's body was tense and on guard, clenching tighter the closer we got. My hand kept reaching for my fae gun, which no longer hung off my belt. I missed it. Though I didn't want to collect fae anymore, I missed the rush the chase had given me. When I quit street fighting, becoming a Collector was a close substitute. I was trained to go in and expect the unexpected. But we went in knowledgeable of the fae we were hunting, the area we were in, and planned exit strategies and backups if we needed.

This was different. We were going in blind and unfamiliar with the area. Ryker and I did a little investigating, and he lent me two of his daggers. But those we were meeting and how many would be there were complete mysteries.

While traveling with Ryker during the last month, I noticed he didn't seem to trust most fae and now seemed apprehensive about this meeting. Another thing we had in common, but we couldn't pass up this chance.

The last bit of sunlight slipped below the horizon, shading everything in a purple hue. There were no streetlights and few buildings out here, intensifying the darkening sky.

Ryker reached over and swung his axe out of the holder. My legs scrambled to keep up with his strides, my boots striking the loose gravel. Flip-flops were never good when you needed to fight or run. He glanced over his shoulder, frowning at my trampling feet.

"What? I've got tiny legs compared to you."

He didn't turn back around, but his free hand found mine and pulled me to him as we walked. "Stay close to me tonight."

I could protect myself, but I also wasn't a fool. Daniel had drilled into me not to let my ego get the better of me. Or do anything stupid because I was trying to prove something. You worked as a team, highlighting each other's strengths. This was Ryker's lead, but I would have his back.

Hopefully, we were simply being paranoid, and it would not come to any kind of altercation. I mean, shamans were healers and usually known to be peaceful, herb-smoking spiritualists. If anything, we should have brought Cheetos.

We stepped off the path where we met with the river fairies earlier. The water was vacant of human or fae. Ryker kept his hand tight around mine but scanned the area continuously.

"She was speaking the truth. It really is you, Wanderer." A man's gruff voice came from the shadows, and a figure moved from behind a tree, followed by a trail of cigarette smoke billowing around his shape. "I thought there was no way the Wanderer would be caught in these parts again. Not after last time."

Last time?

Ryker released my hand and took a slight step in front of me. "And I thought after last time, you'd be long gone, Arlo. Need another reminder?"

The figure wore black jeans and T-shirt, and it took everything I had not to retreat with a gasp. Arlo's face was punctured with deep scars in a zigzag pattern from the middle of his head down his face. The injury puffed up like a long mountain range. Hair no longer grew from where the scar began, leaving a white discolored bald spot on top of his head trailing down to his forehead. His wide-set, beady black eyes glinted in the dark, and his upper jaw didn't seem to line up with the lower one. He was frightening to look at. Not all fae were good looking, and he definitely fell at the far end of the spectrum. He was tall, but Ryker still towered over him, and his frame was thin, though he possessed a power I could not ignore.

"Except you were the one who ran like a coward," Arlo said.

"Coward? I don't think I've ever been called one before." Ryker clenched his axe, his hand strangling the wood. "There were twenty of you and one of me. Didn't feel the outcome was entirely on my side, but I still managed to mess up your pretty face."

Ryker did that?

"What are you doing here, Arlo? Is this revenge?"

"It's been eighty years. You think I would wait this long for payback?" Arlo took another puff of his cigarette and dropped it on the ground, his boot snuffing it out.

Ryker snorted. "Yes."

Arlo shrugged and took a step forward. "In my line of work, you always keep an ear to the ground. Always know what is going on... and I heard you are looking for a shaman, which struck me as odd. Why would you need a shaman? Especially one as powerful as Regnus? But then these astonishing claims floated my way..." Arlo took another casual step over, looking like he was conversing with an old friend. "A rumor you no longer have your magic."

Ryker lifted his chin to the side, where the nerve along his mouth convulsed.

"You can see why I would find this interesting."

Suddenly, I detected more fae around, their glamour skating over my arms. Lots of them. We were going to be ambushed.

"Ryker," I mumbled to him, going on defense.

Only his eyes flicked over to me, and I could see he also sensed them.

"Is this why you have people on the lookout for me?" Ryker said. "And you say this has nothing to do with revenge."

"Maybe a little." Arlo bared his teeth in a sneer. "Water fairies are quite easy to persuade."

I jerked my head around as I felt bodies moving closer around us.

Arlo tilted his head to see me, as if he only just noticed I was there. "I also heard your woman was being held by Vadik."

"Guess you are wrong again." Ryker pushed me farther behind him. It was too late.

Arlo's laugh bounced off the mountains. "Like she

could pass for Amara. The hair kind of gives it away."
Arlo motioned toward me. "A human. Wow. How low
you have sunk. But this only makes the claims seem
more like fact."

"What do you want, Arlo?"

Arlo's lips curled in a smirk. "The stone."

Every muscle clenched across Ryker's back,
stretching his shirt. "I don't have it. Nor would I give it
to you if I did."

Arlo sighed and shook his greasy brown hair. "I was
hoping not to have to play this game with you."

The jolt from the fae moving toward us sent panic
thrumming into me. Heat ignited inside, and I felt the
wind rush in my ears.

Oh hell.

In a blink I was standing in front of Ryker. The
power inside me emerged in a growl, protecting its
owner like a guard dog. I was really going to have to
have a conversation with these abilities because instead
of making me into some cool wolf, I looked more like a
Pomeranian, puffed up and hopping all over.

Ryker's anger crashed into my back. His body
seemed to grow bigger, dwarfing me in his shadow.
The rage wasn't completely directed at me, but I could
feel its impact like a punch in my back. In one
involuntary action, I realized too late I'd showed them
all our cards.

Arlo blinked, shock widened his eyes, then a sly
smile grew on his mouth till it was forced to open in a
hearty laugh. "Gods, this is perfect." He continued to
howl. "Oh, little human, you don't know how happy
you have made me."

Arlo and his men now had proof I contained Ryker's powers. He could no longer play it off as a false rumor. It rendered him vulnerable. To fae it meant death.

A growl erupted from Ryker. He took another step to me, his chest slamming my back. The fury seething in him clawed my neck.

Arlo's chuckle faded into the night air, but a malicious smile took its place. "Is she your bodyguard, Wanderer? Should I call her that now?"

"Leave her out of this," Ryker growled.

"I don't think so." Arlo smirked. "After you give me the stone, you will die and she will become my slave. A man is always on the lookout for a good thief." Slave? Great, another Marcello. Was that all people wanted me for? "Get them!" Arlo's voice called out past us.

Eight men dressed in dark clothing ran out from the shadows, charging Ryker. All had a red bandana tied around their heads. Ryker backed up, and I swiveled, putting my back against his. Most of the men went for the Viking, but a few advanced my way, leering grins on their faces.

The sound of Ryker's axe reverberated off a sword and his body dove forward. He slammed back into me as he retracted and sprang to the side, knocking down several men heading for me. My dagger was an intimate type of weapon and required an assailant to get close. I really needed my gun or a longer sword, but my training never involved those old-fashioned weapons. DMG kept us modern and simple.

As a sword slashed at Ryker's arm, his roar shook my chest. Then he was gone. I whipped around, watching a handful of men barrel into him, taking him down the bank into the river.

Shit.

A hand grasped my shoulder, and I swung around, my fist slamming into my attacker's face.

"Fuck!" The man jumped back, his hand wiping the blood pooling on his mouth. A large mole protruded from his lip near the cut. He looked at his bloody fingers, and a leering smile broke over his face. "Feisty, aren't we?"

He crouched lower, coming for me as another man came up behind. Arlo. *Crap.* Spinning, my blade sliced across Arlo's chest, ripping open his black T-shirt. He stumbled back with a grunt.

"We got ourselves a spirited one here," the mole man voiced. I spun back around as his hand broke across my face in an explosion of pain. Liquid slipped from my nose, and I stumbled to the side. Arlo's arm hooked around my neck, pulling me into him.

"You need to behave, you little bitch," Arlo seethed. Sharp metal scratched against my neck and I stilled. "That's better," he whispered into my ear. In front of me, mole man had stepped away, and I had a clear shot of Ryker fighting Arlo's men.

"Hey, Wanderer. I have your pet."

Arlo's men pulled back on their attack when they heard their leader's voice. Ryker glanced over his shoulder. He looked at the knife and back to me, his eyes wild and fierce.

"One more move and she dies, Wanderer." Arlo held me tighter against him. "I wanted to keep her for the fun of it, but I don't *need* her. If you'd like me to get rid of your human problem, I can do it for you. Say the word."

Arlo's blade dug into my skin, tearing a shallow cut near my jugular. Ryker went motionless. "Drop the axe." Arlo's voice vibrated into my chest. His knife went deeper, and I couldn't stop the hiss of breath exiting through my teeth. Warm blood dripped down my tank top.

Ryker loosened his grip, and the axe tumbled to the dirt.

Instinct to fight, to dig my elbow into Arlo's crotch, twitched my muscles. Normally I would have done it, but it was more than my risk to take. If the blade found its way through my neck, Ryker's abilities were gone along with me. I never feared death, but now I wasn't living solely for me.

"The stone, Wanderer."

Ryker stared at Arlo, and I let out a chuckle.

"You might as well kill me. You're not going to get it."

Arlo yanked me, his fingers now digging into my throat. "Oh, really? I think if it's your life or the stone, he'll choose you."

"Then you're an idiot." I snorted, trying to swallow over his clutched fingers. "I'm human. I am the last person he'd sacrifice for the stone." I was even willing to say he would choose the stone over getting his powers back, which I understood now. The stone, if put in the wrong hands, could destroy the world. Both his powers and I took second place to this.

"Zoey." Ryker gave me a warning look, his voice rigid. His attention went to Arlo. "This is between you and me. Let her go and we can talk."

"What?" I screeched, pushing against my captor. "No. Don't do this."

Ryker ignored me; his gaze fixed on Arlo. "We've got a deal?"

"Sorry, I don't trust that if I release her, you'll be a good boy." Arlo shook his head.

"You have my word." Ryker took a step to us. "Let her go, and you and I can come to an arrangement about the stone."

"Ryker!" I bellowed. Screw this. I was not going to let him sacrifice the stone for me. My head went forward, giving it more momentum as it slammed back into Arlo's face at the same time my elbow went into his gut.

A scream echoed behind me, but as he stumbled back, falling, his blade slipped and sliced into the side of my neck. Hot, consuming pain tore out of my mouth, dropping me to my knees. Then everything went insane.

"Zoey!" I heard my name being called, my gaze catching Ryker bounding toward me at the same time Arlo's men sprang for him.

Out of nowhere, a man dressed in all black jumped into the throng of fae, his sword swinging. It took me a moment to realize he was fighting against Arlo's men. Someone was helping us? It *had* to be a hallucination.

My vision blurred. Ryker suddenly stood in front of me, holding my face, his mouth moving. I heard nothing. A man crashed into him, together they slid across the gravel into the river.

I curled over my knees, wanting to sleep. *Get up, Zoey. You fight till the end. You don't quit.* But I was tired. And numb. I no longer felt pain. Only heat. So much heat I wanted to tear the fire right out of me. The glow spread up my spine and over to my neck. *Get up now! Fight!* I lifted my head, my vision still dim, but I noticed the blood from my wound was already congealing.

Ryker was out of the water, his axe slicing across one of our attackers. The man in black was near him, fighting another group of men with efficiency and a kind of beauty. Actually, he looked bored, parrying and lunging with several men at once. My first thought when I saw him was he looked like a pirate. He had shoulder-length dark hair that dangled in messy strands down to his shoulders and a thick black beard covering his face. Black leather pants, a black shirt, and a long velvet and leather coat completed his look.

He was extremely striking. His face was angular with a long nose, and his dark almond-shaped eyes suggested he had Asian ancestry somewhere. Compared to Ryker he was small, but he still was probably at least six feet. He was thin but defined. He and Ryker made a dramatic pair fighting side by side. The huge, blond, tattooed Viking next to the willowy, dark swashbuckler.

It was only an instant my thoughts wandered, but it was enough. Arms came from behind, scooping me off the ground. A hand covered my mouth. "Shut up, you stupid bitch," Arlo snarled in my ear. From the corner of my eye, I saw blood leaking from his broken nose. "You broke my nose... now I will break your neck. Seems fair."

Wrath detonated in me, locking my jaw down on his fingers.

Arlo let out a wail, trying to shake free of my mouth.

I rolled my jaw, and my teeth sawed even deeper into this skin. The tang of blood glided across my taste buds. The street fighter in me took over. Exhilaration replaced the burning in my lungs.

He dropped me, and without hesitation, I swung around, reaching for my knife. My teeth bared, coated in his blood. I lowered myself in defense.

He probably had never been taken on by a human, let alone a five-foot-five female. But I was no ordinary girl, even before I met Ryker and acquired his magic.

I was a professional street fighter. One who got a crazy high from smashing her fist into someone's tender body parts. Fighting had been my release before I gave it up for my life at DMG. Now that the feelings had been released again, it came back in frightening abundance.

"How adorable are you?" Arlo shook out his hand, hatred drilling deep in his eyes. "Human wants to play a fae game? Come on, girl. This shouldn't take long."

I was used to men underestimating me. At first it pissed me off, now I only smiled and let them believe it. Like a man who thought I was an easy target, Arlo lunged for me. Quick to pick up on people's strengths and weaknesses, I skirted out of his way. My knife nicked at the side of his torso, causing him to grunt. He charged me again, and I twisted around, punching him in the temple. A roar broke from his mouth, and fire lit his eyes. Before he'd gone easy with me, thinking he could take me out with little work on his part. Now he was going to put effort into it.

Bring it, I thought as the buzz of adrenaline spiked a rush of blood through my veins.

He swung around, his fist heading for my stomach. He moved with the uncanny speed of most fae, and his hand made contact, slamming into my intestines. I fell back, rolling into a backward somersault.

There was pain. Definitely. But my anger always pushed it to the side, reducing it to a secondary feeling as I went into the zone.

He jumped down for me, and I rolled to the side, springing back to my feet.

"I'm impressed. Little human can fight," Arlo grunted.

"And like a *girl*." I smiled tartly.

He dove for my legs, and I kicked up, my knee connecting with his mouth and nose. He screamed and fell to the ground, hitting his already broken nose. Blood trickled from his mouth as he spit out a tooth. I jumped on his chest...my knife primed back. "How embarrassing to get your ass kicked by a human girl," I seethed. My hand twitched with the need to drive the blade into his chest. Instead, I dragged it delicately across his face, crossing over his previous scar, playing with him. "X marks the spot."

Before I could drive my blade into the middle of the X, I was lifted off him and pulled back. "Zoey, stop."

"Let me go," I growled, straining against Ryker. He wrapped his arms around me as he stepped on Arlo's neck to keep him from moving.

"Calm down," he mumbled in my ear. "Breathe." He set me down and turned me to face him, his foot pressing harder on Arlo's throat. Once again the moment my eyes met his, it was like stepping into a warm bath. Everything dropped away; my muscles relaxed. The white pools ringed with navy were my anchors. His eyes brought me back from the brink.

He cupped my face, keeping his gaze on me. My legs stayed put, but my upper body sagged in his hands. "I think he's been humiliated enough." Ryker's lip curved in a smile when he glanced down at Arlo, who was struggling to breathe.

"Hey," I huffed.

Ryker rolled his eyes. "Sorry, but you are a tiny human girl who kicked his ass. You think his men will ever let him forget it? If they can even stomach being minions to this piece of shit." Ryker stepped off him and kicked his side. Arlo struggled to get back on his feet, coughing up blood as he sucked in gulps of air.

When he finally rose, Ryker stepped around me, putting himself between Arlo and me.

"You're dead, Wanderer. So is your little pet human there."

One of Ryker's eyebrows flicked up. "Piss off, Arlo, and run fast. I might decide to let her finish the job. It will only take her a moment."

Arlo's bloody face contorted with rage.

"Now," Ryker commanded.

Arlo snarled but took a step back. Then another. A few of his surviving men got back on their feet, and with heads bowed, they hightailed it away from us, disappearing into the darkness.

SEVEN

I let out a staggered breath.

"Damn. Wasn't expecting to see that." The pirate man turned to me, sheathing his sword. "Think I might be scared of you too."

Ryker frowned and twisted me to him. "You all right?" He touched my neck. My hand automatically went to the same area. The torn skin was now molding itself together, the blood drying in clumps, crusting around the wound. Maybe it hadn't been as deep as I thought, and like a paper cut, it felt worse than it was.

Or I was healing like a fae. I pushed the thought away. The idea striking fear into my core. Was I becoming fae?

"Breathe." Ryker sensed my impending freak-out.

"Right. Sure." I licked my lips, my trembling hands continuing to run along the closing gash.

"It's true then." The man strode over to us, avoiding the strewn fae forms on the ground. "Why else would you associate with a human?"

Ryker snarled and stepped in front of the man. "What the fuck are you doing here, Croygen?"

"Is this how you thank someone who just saved your

ass?"

Ryker cocked his head.

"I guess you do."

"When it's you saving my ass, then yeah. You don't do anything which doesn't help yourself."

"Or that I'm not obligated to do." Croygen crossed his arms, resentment darting through his words.

"Believe me, if I could take it back, I would," Ryker sneered.

"Not surprising."

Both men were bristling, and I sensed punches might fly soon.

"Whoa." I stepped between them; my hands went to their chests. "Gathering you two know each other?"

Croygen stepped away from my hand, looking at it with disgust.

I deduced he was also not a fan of humans.

"Yeah. Our pasts go way back," Ryker said. "Unfortunately."

"The feeling is mutual, Wanderer."

Sighing, I rubbed my temples. Another enemy of humans and of Ryker. We were batting zero here. "Is there anyone, *besides* women, who like you?" I glared at Ryker.

"Not really."

I grimaced.

"Thank you for your assistance. You're free to go now." Ryker snarled at Croygen, grabbed my arm, and began to walk away.

"You know it doesn't work like that," Croygen snapped.

"I keep hoping." Ryker was limping, but he continued.

"Still see you have a propensity for finding trouble."

"You should talk," Ryker replied over his shoulder. "As usual, it's been a pleasure."

"I might have someone who could help you," Croygen yelled after us.

Ryker's steps faltered, but he continued to walk.

"I can find Regnus."

Ryker stopped dead, causing me to stumble. He turned toward the pirate. "*You* were supposed to be our meeting?" He said it more like a statement than an actual question.

"Yeah. You think Arlo would do shit for you?" Croygen folded his arms over his chest. "Arlo has been pilfering my runs. Following me. Trying to get a bounty before me." Croygen paused, glancing around. "He obviously offered the water fairies a better deal."

"You always were a stingy bastard." A slight grin hooked at the side of Ryker's mouth.

Now I understood why Croygen showed up out of the blue like Superman. He was the man the water fairies actually sent us to meet. Arlo must have tricked the fairies into telling him who Croygen was meeting and why.

"Regnus is almost impossible to find. You know him. Discovering him on your own will be impossible. But I can help you."

"Why should I believe you?"

"Because I'm hoping it makes us even. Clears me."

Ryker stayed quiet, staring down, his hands on his hips. Finally he declared, "If you fuck with me, you're dead. You know this, right?"

Croygen's lip hitched, but he forced his head to nod.

"I am going to regret this." Ryker breathed out, folding his arms. "Fine. You can help us."

Croygen glared at the Viking, looking as thrilled by the idea as Ryker did. "I'll be in contact with you soon." He pivoted on his knee-high black pirate boots and vanished.

"How did he do that?" I continued to gaze around the empty space. "Is he a type of Wanderer too? He simply disappeared."

"No. The *asshole* is still around," Ryker called out to the shadows. Clouds were moving in, smelling of rain. Patchy clouds drifted over the moon and dimmed the only light source we had left.

"Fuck off, Wanderer," Croygen's voice called back from the forest.

Ryker snarled. "Croygen is a type of dark fae who can blend in with his surroundings so thoroughly it's like he vanishes in front of you."

"Like a chameleon?"

"Yeah, kind of like one. It makes for a perfect thief."

"Ah. Is that how you know him?"

"Yes. We met trying to steal the same object. We go *way* back." He seized my elbow again and took a few steps down the path.

"What about Arlo? You've been in this area before?"

"To Arlo, 'this area' means all of South America. Our paths crossed last in Argentina. Another thief I've had a run-in with. I took his woman and bounty. Didn't seem to want to be friends afterward."

I shook my head. "Shocker."

So, Arlo also had a lot of reasons to hate Ryker and want revenge, which was not good for us. "You have a lot of enemies."

"I've lived a long time." His limp became more and more pronounced the longer we walked. His grip tightened on my arm.

"Are you okay?"

"Fine," he uttered between clenched teeth.

"Stop." I grabbed him. He teetered on one leg, bouncing. Even with the pale glow of the moon through the clouds, I could make out the blood darkening his cargo pants. The back of them had been sliced open and blood poured from the slash across his hamstrings.

"Shit, Ryker." I bent down. The wound cut all the way to the bone, tearing through veins and tissue, but not once did he show he was hurt.

Because others were around. He would never show so-called weakness in front of anyone, friend or foe. *Except me.* A little voice tugged at my heart.

"This is really bad." I searched around for a tourniquet of sorts.

"I'll be fine. Let's get home." Ryker swayed.

"Stop being a stubborn ass." I pushed myself back up, locating what I needed. I heard Ryker snort as I jogged back to one of the dead bodies. Bending over, I unhooked the corpse's belt and tugged it off him.

"What are you doing?"

"This will slow the bleeding. Otherwise you are going to pass out long before we get home, and I can't carry you."

"What? You can't carry me?" Ryker hobbled over to me. "You saying I'm *fat*?"

I laughed. Right. The man didn't have an ounce of fat on him. "You'd be a lot more useful fat, actually." I squatted down, wrapping the belt around his leg.

"What?" Ryker sucked in a breath as I cinched the belt.

"If you were fat, I'd throw your ass in the river and use you as a raft to take us back to our place. But if I did it now, you'd sink. Then I'd have to save you from drowning. There's only so much saving a girl can do in one day."

Ryker shook his head, a smirk playing on his lips.

I finished and stood up, putting his arm around my shoulders. Our progress was slow, and without him knowing I tried several times to jump us, but the powers remained stubborn to my call. When we finally made it back to the room, Ryker was so out of it from blood loss he rambled and muttered incoherently.

Sprig was passed out under my pillow, and I moved him out of the way as Ryker's body crashed on the bed. His eyes already closed.

"Ryker, I need to get your pants off." I shook him.

"About time," he muttered into the pillow. Silence followed and he relaxed like he was falling asleep.

"I need to clean your wound." I tapped on his back. "Come on, Ryker. Help me here."

He only mumbled something I couldn't understand. I pushed him onto his side, unbuttoning his pants. No matter how unromantic it was, my heart still thumped in my chest as my knuckles brushed over his lower abdomen. His body responded to my touch. Rising to greet my hand as my fingers worked at undoing his pants.

Oh. Hell.

His hand came down on mine, pressing me into him. My gaze flew to his, but his eyes were still closed. I froze as he unconsciously guided my hand into his pants.

Holy shit! Alarms reverberated in my head. But none of them stopped me; the need in my fingers to feel him took over. The tips of my fingers grazed the fabric of his boxer briefs, feeling the heat of him pushing past the material.

What the hell, Zoey? I jerked my arm back and stepped away from the bed, putting my head in my hands. A shaky breath emerged from my lungs.

Come on. Get a grip. He's unconscious and hurt. Grow up.

I straightened my shoulders and stepped back, my shins knocking into the bed frame. "Ryker, I need you to help me." I shook him till his lids fluttered.

His hands pushed at the tops of his pants. It took him a couple of tries before he got them over his hips. I let him fall back, face-first into his pillow. I tugged and yanked till his pants peeled from him, taking extra care with the area sticky with blood. His gash was still oozing. This wasn't good. It was becoming more and more apparent I was healing like a fae and he was not.

I went to the bathroom and grabbed the first-aid stuff I had bought earlier: gauze, rubbing alcohol, bandages, and sewing items.

When I stepped back into the room, my stride faltered. Ryker had taken off his shirt and now lay only in his boxer briefs with Sprig curled at his head. My heart fluttered with tenderness. They were all I had left in the world, and they were only temporary. The thought of them eventually leaving me triggered the start of a panic attack; my heart raced and sweat prickled at the back of my neck.

No. Not now. I pushed away the feelings and got back to business. I cleaned and bandaged Ryker's leg, then got in the shower, shrieking at the cold water but relieved to be clean of dirt and blood.

Dressed in soft cotton shorts and a tank, I crawled in bed next to Ryker. Rain trickled at the windows, coating the room with mugginess. I curled myself in the small space his form didn't take up, trying not to touch him. Without waking up, his arm came around me and pulled me to him, his face snuggling into the back of my neck. He inhaled and exhaled, tension leaving his muscles. He drifted off into a deep sleep.

It took me longer, but eventually I succumbed too.

EIGHT

The early morning sunshine and heat roused me. Ryker lay extended on his stomach, his legs and arms splayed out like a starfish, leaving me little room on the mattress. He didn't even stir when I tried to shove him back on his side. Healing produced an almost coma-like state in fae, especially him. Sprig was curled at the head of the bed. Snoring.

I climbed out of bed, stretching as I lumbered to the window. I cringed, my neck and body still bruised and sore, but overall it was shocking how good I felt. The sunlight was creeping over the mountains, hitting the buildings on the other side of the street.

"Another beautiful day in Peru," I mumbled with a smile. Rain clouds rolled through constantly, but they left as fast as they came. Just like the sun in Seattle.

I cleaned the cut on my neck before attending to Ryker's leg. Normally, with a wound like his, a fae would be mended by now. His was still leaking blood. I finished doctoring the wound and wrapped it with fresh gauze.

The air was thick, but a slight breeze trickled through the sheer curtains, brushing lightly over my skin. I plunked down in the chair, curling my legs underneath me. A single papaya chip remained on the table, and I snatched it up, munching.

I sat in silence, devouring the last morsel of dried fruit, my mind going over the night's events. The video camera I was going to watch the other night sat on top of the dresser, drawing my attention over and over. This was as good of time as any.

I had made a pact with Ryker we would deal with the shaman first, but my mind was never far from knowing I was a lab experiment. I mean, how does one even deal with something like that? You technically have no real mother and father, merely donors. I came to life in a petri dish.

The DMG supposedly discovered my abilities and recruited me while I was attending college. Now I knew they had been fully aware of me my entire life. Lying and deceiving me, letting foster parents hurt me. I couldn't regret working for DMG, though. It was where I met Daniel, my trainer, my mentor, the son of the man who created me, and with whom I fell hopelessly in love. Our fates were meant to cross, but sadly our love was not.

The chair creaked as I unfolded myself and leaned over, grabbing the camera. I twisted the screen and placed it on the table. I took a deep gulp of air and quickly stabbed my finger at the on button. Even though I had watched it once before, it wrenched my stomach in knots to push play again.

Daniel's face illuminated the screen, and my heart clenched at his image. It was getting a little easier, but I would forever grieve having him in my life for such a short time. There would always be a "what could have been" if life went another way. But it didn't. And I would have to learn to deal with the loss.

The video rolled with Daniel once again explaining how his father had created a bunch of us in a lab, including Sera and me, the only two still left alive, and the fact I was supposedly dying. "While playing with genes, DMG made a lot of mistakes. Most of the eggs did not make it. And sadly, most of the babies died. Only a few of you survived."

I wanted to believe what Ryker and I talked about, the actual thing DMG was working on to achieve. In small cases they had helped humans recover, but not enough to make a national stand. There was a chance Ryker's fae powers would heal me. It was clear at least they were mending me with extraordinary speed.

Daniel's voice brought me back to the video. "Crush the DMG and find a way to live. You deserve the best this world can offer you. Take Lexie and live the fullest lives you can. Love and have lots of babies. I want all your dreams to come true. If anyone can survive a weakness in her genes, it's you. You are too much of a fighter to give up." He took a gulp. "I love you, Zoey Daniels, no matter how you came to this Earth."

I wiped at my eyes and leaned in to turn it off, remembering it ended here. My finger froze on the button when the video continued to play. Daniel shifted in his seat. His hand ran through his short, dark brown hair, the silver at the temples more pronounced. "I wish this was the end of the bad news..."

What? There is more?

My heart thumped in my chest, recalling Ryker had been the one to turn it off last time. I had only assumed the video had ended. I sat straight in the chair, clutching the camera on either side.

"You have received a great deal of bad news in your life, and you only deserve good." Daniel rubbed at his chin. During the years, I got to know him completely, so with every movement I could guess his mood. His light blue eyes focused on the camera, full of sadness.

My chest and stomach retracted, knowing more awful news was coming my way. "You are going to be upset because I went behind your back, but I talked to Lexie's doctors. Her outlook is not good. I know you were fearful of this, but it's definite. With a few operations, there is a possibility she can live a little longer. She will never have a full life, but even a couple of more years are worth it." Daniel folded his hands over each other. "A year ago, I opened an account in your name and have been depositing extra money in it. You are also my beneficiary; everything I have will be left to you if something should happen to me. Even though the money in the will can be tracked by DMG, the account in your name cannot. It is not something you can do online or by phone. I wanted no ties to the money I left you."

Daniel went on explain where and how to get the money, but my brain couldn't get beyond the fact he had made me his beneficiary. He opened an account for me when he feared he might not be around to protect me. "I want you to use this money to get yourself away from DMG. Give the files to the police and get as far as you can from them. You and Lexie come first. Her medical bills are only going to get worse, and I want you to be able to help her." Tears filled my eyes. I missed him so much. "I also set it up for whoever is left..." His sentence ended, his voice cracking. I understood. He thought I was also dying. So, if Lexie lived longer than me, she would be all right.

Liquid slid down my cheeks. This sweet, unbelievable man. It saddened me we were never allowed the chance to love each other. But I understood all too well life was not kind or forgiving. You had to take what you wanted. Daniel never took the chance, and we both lost out because of fear.

"Which takes me to the last bit of bad news. When I heard of your condition and started researching what DMG was really doing, I uncovered a lot of things. Rapava has stated fae DNA can save human lives. His claims are bigger than his successes. Most humans did not adapt to the fae blood and died. There have been a few who survived, but they haven't discovered why some humans can take it and some can't. Going through my father's research, I learned people with the sight, seers, are those rare people who are immune to fae blood. It doesn't kill you, but you won't benefit from it either. I don't think it's a coincidence that seers are the ones who can see through magic and glamour. Magic doesn't work on you like others." Daniel's blue eyes were bright with unshed tears. "I wanted to believe you could be saved by the one thing we were trying to achieve by collecting fae."

What? But Ryker's powers were adapting to me. I could jump. And I definitely was healing faster. The healing wasn't all in my head, right? Or had I wanted it to be true so badly I believed it to be true? Maybe I could heal externally, but magic was useless in changing my actual DNA?

"My father tested every baby, including you and

Sera, and none of you showed signs of being helped by fae blood. The flaw in your genetic code you were all born with was not altered. He tried hard to save the other children's lives. In the end he could not."

The life raft of hope circling around my soul popped, deflated, and sank to the pit of my stomach. The hope I held for it to be true curled around my abdomen. In my heart I had clung to the notion Ryker's power would help me. But it wasn't true. I was still going to die.

"Again all the information you need is in these files," Daniel continued. "It is imperative these stay out of DMG's hands. I know Dr. Rapava has been searching for this information for a long time. He will do anything to get it. So be careful."

Too late.

I paused the video, no longer able to stop the sobs from wracking through my chest. I really was no different from an hour ago, but hope is a powerful thing.

I cried till nothing was left. Nobody stirred from the bed, which made me feel even more alone, though a part of me was glad. I didn't want them to know the real truth. It was better to leave Ryker thinking the chance was still there. If a therapist was sitting next to me, they would probably also say it was my way of not fully dealing with reality. If I didn't say it out loud, then it could still be wrong.

Reality could bite me.

My heart couldn't take anymore, and I turned off the video, placing it underneath my underwear in a drawer. I sat in silence, staring out the window. Nothing had really changed except now I had money waiting for me in Seattle—if I ever got back there. It didn't help me now; I was exactly where I started when I woke up.

I made the decision I would go on like I hadn't heard this bit of news. I'd pretend the video ended where Ryker had stopped it. My sadness turned to a strong resolve, finding the shaman was the number-one priority. The urgency to get Ryker's powers back to him rang even louder in me.

NINE

Ryker continued to sleep into the afternoon, his body deep in healing mode. Eventually Sprig awoke.

"*Bhean*, please!" Sprig patted at his stomach. "It's not happy. You know if it doesn't get fed, I will die."

I didn't like leaving Ryker unprotected. When he went into this state it was as if he were in a coma. It rendered him completely vulnerable and an easy target.

"Okay, drama queen."

"I can't help it. Sprites have to eat constantly." The Discovery Channel also taught me monkeys never stop searching for food either.

My stomach had stopped growling hours earlier, as though realizing it was pointless since no food was forthcoming. The night before, Sprig had eaten everything in our fridge, which wasn't much.

"Okay." I grabbed some clothes out of the dresser. "But only to get something to eat and come right back."

"Oh, can we go to Izel's?" He bobbed up and down on his feet.

"No." I slipped on my flip-flops, tying my hair back into a ponytail, and scribbling a note for Ryker in case he woke. "We're only grabbing something at the corner store and coming back."

"The churro cart is only a couple of blocks away."

"Okay, churros, shop, back here." I grabbed a reusable shopping bag and the keys to the room. Sprig hopped on my shoulder. No point asking him to stay behind. He wouldn't. And besides actual sit-down restaurants like Izel's, no one seemed to care I had a monkey on my shoulder.

I checked the door twice to make sure it was locked. My stomach knotted the farther my feet took me away from the sleeping man. Leaving him defenseless didn't sit right with me. We had each other's backs, and I felt like I was leaving his exposed.

The sun beat down on me as I rushed to the store. Halfway there I noticed people stringing Christmas lights and decorations along the main drag. You could feel an excitement in the air and watch children running around wearing layers of clothes in vibrant reds, pinks, teals, yellows, and oranges, a vast rainbow of colors and patterns with headdresses and hats.

"¿Qué está pasando?" What's going on? I asked the shopkeeper as I pointed to the street.

"Celebration," he replied in Spanish. "There is going to be a huge parade and party tonight. The whole town comes out. It's a commemoration of an Inca leader, his supposed day of death."

Good reason as any.

"You must join in." He placed my groceries in my bag. I couldn't wait to get access to the money Daniel left me. These people would be getting what I owed them plus a whole lot more.

"Oh, I don't think so." I smiled.

"You won't be able to avoid it." He laughed. "Takes over the town."

I glamoured him into adding the cost to the growing bill, thanked him, and headed out.

"Churros!" Sprig sang into my ear.

"Oh, cork it." I stuffed a banana chip into his mouth.

He batted at it and spit it out. "Ugh, yuck. Banana."

A banana-hating monkey? Go figure.

I bit into my piece. "It's sweet."

He watched me curiously, then grabbed the end of mine, breaking it off. His tongue licked at it with hesitation. "It's okay. Better than the real fruit. But only give me one of these if I am close to death and there is nothing else around."

"So, in an hour."

By the time we got the churros, the streets were filling with people. The late afternoon had turned into evening. A flyer hanging from a pole told me the parade started at six and the fireworks at ten. I hurried back to our room. Panting, I unlocked the door and stepped in.

The bed was empty.

"Ryker?"

No answer.

"Ryker!"

"*Bhean*, listen." Sprig tapped at his ear, settling himself on top the TV.

Trying to hear past the beating of my heart, I finally took in the sound of the shower.

Jeez, Zoey, overreact much?

The water shut off and eventually Ryker came out of the bathroom, steam trailing after him, only a towel around his waist. The memory of him taking my hand last night needled at me. I looked away, putting the groceries on the table.

"You're back." He walked over to the dresser.

"I only stepped out for a moment. Sprig was going to *die* if I didn't get him food."

Ryker snorted and glanced over at Sprig stuffing churros into his mouth.

"True story," Sprig garbled out.

"Yeah, freaked me out when I first woke up, but the note plastered to my forehead kind of let me know you hadn't been kidnapped."

Actually, it said: *Ryker, haven't been kidnapped except by a monkey and his stomach. Be back soon.*

"How are you feeling?" I pointed to his calf. The wound had finally closed, but it looked puffy and raised.

"Fine." He frowned. No doubt he'd noticed he was slower to heal. "What I really need is a drink." He pulled a black T-shirt over his head.

A moment of neither of us speaking suddenly felt awkward and heavy. *Why am I nervous around him now? Why can I only think about what's under his towel?*

"Uh. Th-there's a parade tonight, and I guess it's a big deal." I waved to the windows. "Fireworks and a big party in the streets. Whole town is involved." *Shut up, Zoey.* "The owner at the market said we couldn't avoid it." *Please, shut up.* "Think the parade is at six

105

and the fireworks are at ten or something." And then the worst thing possible happened. A nervous giggle broke from my lips. I usually had a deep laugh. I didn't giggle.

Kill. Me. Now.

Ryker tilted his head, examining me. Even Sprig stopped eating and stared at me.

"Are you all right, *Bhean*?" Sprig's forehead folded in lines. "You look flustered."

Yeah. "No." I pinched the space between my eyes, squeezing my eyes shut. I didn't look up as another beat of silence pounded in my ears.

"Sounds fun," Ryker finally said, drawing my attention over to him. He stepped into a pair of clean boxer briefs, his towel still wrapped around his waist. "Want to start early? Get a drink down the street?"

Drink. Yes. Good idea.

"Uh... yeah." I nodded. "Where are you going?"

"Tulio's."

"The bar we crashed into? The one where he called the cops on us?"

"Don't worry. I've already been back there. Tulio will leave us alone, I promise."

Ahh. That's where he came back from the other night, stumbling drunk. Poor Tulio got glamoured.

"Okay, but I'll meet you there. I want to do something first."

Ryker's brows lowered as he tugged on his last pair of green cargo pants. The other ones were in the trash. Ryker slipped on his boots and snagged a churro out of Sprig's hand, biting down on it. Sprig gaped at his empty hand like he lost his best friend. "You know where to find me." Ryker grabbed a set of keys and left.

"He took my churro..." Sprig's bottom lip quivered as he stared at his empty hand.

"Uh-oh. Will I have to break out the banana chips soon?"

Sprig sniffed. "Maybe."

I shook my head and walked to the bathroom, holding a box I purchased at the store. When I saw it on the shelf, I knew what I had to do. Even if it only fooled people for a moment, it would be worth it. I set the package on the counter. A girl with plum hair stared back at me from the carton. Arlo was the one who pointed it out. Right away people would know I wasn't Amara, only cementing the gossip about Ryker being magic-less and traveling with a brunette human.

Thirty minutes later, my hair was a rich shade of purple. I turned my head back and forth, admiring my new look. My figure was curvier and shorter than Amara's lean modelesque one, but people would notice my shape a lot less than the hair.

Sprig hopped into the room. "Your hair looks like an eggplant."

"I know." The colored locks fell around, framing my face. I actually liked it. A lot. I felt even more like a badass. Sexy badass.

"It actually looks good on you." Sprig leaped on the sink.

"Thanks, I guess."

"Making me crave eggplant lasagna. Or berry pie."

"How about honey-dipped mango chips and a

Spanish soap opera?"

Sprig's eyes widened in excitement, then tempered. "You're leaving me behind again, aren't you?"

"Yeah."

Sprig tilted his head and shrugged. "For honey mango chips I will agree." He sighed heavily. He straightened up, eyes growing wide again. "Oh, Senorita Rosa... I wonder if she will find out whose baby she's carrying." He bounded off the counter and ran to the TV, stabbing at the buttons.

I clicked it on for him. Instead of the soap opera, I found a reality show, which was as good. He climbed on the bed, Pam in hand, and settled onto a pillow. I grabbed a honey bear full of sweet liquid, grasped the stash of mango chips I bought at the store, and handed it to him. He was already in his happy place by the time I finished dressing.

Uncomfortably, I tugged at my skirt. *Was it this short when I got it?* It was an impulse buy. One I was regretting. My nerves rattled around, clenching at my chest. Why was I edgy? It was simply a drink. We'd shared plenty of them before. And it was only a skirt. *My shorts and cargo pants are dirty. This is only thing I have clean*, I rationalized. *Not like I'm dressing for a date or anything.* But with my violet hair, cute A-line, cotton, flared skirt, and tight tank, I felt as if I were wearing a neon sign, like I was *trying* to impress Ryker. Before I overthought anything and changed my outfit, I proceeded to the door.

"We'll be back later." I rubbed Sprig's head on the way out. He grunted and shoved another chip in his mouth as I closed the door.

My nerves doubled the closer I got to the bar. Participants in the parade were starting to gather at the end of the lane. Music swayed down to me as the dancers practiced their routines. Excitement ran like a current through the people. Kids ran around squealing with delight, waiting for the festivities to begin.

It only intensified my knotting gut. "Relax, Zoey. Simply a drink. No big deal," I muttered to myself. What would he think of my hair? Would he think I wore the skirt for him? Did I?

Holy shit! I need a drink.

Inhaling a huge slug of air, I took a step into the bar.

It was packed. Tourists and locals mixed with each other, cheering and singing to the jukebox tunes. People were ready to let loose and have a good time. The excitement and happiness in the air was tangible. I could feel it move across my skin. The parade moved past the bar, and everyone cheered in anticipation of the more "adult" festivities later.

Ryker was easy to spot sitting at the bar. Even with all the other tourists, he stood out. Girls stood behind him in a group, giggling and trying to catch his notice. If he wanted to go invisible, he pretty much could, but he obviously didn't care tonight.

I nibbled at my lip as I made my way over to him. Sensing my approach, he swiveled around in his chair. His mouth dropped open and his eyes grew wide.

"Hey." I pushed through the throng of girls and wiggled in next to him. Several of the girls said something in German and frowned in my direction.

"What the hell did you do?"

My hand grabbed at the ends of my hair. "What?

You don't like it?"

He adjusted in his seat, really taking me in. "I didn't say that."

"Arlo was right. With my brown hair no fae would ever take me for Amara."

"Why would you want to be mistaken for Amara?"

I turned to the bar, searching for the man who stood between me and the alcohol.

Ryker stood up, motioning me to sit. He leaned over, mumbling something in the man's ear next to him. The man got up and walked away. Ryker sat in his vacated chair.

"That was wrong." I scowled.

"Out of all the things we've both done, that is what you think is wrong?"

I smiled and plopped on the barstool. "No. Not really."

"What I thought." His eyes grazed over me again. "You didn't answer my question."

He motioned to the bartender. I recognized him as the man who ran out of the bar the day we arrived, the owner, Tulio. He reacted instantly to Ryker's summons.

"Beer?" Ryker asked.

I nodded.

Ryker held up two fingers and motioned to his bottle.

I looked forward, not wanting to face him. "I'm a liability. They hear the rumors, but until they see me, they probably doubt the truth of them." I picked at a napkin on the bar. "If more people learn you don't have your powers, they will come for the stone. In droves. If for one moment they see me and think I'm Amara and hesitate, it's worth it."

Ryker grabbed my arm, turning my chair to him. He reached out, twirling my hair between his fingers. "

You did this to protect me?"

"Yeah."

Ryker's mouth opened and closed, his fingers trailed through my hair, his gaze growing so intense I stopped breathing.

Tulio set the beers down, the glass bottles clanking. Ryker and I jerked back, turning our attention to the objects in front of us. He reached for his beer and I did the same.

"*Salud.*" Ryker tipped his beer bottle to me.

I lifted my beer. "*Salud.*"

The clink of our bottles was sharp, echoing, but the noise of the bar kept it contained to our little bubble. We watched each other as we each took a swig. My eyes darted away from his gaze as I placed the bottle back on the napkin. My hands shook as my fingers played with the edge of the white paper. *Relax, Zoey. We are only having a drink.*

Pushing back my shoulders, I sat straighter in my seat, holding up my beer. "Here's to us making it through... again." I shook my head, remembering all the crap we'd survived and escaped the past month. "And to us finding someone to help transfer your powers back." I felt no need to keep my voice down. The noise level of the bar was so high I practically had to yell, the celebration energy tingling at my skin.

Ryker tapped the neck of his bottle onto mine. I

downed the rest of my beer. One of his eyebrows hitched up.

"Come on, Wanderer. Keep up." I motioned to the bartender. "I see. Look like a Viking but drink like a pussy."

He snorted and downed the rest of his beer.

The dark-haired, older bartender made his way back to us. There were at least a hundred people in the small bar, but he came the moment I signaled.

"Are you glamouring him?" I asked Ryker. He only smiled in return.

"*Dos cervezas más.*" I held up two fingers to Tulio.

"*Y dos tiros de whisky*," Ryker told the barkeep and turned back to face me, a slight smirk on his face. "Don't challenge me, human."

"Can you really even call me *human* anymore?"

"You're still human. You're not one of us yet."

"Thank God."

His foot hooked the rung at the bottom of my barstool and tugged at it. My arms went flying when I felt my chair go backward. The instant of fear sent adrenaline into my veins. A gush of wind slammed into me. I blinked... and I was standing at the opening of the restroom.

Oh hell.

The place was so crowded no one observed my sudden appearance near the bathrooms—this time. I was going to need to get more of a handle on my emotions. The jumping was starting to happen a little too often. Soon someone would notice.

I pushed through the crowd and made my way back

to Ryker. He sat there sipping his whiskey, looking impervious. My eyes went to his shoulders, searching for the hidden fury, but he was relaxed.

"Now look who's behind." He tipped the rest of the brown liquid down his throat. I slipped back onto my stool. "You obviously didn't go far."

"The bathroom."

He chuckled. "Takes you where you need to go."

"You are being awfully calm about this." I took a sip of my drink. The smoky aroma reminding me of the night we spent in the house together in northern Seattle. The night I sewed him up, and we slept in the same bed. My shift from hate to tolerance had been slow, but from tolerant to... whatever I was feeling now, was fast.

"I'm not." His white eyes turned to mine; the cold seriousness ran deep in his black pupils. "And we still haven't talked about what you did in front of Arlo. But tonight I don't want to discuss any of it. Right now we relax and have fun." He raised his hand to Tulio, nodding toward our drinks. Tulio automatically reached for the bourbon bottle.

The burden slipped off my shoulders as I tipped my head back and finished the liquor. He was right. We needed one night. One night not worrying about anything—to be free and act like we were any other couple on vacation.

Couple? I didn't mean couple as in *together*, I meant couple as in two people being in the same place... *Oh, shut up, Zoey.*

I swallowed the last of my beer, almost choking on it. Ryker's eyebrow was up again. "Whooo." I patted my chest, chuckling nervously. *Dammit! I giggled again.*

Ryker grabbed my chair and turned me to him. "Relax, Zoey." His gaze caught mine, holding it. The alcohol running through my system took the edge off my tension. I nodded, brushing my purple hair over my shoulder.

Ryker pushed the freshly poured drink to me. My fingers wrapped around the glass. The heat of the day had not waned, and the mass of people packed in the bar intensified the humidity in the small space. Sweat trickled down my spine, soaking into my tank. I shoved my hands down, pushing my short cotton pleated skirt between my legs. I felt sticky everywhere. And a lot of it had nothing to do with the temperature in the packed bar.

"How'd you leave without Sprig?" Ryker set his feet on my chair's foot rung and leaned one elbow on the bar.

I brought the cup to my lips. "I left him with a baby bottle full of honey, mango chips, his stuffed animal, and South America's version of reality TV, which is like porn to him. He'll be fine."

"More than fine. He'll want us to leave more often."

I laughed. "You're right. But he better not be doing anything with Pam on the bed we haven't yet." The words were out of my mouth before I could stop them.

Oh. My. God.

"I don't mean together... I meant separate. Not that we could really do anything more than share a bed." My face burned with embarrassment. Laughing, I swiveled my chair to face the bar, and I propped my elbows on it. "That would be awkward."

114

Ryker's mouth twitched with humor. His gaze stayed on me, watching me flounder. I slammed down the harsh liquor, my throat and chest burned in protest. "When was the last time you had sex?" Ryker leaned back in his chair.

I choked, coughing into my hand. "Excuse me?"

"You brought it up."

"I'm not telling you." My head was getting fuzzy, along with my inhibitions. His eyes stayed on me, causing a smile to curl my lips. "Fine. It's been a while," I acknowledged. "But not really my fault. Been kind of busy running from people trying to kill me. Plus, I've been stuck with you." I grinned and took another drink.

"You could have taken the boy we met in the garage who was making eyes at you into a back seat of a Prius. I wasn't stopping you."

"Who?"

Ryker smirked, turning more toward me. "You know who I am talking about. In the garage. The human kid who was totally into you."

"You mean Mr. Kettenburg's son? Andrew?" My nose scrunched up. "Are you serious?"

It was still strange to think of my old teacher and know he had been a plant by DMG the whole time I had been his student—a spy, recruiting me to be their seer soldier.

Ryker shrugged. "He got a stiffy the moment he saw you. You could have been Junior's first."

"Ugh, he was seventeen. I prefer my men *a lot* older." A blush came over my face. Ryker never revealed his actual age, but I knew he was at least a couple centuries old, if not more. "Andrew was not my type at all, but thank you for lowering my standards for me."

"It's the end of the world, and you decide to be picky?"

"Oh, shut up." I smacked at his chest. My arm bounded back like it had hit cement. "Ow." I shook out my hand. "Seriously, you need to put a warning label on that thing."

"I need to put one on you."

"Why? Because you think I'm having sex with a seventeen-year-old in the back of a Prius?"

"A missed opportunity."

"Somehow I will go on." My chair rotated to face him, and I placed my feet between his legs on his foot rung. His heels were hooked on the bar on either side of mine. "What about you?"

The side of his mouth curved up. He emptied his drink and tapped the counter with the glass. From across the bar, ignoring all the hands waving to get his attention, Tulio moved to us.

"Stop doing that."

"I'm not doing anything."

"Oh, right. Like you're not glamouring him?"

"I'm not."

Tulio poured more alcohol and pulled out two more beers, adding them to a tab by the register, before he went back to the other waiting patrons.

I lifted my eyebrow.

"He's doing it out of fear. Not from glamour."

"What?"

"He remembers us. We showed up in his bar out of thin air. Roman Catholics have always held the Devil is real, not a mythical personification." Ryker pointed between us. "Guess what we are to him?"

"The Devil?" I responded. "I can see you, but me?"

Ryker tilted his head forward, almost touching mine. "You probably even more than me. An alluring purple-haired *woman* with magic. Plus, you are with me willingly."

"Yeah. I am pretty scary." I leaned in, and a smile spread across my face. Did he just say I was alluring?

"Tell me about it."

His lips were so close, I could feel the coolness from the beer he drank radiating off them. A voice far back in my brain told me to stop staring at his mouth. Get off my chair and go home. To be smart, or I would regret it.

I was never good at listening. Especially to wise advice.

Feedback from a mic pierced the room, hammering into my eardrums. My head wrenched to see where it was coming from. A man stood on the tiny stage with a band behind him. He spoke in Spanish, addressing the audience before breaking into song. The place went crazy with people screaming and dancing along with the music, the energy level heightening in the dark seedy pub.

My head felt light, all my problems washing away as beer went down my throat. I caught Ryker's eyes on me, examining. My stomach twisted in my belly. Nervous jitters fluttered around my insides.

Danger. Danger.

Still, I could not stop my words or the smile on my face. "You're dodging the question."

"What question?" A smirk lifted the side of his mouth.

Hell. Why was my heart crashing into my chest with his every glance?

Ryker and I had been through a lot together, and somewhere along the way I began to see him as a man. Not fae or a monster, but my partner. When I thought he was dead, I'd felt genuine sorrow. Ryker and Sprig were never supposed to get under my skin, but they had. They changed everything. Now I could no longer see them as merely fae. They were even changing my feelings about fae in general.

"Sex. Last time?" Bringing up sex with him was extremely dangerous territory, but my inhibitions were down and my mouth forgot it had a filter.

"Like you said, I've been stuck with you the last month. Kind of limited my options."

The white bar napkin shredded between my fingers. "I was passed out for a week when we were with Elthia. Don't tell me you didn't take advantage? She clearly wanted to."

A frown tugged his mouth. "Elthia and I are in the past. Plus, I had... have someone." His Adam's apple bobbed as he turned away, taking another gulp of beer. He faced the mirror behind the bottles of liquor. His body a wall.

"Right. Amara." I stared at my hands and drew my legs off his chair.

We stayed silent for a moment.

"Where did you meet her?"

He didn't answer. Silence stretched out. The world continued around us, the singing and dancing, but I barely noticed them.

"We met in a bar, actually. In Romania." He finally spoke, keeping his head forward. "It was instantaneous."

A fist punched through my heart. An automatic reaction. I couldn't stop the consuming hurt and jealousy I felt. I swirled the brown liquid and slammed back the rest in my cup. "You'll get her back," I responded. "We'll find a way."

He nodded absently. Both our bodies faced forward, looking away from each other. Horrible tension filled the space between us, growing so thick it hurt. My lids fell, squeezing together.

"Zoey?" His voice was low and questioning.

I crooked my neck, blocking my face from him. "Can you just go back to calling me human? It's better. Uncomplicated."

He huffed out a long sigh. "Look at me."

I shook my head. I knew if I faced him, he would see what I was feeling. What I still wanted to deny. He grabbed my legs and swung me around to face him. I became overly aware of where his hands touched my bare skin. His fingers trailed over my knees before sliding off.

"Look up." Again I jiggled my head no. "Zoey. Look. At. Me."

Slowly, I lifted my neck, my hair tickling my arms as it dragged up, along with my gaze. Our eyes locked. His demeanor had changed. His eyes blazed bright white; his tattoo on his neck flickered. This only happened with extreme emotions, like anger or lust, but it had been happening less and less since he began to lose his powers.

Air caught in my throat. His expression flamed the desire circling around in my stomach. He searched my face for an answer I wasn't sure of the question, but my countenance must have answered it. Because suddenly his hands gripped the sides of my face, drawing me to him, touching my forehead to his. His breath tickled my lips.

"When did you sneak in?" he whispered so low I barely heard him. "Get this far under my skin?"

It was like a bomb exploded in the room, creating a shield around us. My heart jackhammered against my ribs, my breath shallow. Our skin tingled every place it touched. The need for him consumed every nerve and made it hard to move or think.

His skin glistened under the low light of the bar. A drip of perspiration trickled down his neck, my eyes watched it slide down the curve of his neck into the hollow space at the base of his throat. My hand went to where it pooled. His breath tightened the moment my fingers made contact with his skin. He swallowed but did not move. My brain no longer felt a part of my body. My fingers worked on their own as they trailed up his neck, slipping over his scruffy chin and stopping at his lips. He squeezed his eyes shut as the tip of my finger softly traced his lips.

A rumble came from his chest. I lifted my eyes to look up into his. Need etched deep in his pupils, mirroring my own. His hand slipped farther into my hair, tilting my head. The heat between our mouths increased as we moved in closer. I shut my eyes, anticipating the feel of his lips, when an image of Amara calling out for Ryker slammed into my head. Pain in her eyes as she reached for him.

What were we doing? He had a girlfriend. He was in love with someone else. Fear and guilt washed over me. Air whizzed through my hair and across my skin, making me lightheaded.

Dammit. Not again.

TEN

I opened my eyes. I was back in the ladies' room. A girl was drying her hands and squeaked, doing a double take when she saw me standing next to her. She tossed the paper away, keeping a wary gaze on me before rushing out of the room. I leaned my hands on either side of the sink, taking in a gulp of air.

"What the fuck are you thinking, Zoey?" I addressed the image in the mirror. Nothing good can come of us crossing the line. It would only lead to more heartbreak for me. Something I couldn't handle anymore. He had Amara. It was better if we simply stayed "business partners" until this mess was over. He would return to her and go back to his life free of humans the moment he could. Having his powers within me was like having him on a leash. Once I let him off, he would be gone. Discarded. No. I would not do it to myself again.

Something tickled my upper lip, and I turned to the image in the mirror. A trickle of blood dripped from my nose. Reality. It always came and bit you in the ass.

I wiped away the blood and let the cool water from the faucet wash over my hands and through my fingers, splashing a little on my chest and face. The red-stained water trailed down the drain. With a tissue I patted my face dry and shut down my mind to what it meant.

I felt him behind me before I even looked up, his presence hovered heavy in the air. My lashes lifted, and I saw his reflection in the glass. He watched me with no expression on his face. Somehow I knew he'd been there long enough to see my nosebleed.

A toilet flushed, and a blonde woman in her early thirties came out of the stall. Her gaze darted between the two of us. Her eyes widened, and she scurried for the door, mumbling something in English. She squeezed past Ryker without touching him and glanced once more over her shoulder before dashing out. There was no door on the main bathroom, only an opening. The music and voices seemed distant. All I saw and felt was him.

He continued to stare at me, and his eyes held emotion. Want. Need. I couldn't move, my eyes fastened on his reflection.

You just had another reminder you could die tomorrow, Zoey. Regret what you didn't do... not what you did.

All my fears followed the discolored water down the drain. I wanted him. I longed for him to touch me so much it ached. I could pretend my jumping was because of Amara, but it was a lie. It was fear. I had fought my feelings since the night he saved me from the freezing water in Seattle. I think we both did, but we could no longer ignore it. The elephant in the room was stomping its feet and demanding we take notice.

I watched his eyes move up my figure. My skin tingled every place they went. Then his eyes landed back on mine. Desire charged his expression. The dam we'd tried to build between us splintered. We moved at the same time.

I whirled around as his hands gripped my hips, picking me up and pitching me on the countertop. He spread my legs with his body, pushing up to me. His fingers curled over my jaw and drew my mouth to his. The moment our lips met, the barrier combusted, fracturing everywhere, sending white-hot energy into my chest and limbs. His mouth was desperate. His full lips demanding. Heat traveled down my spine and between my legs. My fingers glided over the braids on the side of his head, pulling him closer to me. His tongue slipped past my lips and an embarrassing moan broke from my throat. His reaction was immediate. His fingers dug into my scalp, drawing me in. Our kisses went from needy to frantic. He tugged at my bottom lip, driving my desire for him into a fury. My legs clamped around his waist. He lifted me and walked us over to a wall, my arms wrapping around his head, pulling me higher on his torso and closer to his mouth. He pushed against me as he flattened me back against the wall, our lips never breaking apart. Through his jeans I could feel him hard and ready. My body responded. I knew he could sense my reaction because he gave a low growl.

Sex. I wanted sex now.

"*Heilige Scheiße*," a voice cried out in German.

Holy shit was right. We both froze and then slowly turned our heads toward the doorway. The group of ladies courting Ryker when I first walked in stood at the entrance. Their eyes wide and their mouths open.

Ryker stepped back, letting me slide down the wall, my feet touching the ground. It felt surreal, like he had taken me to a completely different place and time and now we were jarred back into the present. The women merely gaped at us.

"Leaving." Ryker laced his fingers through mine, tugging me away from the wall, and advanced to the door. I clasped my hand over my mouth, trying to hide the enormous smile on my lips.

As Ryker pushed us past the group of women, one nudged my arm. "Go. Girl." She spoke in broken English, looking him up and down. "He. Is. *Hot*."

I gave her a conspiring smile and nodded.

Ryker weaved us through the throng of dancing couples and groups, out the doors. I stepped outside, expecting to feel the cool air crawl over my skin, refreshing me. Bodies were everywhere, taking up every available space. It was like going from one sauna to another.

Crowds of people lined the street and danced. Floats and groups of costumed dancers paraded down the narrow strip of road. Christmas tree lights and colored lanterns hung from the trees and across wires strung between telephone poles and lamp posts.

The air was heavy with excitement and energy. The late night was turning people's energy sexual and carnal. Bodies pressed together, moving in either dance or trying to get through the crowds. The hot, humid night covered our skin in sweat, sex thick in the air.

Between that, the alcohol, and the fact I was a walking hormone, my mind was on one thing.

And I didn't seem to be the only one. Ryker slithered us through the crowd and then stopped, turning back to me. His eyes hungrily consumed my face, centering in on my mouth. The dense crowd pushed our bodies together. Aligning us. He bent down, his hands cupping my cheeks. I pushed up on my toes. Our lips found each other. It was like I could breathe again. The moment my mouth was on his, the world disappeared.

A body slammed into us, pushing us apart. I didn't want to stop kissing him. I had been kissed a lot in my past, but this was different. It went beyond earth shattering or any other stupid platitude I could think of. I had never felt completely safe before. Always on edge and waiting for the other shoe to drop. Security was always an obscure idea. Something I dreamed about having but never really understood.

I knew instantly what the difference was. *He was home.* It terrified me.

It was worse than any drug I ever tried or heard about. Even if someone had made an ultimatum between my life and kissing him, I wouldn't be able to stop touching or kissing him. I needed him worse than I needed air.

This feeling was unlike me. Daniel never even came close to this. I loved Daniel. He was my bridge to another world. Another life, another me. *I'm not in love with Ryker... so why does he make me feel this way?*

Ryker stripped away all the pretense. This was me: vulnerable, scared, strong, wanting, sad, lonely, crazy, mean, and flawed. A fighter, an experiment, a human, a fae, a Collector, and now one of the hunted.

We were trained to hate each other, but still through it all, we found solace in each other. And I never wanted a man more in my life.

Guilt wiggled deep under the layers of alcohol and desire floating at the top. The thought of betraying Daniel arose, but the whiskey pushed his image away, giving me courage to act on what I wanted right then.

I withdrew from Ryker and grabbed his hand, ignoring the exclamations from the crowd as I pushed through the mob. I shoulder checked a few people before I tugged him past the horde and into an alleyway.

"Ever thought about playing football?" Ryker smirked.

I turned to face him. "Shut up."

"Yes, human." He grinned. He picked me up, my legs wrapped around his waist, and we fell against the brick wall. The smell of garbage and urine was strong, but I ignored it. His hand moved under my skirt, cupping my ass. His fingers nudged under the fabric of my underwear.

My hands ran over his lips and face. "What are we doing?" I whispered.

"I don't know." He nipped at my ear.

"We should probably stop," I said as I continued to explore his skin.

"Yeah. We probably should." He nuzzled into the crook of my neck, his beard tickling it. "Be the smart thing to do."

The thought of him actually stopping charged fear into my lungs. I placed my hands on either side of his face and dipped my head, covering his lips. The kiss started off slow, exploring and thorough. Then it turned, surging with desire. It was so strong and powerful I didn't even realize I was unbuttoning his pants. I slipped past his boxers, my hand finding the length of him. He groaned.

Holy shit. The Viking rumor was correct about their "size," if not a little understated.

Touching him made my entire body more than ready for his. We were in a dirty alley, but I didn't care. I wanted him inside me so badly I couldn't think. My hand explored him. He tipped his head back, taking in staggered breaths. I wiggled down, pushing my underwear to the side. I drew the tip of him to me.

"Zoey. Stop." His voice was thick.

"Why?" Embarrassment and rejection flooded my cheeks. I didn't want to stop. I moved farther down, taking a little more of him to me. I was hot and ready, and he could feel it.

"Oh, gods." He placed a hand on the wall beside my head, leaning against it. He took in a shaky breath. "You are *not* playing fair."

"What? You don't want *this*?" Anger crept into my words, and I released him from my grip.

A burst of laughter came from him, only incinerating my wrath and humiliation.

He tucked himself back into his pants and adjusted me higher on his waist.

"Let me down." I struggled against his hold.

He only smiled, pressing me harder against the brick wall. His face growing serious. "I want this more than you can possibly know. And we will be doing *this*." His voice was confident and it froze me in place. "Just not here." He glanced around. I finally took in the area. I could see vomit in the corner, spoiled food in and outside of the trash cans, and rats scurried in the far dark corners.

Okay, not the most desirable place to have sex, but sadly I'd had worse.

He grabbed my chin.

"Zoey, when I'm inside you, I don't want it to be a quickie in the alley. I want to spread you out and take my time."

Air caught in my chest.

"You got it?"

I nodded.

He put me back on my feet.

"Now, let's try and find the fastest way home or I might forgo that idea."

"Yeah." I was still nodding like a fool. *Oh, I can get us home really fast.* I grabbed his hand, closing my eyes I tried to think of the room we were staying in. I peeked from under my lashes. We still stood in the passage.

"Yeah. Not usually happy about you using them, but right now it would be nice."

"Why doesn't it work when I really want it to?"

"They still haven't fully adapted to you, and it only works when your emotions are extremely heightened."

"My emotions aren't heightened enough for them right now?"

"Obviously not. They seem to come out when you are scared... really scared." He took my face in his hands. "Not horny."

"You should fear me now." I poked at my chest, talking to the powers.

"Good try. Doesn't quite work like that." He turned me toward the entrance of the lane.

It took us more than twenty minutes to get to our room. It was only a five-minute walk from the bar, but between the crowds and many moments spent stopping to fall into each other, it took us a lot longer than normal.

Ryker pressed me into the door before we entered. He kissed me tentatively. He didn't say anything, but I understood. The moment we opened the door and crossed the threshold, everything was going to change. Things were already a bit different, but sex altered the relationship irrefutably. Right now we could blame it on liquor or try and pretend it never happened. I felt deep in my gut sex with him would not be something I would be able to come back from. Not unscathed.

I lived my life in compartments. Sometimes I'd been the responsible girl, sometimes the wild reckless one. Always playing a part. Tonight I was going to simply be me. And I wanted to get in bed with him and never come back out.

My response to his kiss said everything. Without our lips breaking contact, we stumbled inside, banging into everything remotely in our way. The lights were off, but the TV blared in the background, halting me.

Sprig.

Shit.

I searched the room for the little fuzzball and found him passed out on top of the TV. Dried honey-coated mango chips stuck to his fur. His mouth hung open as he snored.

I snorted, covering my mouth.

"No. Way." Ryker stepped around me. He collected Sprig gently in his hands and moved toward the bathroom.

"What are you doing?" I followed.

"He's sleeping in here." Ryker tugged a towel off the bar and balled it underneath Sprig before placing him in the tub. Sprig sighed sleepily and curled up in the cloth.

"Wait. In case he wakes up." I held up my hand and went back into the bedroom. Pam was lying on the bed. I snatched the stuffed goat and took it back to Sprig, placing it next to him.

We watched him for a moment before Ryker touched the small of my back, leading me out of the room. He shut the door behind us. "That was sweet," I said over my shoulder.

"What, locking him in the bathroom?"

"Not tossing him out the window so you could get laid."

Ryker put his hands on his hips and stared at the floor. Silence. I could feel the change in the room. His sudden doubt choked me. "We should walk away."

I whipped around. "Is it what you want?" I whispered.

His jaw clenched. "What I want and what is smart are two different things."

I sank my teeth into my lip. "Yeah."

"I'll find somewhere else to sleep." He kept his gaze everywhere but on me.

"Probably wise." I tried to keep my voice even, but sadness, frustration, and chagrin colored it.

He nodded, staring out the window. The noise from the celebration below came through the open windows, crashing against the suddenly somber mood in the room.

My body was overly aware of his proximity, aching to be touched again. My fingers longed to caress him. "Please go."

His mouth clamped tighter as he rubbed at his forehead, but his feet stayed glued against the wood floor. I could no longer stand there with him this close. The bathroom was my only escape from his presence.

As if our thoughts were on the same thing, we both took a step. I went to the restroom, he for the room door, our figures bumped, blocking the other of their path.

Instantly a lightheadedness swirled my brain. It was like I could feel his hormones. They crawled over my skin, hinting at what they wanted to do to me. We both froze, trapped in each other's space. Only inches apart, our lungs moved in and out frantically.

Ryker lifted his hand, tucking a piece of my purple hair behind my ear. His head dipped lower. His mouth so close it was taunting me.

I never experienced instant desire like this. His hand grazed my skin, and I was ready to jump him. No longer able to hold myself back from him, I went up, crashing my lips into his. Warm. Wanting. Whatever barrier we were trying to build up dissolved, opening the floodgates. The desire for each other hit another level.

He grabbed the bottom of my tank top and whipped it over my head, inciting me to do the same to his shirt.

My hands and eyes took in his chest and ripped abs. The V-line poking out of the top of his pants. His ass. It felt strange I could touch him. Freely. I could finally explore his body without being embarrassed by the thought.

He seemed to sense what I wanted because he stood there, letting my fingers move across his stomach, touching the dented line at his pants line, and over his chest. His lungs pumped in and out faster the more confident I grew in my exploration. One by one I undid the buttons of his pants, letting them fall to his ankles. I walked around to his back, the tips of my fingers never leaving his skin. I traveled over his wide shoulders and strong back, finally stopping at his ass. For a long time, it had goaded me to run my hands over it. Gripping both sides of his boxer briefs, I pulled them down. Ryker took in a deep gulp of air as his boxers joined his pants around his ankles. My hand skated over his buttocks, and muscles flexed under his skin. He had the finest ass I had ever seen on a man. Perky, muscular, and taut. Impulse sent me onto my knees, kissing his lower back and working down.

Ryker made a sound I never heard before, but it got my blood boiling. I wanted to worship his entire physique. I moved around to the front. I took a moment to appreciate the man's form. My hands slid up his legs as I slowly kissed his inner thigh.

His cock throbbed and twitched under my lips. Ryker closed his eyes and grabbed the dresser. I felt sexy and powerful. This was usually something I avoided with other men—it felt more intimate than the actual act of sex. Now I wanted nothing more than to taste every inch of Ryker.

Another moan came from him, and he grabbed me under the arms and threw me back on the bed. "I'm sorry, but I've been waiting too long for this." He kicked off his boots, leaving his clothes behind as he kissed me. His lips were hot and demanding. "It's my turn."

He pulled my skirt over my hips. He dropped the first layer on the floor and came back for my underwear. He tugged them down, his eyes exploring me. He leaned over and unsnapped my bra, dropping it with the other clothing. I was completely naked. He spread me out. His hands skated over my skin, leaving trails of quivers in their wake. He kneeled at the side of the bed, his lips moving up my thighs, until his tongue found its way inside me.

I gasped as he nipped and kissed me. I was usually not a vocal person. The sound coming out shocked me. It only enticed him. His tongue and lips grew more intense. Loud wails of pleasure tore from my throat. Then they grew high, clear, and more pronounced.

"Oh my God, Ryker. I need you now." My fist clutched at his hair. "Please."

He smirked and went deeper. I widened myself, letting him go. He moved with me, building my orgasm until pleasure ripped through me, shaking me to the core.

"Holy shit." I blinked at the ceiling, my limbs limp. "You expect me to be useful after this?"

He gave the sensitive area one last kiss before he moved back out to my thighs, his lips skimmed them. He stood up. I scuttled back to get higher on the bed.

He crawled after me, his body covering mine. His elbows went on either side of my head, keeping some of his weight off me. His white eyes were bright in the dark and glinted with smugness.

"Oh, someone is all puffed up. You're going to be insufferable now, aren't you?"

"Really no different from before." He grinned. "But I do like knowing I can make you scream."

"I've never done that before."

"I'll have to make sure it wasn't only a one-time thing." He leaned down, his lips finding mine. The heat of his mouth, the feel of him pressed against my stomach ignited the fire raging inside. A light breeze came through the window. The sounds of the celebration drifted up. I don't know if it was me taking on fae qualities, but I could feel the energy from the streets, filling me with vigor. Was I feeding off them in some way? Absorbing their energy? Right then I didn't care as Ryker's mouth found my breast, stirring me alive again.

He hitched my leg around him and rolled me over on top of him. We explored and tasted: kissing and nibbling, his skin on mine, his hands touching me, fingers slipping up my spine, his palms running over my breasts, lips on my stomach, my throat, my hip, lower back.

Light from the fireworks burst through the windows, highlighting his face in a ray of colors and reflecting in his eyes. I stopped and stared down on him.

Wow.

I held him at arm's length, never appreciating how absolutely striking he was until now. His chiseled face, the scruff along his jaw, the scars marking his battles, his unbelievable build, and his gorgeous white-blue eyes. His hair, plaited tightly against his scalp, was another shield, keeping people at a distance. I did not want to be kept away so I lifted my hands and threaded my fingers through the braids, loosening them. His soft hair fell around the pillow. Golden and beautiful. He was magnificent, in a distant, don't touch way. With his hair down he appeared far more accessible.

Perspiration glided between my breasts. The humidity swelled in the room. He sat up, his tongue followed the line of liquid, catching it. My skin tingled and craving welled between my legs. Our eyes locked again.

He flipped me on my back, my legs curling tight around him. This went past desire or want. Our breaths were quick as his fingers moved down between my legs, opening me. He barely touched me, and my nails burrowed into his back.

"Now... please," I begged, bucking against him.

He slid down my body then back up, slipping into me. I gasped. There was slight pain as the Viking filled me. He rocked forward, stealing another breath from me. Then again. *Holy hell.* My body was reacting as though I had never experienced real sex before. I felt myself tighten around him, and a deep moan erupted from his throat. Pleasure so intense flickered through me as he plunged deeper into me, our rhythm picking up pace. My legs and nails dug into him. "More... harder." I could not seem to get close enough, to have enough of him. He thrust deeper, harder, until my eyes leaked with water. I still wanted more.

Friction built, creating an even more desperate need

for each other. He tilted me toward him and drove in harder. A cry escaped my lips as I felt my climax coming. My eyes could no longer focus nor could I breathe. I heard him swear, and he pushed my bent leg toward my shoulder. The movement tipped him in farther and with one more deep thrust, everything exploded. Both of us cried out. He drove in once more and ripples of pleasure rocked me. He released inside me, quaking my body again. Every breath I took sent another small orgasm through my limbs.

We laid together, breathing deeply. I had been right: sex with him would not be something I could come back from untouched.

ELEVEN

We carried on for the rest of the night, only pausing for a moment before our mouths would find each other again. The energy from the all-night party swirled in the room, throbbing to the point I could sense my body absorbing it. Energy was addicting, even to humans, but this was different. It was replenishing me. Feeding me. Taking on more fae qualities was no longer the worst thing in the world to me. My fear was not developing more fae traits; it was taking them away from Ryker. Finally around dawn, exhausted and spent, we fell asleep.

When my lids eventually lifted, sunlight splayed through our windows. The pulled-back curtains let in too much light for my sensitive head. I grunted and dug my face into the pillow. Damn whiskey.

It was already hot and sticky, which was not helping me feel better. The sheet clung to my bare skin, and I smelled of sex and sweat. Images of me tangled with Ryker came flooding into my mind. Picking up my head, I peered over at him. He slept on his back, the crook of his elbow covering his eyes. The sheet only lay across his lower torso, but it did not disguise what was underneath. Or how the material tented up. Instinctually I responded to it, wanting to crawl on top of him, feel him inside me again.

I sucked in a gulp of air and turned away. The morning light and blistering headache brought an end to the dream we indulged in last night. In the shelter of darkness, we could hide from our fear, prejudices, and guilt and act out our passions under the influence of hormones and alcohol. But what if he felt different today? What if he took one look at me and realized his mistake? I was not Amara. Not the girl he really wanted, but I was here and available... and willing. We had been through a lot and relied on each other through some extreme situations. After a while you could mix up those emotions, mistake them for more than what they were.

He will leave you, Zoey. You know it is only a matter of time. They always do.

The inner voice pushed me to my feet. Panic and the need to pee took me to the bathroom. I grabbed a clean, folded sheet off the table left for us by the maid and wrapped it around me. I cracked the bathroom door open, tiptoed inside, and closed it quietly behind me.

"Well, well, well." Sprig's voice banged against my skull. I jumped and spun around to see the brown furball sitting on the edge of the tub. "So... how are *you* this morning?" His tiny ears wiggled as his forehead went up and down in a mocking tease.

"Sprig," I warned him.

"Surprised you are walking."

I gripped my forehead. Talking and thinking felt heavy to my brain.

"Seems the human and the Wanderer worked out their differences after all. All night long. And quite loudly I may add."

"Sprig, is it at all possible you can choose this morning not to want to talk to me?" I begged, turning myself to the mirror. I cringed at my image. My hair was so knotted and tangled, it looked like a purple Muppet was sitting on my head. Black mascara ringed my eyes, but a glow colored my cheeks. A lightness and joy lit up my aura, like a girl who had the most incredible sex of her life and who had been so thoroughly satisfied she couldn't even think straight. Against my will a smile pulled my mouth.

"I saw that, *Bhean*."

"Saw what?" I forced the smile off my face.

Sprig jumped down, scuttled across the room, and jumped in the sink. He sat back on his legs, his head tilted. "You like him. I mean really, really like him."

Protecting myself was instinct. I'd always kept people from learning my weaknesses. And my feelings toward Ryker were the ultimate vulnerability to me. Yes. I liked Ryker... probably more than liked. But I would not be the first to express it. It would be too much for me to lose if he did not feel the same. My problem was I either kept people at arm's length or handed them over my heart. Two people prior to Ryker had succeeded in breaking down my walls. Two people. Ever. And both left me.

"No." I shook my head. "It was purely sex. An itch we both needed to scratch."

Sprig crossed his arms. "I don't believe you. It was more than an itch. It always has been with you two."

My tangled hair bounced as I continued to deny Sprig's words. "We were drunk." *He will go back to Amara. You know he will.* "It was a mistake." It almost hurt to say those words, but I couldn't seem to stop them. For my own protection I had to convince myself it was the truth. I could not fall for a fae. No way.

Thankfully, Sprig's attention span was worse than a gnat. "So... can we have breakfast now?" He bobbed up and down on his legs. "I'm soooo hungry. Oh, can we *please* go to Izel's. I *have* to have those Peruvian pancakes, with honey... but make sure it's not the ones with bananas on top." His lip curled. "Because I don't like those. Oh! Or we can go to the churro vendor on the street. He makes the *best* churros. I like min—"

"Sprig?" I leaned over the sink, letting my head drop. The weight of it throbbed in my ears, along with his incessant yammering. "Shut up, please."

"Oh, did someone not get a good night's sleep?" A tiny hand patted my head. "Maybe if you went to bed before dawn. Or didn't keep the entire building awake with sounds only dying animals make."

"Get out." I pointed at the door.

He snickered and jumped off the sink. He opened the bathroom window. "But we are getting breakfast, right?"

"Go!"

He chirped and swung out of the window. I heard him enter the window in the bedroom.

After I dealt with my bladder, I heard movement in the next room. Ryker was up. If only I could hide out in the bathroom the rest of the day. I had to face him, and it was better to see the truth in his eyes than prolong it.

141

I took in a shaky breath, tightened the sheet around me, and opened the door. He stood with his back to me, his hair, free from the braids, lay soft around his shoulders. He was buttoning his cargo pants. His broad back was still unclothed and bore red nail marks down it.

It was embarrassing recalling the many times he had me clawing, begging, and moaning. It was a side of me I never showed. Before, I wouldn't have let a man know he could possess me so completely. With Ryker it wouldn't stay hidden.

The world underneath my feet was unstable, and I hated it. He had broken past many of my walls. He knew more about me than anyone else in the world. It was a dangerous place.

"Hey." My voice came out fragmented and soft.

He glanced over his shoulder. My deepest fears slammed into me, breaking in shards through my gut. His face was hard. Cold. Distant.

"Hey." He nodded and returned to buttoning his pants.

My legs shifted nervously. Oh damn, we ruined it. We finally had some sort of alliance, a partnership, and in one drunken night we destroyed everything.

"I'll go use the community shower down the hall. You can have this one," he said, his voice void of emotion. He walked over to the dresser and pulled open the top drawer. I stood in the bathroom doorway, watching him. His eyes never lifted as he grabbed some fresh clothes.

"Okay. Thanks," I muttered.

He nodded, grabbed a towel off the table, and left

the room. The instant he closed the door, liquid prickled under my lids.

"Think you two need a time-out again." Sprig munched on some dried mango chips he'd left on the TV.

I bit so hard into my lip, the metallic taste of blood coated my tongue. I yanked open the middle drawer and grabbed some clothes.

"Breakfast?" Sprig yelled out as I slammed the bathroom door, rattling the room. I fell back against the door, my hand cupped over my mouth. I would not cry. "So... is that a maybe?" Sprig called.

My response was to bang my head into the door—repeatedly.

TWELVE

Dressed and clean, the three of us headed for Izel's. We'd been there a few times since the first morning. It was family owned and some of the best food I ever had. My hangover was dying for nutrients, but my stomach coiled with hurt and rejection.

Ryker and I didn't speak or look at each other unless it was necessary. The coldness between us was obvious with the two of us sitting there and not talking.

The people here were a lot more open to primates hanging around, but they still didn't like them sitting at a table. The staff would shoo the monkeys away, deeming them a nuisance to the patrons. Sprig sat in my bag, a plastic baby bib around his neck. The way he ate, we needed hazmat suits, but this was all we had.

"If you 'accidently' bite me again, I will bite back this time," I threatened him. He had become a little overzealous in eating the last time we had come here.

"And she will too." Ryker sipped at his orange juice.

A blush colored my cheeks. In anger I had bitten him when we first met. It wasn't why I turned red. Teeth marks, my teeth marks, were currently bruised along his neck and shoulder reminding me of the previous night.

And morning. Even with hurt anchoring me down, the need to crawl over the table and straddle him in the middle of the restaurant gripped me so powerfully I had to dig my nails into my palms to stop myself. He had awakened something in me that did not want to be suppressed any longer. It wanted more.

I swallowed and focused on Sprig. My back was to the customers, so I could feed Sprig easier. Ryker liked being the one to face the door.

"Give me the damn pancake." Sprig strangled the edges of my bag.

"When they get here." I put my finger to my lips.

Izel was the woman who originally opened the diner, but she had passed away several years before. The daughter, Melosa, now cooked and ran the place along with her three daughters, two sons, and husband. She was in her late fifties, with short, dark hair, and big brown eyes. She ran the restaurant like every guest was sitting at her own dining room table. She took pride in every dish and would probably be insulted if we didn't finish everything on our plates. We always did. I think it was the reason she took an instant liking to us. She welcomed our monstrous appetites and appreciation of her food. It was enough for her to look past her automatic suspicion of newcomers and to treat us like locals.

Melosa rounded the corner; our plates lined up her arms. The aroma of hot crepes and butter filled my nose. Sprig chirped and rattled my bag back and forth in excitement. I settled my hand on his head.

She smiled down at him and set my plate in front of me. She had caught me feeding him the second time we had eaten here. She ignored the fact I had a monkey as long as I kept him in my bag and out of sight of tourists and other patrons. I knew we were walking a precarious line. The moment Sprig got overexcited and spoke without thinking, it would be over. She, along with Tulio the bartender, would come after us with pitchforks.

She placed Ryker's dishes in front of him, everything divided into separate small plates. I don't know when she learned of his quirk. It probably was one of the first times when either she saw me switch with him or saw him push his food into different corners so they wouldn't touch.

Melosa was the first human woman, aside from me, Ryker genuinely smiled at. She winked at him every time she went by. When she learned we weren't "together," she paraded all three of her daughters over to him. She would probably try her sons next.

Today, she stopped, peering at us. Her gaze darted back and forth between us, taking in my beard-burned face and the bites on his neck.

A flood of Spanish rolled off her tongue in a giddy cadence, too fast for me to pick it up. My Spanish was good, but I still couldn't understand most of what she said. She gave my hand a squeeze, winked at Ryker, and took off for the kitchen.

"Give me, give me, give mmmmeeeeee." Sprig grabbed for the plate.

I tore off a piece of soft warm dough. Butter and honey dripped off the pancake onto my hand. My mouth watered. Sprig nipped at my finger then chomped down on the piece. He emitted a blissful sigh.

"What did she say?" I slanted my head toward Melosa's fleeting frame.

Ryker cut into his stack. He liked his only with butter.

"She gave us an old Peruvian blessing, wishing us love and a full house." He kept his attention on his breakfast.

"Oh." I picked up my fork.

Everything was awkward now. The sex had been unbelievable, but if it meant we lost our friendship, I'd lose him. I couldn't say it had been worth it.

We ate in silence, my attention mostly on getting dough into Sprig's mouth fast enough. In the middle of one of his bites, his head fell back and his mouth opened as he began to breathe deeply. Out like a light.

I took the unchewed food from him and wiped the sticky honey and butter off his hands and mouth before placing him at the bottom of my bag.

"You act like a mother." Ryker's voice jolted me.

"What?"

Ryker tilted his head toward the bundle in my bag. "Were you like this with your sister?"

The chair scraped the tile as I leaned back into it. "Yeah. Joanna wasn't going to take care of her. It was up to me. At thirteen I was Lexie's mother and sister."

"Taking care of people... it comes naturally to you." It was a statement.

"I did what I needed to survive. For both Lexie and me." I cleared my throat. "And I still failed."

"You didn't fail."

"My sister's dead. You don't call that a failure?"

"Like my sister?" He crossed his arms, inclining back.

"No. It's not what I meant."

"You can take the blame for your sister, but I can't for mine?"

Losing our sisters in eerily similar situations only linked us together even more. There were few people who could really understand what it felt like to watch your house burn with someone you love inside it and not be able to save them. Self-blame was another thing we shared. I could see how it wasn't his fault, but with myself, I couldn't see it as clearly. We actually had much in common, and I didn't want to lose him. If it meant putting my pride aside, I would have to deal.

I sat up, about to say something. Ryker halted the words in my throat. His body was rigid and his eyes were on something behind me.

Oh no

I wrenched around in my seat, ready to stand and run. Ryker had yet to move from his chair, which was the only thing anchoring me to my spot. I spotted the glow of aura, the fae at the door, one I recognized from a few days ago. Croygen. But by then it was too late. Spikes of adrenaline and fear rushed through my veins. I slammed my lids together so I wouldn't puke as wind whipped at my ponytail.

My tender head and stomach did not respond to the sudden trip. The second I opened my eyes and recognized the rumpled unmade bed and spewed clothes on the floor, I ran for our bathroom. My breakfast was coming back for a visit.

"What a waste. Those were amazing pancakes, and you simply tossed them into the toilet." Sprig wiggled free of my bag and climbed out next to me.

My lids narrowed as I flashed him a glower.

"Oh, sprite spit, now you are bleeding." Sprig pointed at my face.

I touched my nose, and my fingers came away dripping red. I squeezed my eyes, rubbing my temples. A part of me still hoped Daniel was wrong, and the truth about seers was incorrect. But the nosebleeds were getting worse.

The sensation of Sprig's feet and hands on my leg tickled my bare skin. I felt toilet paper being pushed against my face. My lashes lifted as he shoved the wad unceremoniously up my nose. I took the paper and dabbed it at the pooling blood.

"Thank you."

Sprig nodded.

I waited a few moments, but like the last dozen times, the nosebleed wasn't followed by a blinding headache, for which I was grateful. The change had to mean something, and it probably wasn't good. Whatever defect was in my brain had probably grown past the headaches and was preparing me for death.

I pushed to my feet and went over to the sink, brushing my teeth and splashing water on my face. Today felt insufferably humid. Clouds were moving in, keeping the heat stagnant over the town. Adjusting my tank top and shorts, I walked out of the bathroom. I wanted to crawl back into bed, feeling exhausted, but I pressed on.

"Where are you going?" Sprig sprinted after me.

"To find Ryker."

"Right." Sprig leaped onto the bed. "Where did we leave him this time?"

"Izel's." I lifted my eyebrow. "Remember? Where you practically had sex with the pastry dish?"

A blissful expression exploded over Sprig's features. Then he looked down and his features turned to horror. "Ugh! Speaking of sex." He hopped back and forth on each foot as if the bed was burning him. "It reeks of you two. You are going to have to burn this bed." He jumped for the TV. He sat, frantically wiping at his feet. "Oh, oak sap! I need to be disinfected now," he whimpered.

"This coming from the sprite who rolled in donkey dung to cool himself off."

"I thought it was mud."

I smirked and went to the door. "You coming?"

"You think I want to sit here in this bordello all day? Seriously, your night of passion has seeped into the walls."

My cheeks heated as another memory flickered through my mind. "If you keep talking about it, I will wrap you in one of the sheets and tie you to the bed."

He chirped and ran for the closing door. Scaling my body, he took a seat on my shoulder. "Poor Pam will have to suffer in your stench all day." He sighed.

I smiled. I had given up trying to convince him Pam didn't have emotions. Actually, I sometimes slipped and treated her like she did. And really, who was I to judge?

The restaurant was only a block away, but I fought with myself to turn back around and go back to bed. Ryker was a big boy and could take care of himself.

My mistake was saying it out loud.

"Yeah, I'll bet he's a *big* boy." Sprig tapped the side of my face with his elbow in jest. "Oh, Ryker, you are *so* big."

"I did not say that."

"Oh, Viking, bang me with your large stick again."

"Sprig, shut up."

He snickered and opened his mouth again to talk. I snatched a banana off a seller's cart and shoved it into his mouth.

"Aaaacck!" He batted the fruit away, scraping the taste off his tongue. "That was mean, *Bhean*. Dirty!"

"Then you stop being nasty."

He tilted his soft head against my cheek. "But you like it dirty."

"Ahhhh!" I yelled and Sprig went sailing off my shoulder and landed in the bushes.

He brushed himself off, scrambling out of the brush. "Dirty and rough."

I flipped him off and kept walking.

"With no sense of humor," he shouted.

I stepped into Izel's with Sprig tucked underneath my loose ponytail. After turning his wide eyes up at me, I couldn't stay mad at him. Melosa's youngest daughter, Raquel, was behind the cash register. Her eyes widened at seeing me, and she shook her head, calling for her mom.

Melosa bustled out of the kitchen, wiping her hands on her apron. She took me in, a frown cut across her forehead. "*¿A donde fuiste, senorita?*" Where did you go?

My eyes searched around pointlessly for Ryker. I knew he wasn't there, but my eyes still went to his vacated chair.

"You two disappeared," she said in Spanish. I knew she meant figuratively, but my shoulders still stiffened.

"I know. I am sorry. Please accept our apologies and add the meal to our tab." Fluent Spanish flowed out of my mouth. "Did you happen to see where Ryker went?"

Melosa slanted her head. She wasn't dumb. Melosa picked up on the fact we weren't quite right, but overlooked it. We *weren't* normal. Superstition was extremely strong in these parts, and they believed in the paranormal more here than Americans did. If DMG was searching for more seers, they should check out this area.

"He and another man were here, but I do not remember seeing them leave or in what direction they went," she responded.

Great. Probably Croygen or Ryker glamouring their exit so no one would remember seeing them depart.

Melosa pressed her lips together and placed her hand on my arm, steering me back for the door. "Be. Careful," she emphasized, keeping her voice low. At first I wasn't quite sure what she meant, but her head tipped to the side, her eyes full of unspoken awareness. My stomach rolled, knowing her warning was more about what she wasn't saying. Did she know what we were?

"And do not trust the man in black." She spoke sternly, almost commanding. Very unlike her normal cheerful cadence.

"What?" I pulled back and heat rushed my veins, turning acid around in my stomach.

"He is not genuine." She glanced around warily. "His soul is corrupt. He will trick and deceive. Neither of you are safe." She pressed her fingers into my arm again and nodded for the door, telling me to go. Find Ryker. The way she talked made me think she was a sensitive or possibly a seer. She understood what we were or at least that we were different, and for some reason she accepted Ryker and me. She nudged her head toward the door once more. "Go. Now."

I squeezed her hand. "*Gracias.*" I nodded to her and Raquel before heading out. Raquel huffed, glaring at me. She clearly did not feel the same as her mother about me. Ignoring her, I hustled out the exit. Melosa's warning clanged in my lungs. I needed to find Ryker.

"Calm down, *Bhean*." Sprig patted the side of my face once we were out of the door.

"I have to locate Ryker." He had known Croygen for a long time. He knew him and what he was capable of more than anyone, but the urgency to find Ryker didn't lessen. I simply wanted to see him, to know he was all right. What if Croygen turned him over to Vadik or some other group willing to pay for the Wanderer and information on the stone?

"Don't worry about him. He can take care of himself."

"I know..." I took a deep breath, scanning the streets for a six-foot-three Viking.

"Geez, *Bhean,* your shoulder is so tight it's like riding a Snathaid."

"What's a Snathaid?"

"A needle glider?"

"A what?"

"I think you guys call them dragonflies?" Sprig rubbed at my shoulder. "Well, they are a little different in the Otherworld. Snathaids are bony and uncomfortable to ride. It's like having a wedgie up your ass."

Forcing my shoulders to relax, I walked to the main part of town. My flip-flops trampled over beer bottles, confetti, random bits of clothing, and who knows what else from the previous night's festivities. I didn't want to think about the bra lying in the gutter or the underwear on the telephone pole. If Ryker hadn't stopped me, mine would be in an alley.

Most people were still in bed, nursing hangovers and wisely staying out of the heat. There were a few men at the far end starting to sweep, but as slow as they were, it would take them days to finish.

I walked from one end of each street to another with no results, only escalating the increasing panic. The feeling something was wrong or Ryker was in trouble stirred my legs and chest in frantic movements.

Minutes, then hours, passed. Sprig eventually passed out in the safety of my bag. Every step I took, the familiar feeling rose in my chest. Fear. Abandonment. It was automatic and predictable, but I still couldn't seem to stop the panic clenching at my lungs, restricting air from passing through. Sprig's outline against my leg was the only thing keeping me from huddling in a ball and rocking.

"Dammit!" I yelled. I hated Ryker had brought out such intense feelings in me. I kept them well hidden before. Not even Daniel provoked this response in me. "Get it together, Zoey, he is fine!" I berated myself. Melosa's warning only provoked all my other insecurities to surge along with the fear for his safety. I knew he hadn't left me, but he brought out the fear in me. I didn't really want to analyze why; it was there, and I needed to acknowledge it and move on. Before I had been a Collector, a hunter of fae, raising a preteen in a wheelchair, and getting myself through school. I was capable on my own and didn't need anyone else. If he ever did leave, for Amara, or any other reason, I would be all right. I was good before he came, and I would be fine after he left.

My heart felt sad at the thought, but I knew I was right. I would be okay.

I took in a deep breath, rolling back my shoulders. The rain clouds trundled thicker in the sky, threatening rain and rumbling with thunder.

The first splashes of raindrops hit my forehead when I finally reached our lodging. I took two steps at a time up the two flights of stairs to our floor. Key in hand, I went for the lock when the door swung open, a large mass blocking the doorway.

"Where have you been?" Ryker's tone was sharp, his face pinched in fury. His wrath took me off guard, and I stood silently in the entry. "I didn't know if you jumped to Zimbabwe or China and couldn't get back."

My brows furrowed. "You're mad at me?"

"Yes," he growled.

I pushed past him, and he shut the door behind me.

"I love you're mad at *me*." I put my hands on my hips, facing him. "You vanished too. Where did *you* disappear to? I've been freaking out all day thinking Croygen turned you over to Vadik or something. If you were really concerned about me, you could have easily found me scouring this town *for you*."

A muscle along his jaw twitched, but he kept all emotion from his face. "I can handle Croygen."

"Really? Melosa thinks we should stay away from him—that he is dangerous."

"What does Melosa have to do with this? How does she know Croygen?"

I crossed my arms. "She knows what we are."

"What?" Ryker froze, his eyes widening. "She knows?"

"I think she is a sensitive." A sensitive wasn't as powerful as a seer, but they still saw more than a normal person. "She warned me to be careful. Said Croygen was not to be trusted."

"She said that? She said to stay away from Croygen?"

"Well, not in so many words. She called him the man in black."

Ryker rubbed his stubble, walking in a circle, irritation riding high on his shoulders. He was silent, but the energy of his anger was loud. He slammed the chair into the table. "Like I said, I can handle Croygen.

And we need him right now. I don't need some crazy kook getting into our business."

"Excuse me? You know I am one of those crazy kooks." I pointed at myself.

Ryker angled his head in annoyance. "Slightly different."

"Yeah, I am crazier."

He took a deep breath, trying to calm himself. His fingers wrapped around the top of the chair. "You never told me where you went."

"Where I went?" I shook my head, confused as to why this was more a concern than Melosa knowing what we were or the danger of Croygen. "I jumped back here and then went immediately back to Izel's. You were gone. All day. So don't give me this fake overprotective crap. I can take care of myself." I stepped to him.

"Fake?" he repeated. "You think this is fake?"

"I somehow got through before you. I think I can survive fine on my own."

A crease wrinkled the space between his eyes. "What are you talking about? I never said you couldn't handle yourself. Are you kidding? You can take care of yourself better than anyone I know."

"Then what is your problem?" I gritted out.

He worked his jaw back and forth, his hand rubbing at his forehead. An aggravated noise came out of him as he turned and walked away from me. "I was worried."

"What?"

He wheeled around; his arms outstretched. "I was worried about you, all right?"

I stood, stumped for a response.

"I didn't know what happened to you, and I didn't like it."

Oh.

My earlier pumped-up self-talk deflated like a leaky balloon.

We both stayed silent. Finally, I cleared my throat. "What did Croygen want?"

Ryker rubbed at his beard. "He found Regnus. We meet Croygen tomorrow morning after daybreak."

"Really? That's great." I forced myself to sound happy. I had to trust Ryker. If he said he could handle him, I had to let it go. Plus, Ryker was right. We needed him.

Ryker's gaze narrowed on the top of my tank, stalking over to me. "You have blood on your shirt." He picked up the fabric, his touch igniting my skin.

I peered at the few spots of red on my top. My mouth opened to tell him the truth, but nothing came out. I wasn't ready. Even more after last night. Deep down, I sensed Ryker knew the truth, although neither of us vocalized it.

He moved toward the door. His shoulders tense around his ears. "Don't wait up."

"What? Where are you going?"

He slipped out, ignoring me.

Ahhhhh! A scream wanted to jump from my throat. Instead, I grunted and slammed the other chair into the table. "Goddamn Viking!" I leaned over the chair, breathing deeply.

"Is it safe to come out now?" A little voice spoke

from the bag still wrapped around me.

I lifted off the strap and set it on the table. He crawled out on the counter. "Sorry, Sprig."

"I don't like it when Mommy and Daddy fight."

I glared at him as I walked over to the dresser, pulling out a clean top.

"You know the asshole, I mean Ryker, is only acting like a toad because he's scared."

"Scared of losing his magic." I huffed and slammed the drawer, the dresser banged into the wall.

"Don't be all martyr-ie."

"Martyr-ie? Is it even a word?"

"Yes." He nodded.

"Adding an *ie* to the end of everything doesn't suddenly make it a word."

He stuck his tongue out at me. "Getting off the point, *Bhean*." He grabbed at a bag of *Cancha Salada*, a form of corn nuts, and started munching on the salty treats. He frowned. "They really should coat these in honey." But he still lifted another to his mouth. "I mean, salt is fine, but I think they would be much better dipped in sweet, lovely, sugary honey."

"Sprig?" I snapped my fingers. "Now you're getting off topic."

"Right." He moved to a grocery bag we left on the table and threw out anything he couldn't eat. All I could see was his fuzzy tail as he rummaged through. "Ick." He tossed a banana over his shoulder. "Ugh." A carton of toothpaste flew out on the table. "Isn't there anything good in here?"

I sighed when another item was disregarded from the

bag. "Sprig."

"Oh, yes!" He wiggled out of the bag, rolling the can of Inca Kola out with him. He fumbled with the lid, rattling the can.

"Let me." I could imagine the cola spraying us, drenching the ceiling and walls with the sticky substance. I opened it and jammed a straw into it.

He took a deep slug of the liquid and groaned happily. "Better! What was I talking about? Oh right! Viking boy doesn't handle showing his feelings well. He will respond in anger or frustration, but he's only hiding the fact he cares for you... a lot."

I plunked down on the bed, noticing housekeeping had made our bed with fresh sheets. A new stack of towels sat on the table, and our disregarded clothes were now folded and stacked on top of the dresser. Involuntarily, chagrin heated my face. The maid only came in once a week, and she had been in the day before. I was aware she lived in the room down the hall. She must have heard us, and knew the sheets would need to be changed again.

"Told you, you were loud," Sprig mumbled between bites.

I leaned over my lap and put my face in my hands. I was embarrassed that everyone on this floor or perhaps the building heard us, but more than anything, I wished to do it all over again.

"*Bhean*." Sprig jumped to the bed, crawling up my leg. "Who knows what tomorrow is going to bring. So why are you sitting here? Go after what you want."

I gulped and looked at my hands. He was right. This was not a time for regrets or fear. I stood up, Sprig falling to the floor with a squeak.

"You're right."

He climbed back on the mattress and bounced up and down. "Go get him, girl!"

I nodded and marched for the door. I wasn't going to waste another second being stupid. Ryker might not feel the same, but at least he would know how I felt.

"Wait! Where are you going?" Sprig stopped jumping.

"To find Ryker." I gave him a bemused look.

"Oh. Now? I was thinking more *after* you got me dinner." He widened his eyes, sweet and adoring. "The honey chicken down at Jose Ricardo's? Oh, pretty please. And several of the *suspiro limeño*. Holy fae poop! Those were good."

I left him still jabbering. He had leftovers in the small refrigerator. He would survive. Without thinking, I proceeded to Tulio's. It's where I would go.

Soft rain pelted down as I ran for the bar. A low rumble of thunder gurgled from the clouds above. It would soon pour. Rain was different here than in Seattle. There it was constant and something you almost could ignore. Rain here stopped everything. It was as if the sky dumped all it had at once.

I wiped my arms and face as I entered the dingy bar. It was quiet, but a few regulars sat at their usual stools. Ryker was sitting at the end of the bar.

I stopped and watched him sip his beer. After every drink he slammed the bottle on the bar, his body language cold and unapproachable. Seeing him made it difficult not to lose the determination propelling me here; rejection and heartache was hard to ignore. But I knew my anger was not at him but our situation. We both were not the type to sit around, depending on others for help. I felt stagnant and lost. We had no real home or place to go. We were waiting. And that killed both of us. At least now, dangerous or not, Croygen gave us a forward moment. It could be our demise, but I think we both would take it over this purgatory.

Tulio gave me a nod, and I settled into the seat next to Ryker. Tulio set a beer in front of me, already knowing my favorite.

"Gracias."

He quickly moved back to the other end of the bar, closer to the TV and away from us. Most of the patrons were watching soccer, ignoring the two outsiders.

"A little predictable, huh?" Ryker brought the bottle to his lips and took a swig.

"Not many places to go in this town."

Ryker snorted. "Jose Ricardo's has a bar."

"And it's filled with humans having dinner."

His nose twitched slightly with disgust.

The sound of thunder quaked through the bar and filled the awkward silence between us. I took another gulp of beer, needing the liquid courage. It also helped with the headache—hair of the dog.

Just say it, Zoey. Rip the Band-Aid.

"Ryker." I turned to face him. "What happened last night—"

"You mean the *mistake*?" He kept his head straight, cutting me off.

Instant knife in the heart.

"Like you said, we were drunk." He shifted in his seat. "We can forget it happened."

My brows scrunched together. *Like I said?*

My hand went to my mouth. "Oh my God. You heard me, in the bathroom, talking to Sprig."

The side of his mouth curved in a sneer. "We scratched the itch. Now we can go back to normal. Disliking each other."

"No!" The word sputtered out of my mouth. "I-I don't want to go back." He finally twisted to look at me. Lightning flickered outside, reflecting in his pupils. "Is this why you've been distant and cold to me all day?" I asked. He glanced back at the mirror behind the bar. "I said those things because I was scared. I was terrified you wouldn't feel the same. I protect myself. It's what I do. Sprig caught me off guard, and it was my automatic reaction." I touched his arm. His eyes darted to my fingers and then to my face. "It was all bullshit. But I'd rather end it than lose you... if it's what you want."

My gaze shot up the tattoo on his neck as it flickered with light.

"I want you in my life. Even if it's only as friends." The words were thick, and it was hard to get them out of my throat. It was the most vulnerable I'd ever let anyone see me, but the floodgates were open, and I couldn't seem to stop the words from coming out. I could feel the tears building behind my lids, but he gave me no time to let the emotion surface.

His hands were on my face, pulling me to him. His lips found mine, and my heart exploded at his touch.

His mouth devoured mine, stealing my breath away. I hated PDA couples, but I couldn't stop kissing him and wanted the world to disappear around us, to leave us alone.

I sent out a "you don't notice us" chant in my head. Hopefully, my glamour worked good enough the other customers would ignore the couple making out at the end of the bar.

Outside the rain pelted the dirt in constant attack. Another boom of thunder rocked through the room, and the lights blinked in retaliation. A strange sense of *déjà vu* hit me as lightning streaked around the sky, illuminating the dark pub.

This time I didn't care if the world crumbled around us. Neither of us seemed keen on pulling away. Our mouths wanted more from the other, both of us gasping for air when we could. It felt good to simply kiss him. It was something I could do all night, though my lower half wanted way more.

Ryker broke away first, putting his forehead against mine. "The entire day all I wanted to do was drag you back to bed. I couldn't stop thinking of you. Wanting you."

Relief came out in a shaky sigh. "Me too."

His fingers went through my hair, stripping my ponytail of its holder. My long dark violet tresses tumbled over my shoulders. Seeing my hair was like a jolt to my fear button. Since we were being honest, I covered the hand he had tangled in my hair and said, "I'm scared, and this is the reason." I nodded to my locks.

His eyes narrowed in confusion, then they grew

wide, the confusion clearing from them. "You think your purple hair is the only reason I'm attracted to you?"

"Uhhh..." A shaky laugh curled out. "Kind of." He leaned back, his eyes searching mine. "I see how it could happen. My therapist calls it transference. You took your feelings for her and transferred them to me. With my hair like this I'm her stand-in."

Irritation flickered in his expression. "A little purple dye, and I become an idiot?"

"Ryker."

He sat back farther from me. "So... every girl with blonde or brown hair is the same girl to me? Thank goodness you and Elthia didn't have the same color hair. I wouldn't have been able to tell you apart."

"Ryker," I tried again.

He propelled forward, getting only an inch from my face. "Believe me, you are nothing like Amara. Nothing. And a little hair dye isn't going to suddenly make you so."

My hands twisted in my lap. My hair fell around my face, blanketing me from Ryker. His hand came through the curtain and curled around my jaw, pulling my head up to look at him. "Shave it, dye it black, it won't make a difference. *You* have gotten under my skin. The stubborn, bossy, tough-as-nails human."

We found each other this time. My mouth tingled as his kiss deepened. His tongue and lips demanded more and mine responded in kind. "You want to go?" he whispered in my ear.

"Oh hell, yeah." I was out of my stool before he could even blink. He smiled and called out to Tulio.

The entire bar was focused on the screen; no one paid us a bit of attention. It probably had less to do with my so-called glamour magic and more to do with the soccer game. Tulio gave us a wave and turned back to the TV. Ryker laced his fingers in mine and together we headed for the door. The smile on my face almost hurt my cheeks, but it would not relax.

Rain poured down from the night sky. The streets were void of people who decided to stay out of the torrential downpour. We had been caught in the rain several times together in Seattle. Never in such sexy circumstances, with teeth-chattering and bone-stabbing cold. This time was different. The cool water felt refreshing against my hot skin, dripping down my head. My hair absorbed the water and hung in heavy pieces down my back.

Ryker watched as water slipped down my nose to my top lip. His eyes locked on my mouth. He sucked the water off my lips, nipping at the bottom one. This boy knew every button to push. He stepped closer, his mouth never leaving mine, and pressed our wet bodies together. The rain slithered in trails down our skin, igniting a fire instead of dampening it. His hands went under my arms, lifting me. "Damn, you're short." I felt his lips turn into a smile. He kissed me again and set me back on me feet. My hand wrapped around his, and I began to walk backward, tugging him with me.

"Actually, I'm pretty average for a girl. You're the Neanderthal."

His eyes sparked and grabbed the back of my head. We dove into another long toe-curling kiss. I became more anxious to get home.

When we finally did, I was expecting to see Sprig

passed out with corn chips stuck to his eyelids. But he was staring at the television like he was in a trance, a Spanish soap opera playing.

"Sprig?"

Nothing. Not even a flinch of recognition.

"Sprig?" I said louder.

Again... nada.

"We could have sex right next to him, and he won't notice." Ryker's lips tickled my ear.

"Ugh." I shuddered. Sprig was like my little brother, a pet, and a son all rolled into one. He was also becoming my best friend.

Wow. My world had changed.

Ryker's warm mouth trailed down my neck, and I grabbed a chair to steady myself. The accumulation of need we had denied all day was starting to reach its breaking point.

The sky streaked with light and a boom rushed behind it. The lights and TV flickered and then went out, plunging the room into darkness.

"What? Nooooooo! She was going to find out whose baby it is." Sprig's wail broke through the shadows. I burst out laughing, which caused him to chirp. "When the hell did you two get back?"

"Time to go, Sprig." Ryker's voice was gravelly. His hand skirted up my back, pushing my hair to the side. His breath hot on my neck.

"Yup. Time to go," I responded.

"Go? Go where? Are we finally going to dinner?"

"No. You are going to your *room*." Ryker stepped away from me, and I felt his absence like a cold wind.

"Room?" Sprig responded. "Oh, you mean the bathroom. Oh, no way. I am not listening to you two go at it again."

"Then I suggest you find somewhere else to go tonight." I could hear Ryker rummaging in the corner. A flick of a match and the room glowed with a single candle.

"Where did you get that?"

"I think power outages happen quite a bit; they have a few stocked in the drawer. And in the storage closet across the way."

"It's like being back in Seattle again."

"Yeah, *exactly*." He moved behind me and slipped a hand down the front of my pants.

"Sprig. Out!" I yelled.

In the glow, I saw Sprig cross his arms and huff. He didn't move.

"Sprig?"

"Not. Talking. To. You."

"Could you not talk to me in the other room?"

"No. I don't want Pam to be subject to this either. We will go find some dinner. I am sure some restaurant will take pity on us."

"Oh, jeez. Fine. You can stay." I threw up my arms. "We won't do anything."

"Nah, I was only kidding. You two go at it like rabbits. I'll be back later." He jumped on the TV and then out the window into the rain.

"Don't pass out face down in the mud or you'll drown," I called after him.

"Not sure that's a phrase many mothers have used

before." Ryker laughed.

I spun around to face him. "I am not acting like a mother."

A grin played on his mouth as he reached out for my hips and twisted me back around, facing the table. "Stay still."

He unhurriedly drew my pants down, his lips gliding over the back of my legs, making his way back up, electrifying every nerve ending with his tongue. Candlelight flickered shadows against the wall as my underwear skimmed down my legs.

"Remember what the river fairy said about me?" He stood, pulling my top over my head.

"You were a fine specimen?"

He chuckled. "That I liked kinky games?"

I sucked in air with excitement. "Yeah."

"Not completely true. I don't like games. But I'm all for the rest." His deep voice skated up my neck. The sound of his zipper and pants dropping to the floor doubled my heartbeat. His hands spread my legs, and he pushed me onto the table. His fingers trailed down my arms till his hands covered mine, then he gripped my fingers over the edge of the table. "Do you want to have a safe word?"

"No," I whispered hoarsely. "Don't hold anything back. I want you completely."

Grabbing my hips, he slipped into me. I bit down on my lip as unbelievable pleasure rocked me. He was not as gentle as he thrust into me again.

"Same."

THIRTEEN

"Wakey, wakey." Fingers patted my face.

I blinked, taking in the brown primate sitting on my shoulder. Ryker's naked form was curved against mine, his face snuggled into the back of my neck. *Déjà vu* flooded over me—to a time before when Sprig found us in bed together, waking us up. Except then we had jumped apart, pretending it never happened.

Ryker stirred behind me, grumbling. "Isn't there an off switch for him? Snooze button?"

"Come on, guys. It's breakfast time." He chirped and jumped up and down on my arm.

"Afraid not." I sighed and pressed my head back into the pillow. My body ached and was tender everywhere—but in an amazing way.

Ryker kissed the curve of my neck and rolled over, stretching.

"There is liftoff." Sprig squeaked and darted off the bed. Looking over my shoulder I saw what he was talking about. "That thing could club baby seals."

Laughing, I rolled over to face Ryker. "Now there's an image that will haunt me."

He pulled me to him and kissed me deeply. I was close to telling Sprig to get lost again when he pulled away. "We better get going."

I nodded and sat up, taking the sheet with me to cover myself. It was possible everything could change today, or at least it could lead us somewhere. There was also a great likelihood Regnus would not be able to help us, and we would be back to zero. My nerves tightened in my belly. I was scared. Ryker's powers needed to return to him before it was too late, but as soon as they did, he wouldn't need me anymore.

If you weren't useful in the world where I grew up, you were dead weight and disposed of. I didn't *think* he would leave me once he got them back, but it didn't stop the fear from curling around inside me, cinching the air in my lungs.

The storm had blown over, and the morning sun was beginning to dry the earth. The humidity from the damp soil clashed with the heat, bringing it to a suffocating level. I grabbed a thin tank top, pulled it over my head, and slipped on a new pair of underwear. At least I was dressed enough so Sprig didn't have to hide. Actually, it was me who had the issue. Fae didn't seem embarrassed or concerned about the naked form. Ryker proved the point as he stood up, stretched, and strolled to the bathroom in the buff. Sprig ignored him as he went through the fridge searching for anything to sustain him till we got an actual meal.

Ryker didn't close the door and the sound of the shower emanated from the room. *Did he want me to join him?*

I still felt shy around Ryker in the morning light. Normally, I was not bashful, but usually I wasn't with my sexual conquest/partner come morning. Sex was something I did and then departed quickly after. Until now, Daniel had been the only one I wanted to be with. Now, I could no longer escape what I felt about Ryker. Surprisingly, I didn't want to.

This was way out of my realm. I didn't even know how to have a normal conversation with him without images of what we did the night before flashing through my head. To pretend my mouth or his lips hadn't been everywhere.

We got ready and grabbed churros and water along the way, which pleased Sprig. Croygen was meeting us out of town at the base of the Huayna Picchu trail. He told Ryker "after daybreak," which could mean any time. Fae didn't seem to have a precise measurement of time.

The trail took a steep incline and my lungs ached at the thinning air, my flip-flops swirling the dirt up off the path. Trees disappeared the higher we climbed, replaced by ancient stone steps left from the Inca, and thick brush wound tightly around the mountain. Green moss and shrubs coated the area, freeing the view to Machu Picchu in the distance. I stared longingly at the ancient ruins, wanting to spread my arms and let the wind fly me over. I still had yet to see them in person.

"We'll get there." Ryker nudged me forward.

"We've been this close and haven't yet."

"I will make sure you see them," he said into my ear, tapping his hand on my ass to prod me to move. We hiked for the next ten minutes, the trail growing so steep I needed to use my hands and feet to crawl up.

Suddenly Ryker stopped. "Here."

"Here?" I asked, peering around. The bit of trail Ryker halted us at mimicked most of the terrain we had trekked.

"Are you going to finish this?" A white sack containing the rest of my breakfast came out of my bag. Sprig opened it up, motioning to the churro.

"This is where Croygen said he'd meet us. If the asshole decides to show up," Ryker responded.

"*Bhean.*" Sprig tapped on my hand.

"At this nonspecific spot?"

Ryker tilted his head and nodded.

"*Bheannnnn.*"

"Okay. Now what?" I continued to observe the location. It seemed like an insignificant place, but maybe that was the point.

"*Bhhhheeeannn*, gimme, gimmmeeeee."

I sighed and handed the rest of my pastry to Sprig. He snatched it from my fingers and shoved it in his mouth, mumbling happily.

"We wait," Ryker replied.

My eyes darted around. "For how long exactly?"

"You already bored?" Ryker smirked, moving his frame close to mine.

"No... yes." I shifted my weight. "I'm anxious."

Ryker nodded and his hands moved to my face. His fingers softly stroked my lips, brushing off the leftover sugar. His gaze was intense on mine. "Still some left." He pulled me to him, his warm mouth covering mine.

"Ugh. I'm not hungry anymore." Sprig gagged but continued to lick every grain of sugar from his fingers.

"Me either." A deep voice came from behind me. I

spun around to see Croygen standing only feet away, leaning comfortably against a boulder, like he had been there for a while. He probably had. Croygen's normal facial expression was to look disgusted at everything, but seeing Ryker and me kissing created a snarl of repulsion over his features he did not try to hide. I could all but hear him think: *a human fraternizing with a fae, how disgusting.* Croygen made it clear how he felt about humans in general, but I seemed to offend him even more.

Melosa's words came back to me. *"Do not trust the man in black. His soul is corrupt. He will trick and deceive. Neither of you are safe."*

My muscles automatically locked up in defense. *We don't have a choice,* I repeated to myself. We have to trust someone.

"Were you watching us the whole time?" Ryker folded his arms. We should have known Croygen was already there, blending in with the backdrop.

Croygen was again dressed in black pants, a long-sleeved black shirt that reminded me of pirates, a long, heavy velvet jacket lined with gold piping, and heavy boots. He seemed oblivious to the heat pounding from the sky. His shoulder-length dark hair was pulled back in a bun, and his thick black beard covered his face. All he needed was a hook and eyepatch.

I was surrounded by a pirate, a Viking, and a talking monkey. Disney had nothing on me.

A sneer trekked over Croygen's mouth as he looked me up and down. "Let's go," he barked at us.

Ryker's shoulders rotated back, his chest expanding. He deliberately moved away from me, showing he would not be intimidated or bossed around.

Croygen's lids narrowed. He was seriously intimidating. Fighting taught me there were those people who put up a front and tried to come across frightening, and there were those people who truly were. Both Ryker and Croygen fell into the latter.

I squeezed Ryker's hand, giving him a tight smile, before letting it drop. I turned and started walking to Croygen. I could feel in my gut our happy little world was about to change. The delicate connection between us was going to be strengthened or broken.

We followed Croygen as he guided us deep into the mountain range, edging along the trails near the high peaks of Machu Picchu but far away from any tourists. Sweat trickled down my face, and I was wishing I had bought more churros and water when Croygen finally stopped. "We go through here."

"Through where?" My head darted between Croygen and the spot he pointed at. I saw nothing out of the ordinary.

"Otherworld door," Croygen sniped.

Ryker leaned into my ear. "Look closer. You should be able to see through the glamour."

I squinted at the area where Ryker was pointing. I didn't know how I missed it. The air vibrated and pulsed like sound waves. I'd never seen one, but Seattle had continuously been a hotspot for these doors connecting our world with the Otherworld. It was how the fae traveled between realms.

"Do you even know how to use these anymore?"

Croygen snapped at Ryker.

Ryker tilted his head and glared back. "Until recently, I didn't have to use these fuckin' things, but it doesn't mean I forgot how. Not really all that difficult." Ryker crossed his arms. "Oh sorry, I meant for me."

Croygen's fists clenched.

Ryker said Croygen was an old friend, right? If this was his friend, I'd hate to see his enemies.

"If your little human toy knew how to work your powers, we could have been there by now."

Ryker disappeared from my side and in an instant was in front of Croygen, grabbing his throat. "Tell me again why I saved your life?"

Saved his life?

"Don't think it hasn't been a thorn in my side," Croygen seethed.

"Why are you helping us?"

"I already told you. Because I want to be clear of my debt."

Ryker's grip constricted around the pirate's neck. "Why don't I believe you?"

"Because you're an untrusting, cocky son of a bitch!" Croygen hissed, saliva spraying from his mouth.

"If you betray me or Zoey, I will hunt you down to my last dying breath. *That* is my oath to you." Ryker shook him, his eyes burning.

Croygen licked his lips as if to say "bring it." These two were on the verge of tearing each other apart.

"Ryker, stop." I touched the arm holding Croygen dangling from the ground. "We don't have time for this crap. Kill or make out with each other later. Right now we need to go."

"Ahhh, come on, *Bhean*. Some popcorn and a soda and this would have been like watching gladiators."

"Real gladiators or the movie?"

"The one with obstacles and spandex."

"Of course."

Ryker let Croygen go, his neck imprinted with Ryker's fingerprints. Croygen straightened his shirt out, his glare still on Ryker.

"If you only knew what is ahead of you." He smirked, shook his head, and walked away. Only a few feet into his steps he vanished.

My stomach gurgled with his words. Was it too late to run? What were we getting into? I took a few steps backward then stopped. Ryker looked over his shoulder and held out his hand. He didn't say anything, but I understood the gesture. We would do this together. Whatever was ahead of us, we would deal with it. It's what we did.

"I'm going home!" Sprig chirped excitedly as he held on to the flap of my bag and hopped up and down.

"We're not actually going to stay in the Otherworld," Ryker said to Sprig.

"I know, but even to feel its magic again when we pass through the doors will be enough."

Ryker tugged me forward and we stepped through together. Immediately a bustling energy sizzled through me. The air was thick as it brushed against my skin, sending my hair on end. The magic rushed through the space; my lungs struggled to breathe. Ryker kept his fingers securely through mine, never letting go. He escorted me in and out of doors so fast my head spun.

We exited briefly into cities, like Paris and Sydney, to rural areas I didn't have time to recognize. Finally, we caught up with Croygen, and together we all stepped through another door.

My flip-flops crunched down on a bed of white powder. My skin prickled as cold snowy air circled around us. I clutched myself to hold any warmth to my body. "Shit! You could have told us we were going to the snow," I exclaimed.

Croygen smiled, his eyes glinting with delight.

Now his outfit made more sense. I glared at him, but he was loving my discomfort too much. Sprig, in his excitement at our field trip, had passed out. He was warm and snug, curled in my bag. Lucky monkey.

Croygen pointed ahead to a yurt.

"Where are we?" My teeth were already chattering.

"High in the mountains of Mongolia."

Ryker's forehead furrowed, but he put his hand on my lower back and urged me forward. A tent would at least block some of the icy wind.

As we got to the entrance of the tent, Croygen's voice wafted over to us in a taunting jibe. "Good luck. I'm going to stay out here for a bit."

Ryker ignored him but took a deep breath.

"Whatever happens, we'll figure it out." I looked at him. "Together." He nodded; his lips were compressed into a thin line. Then we walked through the canvas flap.

It was dark, lit only by a fire in the middle of the room and decorated simply with two cots on one side layered with furs and blankets. The other side held a table with maps and stacks of books. Four chairs, also adorned with soft pelts, circled the firebox.

There were no herbs hanging or concoctions boiling in a cauldron as I'd imagined. Okay, maybe my idea of a shaman's place was skewed from TV, but this seemed too minimal for even a hermit to live in.

"Ryker?" A woman's accented voice broke through the dimness. Our heads jerked in unison to the dark figure in the corner. A tall but thin silhouette emerged from of the shadows. A gasp tore from my lips.

Ryker stiffened next to me. There was a pause before he muttered, "Amara?"

FOURTEEN

Amara?

Here?

Her waist-length plum hair sparkled under the firelight as she ran for the man next to me. Her small face and perfect lips were set in utter joy. She jumped into his arms, her mouth crashing against his, kissing him with a passion of two lovers who had been separated.

Ryker didn't counter with the same zeal, but it didn't matter, he *did* respond. And seeing them together was like stepping into a frozen lake. Ice poured down my spine, waking me out of a dream. They looked ideal together. She was exquisite with her long elegant nose, perfectly symmetric face, dark eyes, and olive skin. She was clad in black military-style pants. She wore brown ankle boots and a long army green winter parka lined with brown faux fur. She was taller than me but small boned, and possessed the regal posture you only see in women who know they are stunningly beautiful. Amara's beauty would be celebrated, remembered in history.

The only blemish to her magnificence was a huge bruise near her eye and cheek and scabbed cuts over her face. She had been beaten.

Ryker pushed her back from his lips, his mouth still ajar. "Amara, what are you doing here? How did you get away?"

She glanced over me; from the top of my head to my shoes, she took me in. A frown creased her forehead. Her accented voice sounded snobby when she spoke. "This is the human Croygen told me about?" Her nose crinkled, as though I smelled bad.

My shoulders naturally went back in defensive pride. "My name is Zoey."

"Zoey." She repeated it like she'd said a bad word. Her eyes caught at my hair. "Why is this human *trying* to look like me?"

I clenched a fist and felt my legs tense as though to spring at her. My inclination when insulted was still to fight. It had taken years for me to get this in check. Now with one look, one word, I was ready to throw her down.

Ryker brushed past her questions and continued. "Tell me how and why you are here."

"It's a long story. We can talk of those things later. I have missed you." Her voice was deep and still inflected by her Romanian accent. She stood on her toes, kissing him again. This time he did not kiss her back. His eyes darted to me then away.

I felt another stab, directly into my heart.

"No. Now, Amara." Ryker cupped her shoulders and pressed her back down on her heels.

She frowned but nodded. "Fine, but let us have a drink first." She motioned to the fur-lined chairs around the fireplace and the kettle cooking on top of a metal box. The steam from the pot found its way to my nose, the smell of herbal tea seeped in.

"Mara!" Ryker exclaimed. "What is going on? How did you get free? Where is the shaman?"

She walked over to a boiling tea kettle; it hissed angrily. She grabbed a mitt before picking it up and pouring out *two* cups. The slight was not lost on me. I was human. She would not acknowledge me.

"There was no shaman," she finally replied as she added a splash of milk to both cups.

"What?" Ryker's brows furrowed. "What are you talking about? There is a shaman. I've met him... through you."

Her purple locks danced as she shook her head. "No. I mean I arranged this. He knows nothing." Her dark eyes darted to me. "It was always me."

"You set this up?" Ryker strode to the fireplace, closer to her.

I was locked in my spot. Shock, hurt, bewilderment, jealousy crashed inside my chest keeping me in place. I no longer felt the cold drifting in that had been wrapping around my legs and arms. The only outside sensation was Sprig's rhythmic breathing inside my bag. It was the only thing grounding me, keeping my claws retracted. Pure jealousy worked its way through me like poison.

"Please sit." She picked up a cup, handing it to Ryker. "I will explain everything. I promise."

Ryker took the cup absently and sat in a chair, setting it on the ground next to his feet. He positioned himself on the rim of it, leaning his arms on his legs. The muscles in his shoulders curled up by his ears and the familiar tick at his jaw told me he was really on edge.

Amara took a sip of her tea and sat across from him.

Ryker peered over his shoulder, careful to not make full eye contact with me.

"Zoey?" He nodded to a chair next to him.

"Maybe I should go." The words were out of my mouth before I could stop them. It was a knee-jerk reaction. The long-lost lovers were reunited, and I didn't want to be anywhere near them. If I had to see her kiss him once more, I was going to vomit on my shoes. And I was wearing flip-flops.

Ryker's white eyes fully sealed on mine. They were emotionless, except for a slight annoyance under the surface.

"That might be better." Amara reached her hand out for Ryker.

He shook his head violently, his voice gruff. "Sit, Zoey."

My teeth ground together as I stepped around and sat down. I was normally good at hiding the anger and bitterness I felt, but I struggled to keep my resentment from broadcasting off my features like a TV screen. The wall I'd kept between us for so long was back in place.

He must have seen the animosity in my face and turned away from me in a grumble. "Amara?"

Amara shifted in her seat, taking another sip of tea. "After Garrett kidnapped me, he took me to Vadik." Amara's words reflected on Ryker's jawline. "They hoped at first if they tortured me enough or starved me,

I would talk and tell them where the stone is."

"But you don't know," he growled. It was true. Amara didn't know. He told her the stone was somewhere in a cave near Mongolia. My gaze struggled not to look at his boot, the true location of the stone.

She touched his hand again and despite myself, my eyes followed her fingers as they stroked his skin. "Vadik did not believe I knew nothing. After a while they discovered I would never tell, no matter how much they beat and tortured me." She squeezed his hand. "We made a pact."

His face softened, his eyes taking her in.

"I think they hoped you would come for me. Make a trade. I merely laughed at them and told them to kill me because they would never get anything from me."

What a martyr. Okay, I was being a bitch, but I didn't trust her self-sacrificing story.

"How did you get away?" Ryker asked.

Amara's head flicked toward the open door. "Croygen."

"Croygen?" Ryker stared at her with a guarded expression.

"He heard I was taken." Amara licked her lips, and Ryker shifted in the chair. Their body language conveyed to me there was more to this story than what she said. "He broke in and got me. He lost a lot of his men. But you know him. He wouldn't stop until I was free."

Ryker stood up, the chair tipping over as his weight left the stool.

"I knew with his connection to you, it was the only way I could find you." Amara stood with him.

"Croygen made sure I was safe here and went to find you."

Ryker folded his arm, staring at the ground. "I couldn't come for you. I am sor—"

"Stop." Amara held up her hand, flattening herself to Ryker. "I know." An intense moment passed between them; their eyes communicating an intimacy they had shared.

I wanted to jump, to be kidnapped, anything to get me out of the room.

Another man risking everything to save Ryker's woman when he couldn't had to rub Ryker's pride wrong.

"I heard what happened... with your powers." Her hands glided up his arms. He jerked back. "Croygen told me. I didn't believe it till he revealed that he'd seen it happen. Is this why you want to find Regnus?"

"Do you know where he is?" Ryker came back at her with renewed interest. "I think he might be the only one who can possibly help us. Get my powers back to me."

"If anyone can, it will be him." Amara nodded. "You are right to try and find him. He is probably the only one with enough magic to transfer them to you."

"We need to find him," Ryker demanded. "Before it's too late."

Amara's head dropped, her hair covering her face from view.

"It will be difficult."

"Why? What's going on? Where is he?"

She pressed her mouth together.

"Where, Amara?" Ryker grabbed her shoulders.

"Don't fuck with me right now. Tell me."

My stomach dropped as she turned her face to him, anguish etching deep in her expression.

"He has him," she whispered.

"Who has him?" Ryker gripped her harder.

We all knew who she was referring to, but I needed to hear her say it. To confirm the wrenching sensation inside me.

"Vadik."

The tattoos up Ryker's neck flickered. He stared at her with strained tension. "What?"

"Vadik took him to control me. He knew how close we are. He will do anything to get the stone, and he thought using Regnus would get me to finally confess."

"Vadik has him," Ryker repeated.

Pain shot up my arm. I looked at my hand and my nails dug deep into my palm, drawing blood. All our hopes had been on finding this one man.

"It was hard for me to leave him. You know he's like a father to me. The only kind man I knew growing up. I don't think Vadik will hurt him. He will use him as leverage. We have to get the stone."

Ryker pushed away from Amara and ran his hand through his hair. "Fuck!" he yelled, making me jump.

"If we get the stone, we can offer it to them as a bargaining tool for Regnus."

"What? We are not giving up the stone." My voice found its way up my throat.

Amara whipped around, her narrowed eyes stormy. "I never said we'd give it to him, but we need to have it. We need to get Regnus. I will not watch Ryker *die* because of you, and he seems to want you to live."

It was like a brick slammed into my chest. "What? What are you talking about?" My gaze drifted from Amara to Ryker. His skin pinched around his mouth, not combatting her words. What the hell was going on? What had he not told me? "Ryker?"

He cleared his throat, and his white eyes turned to me. "If fae lose their powers, it will eventually kill them."

My eyes widened as the information sank in.

"Not right away. It will be years, but from the moment you fully take the powers, I'm doomed."

The world collapsed around my feet. "Wh-why didn't you tell me?"

Ryker shrugged his shoulders. "Because."

Ryker's layers went deep, and I still had not reached the one where he felt he could completely trust me. The sting of it lashed me across the heart.

"Why would he tell you?" Amara looked at both of us. Irritation flickered behind her eyes. "Your kind would only use it against us."

"I would never—"

"Really? I know what you are. A Collector for DMG. Isn't that entirely what you do? Find our weakness so you can hunt us down?"

My mouth opened to retaliate, but no words fell out. It was exactly who I was, once, until Ryker and Sprig changed me. I was no longer a Collector.

"I thought so." She nodded and turned back to Ryker.

"So, what do we do?" I struggled with the idea that Ryker was dying. If *I* didn't die, he would.

"We get Regnus," Ryker stated.

"We get the stone," Amara said at the same time.

My words belted out at Amara before they had approval to do so. "We will *not* barter the stone, no matter what. I thought that was the pact."

Amara's lids narrowed. "And what do you know of it, human? You think because you have been with him a few weeks you understand what is going on? You know nothing."

My feet moved toward her, but Ryker stepped between us before my fist could encounter her perfect face. "Whoa." He grabbed for my wrists, holding me back. "Zoey, look at me."

My eyes were still locked on her. She wasn't scared nor was she taunting me; she merely watched me with curiosity.

"Look. At. Me." He damn well knew with one look he could calm me, but I didn't want to be soothed. I wanted to punch and kick, releasing the anger, frustration, and sadness building up. Ryker shook me. "Zoey?"

Blowing out air, my gaze went to his, falling once again into the icy pools of his eyes. *Damn him!*

He squeezed my hands and let go, turning back to Amara, his voice forceful. "Do not insult her again."

Amara studied both of us. She kept her shoulders back, her head held high. The woman did not lack confidence. The way she watched me didn't seem to hold jealousy or fear that something was going on between Ryker and me. More like I was a bug. A gross, disgusting insect that needed to be squashed. "Without the stone, you won't get Regnus. My escape only made Vadik more cautious and guarded. Croygen can tell you it was almost impossible retrieving me." Amara folded her arms. "But if you don't want to get Regnus, there is another way."

"Another way for what?" I placed my hand on the warm spot on my bag. Feeling Sprig's body heat comforted me.

"To get your powers back." Amara still faced Ryker, but shrugged over to me. "Get rid of her."

"What?" Ryker and I said in unison.

"As soon as Croygen told me about your predicament, I recalled a memory from my childhood, and I found something that might help." Amara sauntered over to a desk against the far wall of the yurt and picked up an ancient leather-bound book. Faded gold writing scrolled across the cover and spine. The aura of the book twinkled with deep golds and sparkling silvers. I once touched a fae book and almost passed out. Their history was alive between the pages, and it showed images along with words. Kind of like the stone. I could feel the book in her hands waiting to share its story. "I had Croygen bring me these books, and yesterday I found what I was looking for." She flipped through the yellowed parchment pages of the book. "I remembered an ancient legend. It was a fable Regnus told me when I was a child about a boy who loses his powers to a witch and gets them back. I can't believe you didn't think of this yourself."

"I was raised by humans. I don't know any fae

legends or bedtime stories." Ryker walked up next to her, peering at the pages held in her hands.

"In the story, a witch steals the boy's magic. Growing weaker and weaker, he continues to search for a way to retrieve his magic. Finally, one day he runs into a raven who tells him how to get them back from the witch."

"And how does he get them?" Ryker questioned.

Amara's head lifted up, her gaze falling on me. "He has to kill her."

FIFTEEN

Kill her.

Of course that was the answer.

"What?" Ryker shuffled back, his gaze bouncing from me to Amara.

"If the vessel of the thief dies, magic will be restored to the original possessor. If the magic familiarizes fully to the vessel, only death from the original possessor's hand can undo the spell," Amara read from the book.

"What does that mean?" My voice came out in a croaking sound.

"It means..." Amara cleared her throat and glowered at me. "If Ryker's magic fully acclimates to you, the only way the powers will go back to him is if he is the one to murder you."

"What if I die before that?"

"If they become fully yours and someone else kills you or you die, he will never get them back," Amara replied.

"But right now... if I die... he'll get them back."

"Yes. But the moment they become fully yours, the only way for him to get them back is if he takes your life."

Ryker reached over, ripped the book from her hands, read the passage, and then slammed the book shut, searching its bindings and cover. "This is a fairy tale. Doesn't mean it's true."

Amara placed her hand on his arm. "Ryker, our fairy tales *are* real. They are stories passed from generation to generation, but they are based in fact. There is truth in all the fables you read. Only humans think they are made up."

Ryker looked back and forth between us. "No. No way." He threw the book back on the table, like it was burning his hands.

"The only other way is we find the stone and pretend to trade for Regnus. He is the only one with the power to *possibly* get your powers back with both of you unscathed."

"Then we get him," Ryker stated. "Even if it's a slim chance. It's the only option."

"Ryker?" I stepped to him. It wasn't the only one.

His head jerked up. "No."

"Ryker..."

"No. Stop right there."

"But—"

"I said no, Zoey. There is only one route here."

"I'm already—"

"I am done with this conversation." He stomped for the door, whacked at the canvas entry, and stormed out.

I stared after him, a lump choking my windpipe.

Amara took several steps toward me. "He is in danger the longer he is without them." Amara moved to my side. "You want to do the best for him? Either you help me convince him to get the stone, or he kills you. I am sorry it has to be this way; I really am. But this is bigger than you or me." Her dark eyes challenged mine. "I was willing to make the ultimate sacrifice for him. Are you?"

My frozen toes sank into the snow, causing me to falter as I ran after Ryker. Even if I weren't already dying, I probably would have been willing to sacrifice for him. Too many people had died because I couldn't save them. I could help Ryker.

"Ryker!" My screams pierced the high snowy peaks, bouncing back to me. His form in the distance stopped, but he kept his back to me. At least running warmed me a little. The high altitude rendered me breathless in no time, and I stumbled to him, gasping for air.

"What are you doing out here? You're going to get hypothermia." He swung around, rage thumping off him. "Again."

"Needed..." I struggled to breathe. "Talk... to you."

"I told you I'm not discussing it. Now go back before you freeze to death."

I shook my head violently. "No, not till you..." I gulped in air. "Hear me out."

"Zoey!"

"Ryker!"

His hand crashed into his forehead, rubbing furiously. "You are so fucking stubborn."

"Yeah, and you're so compliant." I snorted. Then seriousness settled back in. "Before you start saying 'no' or tune me out completely, please listen to what I have to say."

"Not with you trembling like that." He only had his T-shirt and cargo pants on, but he ripped off his shirt and shoved my head through the hole. The warmth of his body heat clinging to the shirt felt like heaven. It wasn't much, but it was better than my thin tank top. But now I had to talk to his bare chest.

"We both knew this was coming."

"Zoey," he warned.

My feet wiggled under the white ice covering them. "Why didn't you tell me?"

He sighed, shifting to the side. "You couldn't do anything about it. Why put extra pressure on you?"

"That's not the point." Someone could write "hypocrite" on my forehead. I was hurt he'd kept this from me, but I was keeping the same sort of information from him. My tongue curled around the vowels, ready to confess my own secret, but nothing came out.

"What *is* the point, Zoey?" he exclaimed; frustration crimped his face.

"I want you to talk to me."

"You want to talk about the fact that you having my powers is slowly killing me? That when you take them completely, I will grow weak and be vulnerable to both human and fae deaths? Is this what you want to hear?" He shook his head. "No. There is no reason to dwell on something *we* can't change."

He was right, I didn't want to hear it, but I needed to. His declaration only solidified the reason I ran after him.

"There's no other choice. We have to barter the

stone for Regnus."

"You don't have to," I declared.

He opened his mouth to argue.

"And what if he can't help us, anyway?" My hand went up. "There is no good side or way out of this. I'm not saying kill me right this moment, but if we don't get Regnus, promise me you will." I took a quick breath before he interrupted. "We have a limited window of getting them back to you."

He put his hands on his hips. His lashes fluttered closed, and he squeezed his lids shut.

"Ryker, you know it has to be this way."

His head tipped back and his eyes shot open. "Absolutely. Not." Fire burned through his gaze as his lids narrowed. He took a step back, his pectoral muscles twitching. "No. And we are done talking about this." He turned to leave.

"Wait." I grabbed his bicep. It tightened under my grip. I could feel the anger raging under the surface.

"*No!*" A bellow hurled out of his mouth. "Do you grasp what you are asking of me? I am *not* going to kill you, Zoey." He shoved my hand away from him and swung around, stomping through the thick snow. There were few times I had seen him yell or let his emotions come to the surface. Usually his fury was contained— rumbling underneath.

"I am dying anyway," I screamed at his back, desperate for him to understand, to hear me. I didn't feel the cold any longer.

He stopped dead in his tracks, his back still facing me. "What?"

"I am dying, Ryker. There was more on the video

Daniel left. Seers are immune to fae blood."

"But you are starting to heal faster, and you can jump."

"I know, but it did not affect my DNA. They tried it on us when we were babies. None of us responded to it, and all except two of us are dead."

His head shook back and forth. "No. My powers changed you."

"They definitely changed me. You changed me. But not the flaw in my genes." My words hit his back. "Nothing you can say or do is going to stop it. You can't pretend it away or deny it's not happening. Because it is."

He lifted his hands to his face, rubbing it furiously. His shoulders curled forward. I could sense my words finding their way in. "How can you ask this of me?" he mumbled under his breath, slowly twisting back to face me.

"What if roles were reversed?" I inquired. "Wouldn't you want me to do the same for you?"

A low growl rose from the depths of his chest. He knew I had a point. We both stood in silence, neither of us ready to give in.

"I can't..." His voice broke, and he blinked rapidly, shaking his head. "I don't want to lose you. I won't..."

Without thought, my feet moved to him. I reached up, cupping his cheeks. "I don't want to lose you either, but this is no longer about what we want."

A choking noise came from Ryker's throat, his forehead knocked into mine, his hand skirting the back of my neck, holding me closer. We stayed like this, halting for a moment in time.

"I want you to kill me, Ryker," I whispered. I heard another sound come from him. "You have to promise me you will do it."

"A promise is binding. I will have to do it no matter what. I can't... I won't."

"You must. Before it's too late. You heard her. If I died now, they go back to you. But if we wait and they become mine... Either way I won't survive this. You need to get away, jump far from here, and protect yourself and the stone."

His head stayed still, but his grip on me constricted.

"Promise me."

"No." His head rubbed against mine. "Not yet. There is still the hope of getting Regnus." His hands rubbed up and down the goose bumps on my arms. "Not giving up yet. Don't you either, okay?"

Breathing out a heavy sigh, my shoulders fell in agreement. "For now."

His only response was to bring me closer against him, crushing me to his chest. I tucked my head into him and for one moment let everything disappear. There was no one chasing us, no one trying to kill us, no DNA fuck-up, no magic stone, and no ex-girlfriends waiting back in a tent.

Nothing but him and me.

"Is it okay to come out now? Getting a little smooshed in here. Like a sandwich," a voice came from my bag. "A peanut butter and honey sandwich or maybe a panini with melted cheese. Ohhh, a peanut butter and honey panini." A giggle burst from me. Hell. I totally forgot about the little fuzzball. "Is it lunchtime yet? Please," he begged.

My happy place was right here with Ryker and Sprig. The rest of the world could disappear.

Especially Amara.

When we returned to the yurt, Croygen had joined Amara inside, and they were searching maps. Hiking gear sat in a pile on the rug near the stove.

"What's going on?" Ryker folded his arms, his torso probably only slightly chilled from the cold. On the other hand, I was beet red, stiff, and shivering. The heat of Peru sounded like heaven. Sprig stayed in the warmth of my bag with Pam. I could hear him jabbering to her.

Amara glanced up from the table, her eyes darting back and forth from Ryker's shirtless frame to me. His shirt was thin but covered a lot of my exposed legs. Her eyes narrowed, lips pressed, before peering at the map. I couldn't blame her. As far as she knew, she and Ryker were still together and happy. She probably never imagined a human coming between them.

"Good. You're back. We don't have a lot of time. We need to retrieve the stone as soon as possible." She waved Ryker over. "You said in Mongolia close to the China border, right?"

My head turned to Ryker. He kept facing Amara, but I saw his jaw twitch. "We are heading back to Peru first. We will devise a rescue plan there."

"What?" Amara placed both her hands on the table, gaping at Ryker. Croygen stayed quiet, but watched Ryker skeptically. "Why? We are in the perfect location to go get it. It's why I picked this place. We need to go now. There is no reason to wait."

"There are plenty of reasons to delay."

Amara shook her head, coming around the table to the Viking. "I don't understand. We need to get it before Vadik does."

"Believe me, it is safe." He shifted when she placed her hands on his crossed arms, tugging them loose. When they fell to his sides, she laced her hands with his.

"We are here. Now." She squeezed his fingers. "If you had your powers, it wouldn't matter, but you don't. Do you want to risk coming through the doors again to get all the way back when we're already here?"

"Amara." Ryker tugged away from her, his voice growing hard. He turned for the door. "We are going back. Zoey is not dressed for this climate, and we need more time to plan."

Why was he not telling her the truth? There was no reason to go traipsing through the countryside for this stone. It was always with him, located in the heel of his boot.

"Do you understand the importance?" Amara threw up her arms.

"Yes!" Ryker whirled around, bellowing. Amara stumbled back. "I get the urgency, Amara. Believe me, I do. You can stay here if you prefer, but *we* are going back."

She jerked back as though slapped, her face contorted into a shocked expression. "What?" she whispered.

"That came out wrong." He glanced at the ceiling.

"No, it didn't," Sprig's voice burst from my bag.

Amara's head whipped around, glaring at me. "What

did you say?"

Sprig's head poked out of the top, waving. "It was me, Medusa."

Amara screamed and jumped back.

"Now that was rude. A simple hello would have sufficed."

Sprig climbed the strap to my shoulder, his tail wrapping around my neck.

"What is that?" Amara pointed at him.

"Haven't you ever seen a sprite-monkey before?" Sprig pointed back at her, mimicking.

"No."

"Of course not. I am one of a kind. There is only one of me."

"Thank the gods," Ryker scoffed.

Sprig stuck his tongue out at the Wanderer.

"We can discuss Sprig's existence later. Right now we need to go. Before *some* of us get frostbite." Ryker glanced over to me.

Amara's head snapped back to Ryker. The shock from Sprig now replaced by her earlier irritation. "Ryker, you are not thinking this through."

Croygen had been silent while observing, blending in with the background. I forgot he was there. "I'm with Amara. If we are going to get the stone, we should do it now."

Ryker stiffened, his eyes flickering over Amara's head to Croygen with distrust. "That would be convenient for you wouldn't it, Croygen? You'd love to have the stone. How many of your problems would disappear if you had it, huh?" Ryker challenged. "You are not part of this. Just go. You're done with your obligation to me."

"If it could only be true." Croygen's boots met Ryker's, and he leaned his head back to stare the few inches up at the Wanderer.

"Still hovering around, waiting for scraps." Ryker's lip curled.

"Yeah, and you're such a catch. Leave one woman in a prison to be tortured and beaten while you're getting your rocks off with another."

The moment before you move to attack someone holds a palpable pressure, like a drop in the barometer. I knew it well from fighting. I instantly grabbed for Ryker, pulling him back with little effect as Amara jumped in between them.

"Stop!" She hit her hands on both their chests and turned to Ryker. "Croygen saved my life. And if *she* is a part of it, then so is he." Amara jutted her chin to me.

"Mar—"

"No, Ryker." Amara waved her arms. "He has as much right as her."

Ryker breathed in, his lungs expanding.

"Either it's only the two of us, or it's the four of us." Amara motioned to herself and Ryker. She leaned closer, expressing this was her real wish.

Croygen's annoyed glare flicked to the side, and he stepped back. Ryker's face was expressionless.

"Fine," Ryker stated. "But we go back to Peru."

Amara observed him for a moment and swallowed. "As usual, it's always by your rules." She straightened her shoulders and clomped over to the table, rolling up the map. "Fine. Let's go." Her rage charged the air. So much magic rippled off her it blurred the edges of her body.

"Medusa's getting stone-cold mad," Sprig said. Silence filled the area. "Get it? Stone-cold... You know, because Medusa—"

All heads swung to the animal on my shoulder. "Sprig," I warned. "Shut up now."

"Jeez, you guys have no sense of humor."

Croygen directed us to the Otherworld door, not hesitating before he crossed over, disappearing. I was next to follow, but a hand came down on my shoulder.

"If you are the reason Ryker dies," Amara's voice whispered harshly in my ear from behind, "I will kill you myself." With a shove, my body stumbled through the door.

I whirled around to retaliate, but halted when both she and Ryker stepped through together. Looking like an idyllic couple, her arm looped through his.

He seemed oblivious to her territorial claim. He listened as she filled him in on what happened to her as we made our way back through the doors to Peru. His only interruptions were to ask her more about Vadik and everything she could remember about the infamous man. No one had seen him before, and Ryker was intent on learning everything he could.

Finally we reached the entry we used in the forest of Peru. The moment I stepped back into the warmth of South America, I moaned happily. Thawing, I rubbed at my fingers and toes. We hadn't been in Aguas Calientes long, but it already felt like home. Seattle held much sadness and death in my memory. This place was a new beginning, and I liked the life Ryker, Sprig, and I were forming here—a happy bubble—a fragile haven, which burst the moment we stepped into the fae door. It would have happened eventually, but I wasn't ready for it to end this soon. We had finally let our walls down, let each other in, and now the close feeling was gone. What if I would never have his lips on mine, or feel him inside me again? I shook my head. *I can't think of it right now.*

If it was possible, the trek back to the village felt even longer. Watching Amara walk next to Ryker and touching him every chance she got, the reality of the situation was setting in. It was like someone was grinding my heart, mincing it into slop. Anger and agony pressed down on me, weighed my body down, and there was nothing I could do about it. I was the other woman. The bitch. The one who slept with an unavailable man. I had known this was coming, but I heedlessly jumped anyway.

Stupid!

My ribs crushed down on my lungs, strangling the air from my lungs. Hurt tore into my soul, causing me to stagger to the side.

"You all right, *Bhean*?" Sprig was still on my shoulder, his hand touching my cheek.

"Yeah." Of course I wasn't fine. About anything.

"You don't look so good."

I couldn't breathe. I grasped at my chest, my feet tripping over a shrub.

"Whoa." Sprig's nails dug into my skin as he clung on. "Viking?" he yelled for Ryker.

Was it finally happening? Terror ran cold down my spine. I didn't know if I'd die slow or fast. It wasn't a detail Daniel ever got around to explain. I was really hoping it was the latter.

"Zoey?" I heard Ryker call for me.

If we were alone, dying in his arms would be a good way to go, but I didn't want Amara and Croygen there. I wanted to be home, safe in the bed Ryker and I had shared many nights.

The world around me swirled, making me dizzy. I heard my name again before my eyes shut and a rush of air swished past me. I felt the soft mattress beneath my body before anything else. Without opening my eyes, I knew I was back home.

"Dingle droppings!" Sprig's arms and legs were wrapped around my neck, holding on for dear life. He eventually untangled himself and lay on the pillow next to me.

My lids lifted but my head still spun, and I quickly shut them again, bile rumbling around in my stomach. Guilt twisted it even more. Every time I used his magic, Ryker's powers became a little bit more mine. In a way I was murdering him. Slowly and torturously.

"Uh-oh. Code red." Sprig's voice opened my eyes again. "All over the sheets."

Blood dripped from my nose and soaked into the newly changed white bedding. The poor maid should be getting overtime with us. Disappointment slammed into me; it was over now. Would the housekeeper have to change the sheets for Ryker and Amara? I barely got to the toilet in time.

Heaviness dropped me to my knees. Utter loneliness

I hadn't felt since before Lexie came into my life constricted my chest. Dying only roused the feeling stronger. Isolating me. It sent thoughts of Sera into my mind. She would understand. If she only believed me when I told her we were DMG's experiments. I didn't blame her for not trusting me; it did sound crazy. And it's not like we ever liked each other.

I truly had no one, and it almost crippled me. When I was young, I turned the emotion to anger and lashed out.

It was not so simple now.

Blood poured from nose, zapping me of energy. By the time it stopped, and I cleaned myself up, I barely could get back to the bed. I crumpled onto the mattress and wrapped my body with an extra sheet left on the table. Sprig was sound asleep on the other pillow, his snores fluttering in the air.

My lashes dropped, and I quickly joined him, letting sleep take me.

SIXTEEN

Heated voices roused me out of my slumber.

"I'm sorry, I'm confused. I don't understand what is going on here, Ryker. Do you *care* about her or something?" Amara's voice stirred my lids to open, but I closed them tighter. "She is *human*."

"I know that," Ryker's deep voice responded. The room was tiny, but it sounded like they stood at the foot of the bed by the table, underneath the windows.

"You *despise* humans."

"I still do."

Ouch.

"Or at least I used to," he huffed. "Look. I don't want to discuss Zoey with you, but she and I have gone through a lot. She's made me see things differently."

I could no longer keep my eyes closed. I cracked them enough to let a sliver of light break through, to watch them without them knowing I was awake.

I was not above eavesdropping.

"See things differently?" she repeated. "If I didn't know you as well as I do, I'd say something was going on between you. But I know you would *never* fall for a human. Ever. Especially when your *girlfriend* is locked in a prison being tortured. For you!"

"Mar—"

"Be careful, Ryker. You might tolerate her, but she clearly has a crush on you. You need to stop it now. I am back. She needs to understand her place."

Understand my place! Excuse me?

Ryker's silence cut into my heart.

"The girl already has to die for you. You should simply help her do it now and get it over with."

"Amara!" Ryker seethed.

"What? It's the truth. She has to die, Ryker. You need your powers back. Her life is a blink of an eye to ours. She could step out tomorrow and get hit by a car or something. Humans are fragile. You were the one always telling me that."

"Yeah, I did." He let his sentence trail off. "But she has shown me they are not as delicate as I thought. At least not this one."

"Wow," she snorted. "She has really made you soft."

"Excuse me?"

"Where is the intimidating Wanderer I knew? The *man* I knew? Can you still lift your axe, or do you need help with it?"

Ryker growled, grabbing her arm.

"There he is." She let her head drop back, pushing herself in. Her hand went for his cargo buttons. "Oh, it looks like all of you are here."

The impulse to lunge for her, ripping her away from him, sawed my teeth together. My fists were always my first reaction. And I struggled to not let the Avenging Angel come to the surface.

Calm down, Zoey. Busting her lip and breaking her fingers will not help the situation.

But I really wanted to.

"Stop." He gripped her wrist tighter.

"Why?" She glanced at me and back to him. "She's out cold. Croygen has vanished. And don't tell me you haven't been dreaming about this for the last month." She pulled the first button free. "My gods, do you know how many nights I dreamed you were inside me, recreating the night we had in Rome?"

Ryker's lids shut, squeezing them tight. "Stop," he whispered hoarsely.

"You want to fuck me, Ryker. Don't deny it." She leaned up, her voice husky. "Right here."

Frozen. I had no air. Not a muscle twitched.

Ryker inhaled and exhaled rapidly while Amara undid the rest of his buttons.

I wanted to scream. To stop him, but nothing came out.

"No!" Ryker barked, moving out of her reach. She stilled, shock furrowing her brow. "Things are not the same as before."

"What are you talking about?" Amara's head once again flicked over to my "sleeping" form. "Are-are you telling me you don't love me anymore?"

"Mar, come on. You know I am not capable of loving anyone. And you can't say you ever really loved me. It's what made us compatible."

"I didn't love you? I was tortured for you!" She shoved at his chest.

They both stood there, breathing heavy.

"Oh my gods... have you fallen for *her*?" Amara's voice rose in astonishment, like it was the first time she considered the notion an actual possibility.

Ryker shifted on his feet. "This has nothing to do with her."

"Not an answer, Ryker. Do you love her?"

"No. Of course not." He rubbed the top of his head. My eyes squeezed together to push out the pain that barreled down on me. Did I think he *was* in love with me? No. But it still hurt to hear.

"Ryker, you know I've always been open to other girls. As long as there were no feelings attached, it didn't bother me." Amara pushed her violet hair over her shoulder.

"I nev—"

"I know. You are as loyal as they come. And I know you and I are always going to come back to each other, no matter what. I was always okay with the fact you didn't love me. No one else will tolerate it. Like you said, that's why we work. You know it, and I know it. All the others are temporary, and it will always be us," Amara huffed. "She is only a blip on the radar, and you will forget her soon enough."

Ryker opened his mouth to speak, but Amara raised her hand. "Right now we have more important things to deal with. If you want to play this little game of yours with the human, that is fine. At the end of the day, I know it will be me you come back to." Amara turned and went to the door. "I am going to go find more clean sheets. Those are covered with blood and smell like her and that monkey." She stepped out the door, shutting it firmly behind her.

"What. A. Bitch." Sprig popped up the moment the door shut. I should have known I wasn't the only one eavesdropping.

Ryker rubbed his face, plunking down on the bed, his back to me. "You can stop pretending, Zoey. I know you're awake."

Oh, was this the reason he stopped her? Because he knew I was awake? Of course his feelings for her wouldn't simply disappear. I knew this time was coming. It was probably better now than later.

I sat up slowly.

He twisted his head to glance over at me. "You all right?"

I tilted my head, raising an eyebrow.

"Yeah." He scrubbed his head where his hair laced in firm braids. "We need to—"

I put my hand up. I couldn't handle the impending rejection. "Things have become complicated. Amara's back. Till this is all over, we will return to solely being partners. Focus on what is really important."

His jaw twitched. "Pretend nothing happened?"

"Yes."

"Can I do it too?" Sprig raised his hand. "Otherwise your therapy bill is going to be extensive."

We both shot him a *shut up and go away* look. He squeaked and dug himself under a pillow.

"Is that what you want?" Ryker's voice was void of emotion, which pissed me off.

"It's not about what I want, Ryker." Anger moved me out from the twisted sheets, standing.

"What. Do. You. Want?" Ryker rose off the bed, his figure towering over me.

"What I want is to live a long, happy life. To have my sister and Daniel alive. To not have *your* fae powers trapped in me. To be free of all this. *Of you and her.*" I wanted to bite my tongue. It came out wrong. Jealousy of Amara was coating my every thought.

His eyes flashed.

"I didn't mean it."

"Yes, you did." He took a step away from me.

My mouth opened to say something, but he was out the door before I could utter a sound.

Shit!

I flopped back on the bed and tugged the sheet over my head. Everything was so messed up. And as usual I only made it worse.

Sprig's little fingers tapped on the blanket at my forehead. "Not to bother you or anything, but are we getting dinner anytime soon?"

Muscles pinched in my arm and I wiggled, trying to find a more comfortable arrangement. My mind churned with the frequency of someone turning the channels nonstop on the TV. Even with everyone asleep, or pretending to be, the tension in the room was dense, each one of us fighting for dominance. The dislikes outweighed the likes in the room, and most were pointed at me, except from Sprig.

Trying not to toss and turn was torture. Amara's sighs of contempt every time I rolled over were enough to force me to hold still. I couldn't blame her. She didn't like this setup any more than I did. If it wasn't for the fact I lay next to her, I would have laughed. She probably never imagined one day, per Ryker's request, she would be sleeping next to a human.

Earlier in the evening, after Amara had remade the bed, she voted I go grab dinner. The only reason I complied was because I wanted nothing more than to get out of the room. Away from her and Ryker. He had stopped speaking to me, and the small room became insufferable. Croygen returned after I brought dinner back. The four of us and Sprig ate pizza in mostly awkward silence.

"The girls get the bed; Croygen and I are on the floor," Ryker stated, heading for the bathroom.

"What?" Amara jumped up from the bed. "I am not sleeping with her!"

Ryker stopped, turning slowly.

"I actually second that." I folded my arms, leaning back in the desk chair.

"I don't care." Ryker scowled. "That's how it's going to be." He whipped around and slammed the restroom door behind him.

Amara huffed, falling back on the bed in a pout, shooting a glare at me like it was my fault.

In a way it might have been. There was no way one of us would let the other one share the bed with him, so this was the best arrangement without it getting into a full catfight.

It still pissed me off.

Almost like Croygen was reading my mind, he motioned to the two of us. "If you girls decide at any time you are going to wrestle, let me know."

"Why would we fight?" Amara twisted her lips up. "She *doesn't* have anything worth fighting her for."

Oh, she was asking for it.

She got up and began preparing for bed.

Now she and I were stuck sleeping next to each other. I rolled over, tucking in on my other side. She was a snobby bitch, especially about humans. The problem was I wanted to hate her for more than just Ryker, to think she was a spoiled princess, but I couldn't. She didn't back away from hard work. She dove in, remaking the bed and scrubbing the bathroom because she found too much of Sprig's fur everywhere. Maybe she was a bitch, but one with a solid work ethic, which was hard not to respect in a way. The feeling only stirred more unease in me.

It wasn't merely because I was sleeping next to Ryker's girlfriend. It went deeper than that. Being this close to fae dragged up all my old prejudices. I still was not comfortable with *all* fae. I had grown accustomed to Ryker and Sprig. In my head I put them in a separate group, and all the other fae we came into contact with were kept at a distance. Here there was no distance.

Though, I would be unrecognizable to my Collector group now. Sera once slandered me when she believed I had slept with a fae. The idea at the time repulsed me. *Disgusted* me. Now look at me. I really had crawled into bed with the enemy.

I glanced at Ryker on the ground beside the bed and then over to Amara, sleeping next to me. I rotated over again. The bed felt like a torture device. The other night Ryker and I were having sex in this bed, now his girlfriend was in here with me, and he was on the floor.

Everything that made me feel secure and happy vanished. It felt like I was standing on the top of the tallest building and the floor evaporated under my feet, leaving me scrambling and flailing for anything to break my fall. My stomach plummeting as I dropped into the abyss.

I was used to change, feeling unstable, but I had kept my guard up, never letting hope in. Ryker pushed down the wall, and now I was left scared, unsure, and lost.

My arm twinged with discomfort. I let out a low sigh. Only a baseball bat or bottle of whiskey was going to help me relax tonight. I kicked at the sheets, which tangled around my ankles. A hand landed on my calf, pressing it down on the mattress. My head jerked up. Ryker still lay on his back on the ground, one elbow bent, covering his eyes, his other hand on my leg. His thumb rubbed in soft circles above my ankle bone. I watched him for a while before I laid my head back down, tucking into the pillow.

His touch could ignite my blood but also calm me. Tonight I was going to focus on the soothing option since the kindling would only get me frustrated and more restless. I let my lids drift close, absorbing the rhythmic motions on my skin.

All I wanted was to have time with Ryker and Sprig and live a life free of DMG and Vadik. I wanted nothing more than for Amara to disappear. Sadly, no matter how much I wished her away, she would be the one who ended up with Ryker. Even if I did live a full life, it was still a human one. Compared to Ryker and the years he already lived, my life was a blip. I could see why he cut off humans after a while. Why grow close to someone who would not live as long as you?

But you could live forever. You could have Ryker and all you ever dreamed of, a voice deep in my heart said. My eyes opened, and I glanced over at Ryker's boots. The unassuming worn boots sat next to the dresser. The power that lay at the bottom of one of the heels was immense but chilling. And very, very tempting. All I had to do was agree to let it in, and it would give me all I ever desired. Didn't I deserve it? My life had been full of pain, fear, hurt, and sadness. Wasn't it my turn to have some good things come my way? It wasn't like I wanted to take over the world like others did. I wanted a family, my sister back, Daniel alive again, a mom and dad. Money, home, security.

And Ryker.

After the stone's touch had worn off, I was able to put it out of my head. The temptation not strong enough to lure me to hold it again. But curled in bed next to the lover of a man you were falling for did something to a girl.

So many of our problems could be solved if I simply agreed to the stone. It might suck the life from me, but that was happening anyway. Really, what did I have to lose?

Lost in my thoughts I didn't notice Ryker's hand had slipped back to his side, his chest moving up and down in metered repetition. I lifted my head, slowly looking over the room. Everyone was fast asleep. I could even hear Sprig's heavy breathing from inside the dresser.

The bed squeaked as I sat up. Everything in the room was old, and no matter how slow you moved it protested. Inch by inch I lifted myself off the bed, careful not to step on Ryker's limbs. Playing a solo game of Twister, I stretched my way over to the bureau, snatched Ryker's boots up, and shuffled to the bathroom, closing the door quietly behind me.

I flicked on the light and settled on the rim of the tub, dropping the lighter boot on the floor. The other I cupped in my lap, my fingers tugging at the sole of the boot. Glee filled me at seeing the gray smooth stone at the bottom of the heel. He hadn't moved it. He really did trust me.

Shame spread over me and caused by cheeks to flush. *It's not like I'm destroying the world,* I reasoned with myself. *Wouldn't he want this too? We would be happy. Neither of us would have to live in pain or fear anymore.*

I reached down, my fingers sliding around the rock. The instant my skin touched it, energy blasted through my body. The bathroom disappeared, sucking me away from the present.

"I knew you would come back, Zoey." The stone's comforting voice spoke in my head. "You are different from the rest. Special." A warmness swirled in my chest, creating a sense of love and safety.

"You and I will help many, Zoey. The lives you will change and save. The happiness and fulfillment you will have in your life. Every bad memory will disappear."

It all sounded wonderful.

"I can bring your sister back to life, healthy and happy. You can have the parents you always fantasized about, but we can do even more than you even dreamed. We can lead the world in stopping diseases and preventing children from being born with disabilities. And this is only the beginning. Don't you want to stop children from hurting? To provide better homes for children in foster care? To be the one who has the power to save lives? How about all those who suffer at fae's hands? *You* could protect the human race."

This all sounded amazing. How could helping to stop cancer or children from being abused be a bad thing? Humans no longer the unknowing or unwilling victims of fae. I could do it all. The girl from the wrong tracks saving the world. The stone was right. I had been thinking too small.

"Yes, Zoey. There is not a limit to what we could do together. The people who thought you were nothing, who didn't want you, treated you horribly... they will be sorry. All you have to do is say yes to me, Zoey. Take me in willingly. And everything you've ever wanted will be yours. Don't you think you deserve happiness?"

I did. I really did.

"Zoey!" A sting slashed across my face. Ryker's voice broke into my mind.

"Ignore him. He doesn't see how much happier he will be as we do. He'll be so grateful. He wants his own pain to end as well. He doesn't think he is capable of love. But he is. And you will show him."

"Dammit, Zoey. Let go!" A growl echoed in my eardrum.

"Don't you want him to be happy, Zoey?" the stone questioned. "Do this for him too."

There wasn't anything I wouldn't do for him.

"Ye—" A pain so intense clogged my throat. My word turning into a scream. I burst from the space, my eyes jerking open, my hand releasing the stone, which crashed onto the tile floor and slid away from my grasp.

Ryker squatted next to me, a lit match between his fingers. He huffed out the tiny fire. His mouth clenched in a firm line.

I seized my hand, turning the sensitive part to me. It was red, and a small welt bubbled around the burned skin. "You burned me?"

He glared at me, his head lifting in a challenge.

"What? You couldn't actually pry my tiny little hands open?"

He snarled and grabbed my arms, sitting me up, pushing me against the tub. When did I get on the floor?

"The stone gives whomever is holding it unbelievable power and strength. It doesn't want you to let it go. I couldn't have pried your hand open with a crowbar and the strength of four more men. You had to do it yourself."

"You had to burn me?" I mumbled to myself, holding my blistering hand to my lips.

"Don't even fuckin' start with me." Fury smoldered in his irises; every word he spoke was clipped and forced.

The shame I pushed away earlier came flooding back, scalding my cheeks. What could I say for my actions? I wanted to do it. My attention landed on the stone, innocently lying on the floor under the sink. I wanted to crawl after it. It was still under my skin, the voice calling to me to pick it up again. To let it and myself have all we ever desired.

Ryker stood, with a hand towel he grabbed the stone and shoved it back in his boot. I fought the desire to go after it.

"Zoey." Ryker snapped his fingers in my face, drawing me back to his crouched frame in front of me. When he had my focus, he tilted his head as if to say, *What do you have to say for yourself?*

I pulled my knees to my chest, covering my face with my hands.

"Do you know how dangerous and stupid touching it was?"

"Yes."

"Then what in the hell were you thinking?" He stood, rubbing at his head, his voice a hoarse whisper. "Tell me!"

I bolted up, not liking him towering over me. I already felt like a child around him. "I'm sorry," I spat at him.

"No. This was far too reckless for an *I'm sorry.*" He folded his arms, his face red with anger. "Not even considering the fact Amara and Croygen are in the other room. What if Croygen was the one to find you? Game over. He would have the stone halfway to the Orient by now." He struggled to keep his voice at a low volume.

"Why haven't you told Amara the truth?"

"Oh no. We're not talking about me," he growled, taking a step closer to me. "What the hell were you thinking?" he repeated.

Embarrassment fueled my own anger, and I challenged his step with one of my own. "I wanted for one second to have my happy ending. To have the life I always dreamed about. The ones I've seen on TV. To have more than the sucky life I was given. Because it seems the moment I might get something good," I took another step, my toes flushing up to his, "it's taken from me."

My meaning was not lost on him. His eyes softened before he squeezed them shut, then opened them to stare at the floor. "I understand the impulse. Don't think I haven't wanted to do it myself a time or two, but you need to be stronger than the stone. There is a reason what it offers is too good to be true... because it is. The legends of this stone and the consequences—the devastation, greed, and death it has caused—no matter how innocent people first start out thinking their wishes are, it's not worth it. You think bringing back people from the dead is natural? There are always costs. Huge ones."

The hope of my dreams coming true popped. I gritted my teeth, forcing back emotion. Ryker drew me into his chest, wrapping his arms around me. "I am sorry, Zoey. I know how much you want Lexie and Daniel back. To have a different life. To be away from all this."

I raised my chin up, my gaze meeting his. "Not from you."

He stared at me for a couple of moments. His hands slid up my neck, cupping my face. He leaned in to kiss my forehead. "Promise me you will never handle it again. We've been through far too much shit for me to lose you to a *rock*."

I nodded my head against his shirt. "I promise." There were several other things he'd lose me to first. His arms constricted around me and his lips pressed against my forehead again. I let myself drown in his smell, his huge arms, and warm body. This was all I needed. Where my true peace and happiness lay.

My determination to stay away from the stone was ardent, but I also knew how quickly the resolve could change. It knew my cards and would play them against me. There was no question I had my weaknesses, and the stone would find ways of breaking me. I only hoped I wouldn't shatter when we collided again.

Ryker escorted me back to bed, making sure I stayed there. He laid on the floor next to me, his eyes glued on mine. After a while I could no longer handle his guarding gaze and rolled over to my other side.

Brown eyes glowered into mine, flaming with wrath. Amara shifted, sliding her face closer to mine. "If I see you go off with him again or are alone with him in any way," she whispered, "nothing will stop me from butchering you into tiny chunks and feeding you to your monkey. Stay away from him, human. You do not belong in our world, and I will take you out of it if you persist." Without letting me respond, she whipped around to face the other way, her hair slapping me in the face.

My blood boiled with the need to fight her—to take my pillow and shove it over her face. The day she and I will come to blows, one of us might not be walking away.

SEVENTEEN

Hostility rose along with the sun, clogging the room with a suffocating presence. We couldn't help but knock into each other as we got ready, but it made us recoil and back away. Everyone moved around each other like bumper cars. Amara and Croygen circled me like I had cooties. Human cooties. The feeling was more than mutual.

Setting a bag of honey mango chips in front of Sprig, I got dressed. It would only tide him over for a while, but he sat quietly on the windowsill, eating his pre-breakfast.

"Can't we glamour the guy downstairs and get another room? Or how about we go to a nice hotel?" Amara grabbed the thick long-sleeved top she wore yesterday, holding it with a frown. "It's so hot here." It actually was a lot cooler today, but compared to the snowy mountains of Mongolia, it was blistering.

All morning she pranced around in her bra, repeatedly turning down my offers to borrow one of my shirts. Normally, it wouldn't bother me. It was no different from a bathing suit, but besides her clear insult to me, her confidence in being so minimally dressed drove me crazy. She knew she was perfection, causing people to stare, and she enjoyed it immensely. She banged into Ryker whenever she could.

Croygen, dressed in his leather pants and black shirt, nodded in agreement. "I'm used to heat, but I'm usually on a ship with the cool wind blowing."

"Ship?" I smiled. "You really are a pirate, huh?"

"Tradesman."

Ryker snorted, earning a glare from Croygen.

"If we are going to stay here another day, I need new clothes." Amara threw the top on the bed, brushing back her hair off her face. It fell back over her arms, cascading in dark violet waves.

A scream built in my chest. I needed to get away from this room and the people in it.

"We're staying here." Ryker sat down, giving me a sharp look, before he turned away, pulling on his boots. "I'm not dealing with Vadik without a solid plan. We have one chance. We can't blow it."

"We can make a plan, but why don't we get the stone first? Make sure it is protected." Amara rolled her hair back into a messy bun. "I don't understand your delay in getting it. We are only risking it being taken."

"We are doing this my way." Ryker stood.

Amara groaned and rolled her eyes, mumbling something under her breath. All I could make out was "stubborn" and "just like him."

"If you don't like my decisions, there's the door." Ryker's arm was rigid with tension as he pointed.

Amara sucked in a breath, her lids lowering. Friction zipped across the room, settling on each other's locked gazes.

In the last day, I'd seen Ryker lose his temper a lot. It was strange, but Amara brought out the worst in Ryker. It also clarified their relationship to me. They probably fought constantly, but they made up with the same intensity. My lungs clenched inside the walls of my chest as an image of their tangled bodies, wrapped in heated passion, occupied my thoughts. My shoulders shook, trying to brush off the vivid illustration. My hands balled into fists, my nerves twitching under my skin. I knew my temper. If I didn't get out now, it would not be pretty.

Ryker's gaze drifted to me, his eyebrows lowering as I shoved on my boots.

"You guys do what you need to; I'm going out." I grabbed my bag.

Sprig squeaked and moved toward me.

"Sprig." I held up my hand. "I need to be alone for a bit. Stay here."

He stopped, dropping his arms at his sides, staring at me.

"Where are you going?" Ryker strode across the room, following me.

"*Bh-ean?*"

Ignoring Ryker, I addressed Sprig. "I'm sorry, buddy. I know sprites don't understand being alone, but I need an hour or two. Okay? I'll take you to Izel's tonight."

He nodded. "It's enchilada night." He stuffed another chip into his mouth.

Ryker's hand grabbed my elbow, stopping me from reaching the door. "Where the hell are you going?"

I yanked free of his grasp. "I don't know. Anywhere.

I simply need to get out of this room."

"Let her go, Ryker." Amara waved at the door. "She needs some time to herself."

Some might think she was being supportive and nice, but I knew better. Everything she said was designed to get me as far away from Ryker as she could... then she could move back in.

Ryker noticed my mood and stepped between Amara and me. My body convulsed with the need to end our feud now, along with the necessity to let out all my pent-up anger and sadness.

"Zoey," Ryker said my name softly. When it didn't break my attention on Amara, he grabbed my chin, turning my face to his. His navy-blue rimmed white irises stared down on me. My shoulders drooped, my breath exiting from its tight hold.

"Why don't you guys go and get what you need? Get the lay of the town. We're going to go out for a little while." Ryker kept his gaze on me as he spoke. "We can reconvene tonight and start planning."

"But—" Grabbing Amara's arm and shaking his head, Croygen stopped her mid-sentence.

"Sprig, there is food in the fridge. Honey on the counter. You will have to survive till we get back." Ryker left no room for a debate. *Amara's going to love this.* He turned me around, opened the door, and walked us through it. The instant the door clicked behind us more tension drizzled from my muscles. His hand stayed on my lower back as he walked me downstairs.

Now it was my turn to ask, "Where are we going?"

The side of his mouth hooked up. "It's a surprise."

A light breeze wafted gently through my hair, pushing it back off my face. The afternoon sun sparkled off the ruins and turned the shaded areas purple and blue. Crumbled stone structures, which once stood tall and strong, now appeared as ghosts of what they once were. Vibrant green grass lay in a striking contradiction to the rugged, dark mountain peaks. Clouds circled the crests like hula hoops.

For more than a month we'd been only miles away but never made it to Machu Picchu. Many other things had taken priority, so it got pushed back.

"I knew how much you wanted to see this place. Sorry it took this long for us to come here," he said when we arrived. Ryker couldn't have chosen a more perfect spot to take me. My bad mood vanished, and I became a kid: exploring, touching, reveling in the place I dreamed about visiting for such a long time. People stayed clear of the large daunting Viking with an axe strapped to his back, letting us have more freedom to explore the inundated tourist spot. I spent the day reading every bit of information I could, eavesdropping on the tour guides' speeches, and discovering firsthand the beauty of the place. Death, fae, DMG, stones, and all other negative things were forgotten.

Machu Picchu was magical. And not merely hypothetically. I could feel power pulse from the ground and the stone ruins and throb into my feet and body. The energy coming from the earth was so intense, I didn't doubt most humans could feel there was something special here.

"Were the Incas fae?" I asked, feeling Ryker come

up behind me.

"You can feel the magic here, huh?" He shoved his hands in his pockets and stopped next to me.

"It's actually making me jittery." I rubbed at my arms. My goose bumps were not from the slight chill in the air or from being this high; it was from fae magic. "So, were they?"

Ryker put his hand to his forehead, blocking the lowering sun from his eyes. "No, they weren't fae, but they held magic. They were the South American equivalent of Druids."

"Druids?" My eyebrows arched in curiosity. I had heard of Druids, and my reading while at DMG taught me a little more about them. All I knew was before fae went into hiding, a group of humans learned fae magic. They worked and served many of the fae rulers. They grew in favor with the Celtic god and goddesses, and they became more powerful than the fae. Then, like the civilization here, they disappeared. The entire Druid race vanished.

"The history says the Incas disappeared after the Spanish Conquest, most probably from smallpox or other diseases foreigners brought in. That did happen, but it is not the reason *this* Inca civilization vanished."

"What was the reason?" I peered over at his profile. I sometimes forgot how long he had been alive and how much history, the real history, he knew and experienced.

"The Seelie Queen." He licked his lips, and I forced my head to turn away.

"The Seelie Queen? What do you mean? Did she kill them or something?" I laughed at the thought. I heard rumors she hated humans and was a bitch, but this was genocide we were discussing.

Ryker gave me a nod that suggested bull's-eye.

"What?" I exclaimed. "She eradicated this entire village?"

"No. She exterminated the entire Druid race."

"What? Why?"

"There are a number of rumors and theories. As far as I gather, she hated the fact the Druids were extremely formidable, and she couldn't challenge some of their magic. As Queen, she doesn't like anything more powerful than her."

"So she had them executed." I stared out at the ruins. Another chill ran up my neck. The place held so much energy I felt I could see the ghosts of the past. Knowing the truth of what really happened to the people connected me even more to the land. The secret of Machu Picchu will never be known to humans. Always an unsolved mystery. There were probably many unsolved cases we could blame on the fae.

"What?" Ryker stared at my profile.

I scrunched my nose. "I don't know, but it feels strange knowing the truth when no one else here does. Before I could feel magic, but now I sense *their* magic. Their blood saturates the earth, like they are still here."

"They probably are." He continued to watch me till my skin tingled. Finally, I shifted my head, my gaze finding his. Neither of us looked away. The sun slowly dipped behind the peaked mountain. Orange and pink reflected off his white eyes, highlighting the rings around his irises. Nerves took hold, and I licked my bottom lip. His eyes dropped to my mouth.

The memory of the way his fingers ran up my body, how his lips felt, trapped air in my lungs. I wanted him to kiss me.

Badly.

Ryker leaned forward, his breath gliding over my mouth. My lids drifted half closed, waiting to feel his lips on mine.

He jerked back. His head darted away as his hand ran over the top of his head. "We should get going before it gets too dark." He jutted his chin toward the path on the other side of the ruins.

"Uh. Yeah. We should." I nodded, shoving my hands in my pockets.

Most tourists were on the last bus heading back to Aguas Calientes, leaving the heritage site empty. Deep reds like cabernet colored the sky, painting the light fog ringing the mountain.

Ryker's elbow nudged at my side. "I'll race you."

A conspiratorial smile grew on my face. I might have little legs, especially compared to him, but I was fast.

We both zoomed off at the same time. Three of my strides were one of his, but I pressed harder into the dirt, which moved me past him as we glided down the hill. We neared one of the stone structures and just as I reached out to touch it first, hands clapped on my hips, yanking me back. I yelped as we tumbled to the ground, rolling.

My back landed in the dirt; my limbs spread out. Ryker lay a little away. I rolled to my side, smacking his leg. "Cheater."

He propped his elbows on his knees holding his chin

in his hands and chuckled. His laugh halted me. It was rarely heard, and it stopped my heart. He winked. "Damn right."

I grinned back. "Just know, every night when you cry yourself to sleep because of the lack of your manhood... think of me and how I kicked your ass."

"I am sure *I* will." He stared intently, his voice thick.

His meaning went into an area that clouded my thoughts and restricted my airways. Jumping to my feet, I tried to break the nervous energy gliding through my veins. He sat up, his finger catching one of my belt loops, and tugged me back down. I fell on top of him. He rolled me over, pinning my arms above me, his form hovering over mine. He blinked, freezing, almost like he couldn't believe what he had done. But instead of withdrawing, he pressed his body firmer into mine. My body absorbed his heat, and his erection pressed against my hip.

One hand loosened from my wrist and trailed down my arm to my face. His thumb traced my bottom lip, tugging at it. I stayed motionless, afraid if I moved, he would realize what he was doing and stop.

Two fingers snaked from my lips down the middle of my neck and followed the route to my breastbone. His gaze was fixed on mine as he drew a line down the middle of my chest, taking my tank top lower as he inched between my breasts. His touch was fire to my blood, boiling it to the point I couldn't breathe.

I bit down on my lip. His fingers followed the edge of my bra, the skin along the perimeter burned as he continued to explore both sides. I could no longer control my actions. Between him and the pounding magic in the earth, I trembled with energy. My leg snaked around him, pulling him into me. My free hand curled around the back of his head.

A rumble came from his chest, and he crawled between my legs, his hands running up my sides, taking my tank top with them.

A single spark and we were lost in the flames.

My tank top went over my head, and his erection rubbed against me when he moved, spinning my head. My hands went for his pants, wanting him so much a few seconds felt like a lifetime. He grabbed my face, turning it to him, a growl of desire emanated out his throat. My fingers continued to work on his buttons as his lips came down for mine.

"Park's clos—" A man's voice spoke in Spanish behind us. Both Ryker and I stilled. "Hey! What are you doing?"

It was a rhetorical question. With a man between my legs and my shirt disregarded several feet away, it was clear what we were doing.

"You can't do that here. You need to leave now." I looked around Ryker to see a man in a park service shirt.

"You're fuckin' kidding me," Ryker mumbled. The absurdity and embarrassment of being caught like two teenagers made me laugh. Ryker sat back on his heels, pulling me up while he stood. He reached over and grabbed my top, handing it to me before he turned to the ranger.

"Walk away. You never saw us," Ryker said.

The ranger blinked, a frown cresting his forehead. He absently rubbed at his head. "You... you need to leave. Now."

Ryker stiffened, a scowl forming on his forehead.

"Walk away. You. Never. Saw. Us," Ryker repeated.

The man shifted, his brows furrowing deeper, but kept his stance. My stomach sank, understanding what was happening.

Ryker's magic was dwindling, taking his power of glamour away from him.

I pulled on my tank, but guilt coated me thicker than any clothing. It might not be my fault, but I was still responsible. I was gaining while he was losing... dying. And it was the last thing I wanted to do to him.

"Leave. We were never here." I came round Ryker, squinting at the park ranger.

He shuffled his feet again, lines folding on his forehead. "This is the last time I tell you. Leave now."

What the hell? I could no longer glamour either? Ryker's magic was dwindling, I understood that, but mine should be growing.

Ryker's lids narrowed on me, then back to the man.

"We're going." I pulled on Ryker's arm, leading us to the trail. Ryker followed but his eyes still watched the guard. When we could no longer see the ranger, Ryker turned fully around, tugging free of my hand.

Anger simmered under every breath he took. Not pointed directly at me but at everything. At the moment I was the last person he probably wanted to talk to about it. He wasn't exactly someone who talked to *anyone* about his problems. He was losing control of himself, and he could do nothing but watch it happen.

But what about me? Why did they fail me? I couldn't remember the last time I used glamour. The knowledge that my usage only solidified them more to me kept me from utilizing them unless I had to. Jumping was never in my control, and I only glamoured when I went shopping by myself. Still it should have worked.

We followed the trail back to the village, both lost in our thoughts. The dense forest darkened with each step, the trees and mountains shielding us from the last rays of sun.

The unspoken moment earlier congested the space between us. All the tension I let go over the day reassembled back up my spine. I wasn't one for small talk and knew it was better to stay silent.

We were halfway back when my skin began to tingle. Warning me.

Simultaneously, Ryker and I halted our steps.

"You sense it too?" he muttered while scanning every inch of space.

"Yeah." The word wasn't even out of my mouth when another wave of magic plunged down on us. My nerves and skin jumped with the overload of energy. I swallowed and slowly circled the area, my heart picking up pace.

Ryker grabbed the axe attached to his back, gripping it between his hands.

A low growl reverberated from the forest. We swung around in the direction of the noise. A shimmering glow from the dense brush confirmed fae were coming for us. Then like fireflies, dozens of yellow lights gleamed from the foliage. It took me a moment to realize they were in pairs... eyes... wildcat eyes.

Wordlessly, Ryker ripped a dagger from his halter

and tossed it to me.

The leaves rustled and a paw stepped out from the shrubs but was hidden in the shadows. All I could see was black outline with yellow glowing eyes.

"Fuck," Ryker uttered.

"What?"

"It's a balam," Ryker said to me, his eyes never leaving the animal.

"Balam?" The name rang in my memory, remembering it was a type of fae, but I couldn't place what it was. "What is it?"

"Every country and region have their own mythology and names for a certain fae. Here a jaguar shape-shifter is a balam, and unlike the real animal, they run in large packs. Real jaguars are dangerous and can easily take down a human, but most are solitary animals and fear humans more than wanting to attack them."

I nodded. I'd heard that in my studies. Balam were known hunters, fully taking on the cat's predatory nature. They usually left humans alone unless the human ventured too far into the jungle and saw something they shouldn't. I never had to deal with one before. Jaguars would be a little out of place in Seattle.

I gulped and gripped Ryker's wrist, my other hand squeezing the handle of the knife as several of them stalked slowly out from the bushes.

Oh hell, that is a big kitty.

These jaguars were three times the size of a normal wildcat. One ordinary wildcat was scary. Fifteen huge yellow-eyed fae beasts were pee-your-pants worthy.

"I don't know what they want. They usually stick to

themselves. Leave other fae alone."

A growl erupted from the biggest cat, and a claw the size of my head dipped into the soft dirt. His muscles rippled, displaying the soft brown spots dotting his black fur.

"Usually?"

"Generally."

"Generally?" I exclaimed.

"Mostly." Ryker shrugged, drawing me into him. "This doesn't look like one of those times."

Dark fur glinted in the dying light. Their long claws drove into the earth as the pack moved slowly toward us. The front cat snarled, displaying long white fangs.

The back of my neck prickled as more fae surrounded us from behind.

"We have no dispute with you. Let us pass. I don't want to spill fae blood tonight," Ryker called out to the shape-shifters. They couldn't talk back in this form, but they could understand us.

The cats hissed; the exhibition of sharp incisors reflected the twilight.

"Yeah, they seem terrified of you."

Ryker cast me a look.

"It will be your blood spilled tonight, Wanderer. You and your human's," a heavily accented voice came out of the darkness. A tall willowy man appeared wearing a long white cotton abaya, customary to the men in Turkey or the Middle East. His dark skin only highlighted his white, wiry hair and beard. The man stepped in front of the pack. His eyes glowed with the same unnerving yellow as the jaguars behind him. The aura around him confirmed he was also a shape-shifter.

"Kanaima." Ryker shoulders tensed at the sight of the man.

Again the word *Kanaima* struck a familiar chord with me, but I struggled to place it. There were many fae to learn, along with their names and powers.

"I have no quarrel with you, shaman. I already found the one I need."

Right! Kanaima was a South American shaman, and if I remembered correctly, leader of the jaguar shape-shifters and not a nice guy. Evil. Goody for us.

"Unfortunately, Wanderer, we have a dispute with you."

"What did you do now?" I demanded.

"Nothing." Ryker shook his head. "I swear."

"He seems to think you did." I waved at the man. "Is there anyone you haven't pissed off?"

"Only the ones *you* haven't yet."

"Then your list should be a hell of a lot shorter!"

Kanaima cleared his throat, his staff striking the ground with force. "Enough!"

I drew back, but Ryker tensed like he wanted to rush the man and tackle him.

"What is it you want? My patience is running thin, old man, and we have enough people after us."

"We want the same thing as the others... the stone."

Ryker's brows furrowed. "How would you learn of the stone's whereabouts? You live in the middle of the jungle."

A slow, frightening smile crept upon the Kanaima's mouth. "We have our sources."

"Why would you even want it?" I couldn't help but

ask. They didn't seem like the take-over-the-world type. Their intent might be simpler, but the stone had different plans. It wanted power and dominance and would twist, corrupt, and suck you dry till it got it.

"Probably the same reason as you, human. To change the fates. We want to return to a better time when our land wasn't being ripped from us and destroyed by humans. We were the alphas of this land once upon a time. We should be the rightful leaders again." He tilted his head, examining me. "Fascinating. There is becoming less and less of you that can still be called human." He licked his thin lips and took a step toward me. Ryker growled, triggering the pack of jaguars to recoil, though they were still ready to pounce.

Kanaima put his hand out, indicating the shape-shifters to stay put. He didn't advance toward me again.

"You are extremely intriguing. I have never seen this before—a human procuring fae powers in this way—stealing them away from their master." His yellow eyes scanned my body. "The more you gain, the more he loses. Bit by bit you are stripping him. Forever."

Ryker bristled and subtly shifted his weight closer to me.

"I have seen many humans become fae by eating Otherworld food, but this is not what I observe here. I see electricity. Fire. Light. Boom!" His excited voice rang into the evening sky, raising goose bumps along my flesh. The moon peeked behind the mountains, shining an eerie light around us. "You are strong, human, hindering and pushing against all that wants to be claimed."

Huh?

"I think it's time we were going." Ryker's hand went around my hip. "It is better for both if we walk away peacefully."

Kanaima chuckled, his eyes wild.

Ryker took a step back and those same eyes narrowed into a pinpoint focus.

"I want the stone, Wanderer, and you cannot speak falsehoods to me. I see its power *on* you."

"Zoey," Ryker said.

"What?"

He shoved me behind him, lunging at the shape-shifters. They reacted instantly to his threat and leaped for him.

Seeing Ryker threatened inflicted anger in me I could not control. The mass of objects coming at him from all different angles reminded me of the night Marcello and his men used me as bait. Even though each swing Ryker executed had been lethal, there were too many of them at once. I think it was that night, thinking he was dead, when my feelings for him started to take root.

I kicked, hitting a big cat in the side and toppled it to the ground, swinging around to the threat behind me. My dagger nicked at the new danger, ducking out of the way of the searing claws swiping at my head. Ryker fought next to me, trying to keep close, but the cats came from all angles, creating a wedge between us.

"Zoey!" Ryker bellowed, fear striking his face as he looked past me.

The instant I heard my name I knew I was in trouble. My neck and back prickled. I whipped around. All I saw were claws, a large pink tongue, and enormous white daggered teeth barreling toward my face.

Oh hell. This is it.

I shut my eyes, anticipating the moment the teeth and claws would find their target. A force knocked me off my feet, my head smacking on the rocky trail. The dagger flew out of my hand, resonating across the rocks as it tumbled into the bushes. My head spun from the impact. My lids squeezed even tighter and waited for the jaguar to sink its teeth into me... and waited.

Then I sensed cold stone rigid underneath me, my skin instantly suffering the harsh chill of the air. *Cement? Cold?* I blinked, opening my lids. Only gray metal was in my line of sight. Blood leaked from my nose and I sat up, wiping it away. My head tumbled around from the sudden trip and the hit it took on the ground. When the room halted, my eyes fixed on the space around me.

Oh God, no.

I rubbed my red fingers on my pants as I clambered to my feet, circling around in utter astonishment and fear. I had gotten used to returning to our room, a place of safety. It never seemed like it was a big jump when I was still in the same town. Almost like it didn't count.

This was a big jump. Of all the places in the world— what brought me back here? Why this place?

"Hey," a woman's voice bellowed from the top of the stairs. "What the hell are you doing in here?"

I whirled around to face the girl. Both her eyes and mine widened into saucers.

No. This can't be real.

Her shock quickly fell from her face, replaced by a

smirk. "I knew you'd come back someday."

Jump, Zoey. Jump now! Nothing.

"You'd miss the excitement too much. Money, drugs, security. It will always be a stronger pull than freedom." The woman took a step down. "Not that I won't punish you first for what you did to my brother and to me, but you bring in far too much money to do too much damage."

Brother. Marcello.

Maria's lips curled in a malevolent grin. "The Avenging Angel has come home."

EIGHTEEN

My boots squeaked as I turned to run for the door. A high-pitched laugh bounced off the metal, assaulting my eardrums.

Men came from all directions; some I recognized, but most I didn't. I kicked out at one, using his leg to twist myself around and jab at an Asian guy behind me. The man fell back, and I dove into him, using him as a plow, pushing a few more men behind him to the ground. A punch slammed into my ear, another into my gut, and I stumbled to the side. Weaponless, I was fighting a losing battle. The knife Ryker gave me was still on the ground in Peru.

Ryker. Was he all right? Did he make it out?

Dozens of hands grabbed at my shirt, arms, and hair, stopping any further movement. Pain stung my head as one yanked my ponytail back with a sharp snap. Then I felt pressure against my temple, cool metal pressed into my skin. "Don't move."

I stilled. I couldn't outrun a bullet.

Jump. Dammit. Jump! I screamed at myself. Again, nothing happened.

My focus locked on the girl approaching me. I tried another tactic, repeating over in my head, *Let me go. Forget you ever knew me.*

Maria didn't even flinch as she slithered through the throng of men, a sneer playing over her red painted lips. "Talk about predictable. You really think you could escape?"

You will let me go, I demanded. She only folded her arms, shifting her weight. What was happening to me? I could no longer jump *or* glamour.

"I gave it the ol' college try."

She nodded. Her long, curly brown hair bouncing as she did. "I understand it's in your nature to do what you do best. Fight. No matter the odds. It's who you are. You will never be able to leave this life behind... and by the looks of it," she motioned to my bloody nose, "you haven't." A strange mix of understanding and kinship filtered over her features before she turned aloof again. Her eyes wandered over me, a sneer wrinkling her nose. "I *love* what you did with your hair. Fits you. The Avenging Angel looks even more ethereal, like you don't belong to this Earth." Her voice was soaked with mocking and jealousy.

"Tie her arms." She nodded to my hands. "Use the cuffs. You don't want to underestimate this one." She motioned to the men around me and pivoted, heading back for the stairs. "And bring her to my office."

Her office? For the first time I really took in the people and changes around me. Maria was in charge. She would only be running things if Marcello was dead. I wasn't too surprised; Ryker had bashed his head in with his axe.

Some of the men I recognized from my days here with Marcello, but more than half of these men were Asian. During my last stay here, all of Marcello's men I encountered were Hispanic, Italian, or Caucasian. It didn't really make sense Maria would change that, but it wasn't really important, my mind was centered on more crucial things. Like getting the hell out.

Maria's crew dragged me forward, but stopped at the bottom of the stairs. A skinny dark-haired boy stepped in front of me, handcuffs in his hands.

"You will pay." The boy glared at me with unabashed hatred. "My sister will never be the same because of you." He squeezed my wrists so tight against the metal, I cried out.

Sister?

"Hiro." The man next to him nudged his arm. Neither one could have been more than eighteen.

Hiro's lip crooked, and he begrudgingly stepped to the side. The men behind pushed me up the stairs. I knew my way. This wasn't the first time I had been locked in this warehouse. Fear for my life and my anger at putting myself here made it difficult for me to keep a clear head. All I knew was I had to escape.

Only five of the men who attacked me downstairs came upstairs with me. Guess they figured I'd be obedient handcuffed with a gun to my head.

The office I stepped into was not the one I had left. It still had the old wooden desk, but several chairs were placed on the opposite side of the desk, allowing visitors to sit. Two file cabinets had been added, along with several detail maps of Seattle. Red ink and flags decorated the charts. A small generator sat in the corner, and on top were a dozen walkie-talkies being charged. More sat on the shelf. On the upper shelves behind the desk were ten to twelve black binders, some labeled: Outgoing, Payments, Received, Fights, Girls.

Compared to Marcello, Maria looked to be running a business. When I was here last, she was managing the underground fight club. She was more efficient in business, coordinating and handling the fights. Marcello liked the presentation, to be seen, and have the hoopla feed his ego. Maria was the one who did all the work.

"As you can see, I am running things now." Maria leaned against the desk, staring at me with regard. "How is it one insignificant person can bring such destruction and havoc? How were *you* capable of completely changing my life?" Fury flashed in her brown eyes.

Neither one felt like questions to me, so I didn't respond.

She cleared her throat, anger vanishing from her expression. "Come. I want you to see what you are responsible for." She motioned for the men to follow her. She walked me back toward the room I was all too familiar with. My stomach twisted in knots recalling my last stay in the back room of the warehouse. I was left for two days chained to a water pipe, only in my underwear.

Maria unlocked the door and slowly opened it. She peered around the corner before turning back to me. "See for yourself."

The men shoved me into the room, and I stumbled past the door. The room had been bare last time—only me, chains, and the water pipe above. The room now held a cot pushed against the wall, a bed pan, a side table holding a glass of water and bottles of medication. The man on the bed stared absently out the window at the pigeons nestled at the broken window.

I gasped.

Marcello.

The vacant expression on his face only emphasized the side of his head, which was completely caved in. It was wrapped with gauze as not to display the grotesque deformity. His eye on his bad side was closed and drooped down to his mouth. The features on his good side had slid down an inch. Acid careened around into my stomach, blending both guilt and anger together. My emotions mixed with extreme loathing for seeing him still alive, remembering all he did to me, and the revolt at seeing his condition.

"Marcello, look who's here." Maria spoke sweetly, but her expression was crammed with disgust and hatred for me.

Marcello jerked his head, his one eye landing on me. He watched me for a while, with no recognition or response in any way. I could have been another pigeon to him.

"He can't form sentences anymore. And I don't even know if he recognizes who I am. He wakes me most nights screaming."

My lungs felt like two blocks of ice. I didn't know what I should be feeling. I was sick at the sight of his disfigurement, but he had hurt many of the girls and had beaten me, and if Ryker hadn't come, he would have used me as his sex slave. Now the ruthless, merciless man was nothing more than a drooling mass of bones and skin.

"He still seems to know how to eat and go to the bathroom by himself. I've been told when those abilities go... so does he."

"Been told?"

"You think he was the only one affected by you?"

Technically, Ryker had done this to Marcello, but I was the reason Ryker acted against them. And I can't say he would be upset by Marcello's current condition. I wasn't even sure I was.

Maria turned to the men behind me. "Leave us."

"Ma'am." One of the guys I recognized from my stay before spoke.

Maria leaned over and took the gun out of his hand. "She is not going anywhere. And I think I can handle her."

I wouldn't bet on it, Maria. I have fae power in me now.

He nodded, and the rest of the men retreated out the door, closing it behind them.

The gun barrel pointed at my face. "Don't think about it. It's taking everything in my power not to shoot you in the head now." She stepped to me, the gun pressing into my skull. "But you will be my security here. Like you, I am a survivor. I will do what I need to get by. Unfortunately, right now this means not killing you."

A tortured grimace flicked the edges of her mouth. "I wish he had simply died. But now they have leverage on me. They know I will do what they say."

"What are you talking about?" I stepped back.

Maria shoved me, my back slamming into the concrete wall. She rammed the mouth of the gun into my forehead. "My brother might have been a bastard, but he is my family. I love him. Now they have me trapped as their puppet." She gulped, tears reflecting in her eyes. "Do you know how it feels to wish your brother actually died that night? How much easier it would have been. I could have run. Gotten away from here... from them."

"Gotten away from who?"

The weapon pressed harder into my head, causing my eyes to water, before she relented and stepped back. "The Scorpions." Her arm dropped to her side. "Duc."

Everything came into sudden focus. Now it made sense why more than half the men downstairs where Asian. The Scorpions, a rival gang in Seattle, had swooped in when Marcello could no longer fight them, and taken over. I understood who Hiro was talking about. There was little doubt the sister he mentioned was Crazy Kat, the girl I almost killed in the fight against the Scorpions.

Hell.

"They have taken over Seattle, running everything. Marcello was the only one formidable enough to keep them in check. Now no one curbs Duc's greed for supremacy and control."

"I'm surprised they kept you alive."

She shrugged. "Duc is exceptionally shrewd. He saw how I ran the girls here and coerced me to keep managing them. I live as long as the girls keep winning their fights. I run a tight ship, so I'm allowed to have some freedoms and authority, but it's all an appearance.

The moment I step wrong, I'm dead." Maria glanced back to the form on the bed. Marcello glanced up and waved to us, an innocent grin on his mouth. Maria nodded at him, then turned back to me. "First they will torture him to death."

Even after the shit I went through here under Maria and Marcello, I couldn't help but feel sympathy for her. I understood how it was to live in fear every day or to stay somewhere you hated because of family. Lexie might not have been my real sister, but I couldn't have loved her more. I stayed because of her, living life as a caged rat. But I wouldn't have done it differently. She was everything to me.

Maria's threat was quite real. I didn't necessarily think it was my fault, but I was a huge reason it all came to be and why she was in this situation. But like Maria said, she was a survivor, and my sympathy would be fleeting because I was the one she was going to throw under the bus.

Almost sensing my train of thought, Maria drew her arm up, pointing the revolver at me again. "God dropped his Angel on me again, and I'm not letting you get away this time. You are going to secure my survival."

A squeal behind Maria directed my focus past the gun. Marcello cowered on the bed; his eye locked on the gun in Maria's hand.

"I'm sorry, Marcello. I know guns scare you." She slowly backed up, keeping the gun on me, reaching back with her hand to touch him.

Guns scare him? Wow. Things had changed.

Marcello curled tighter into a ball the closer she

came. Terror warped his expression. His eyes fixed only on the weapon.

It was kind of sad to watch, but I had to keep reminding myself this was a man who raped and abused many women.

"Drop the gun. Forget I was here." I stared deep in her eyes, hoping this time if I said it out loud it would work.

She tilted her head to the side, studying me before she burst out with a laugh. "I don't think so." Her finger twitched. "Now let's move, girl. Your fellow bunkmates will be eager to have such a legend in their midst." For a moment Maria peered over her shoulder to comfort him. "Marcello, it's all right. No one is going to hurt you." I wasn't about to let any opportunity to escape get by me.

I leaped forward, my hand reaching for her wrist, and knocked her hand holding the gun. *Boom!* The gun went off, exploding in my ears. The bullet hit the ceiling, bouncing back. Maria and I jumped back, ducking out of the way of the ricochet. The slug hit close to my foot, embedding in the floor.

Marcello's screams broke through the ringing in my ears.

"You crazy bitch!" Maria bellowed over her brother's wails.

"I'm the crazy bitch, seriously?"

Feet pounded outside the door before breaking through. "Maria!" A familiar dark-haired boy, his lip scarred and misshapen, was the first to cross the threshold. "Are you okay?"

"I'm fine, Carlos." She brushed ceiling debris off her

pants. He watched her, bobbing back and forth on his feet, debating whether to run to her side. I remembered him. Carlos, the boy with the hair-lip, was the one who saved me from another one of Marcello's groping men, Pedro. Pedro was a victim of Ryker's wrath the night of the fight. I felt no sadness that asshole was gone.

Marcello continued to whine, curled tightly around his blanket. Maria picked up the gun, handing it to Carlos, needing to get it out of the room, away from Marcello. "Take her across the street and put her in the room. I'll be over in a bit."

"Come on." Carlos grabbed my shoulder and pushed me out of the room. Normally, I would work him, play with his emotions to help free myself. The expression he gave Maria when she wasn't looking told me pleading my case would be pointless; he would do anything she asked.

My escape would have to come another way. If only for one moment, maybe the powers would work in my favor, instead of at inopportune times. My body jumped at the bar when Ryker was about to kiss me, but not now. Go figure. Until they decided to come back, I had to stay smart and alert. Just like old times.

Carlos and a few others walked me away from the warehouse. Evening was slowly descending on Washington. It felt strange to be reliving the same sunset I'd just seen in Peru. I hoped Ryker wasn't worrying about me and had escaped the throng of jaguars.

He did. He had to, I told myself. And he was back safely in our room, freaking out, realizing by now I was not at the usual places I jumped to. Even if I were free, there was no way I could have contacted him to let him know I was okay. The inconvenience and frustration from the lack of modern technology in this area in the last few months was getting easier to deal with, but at times like these I really wished for a cell phone.

Even though I had only been gone a short time, I was curious how Seattle was doing. The generator in Maria's office led me to believe there still was no electricity. At least not constant. Had anything been done, or was Seattle still stuck in the waiting game?

Carlos marched me across the road, giving me no opportunity to get any of my questions answered before hauling me through the doors of a warehouse. Another one vacated, left for gangs like the Scorpions to take over.

The bustling noise of people talking and laughing echoed off the tall roof. Thirty or more tables lined one side of the warehouse, the other filled with cots. More than a hundred women and younger girls lounged across tables and beds. Makeshift lighting connected to generators spotted the room, giving a low glow to the darkening space. A cafeteria-type space sat at the far end of the building. More women in aprons went in and out of the back doors into another room, bringing food in large tin containers and placing them inside the buffet station. Seven guards stood around the premises with guns hooked to their waists. Seven guards could be taken down by a hundred girls who were trained fighters. But compared to what was outside the penitentiary, inside seemed a better option. Food, bed, clothes. If they left, where would they go? And if you did escape, Duc didn't seem like the type of man who would simply let you go. He would track you down and kill you.

A group of girls who played cards at the first table looked up when Carlos walked in. Their eyes landing on me, analyzing me from top to bottom.

"Fresh meat," a girl cackled, her black eyes flashing. She yelled to the room behind her, "We got a newbie, ladies." Everyone stopped what they were doing and stared at me.

Just like prison these girls were deciding quickly to either take me down or make me their bitch. I would be neither. There was a reason they called me the Avenging Angel. I couldn't match a bullet, but I could fight any one of these girls.

Carlos gripped my arm. "You don't want to fuck with this one, Jada."

"This tiny white girl? Pleeease." She waved her hand at me. "I wouldn't even have to get out of my seat."

Carlos smirked and tugged me to follow him. "Don't say I didn't warn you."

Rewind four years and I would've ripped out of Carlos' hold to show Jada how much she'd misjudged me. I could protect myself, but I didn't have the desire to battle for no reason like I used to. Since meeting Ryker, my bloodlust had plummeted, probably because during my time with Ryker my fights were not about releasing my pent-up anger or proving myself. They were life and death.

Also, being with him made me happy. Nothing kills your savagery like happiness. Damn him. He was making me soft.

"You know, if they find out who you really are, it will cause more problems for you." Carlos turned us in the direction of the stairs. The setup of this warehouse was similar to the one across the street, so I easily took the lead up the steps.

"I can handle them."

He scoffed. "There are over one hundred fighters here. Each one would love to claim they took down the Avenging Angel."

He was right. A dozen or so I could handle. One hundred sounded exhausting.

A guard standing at the entrance of the stairs nodded at Carlos and stepped out of our way. His eyes widened at me, and a curse mumbled from his mouth. Another one of Marcello's men who remembered me.

"I seemed to have made an impression on you guys."

"Let's say you and your friend left a mark." Carlos' lip hooked up even higher than normal in a sneer. "I will be extremely surprised if you make it out of here alive. I'd keep one eye open when you sleep. Too many of us want you dead."

"Take a number," I mumbled to myself.

The room where he led me was only a ten-by-ten, windowless cell. Chains hung from the wall. It smelled of blood, body odor, and urine.

Oh hell no.

A guard in the assembly walked over, nudged a firearm into the back of my head, and urged me to continue into the space.

I tried to glamour, again; to no avail. *What the fuck?*

Carlos pulled me over, latching me into the shackles.

I hadn't realized how much I'd begun to respect fae's rules of battle. They still were old school, and few fought with guns, choosing blades instead. There was an honor in that. It was about who was a more skilled fighter. It was about smarts. Guns could render the slowest person a winner in a duel. But in the general sense, I liked the concept of "may the best fighter win." I went into all my fights with only my fists and wits.

It rattled my bones to be forced to do something without a fight. Until I jumped, I would watch for any moment their defense went down.

The metal clasps around my ankles and wrists allowed me to move only a foot in any direction. Carlos rechecked all the fastenings, testing for a weak connection. "Get comfy, *bruja.*" He and his two other minions walked out and slammed the large iron door behind them, plunging me into sheer blackness. My stomach screwed into a lump, my breath immediately becoming short. Being tied in a dark room brought back too many horrible memories. My first reaction was to soothe myself and go to my happy place. But at the same time, there was a chance if I worked myself up enough, I would jump. Fear seemed to be my trigger.

I let the dark soak into my skin, focusing on the ties binding my wrists and ankles, remembering my younger self confined in small quarters in utter darkness, left for hours with no food or water. A mist of sweat beaded my forehead. My heart beat irregularly in my chest as I focused on the memories.

Why am I not jumping? I yanked at the chains in exasperation. *Why isn't it working when I need it?*

Indignation at myself, at my situation, prickled at my eyes, but I was far too angry to cry. The girl who held so much rage for life, for the cards she was dealt, was bounding to the surface again. The girl who could only solve things with her fists growled inside, wanting to break out like a caged animal.

I seethed for hours in the dark. I'd promised myself I would never be a victim again. Even if I were forced to a wall, they would not possess me.

The door swung open and dim light leaked into the small room. Maria's shoes clicked on the stone as she sauntered in with Carlos and two other men behind her.

"Not sure if the sight of the Avenging Angel chained could ever get old to me." Maria's brown eyes glinted with amusement.

A slow methodical smile grew on my mouth.

Maria blinked, glancing over her shoulder, and then back at me. "What are you smiling about?"

My grin expanded.

"Stop it," she demanded. "Why are you smiling? You're chained up. You have no way out. Your life is now mine. I *own* you."

I only smirked.

"Stop that!"

Damn, she was easy to rile. It was one of her biggest flaws. Quick to anger and quick to act.

"I tell you when to eat, sleep, and shit. Don't you understand you are mine now?" She grabbed my face, squeezing my jaw.

In this moment she reminded me of her brother. Marcello's need to fashion himself above everyone else by control and dominance. The power he felt when someone cried or showed fear had governed his existence. When someone didn't give him this, he got angry and unsettled. She was exactly the same way. It was amusing to watch. Even if I knew there were reprimands, it was worth it.

Like the time before, she did not fail me. Her slap whipped my head to the side. The bubbling of rage tickled my gut. I chuckled.

"Dammit, you bitch!" Maria closed her hand. The punch hit my upper lip and nose, slicing my gums and cracking the cartilage in my nostrils. Fresh blood broke free, sliding over the previous nosebleed, crusted above my mouth.

Come on, Zoey. Jump!

My body stayed in place. Extreme emotion was usually the source of my previous jumps. Anger, sadness, fear. I hoped one of these would finally click in and work.

Anger was an emotion I understood well and was easy to invoke in me. Once I started down the path, it took a lot for me to come back. Like a bull, all I saw was red. The more Maria hit me, the more my emotions narrowed down the tunnel, inciting my wrath.

"Still can only fight me when I'm chained up, huh?" I taunted her.

A punch to the stomach.

I bent over, coughing. "Poor Maria, you were never any good at fighting. Hope you are better at changing diapers. Looks like your brother might need a nanny."

Whatever switch I snapped in Maria, it flooded her with a billowing rage. She cried out and came after me with all she had.

I closed my mind to the pain and centered on escaping. My muscles twitched with the need to act. I could feel the magic in there, but for some reason it was not coming to the surface.

Another jab to the stomach doubled me over, gagging. A cry mixed with annoyance and agony tore from me, bringing me back to my outer shell. Blood gushed from cuts on my face. My eye already puffed, pulling the lid shut. The taste of blood coated my teeth.

"Maria," Carlos shouted over her wails. I lifted my only operational lid, seeing him pull her off me. "Stop." He wrapped his arms around her, keeping her still. *"Detengase, mi reina." Stop, my queen.* He whispered so low I knew I was probably the only one who heard him. Maria's attention was still locked on me so she didn't seem to hear or see anything else.

Saliva dripped from my mouth and I spit, feeling the thickness of the blood mixed in.

"That was for my brother." Maria ripped from Carlos' hold, coming back for me. "And this is for me."

I felt and heard the crunch to my cheek as her fist collided with my face. It was the only sensation I had before everything went dark.

NINETEEN

A faraway squeak of metal brought me out of my hazy dreams. Right away I wished I had stayed unconscious. My face pounded in sync with my heart, shooting ice picks into my temple. Soreness rumbled over my ribs and tender bruises flickered their own torture over my stomach and face. My head lay on a cold, unforgiving ground, and my body huddled in a tight ball. I shivered from the icy room.

Soft footsteps on the stone pulled my one lid up. The other partially opened, but it felt better to keep it closed. In the shadows an outline of a girl bustled through the door, her hands full. Two guards stood on the other side, holding the door open for her. The only light came from a flashlight one of the guards held. I had no idea what time it was, but it seemed late night. The girl moved to me.

I always had sharp senses. Probably something DMG made sure was in my coding. Now with Ryker's powers, they'd heightened to extraordinary. Similar to someone blind, my senses were tiny fingers, making out faces, bodies, and auras in the dark.

Human. Girl. Young. Timid. The taste of her fear glazed over my tongue.

An Asian guard I recognized from earlier, Hiro, pushed around her, a semiautomatic hanging from his side. "If you make any move, I will put a bullet into your brain."

I wanted to laugh. I was chained to a wall, beaten, and so cold my muscles decided to go into hibernation. In a few months I had acclimatized to Peru's heat. I missed it.

Hiro grabbed my shoulders and propped me against the wall. Air hissed between my teeth. The girl kneeled in front of me with a bottle of water, rags, bandages, and antiseptic. Her hands shook as she dampened the cloth with the disinfectant and reached for my face. I hissed when the alcohol touched my cuts, rearing my head back to the wall. The girl jerked her hand back.

She was clearly terrified and a pretty little thing, only about fifteen. Naturally skinny, but the sharpness of her cheeks told me she was being underfed. Dirty, knotted beach waves of long dark blonde hair tumbled over her shoulder out of her loose ponytail. Her light blue eyes reflected in the torchlight as she reached for me again. I bit on my lip and forced myself to stay in place as she dabbed the wounds. She continued to clean my cuts, keeping her gaze away from mine.

"You're scared of me." It was a statement. She set the cloth down, picking up the bandages. I saw her nod. "Why?"

The guard grunted in warning but didn't stop me from interacting with her.

"Why are you afraid of me?" Her fear might also be of the guards or even this place, but I could feel it was mostly directed at me.

"You are the Avenging Angel," she whispered, voice shaking.

So much for keeping my identity a secret. "Yeah, so?"

She frowned, like her saying my moniker was enough of an answer. "People have told me about you and what you are capable of doing."

"Enough talk. Keep working." Hiro nudged the girl with the handle of the gun. She quickly got back to patching me up.

"What are they saying about me?"

She pressed the bandage to my cheek. "That you are a killer. You enjoy the taste of your victims' blood and drink it after you've murdered them."

Wow! Okay. Now they had turned me into some dark fable, scaring children.

"What's your name?"

The girl tugged at the bottom of her lip before answering. "Annabeth."

"Annabeth, look at me. Do I look like a murderer to you?"

For the first time, her eyes met mine, and her gaze bored into my soul. I can't say what it was, certainly not her looks, but something in the way she met my gaze reminded me of Lexie. Like they could see past all the bullshit people used to hide themselves and really see the person underneath.

Her head shook back and forth. "No."

"Not to say I am not capable of it; we all are. But you don't have to fear me."

A smile hinted at her mouth, and she nodded.

"But only you." I winked. It was good if most of the others feared me. Kept me protected. For some reason I didn't want her to be afraid of me. She was already scared enough.

"What are you even doing here?" I asked.

"That's enough." The guard tapped on Annabeth's shoulder. "You are done here."

She nodded and collected her items. "The water is for you." She stood and was escorted by the guard. The metal door clanked as he shut it, plunging me back into pure darkness.

Annabeth stayed in my mind till I drifted off. I wondered how she became a part of this group. Was she kidnapped? Joined willingly? She didn't have the body language of someone who spent time on the streets. My intuition told me she came from a sheltered, loving world. She could not possibly be a fighter. Skinny and timid, she would be eaten alive out in the ring. Why was she here? What use was she to them?

I knew I would not like the answers to my questions. But with this one girl, I felt I could no longer run away and forget she existed. I had done that once, and there was never a day that went by I didn't regret it. I hadn't stopped the man who abused me from doing it to other little girls. This time I would stop it. Make sure these girls got free of this life.

When I was awakened again, daylight streamed in from behind Maria as she entered. A frown creased her forehead at seeing me. "You seem to be healing."

My fingers reached up, touching my face. The cuts were swollen but closed and on their way to mending back together. My bruises felt less tender and my lid could almost fully open. This might raise questions if she kept hitting me and I kept healing in only a few hours.

Humans would find a way to rationalize it in their heads till it made sense to them. Air caught in my throat. Did I just call them *humans*? Like I was no longer part of them? Shit. I'd been with Ryker too long. The thought of him sent a fire to my heart. Damn, I missed him. I wanted nothing more than to feel his arms around me. I needed to believe he was okay. I couldn't fathom my life without him now.

"I guess that's a good thing since Duc will be here tomorrow. He will want to see you healthy and ready to fight." She motioned with her head to someone behind her to come forward. "You have two options. You can behave and be allowed to go downstairs with the rest of the girls." A wicked grin curled at her mouth. "They are quite eager to meet their new bunkmate. Especially when I told them who has graced us with her presence. You are quite famous here."

Carlos shifted behind her, a frown twitching his mouth. Did he disagree with Maria's decision? Well, if so, I was definitely on his side. Telling them only would cause problems. Girls would want to take down the legend to become one themselves. The guards were few in number; now they would have to be on constant defense and ready to act. Maria was far more business savvy than her brother, but when it came to me, both of them lost their reasoning.

"Your other option is to stay chained here with no

food."

I sighed dramatically. "So many great options... I hardly know what to choose."

Maria sprang to me and sank her nails into my neck. Carlos was right behind her, tugging her hands free of my skin. He pulled her back, her chest rising and falling.

I touched the scrapes around my neck; a drip of blood stained my fingers. "You definitely need to reel in that temper of yours. You make it so easy."

Maria took a deep breath. Carlos let her go, but he didn't back away. "What is it about you?" She shook out her arms, trying to free herself of the anger. "Just looking at your smug, perfect face makes me want to tear you into little pieces."

"How sweet."

Her lip lifted in a snarl. Carlos put his hand on her shoulder to calm her. "So, what do you choose? Eventually you are going to realize you are mine now, and you have nowhere else to go."

I was unsure why she would let me roam freely downstairs. I didn't want to pass up the opportunity to get out of these chains. Free of the cuffs, I had a chance. I pushed to my feet, shoving my hands out to her. "I'll be good. I promise."

"Maria?" Carlos shook his head.

"No, if she wants to go, we shouldn't keep her from going."

I was being set up, but I didn't care.

Maria pulled a key from her pocket and unlocked my binds. "But I forgot to tell you." Here came the conditions. "If you go downstairs, you have to wear this." She grabbed an item out of a guard's hand and held it up.

It was a leg cuff, the kind you see on people under house arrest.

"This one has been modified." She pushed a button and the manacle vibrated with electricity. "One wrong move and every muscle in your body will lock up, and like a block of wood, you will crash to the ground."

Fuck. Still, the possibilities outside this cell were better for me than inside them.

I nodded. She smiled. She was looking forward to pushing the button.

A brown-haired guard, one of Maria's first tier, latched it around my ankle. It clicked as he locked it.

"Every guard, and myself, have a remote to detonate it. Also, it's rigged to go off if you get too close to the outside doors." Maria brushed her curly hair off her shoulder and opened the door. "Have fun getting acquainted with your new friends," she sang before disappearing.

Carlos heaved a sigh, walked to me, and unlocked me from the wall manacles.

"You don't agree with her, do you?"

He let go of the shackles, allowing them to fall to the floor. "No. Keeping peace here is hard enough. You only bring misery and evil to our doorstep."

"So you like me then?" I was easily returning to the life of living where I felt I had to show different sides to each person I interacted with.

Carlos walked me down the stairs. Counting the guards, more than a hundred pairs of eyes were on me as I descended. As I predicted, there were a few already mumbling I looked more like a little cheerleader than a fighter, scoffing at the idea they couldn't handle me.

"She's the so-called legend? The Avenging Angel?" The girl, Jada, was the first to vocalize it loud enough for everyone to hear. "Please, my eight-year-old niece could take her out."

I loved it when they formed the wrong idea of me. It actually helped me more often than not.

"She's so cute. Like a Barbie doll." Jada sniggered, others growing in confidence to join her. "No, sorry, make it a Skipper doll."

This is what I lived for. Girls getting lippy in their overconfidence. Their fall was always much sweeter. I learned to stay quiet, letting the insults roll off me. The other girls had a hard time with this. The loud boastful ones hated when their slights were met with silence and calmness. I would only grin like they were praising me. It always provoked them to act rashly. Predictable. First Maria, now Jada. It was getting boring.

"Jada." Carlos stared her down, moving me past the hecklers. She crossed her arms, her eyes still roaming over me. She was at least five eleven, thin, but fighting gave her a toned body women killed for and men desired. Her curly black hair was tied back, and her dark skin was lined with scars. All the women were dressed in a uniform of black leggings, a nondescript gray sweatshirt, and cheap white tennis shoes. Duc must have raided a Walmart.

"I want no problems. Got it?" Carlos yelled out to the group. Only a few nodded. "Go back to what you were doing."

The girls in the kitchen area returned to their work,

putting food out. My stomach growled at the smell of cooking eggs. Carlos directed me underneath the stairs where there were toilets and communal showers.

"You have water?"

"*Borrowed* by the Red Cross. You can only shower for three minutes. And a forewarning... it's not heated." He grabbed a toothbrush, paste, towel, and fabric from the shelf, shoving it at me. "Take care of business and change. Breakfast is in ten minutes."

I glanced at the clothes in my hand. Black stretch pants and a gray hoodie. I wanted a shower, but I was already shivering. Icy water did not sound pleasant. I could push it another day. I went into the bathroom and changed. Peeling off the ripped cargo pants and stained shirt was another reminder this was not some screwed-up dream, and I was no longer in Peru.

For my own sanity I convinced myself Ryker had escaped from the balam and was fine. What did he imagine happened to me? What was he going through trying to find me? He had to be frustrated knowing he could do nothing but wait. He had no idea where I'd gone, or if I could get back, but he also couldn't leave Peru, knowing I would return the moment I could.

I pushed thoughts of Ryker away. While I liked the softness he created in my heart, here I had to be stone: no emotion, no sentiment, no cracks in my walls.

I finished dressing. The hoodie was thin, but it gave me a little more protection than my tank top. Using the supplies he'd given me, I cleaned my teeth and washed my face.

When I came out, Carlos was waiting for me. "Your bed is over here. All your stuff will go into the basket under your bed. We do random checks, so don't bother trying to hide anything. We have our fight training in the yard." He nodded to the back doors.

"You worked at a prison before this, didn't you?" I teased. By his pointed glare I realized I hit on something. "Resident?"

Carlos moved till he was only an inch away from my face. He was only a few inches taller than me. His voice razor sharp. "Five years at the King County Correctional Facility, and I didn't become anyone's bitch. Got me, *perra*?"

Touché.

He didn't scare me. Instead, I respected him a little more, but I didn't want to purposely piss him off. I gave him a curt nod, and he stepped away.

"Watch your back." He knew, as well as I did, there was a large target from all sides. His disfigured lip curled with amusement, then he walked away out the main doors. Probably heading across the street to Maria. The boy had it bad.

The springs of the cot protested as I sat. It was adorned with only a pillow, sheet, and scratchy wool blanket. I slid the basket from under the bed and placed my newly acquired items in the holder.

"How are you feeling?" A small voice turned my head up. Annabeth stood in front of me. She wore the uniform of yoga pants and a hoodie, her hair knotted back in a loose bun.

"Hey." I smiled. "I'm feeling better. Thank you for patching me up."

Her critical gaze roved over my face, her brows

hitching together. "You are almost healed."

My hand automatically went to my face, brushing over my bandages and bruises. My eye was practically back to normal, no longer swollen shut. "Uh... yeah."

Her eyes narrowed on me suspiciously.

"Chow time." A woman's voice accompanied a loud bell.

"Hell," I mumbled. "I feel like I'm in prison." I rubbed my hands over my face.

"No." Annabeth shoved her hands into her pockets. "You're in hell." She turned and walked to the line forming at the buffet.

TWENTY

How true her statement became.

On my way to get in line, I was tripped, shoved, and insulted in every way. They only backed off when I stood next to Annabeth. I guess I wasn't the only one who felt like protecting, instead of harming, this girl. She brought out the same instinct in me Lexie had. I didn't know how long I'd be here, but until then, when I was around, no one would touch her.

I lifted my tray, holding it out for food to be slopped on it. The women ignored me, pushing it out of the way as they served the other girls. My head already pounded with annoyance. I wanted to drop the tray and go back to my bed and crawl into a ball. What I wanted to do and what I had to do—polar opposites.

"You really want to start out like this?" I shoved my platter back at the girl serving, my tone walking a thin line of bemusement and threat. "It's really early to get on my bad side."

The girl lifted one eyebrow in a challenge.

"You know those rumors about me?" I giggled, sounding a bit crazy. "Like I enjoy drinking the blood of my victims?" My face fell, and I reached over and grabbed the girl's throat. "They. Are. All. True."

Whatever it was, my expression, my tone, or the dead seriousness she saw in my eyes, she placed food on my dish. "See how easy it was?" I let go of the girl, patting her face, and continued down the line, humming. Unstable was a good trait to use. People didn't like being unsure; it created insecurity and fear. I might be small, but they'd learn I was not someone to mess with. I earned my reputation.

I settled at a table, and Annabeth sat next to me. She was wise. Even though most were taller or bigger than me, she was insightful enough to sense my underlying power. I was someone to align with, not challenge.

But not all took the wise road.

"Oh, AB, has she already made you her pet?" Jada came to the table, leaning between two girls on the other side of me. "You're a sweet kid, but not too bright."

I took a bite of my eggs and snorted. Talk about not too bright.

"You have something to say, Skipper?"

"I would have to talk too slow... and I simply don't have the energy for stupid this morning." I took another bite. The powdered taste reminded me of the breakfast at Red Cross, which probably wasn't a coincidence. Everything here, including the water, appeared to be stolen from them. Maybe it was the red crosses displayed on everything, including the tray I was eating off, that tipped me off.

Jada's shoulders hunched to her ears. "Oh no you didn't." She swirled her finger at me. Seriously, I could take a nap while she worked up to the point.

I shoved a piece of toast into my mouth, ignoring her

insignificant chatter. Annabeth sat rigid next to me and everyone, including the guards, watched us. Even they knew a fight would happen between Jada and me, but until then it was all talk. Supremacy only had room for one, and sooner or later she and I would have to fight for it. I wanted to fast-forward to it, but she seemed to need the foreplay.

I sighed. *Foreplay.* The only foreplay I wanted was with Ryker.

"What the fuck are you smiling about, cunt?" Jada's fingers grabbed the lip of my tray and flipped it up. Oatmeal and runny eggs slipped onto my lap with a slopping sound.

She wasted my food. Now I was pissed.

"Dammit!" I rose to my feet like a phoenix. "I wasn't *finished* with my meal yet."

"Oh, does the little princess want more eggs?" Jada taunted.

"Yeah, actually I do. Thanks." I waved her off like a servant.

It was only a blink, the calm before the storm where you could hear everyone suck in their breaths, then the storm crashed onto the shore.

People wailed with excited cheers as Jada flung herself over the table, her nails coming at me like missiles.

Finally.

The guards yelled as they moved away from the walls.

I snapped up the empty tray on the table and swung it at her face. The plastic vibrated as it made contact with her head.

Hoots and whistles buzzed in my ears along with the adrenaline. The noises became background as I focused on my target. I needed to learn her weakness.

Jada continued to smack talk, but she did not hesitate in striking out at me. She had the tendency to claw at me in between punches. Old schoolgirl fighting—scratching, pulling hair, and nail gouging.

I nailed her in the eye, knocking her across the table. Her back slipped over gooey oatmeal, and orange juice spilled into her eyes. She touched the back of her head, where oatmeal and egg clung to her curls in globs.

"You bitch." She grabbed a tray, ramming it into my stomach. I curled over. She flew at me, knocking us both to the ground. She seized my hair, banging my head against the cement. I curled my elbow in, stabbing her in the soft part of her throat. She rolled to the side, coughing. I took advantage, obtaining the upper hand, literally. I climbed on top of her, my hand connecting with her mouth, cheeks, and eyes.

The girls cheered as we fought.

"What the hell?" Carlos' voice reverberated from the doorway. "Stop this!"

The guards who had been letting us go at it suddenly jumped in, trying to split us apart. "Get a hold of her." My body was pulled back, a voice yelling in my ear. But I wasn't done. She needed a final lesson.

"Stop." Carlos grabbed for my arms, trying to contain them.

"No." The word almost came out inaudible.

"Okay, I warned you."

Suddenly my body was on the ground, twitching and flapping around like a fish. Pain so intense I couldn't see pummeled down each vein, shredding them. My muscles seized, ripping the air from my lungs. My eyes were still open, but I could not focus on anything. My thoughts retreated to the faraway depths of my mind.

Finally, oblivion consumed all my senses.

I scanned the area. The off-white walls were blank, but I knew them well. The DMG training room was like a second home to me. The floor was adorned with black mats, which Daniel had thrown me down on way too many times to count. A girl stood a short distance away, her back to me.

"Hello?" I called out.

She turned around, and I let out a gasp. The girl staring back at me was me.

"You are a pain in the ass, Zoey Daniels." She walked to me.

"Excuse me?"

"You are trapping us in this hell."

"Since this is a dream, it's you who dragged me here." I motioned around the room.

"No, not here, here." The other me rolled her eyes. "I mean here as in this prison camp you have stranded us in."

"Do you think I want to be here?"

"No, but you are the one keeping us here."

"What?" I exclaimed. "How am I keeping us... me here? I have a monitor strapped to my ankle and over seven guns trained at my head at any given time. How is it my fault?"

"Because the decision is yours."

Annoyance at myself was growing, shifting my weight between my feet.

"Don't you see? You're the one blocking it," her voice echoed my irritation.

"Blocking what?"

"The magic." Without warning she swung her arm. I barely ducked in time, feeling her arms skim over my head. I jumped up and danced back. A smirk grew on my other self's face. "Stop fighting it. Let it in... don't you feel it? Wanting to come out? To be part of you? As soon as you heard about him, how it was killing him, you cut it off." She lunged forward, and I fell, somersaulting backward till I was on my feet again, pushing her back.

"You don't think I haven't tried to bring the powers out? To get the hell out of here? But nothing happens."

She wrapped her leg around mine and ripped my feet out from under me. I hit the mat. "The problem is you can't lie to me. I know." Her hand came for my throat, and I rolled out of the way, bounding back on my feet. "You're blocking them because you're too scared to fully accept them. To take them from him."

I hooked my arm in a punch as she bobbed near. She weaved out of my reach.

"He has made you weak," she sneered. "Love has turned you soft."

"Love?" I scoffed. "You think I'm in love with him? I care about him a lot, but—"

"Yeah, keep telling yourself that." My twin circled me, trying to move in closer. "It's killing you. Holding on to the idea of one, while loving another."

I immediately wanted to dispute her claim. Daniel

275

was the only man I would ever truly love. The image of his smiling face, all he had sacrificed for me. Guilt twisted my stomach. No. Only Daniel. I cared for Ryker, but not loved. I did not throw that word around. Love was frightening and held enormous power for me. Only two people ever reached that level with me. And after losing them, there was no way I'd let in a third.

Especially Ryker.

There was no doubt he'd wormed in enough that I would do anything for him, protect him with everything I had, but I did not love him. I couldn't.

Her foot came up, slamming into my stomach. I went sailing back, hitting the ground with a thud. I couldn't move. My own face came into view, leaning over.

"It is up to you, Zoey. You can change your own fate." She moved closer to my face, her features turning fuzzy the closer she got, till I could no longer make out my own appearance.

"Hey?" the blurry figure said. I saw her hand move and a sting zipped across my cheek. My vison cleared. Maria sat in front of me with a frown etched on her face.

I blinked, trying to sit up. Instead, I continued to lie there, my muscles unresponsive.

"Your body is traumatized. It will be a couple more hours before it will fully function again." She sat back on her heels. "I am really sorry I missed you being electrocuted. I would do it again simply to watch it for myself, but Duc will be here tonight, and I need his new prize not to be shitting herself." She pressed her bright red lips together, barely containing her laughter.

Oh hell.

"Regrettably, you only peed yourself. Still funny though." She got back on her feet. "But because of this incident, both you and Jada are in confinement. We need to keep order and can't have our girls fighting each other out of the ring." She grinned. She knew perfectly well bringing me down would cause a fight. She wanted this to happen.

Maria stepped to the door and another figure joined her. I didn't need to see him to know it was Carlos. His hand went to her lower back, escorting her out of the door. The door clicked shut behind them, the room going dark.

I was back in the room where I had been before. Though I couldn't move, I felt the shackles back around my limbs, the ankle device replaced by a metal one.

I could also feel my pants were soggy at the crotch. Awesome. When you are stunned with what seemed like thousands of bolts of electricity, losing bladder control was the least of your problems. But the chilly stone floor only emphasized the dampness and caused my muscles to lock up more.

It is up to you, Zoey. You can change your own fate, a faraway voice in my head spoke.

Was I the only reason I was still lying here in my own urine? Was I blocking Ryker's powers out of fear or guilt? Because I cared too much about him? My brain wasn't ready to mull through heavy thoughts. Instead, I concentrated on trying to get my muscles to move.

It took me fifteen minutes before my fingers and toes could wiggle. In twenty, I was able to sit up but left drained. The simple movement of trying to lift my head was like pulling it out of drying cement. A weight of a bowling ball attached to my shoulders made it hard to curl forward, propping myself up higher. My arms hung lifelessly, prickling as sensation started flowing down to my fingers. My forehead lined with sweat, I leaned back against the wall, spent.

The door squeaked open, and Annabeth and Hiro ventured into the room. Annabeth carried a fresh pair of yoga pants and Red Cross issued underwear. I was all too acquainted with the generic brand of underwear they used, stealing many myself.

"I need to get her in clean pants." Annabeth pointed at the cuffs around my ankles.

Hiro grunted, shaking his head.

"I can't get pants off or on with the ankle chains." Her voice was soft, but determined. "I need those off. She can't do anything with her arms still bound."

"I'll be good." The words slurred out of my mouth, my tongue still having problems coordinating itself.

Hiro finally relented and pulled a key from his belt. There was a moment I thought about betraying my word and attacking him the moment he mobilized my legs. But I wasn't strong enough yet, and there were too many guards outside the door to get through. My energy would be wasted, and I'd probably be beaten till I blacked out again. I would wait. Bide my time.

My ankles were released from the binding and Annabeth kneeled in front of me. She glanced over her shoulder. "You don't need to watch."

Hiro's eyes widened then narrowed into dangerous slits. His face gave the impression he was horrified at the thought he might enjoy watching me be changed.

He walked out mumbling words in Chinese. I didn't understand them, but by the tone I could tell they weren't pleasant. He kept the door partway open and stood rigidly on the other side. It was more privacy than I expected.

"Here, I brought you this." She held out a granola bar. "It's all I could grab undetected."

This girl was officially on my "favorite people" list.

She unwrapped it and handed it to me. I grabbed the familiar item, shoving it into my mouth. If I weren't starving, I probably would have gagged. Even the wrapper reminded me of the countless days these bars were my breakfast, lunch, and dinner. I grew to despise them, but hunger always won out over taste buds.

Annabeth went quietly to work changing me.

"Thank you," I forced out. It was slow and choppy, but at least they sounded like actual words. Annabeth nodded, not looking at me. I watched her. She possessed a quiet strength, holding her shoulders back while keeping her head downcast. It was like she hoped to go unnoticed, but an inner strength was ingrained in her, something you perceived no matter how invisible she wanted to be. Someone who probably curled in a ball and cried quietly to herself, but rose each morning without complaint, doing what she needed to do to survive.

"How did you get here?" Her light blue eyes flickered to mine then back down. "I promise, Annabeth, I won't hurt you. I want to help get you out of here."

"And go where?" Her brows furrowed.

"Don't you have any family? Friends?"

Liquid coated her eyes before she blinked, pushing the tears back, her voice barely above a whisper. "No." She swallowed, feeling my curious gaze on her.

"My family was killed in the electric storm. The apartment building we lived in collapsed, and they weren't able to get out." Her voice trembled, but didn't crack. "I was at school. A volleyball game. My entire school was destroyed... I don't know how I got out alive; only a few of us did. We tried to stay together, but I heard about the Red Cross tents, and one night trying to get there I was kidnapped and brought here."

"If you could escape, do you have any extended family you could go to?"

One of Annabeth's shoulders raised and dropped. "My dad's parents live in Wisconsin, but I was never close to them. I only visited them once when I was a child before my dad had a falling out with my grandfather. I don't even know where they live or their phone number."

"We will find them," I pronounced, her gaze met mine. "I promise I will get you out of here."

A flash of hope glinted in her eyes before her head dropped, and she went back to finish what she was doing. With what little movement I could manage, I helped her put fresh leggings on me.

"Thank you, again. I will not forget this, and I never make promises I don't intend to keep." A thin empty smile curved her mouth at my words. "Can I ask you one more thing?"

She nodded.

I gulped, forming my dreaded question. "What does

Duc have you here for? You are clearly not a fighter." *Please, don't let it be what I think it is.*

Her lips pressed together, folding her hands in her lap. "Duc wants to have girls at the fights walking around and serving. He said my role would be more of an ambassador."

The knots in my belly folded over themselves. Duc could sugarcoat it all he wanted, but I knew exactly what it meant. They were there to satisfy whomever Duc wanted to please in whatever way they desired. He was prostituting all of us one way or another.

At first, I'd thought coming back here was a mistake, but what if Annabeth was my reason?

I knew I couldn't do shit tied up in this room. I wasn't even sure I could do much from the inside, but I needed to try. But even if I could convince everyone to escape this warehouse, where would they go? Duc wouldn't simply let them go, and they wouldn't be able to hide at the Red Cross. The police had too much on their plate to do anything. Some of the girls might not even want to go. Their lives might be better and more comfortable here than they were before.

If I could get a few to safety, the ones who had families, who wanted to be free of this life, it would be good enough.

When Annabeth left and my legs were once again restrained, I knew what I had to do—let down my walls and release Ryker's powers. The dream of arguing with myself rang through my memory. I was the one blocking them. I had to change not only my fate, but every girl's here.

TWENTY-ONE

Sweat poured down my face, my concentration wobbling. *Come on, Zoey. Try harder!* So far I only was able to give myself a crushing headache. There was one moment I felt myself jump. I stayed inside the cell, but I jumped to the other side of the room then snapped back. It happened so briefly I was starting to doubt it even transpired. Still, it gave me hope to continue.

Deep down I understood what was really blocking me. I cared about Ryker. A lot. No matter how I tried to talk myself out of the fact or denied it, it was true. I would not let myself give it a name. I'd never experienced anything like this. It felt different from Daniel. This was the exact thing blocking me from taking Ryker's magic completely. When I first met Ryker, I would have taken his powers from him, no question, no matter what it caused him. I could no longer do that.

Somehow, I was going to have to do it, and it killed me to know what the consequences would be after I did.

The room was perpetually pitch black, so I had no concept of time. But when my stomach gurgled past growling and my eyes grew heavy with sleepiness, the door to the cell unlocked and flew open. Generated light streamed in behind the figures, outlining them. Flashlights flicked on, blinding me.

"Get up," a man's voice barked at me.

The guards didn't even wait for me to respond before they grabbed me and yanked me to my feet. Between the torchlight and the light outside the room, I could make out Duc's slight form walking toward me. He looked exactly like I remembered, down to the suit he was wearing. The fabric was thinning from incessant wear. Threads hung from a few buttons, and it was wrinkled, but the man in the suit still held himself like he was in Armani. He had thick dark hair, small dark eyes, and a thin mouth. His face was strong, his cheekbones defining his angular face. Power and ruthlessness pulsed off him, instilling fear in those around him. I pinned my shoulders against the wall and kept my head up. I would not show I was afraid.

Maria stepped in the room after him. She also tried to hide her fear, although it seemed etched in her stance and her wringing her hands. "See, Duc? I got the Avenging Angel for you. I was not lying."

He grabbed my face, his nails digging into my chin. His eyes ran over me critically. He had seen me at least once before—in the fight with Marcello—the one when I almost killed his star fighter. That night I had been adorned with wings and heavy black makeup.

"Yes, I remember you now." His lips pinched. "You will compensate for the girl I lost." Duc's eyes drifted over to Hiro's, giving him a nod. Hiro's hatred for me grew in his expression as he clenched his jaw. "Your name will bring me money."

It didn't seem I was really needed in this conversation, so I kept my mouth shut.

He swung around. "Maria, announce her return at tomorrow's event. She will fight in Friday's match. I want flyers all over this town. Pictures of her if we can. Let's increase the excitement and up the bets."

Maria nodded obediently. "I have photos of her from the last fight." She shifted from foot to foot, not looking at him.

"If you lose or throw this fight..." Duc grabbed my face again, letting the unsaid threat hang in the room. He did not need to continue on. I understood perfectly. The rumors of the types of torture he delivered would make men trained in combat weep. "You will be reprimanded. If you try to run, there is *nowhere* you can go I would not find you." Duc motioned to the guard next to him. "Release her."

"What?" Maria bolted forward. "Sir, I don't think that is wis—"

Duc shot her a look, slamming Maria's mouth closed. A creepy smile grew on his face as he stared back at me. "I think she comprehends what disobeying me would entail. Don't you?" His fingers nipped at my chin. "Keep the monitor on her if it makes you more comfortable. But she will eat, sleep, and train with the others... and do everything I say."

A guard unlatched my restraints. Then Duc swiveled around and proceeded to the door. Maria glared at me before following Duc. The sound of the group marching down the stairs echoed in my chest as I fell back against the wall and slithered to the floor.

Every moment I could spare, I was going to work on getting out of here. It felt like the moment I stepped into the ring, Duc would truly own me.

I would forever be lost.

I peeked through the curtain at the hordes of people packing the warehouse, chanting and cheering at the two girls in the center of the fighting ring. My legs trembled as the shouts of the crowd escalated.

Training filled almost every waking hour till the night of my fight, leaving me exhausted. I could barely focus on trying to jump, but it didn't seem to make a difference. Whatever was blocking me held firmly in place.

Another roar of the crowd skated over my skin, giving me shivers. The energy all around pumped against my spine, dancing my legs about. Screams and bellows of the enthusiasts vibrated against the walls of the abandoned warehouse. Duc had taken the fights to an industrial area by the railroad tracks, a good forty-five-minute walk south of Seattle. From the unrelenting line still flooding through the door as hundreds of bodies and shoving themselves into every free space around the ring, the distance hadn't deterred them.

It wasn't the fight causing my nerves, but the sensation of human energy drenching me, like I had electricity coursing through my muscles. Getting a high off energy was normal for humans. What *I* felt wasn't. Like the night Ryker's powers were hurled into me, I could feel my body absorbing the force coming from them. There were fae around too. Their multicolored auras blinked constantly through the mass of people. I shouldn't have been surprised; many dark fae lived off energy like this. Wrath, greed, pride, envy, and probably lust dangled in the air like dust particles.

Even in a month, the fight scene had tripled. At first people thought the devastation in Seattle would be temporary, but hope was dwindling, and the worst in human nature was taking precedent. More people were desperate for an escape from the life here in Seattle.

Fae were probably having the time of their lives, loving this new turn of events, which created even easier victims. I could no longer exclude myself. I was also sucking up the human energy, like a sports drink powering my adrenaline. I could now see why fae were addicted. It was an unbelievable high. Maybe I should have been shamed by my thoughts, but things were not cut and dry to me anymore.

The crowd gave up a final cheer or hiss, the fight in the ring coming to an end. Energy circled, tumbling nervously around in my stomach.

The opening fights were over, now it was time for the headliner to come on stage.

"You're up." Maria pulled me away from the curtain, placing the mask on my face, letting the bands snap on my ears. Carlos stood guard at the doorway. The crowd on the other side of the curtain chanted a shortened version of my moniker.

"AN-GEL!" The pounding of feet and hands set the rhythm of my heart.

"They are riled tonight." Maria came around, straightening the wings on my back before kneeling down and releasing me from my charged ankle shackle.

"You better not fuck this up. And if you try to run. He will hunt you down and kill you." Her threat would have meant more if the real fear for her own life didn't break through, flooding her demeanor. She stood and walked over to the table, grabbing something out of her bag.

She tilted the needle up, tapping the air bubbles out of the syringe with her fingertip.

"No." I stepped back.

"It's merely vitamins." A smirk rolled her mouth.

"Vitamins, my ass."

My feet struggled to maintain their ground as she walked to me. Whatever she injected me with last time had caused withdrawals, nausea, and a fever.

"You will thank me later, when you are numb to the pain."

I shuffled back. "No, I don't want drugs."

"It's not heroin." She advanced toward me. "We don't want our girls becoming junkies. This merely gives you energy and dulls the pain."

A set of hands came behind me, pinning my arms against my body. Carlos locked me in place. Maria was fast, jabbing me with the needle before I could wiggle out of Carlos' hold. I sucked in a hiss, my eyes narrowing on her. She patted my arm with a cotton ball and flashed me a smug grin. The heat in my veins was instant, working down my arm and across my chest.

"Ladies and gentlemen..." The room filled with the announcer's voice. It was the same guy who introduced me last time. His words rose and fell with emphasis, rallying the audience and teasing them. "Descended from the heavens above, our own fallen messenger has come back to fight for us. Let's all welcome... THE AVENGING ANGEL!"

"Okay, it's time." Maria swung away from me and opened the curtains.

The rush of blood to my ears almost drowned the cheers. Hundreds and hundreds of people jumped up and down, creating rolling waves. Signs and hands jostled around, making me nauseated with adrenaline.

This was all for me. Well, not for me, but for the hope I gave them.

The poor girl they had me fighting stood to the side, adorned only in a red cape and mask, in some pathetic excuse for a superhero. She was tall, lean, and fit, but her body didn't look like being this thin was natural for her. Her sharp cheeks protruded as if malnourished. She pinched her mouth together and raised her shoulders with determination. But there was no denying the terror in her eyes as she watched me walk toward her, my green eyes ringed with black kohl and my wings flapping behind me like I was about to take off into the air.

I had seen her around the warehouse. Duc owned almost all the underground fighting girls. We ate, slept, and trained together. Some becoming friends. Then we would have to turn those feelings off and become machines, tearing each other apart in the ring. In this modern day, we were no more than gladiator slaves, fighting for the money and amusement of our "owners" and the masses.

This girl, whose named I never learned, was nowhere near my league. It was exactly how Duc wanted it. My first fight was merely pageantry. Over time he would build up my opponents, wringing money from the spectators as excitement grew.

Duc walked to me with his two henchmen who kept their eyes roaming for any sign of a threat. "You make this fight last." Duc tugged at his shirt cuffs, keeping his voice low and threatening. "People paid good money to see you fight, and I want them to keep paying." His dark gaze took in the hordes. "Next week I will introduce my companion girls for the top donators. Give them a show so this crowd and the bets will double."

Annabeth. My fists clenched until my nails cut into my palms. Biting words rolled around on my tongue. What he was doing to all of us was bad enough, but I was disgusted by his attempts to groom naïve, sweet girls like Annabeth into escorts.

Duc walked away.

The light around the warehouse from the generators darkened as the spotlight on the ring intensified, and I stepped inside. Maria came to my side, liberating me from my mask and wings.

The ground shook as people pounded their feet on the cement, crying out as I stepped into the ring.

Then the tall brunette strode to the opposite side, bringing up her arms in defense.

The two of us circled each other. The adrenaline from the crowd, now running in my blood, bounced my feet excessively. It took all my concentration not to take her down right away. She had several weaknesses, which were like beacons. Comparable to a bad poker player, she did a double bounce and hesitated every time she went in for a hit. To keep the fight going, I let her get in a few strikes. Never fun, but it was something I was used to.

The crowd gasped when she clocked me in the eye and then split my lip. My retaliation caused her ass to hit the floor with a thump.

"Get up," I mumbled to her when she didn't jump back up immediately.

She slowly climbed to her feet, the fight gone from her shoulders. She put her arms up, with little effort to block me. "Hit me," her soft voice pleaded.

My gaze turned to her. "What?"

"Hit me." Her expression held a sadness. "Just end this. I am *so* tired of fighting."

My gut wrenched. Something in her demeanor told me she wasn't merely talking of this match.

"Just end it. Give them what they want and Duc a good show. Make sure it's a good hit."

I heard a lot of talk, excuses, taunting, threats, but never had someone's words knocked me off my game. Staggering back, I let my arms drop.

The girl glanced around nervously. "What are you doing?"

Low booing hummed in the air.

"Come on. Do it. Now," she hissed. Her forehead lined in frustration. "Hit. Me!" She stepped into my face, shoving me.

"No." Normally I would have no problem, but her sorrow ripped the bloodlust from my chest. It felt wrong.

"Come on." She pushed me again, her brown eyes

narrowing. Then she did something I wasn't expecting. She grabbed the back of my head and pulled my face into hers, our heads touching. "*Pleeease!*"

The desperation in her voice tapped at my heart. "Okay."

"Thank you," she whispered and pushed off me. The crowd's boos turned to cheers as the fight looked to be resuming.

While she bobbed around me, I shut my eyes and swallowed before I lifted my lids. I didn't have it in me to truly hurt her. I never "professionally" fought someone this far below my level and who didn't want to be in the ring. This entire fight sat wrong with me.

My punch was light and only knocked her to the side. I dug my elbow into her gut, crumpling her to the ground, and leaped down, looking like I would continue to hit her.

"I'm sorry," I leaned over and whispered into her ear.

She snorted, blood pouring from her nose. "One more. Duc won't be happy until you knock me out cold."

I bit down on my lip and nodded.

I was about to strike one last time when I felt a sensation come over me. The awareness of one pair of eyes, among masses, on me, like the last fight when I looked up to see Ryker standing there, still alive. My head jerked up, my gut twisting with hope. Did Ryker find me?

My gaze locked on a pair of familiar *green* eyes.

Oh God.

I blinked, wiping the blood and sweat from my face.

Please, no. But there was no denying it. Garrett stood across from me at the edge of the ring, his gaze fastened on me, a rolled flyer in his hand.

Of course. How stupid of me to think it was only Duc and Maria I should be afraid of here. Flyers adorned with my picture filled the city. Even with wings and a small mask, it was not hard to make out my face.

The redheaded Irishman worked for Vadik as his lead henchmen. No one had met Vadik in person; he used Garrett and his men as his face and muscle. It had been more than a month since I last saw Garrett searching for me at a Red Cross. I'd gotten away only by luck and glamour.

Both of those had run out...

Finding me was surely Garrett's big break. Now he could locate the Wanderer. Ryker might not be physically in Washington, but if Garrett captured me, he would find a way to let Ryker know he had me. If Garrett caught me, it was all over.

A slow smirk twisted Garrett's lips; his eyes ignited with delight. There was nothing that would get in his way of acquiring me. Not even Duc could stop Garrett. No human could.

He nodded and his men stepped to the boundary of the ring. My skin prickled as fae surrounded me.

"Finish her!" some of the crowd barked at me. The other half were chanting, "Angel."

Their words fell off me as I blocked out anything but the fae coming for me. It was now or never. They would only wait until the fight was over to grab me, so I had to move immediately. I took one last breath, then bounded up off the girl and darted into the throng of onlookers. The disbelief at my irrational behavior only lasted a beat before the place broke out in chaos. The slight advantage was not something I could waste. I shoved and elbowed my way through the first layer of bystanders. Most stood in shock, but I felt Garrett's men moving, propelling quickly toward me.

"Hey, the fight is back there."

"What the hell are you doing?"

"Finish the fight. I've got a lot riding on this!"

Voices bombarded me as I pushed through the crowd and veered and wiggled through the mob blocking my getaway. Shouts reverberated out from the speakers, but it was all white noise to me, my heartbeat thumping in my ears.

Fingers grazed my elbow, a body moved in close behind me. "I'm looking forward to killing you, like I did your human partner," the voice mocked in my ear. My neck twisted to see a man with long blond hair and blue eyes behind me.

Maxen. The fae who killed Daniel.

He reached out for me, his hand brushing across my shoulder blades. I twisted and curved in a different direction, ducking between two large men and knocking over their beers. Cold liquor dumped down my shirt, the sharp tang rising up my nose. They turned, yelling at me, blocking Maxen's direct path to me.

A small victory, but I was grateful for any extra moment I could break away from them. I looked up to see the exit sign only yards away.

They would pursue me to the ends of the Earth, but if I got through the doors, at least I had the chance to lose them in the streets, dissolving in the evening darkness and between the fortresses of buildings. I barreled for the doorway. The density of people thinned a little, and I impelled my legs toward my escape. Whatever Maria injected in my system pumped into my feet, driving them harder into the ground. The taste of hope dusted my tongue. *Only a few more feet, Zoey. You can do this.*

Suddenly several of Garrett's men stepped in front of the door, blocking my way. Panic boiled in my head as I peered around seeing another group coming in behind me. *Shit!* They were surrounding me. *Noooo!* A bellowed scream shook inside my head. I would not let Garrett beat Ryker this way. I would not be his downfall. I would do *anything* to protect him.

Something deep in me broke. Pain and fire combusted inside, taking me to my knees with a cry. A scorching inferno sliced throughout my body, like a hundred branding tools. My back hit the concrete and my head bounced on the ground, but I didn't feel anything but the scalding lava. It expanded, consuming every inch, until I thought I would melt.

"Grab her," a voice yelled, and figures moved for me.

I'm sorry, Ryker.

The room spun and my lids fastened together as everything whirled around me. A scream budded at my lips, but nothing came out. All my senses disappeared, and I felt like I was no longer in my body.

Then a tsunami of emotions and sensations flooded back in, and I screamed. My eyes shut from the onslaught of pain. The roar of the crowd exploded then went silent.

TWENTY-TWO

The heat quickly evaporated, and I felt myself gasp for air. I could tell I was lying on a floor. Uneven wood planks dug into my shoulder blades. My lashes fluttered open and my vision adjusted, focusing clearly on a chipped white ceiling.

"Holy fuck," a deep voice spoke from somewhere close to me.

"What?" a woman's voice asked.

"Look," the man said.

There was a squeak of metal. "*La naiba!*" The woman swore, her voice coming from somewhere above me. "You better go get him."

I rolled my head toward the speaker. Sitting on the edge of the bed, leaning over, a stunningly beautiful woman with plum-colored hair stared at me. A sensation of familiarity tickled in my mind.

I knew her.

The animosity I felt for her was instant, but it was diluted with so much jealousy. I knew she was not a physical threat to me.

"Yeah." A man's face peered over me. His dark hair, eyes, and beard hit a memory. I also recognized him.

Pirate, was my first thought at seeing him.

"Damn, she looks like she's been beaten up. A lot."

"Go." The violet-haired beauty pointed to the door. "If he finds out we didn't go get him the minute she returned, he will kick both our asses."

The man frowned. "She's human. I don't see what has his panties in such a twist. But if her being back makes him a tad more pleasant, I'll take it."

"It's not *her*. It's because of the powers." Hurt colored the woman's face and words.

The pirate man snorted. "Okay, Mar. You keep holding on to your delusions." He turned and left the room.

The woman's eyebrows furrowed as she glanced at the ceiling and let out a long exhale. Then she unfolded herself off the bed and came to my side. "Can you sit?"

I stared at her.

"Zoey?" Her voice was sharp and rung crisp in my ears. "Hey," she shouted at me again. Loose strands of indigo tresses trickled my arm. *Her hair is so beautiful.* Unlike mine, her hue was naturally that color. *There is a reason my hair is a similar color as hers, I know it.*

"Zoey!" A hard slap zinged across my cheek. Like being dunked in ice water, my mind was shocked out of its anesthetized state, letting images and memories flood back in.

Holy shit. I was back in Peru, in the room I shared with Sprig and Ryker.

Ryker! My heart screamed, and I lurched to my feet.

Amara stepped away, startled by my sudden movement. "Are you all right?"

"I'm back." Relief teetered on the cusp, hoping it was not a dream. I grabbed Amara's arm. "You're real."

She eyed me skeptically. "Yeah."

I dropped her arm, curling over myself as happiness gripped my air passages. "I'm back," I cried with relief and joy. The fire in my veins had relinquished its hold, but I could feel it was replaced with a heavier presence—Ryker's powers. Whatever barrier I had been keeping around them, protecting them from me, had shattered into a million pieces.

The last time Maria inserted a needle in my arm, I was able to jump the next day. Once again whatever she gave me seemed to prompt Ryker's abilities to acclimate to me. This time it was for good.

"What happened to—" Amara's sentence trailed off as the sound of footsteps bound up the stairs.

"Zoey!"

Ryker.

The door swung open, and the enormous Viking pushed into the room and stopped. He stood in the entry; his gaze locked on me. Croygen stood behind him, his expression bemused.

Breath evaporated from my throat. I wanted to run to him, but the feel of Amara's eyes boring into me kept my feet in place.

"*Bhean,*" Sprig squealed from Ryker's shoulder and scrambled down, running for me. I bent down and picked him up. His tiny arms wrapped around my neck. "Sprite-spit, I've missed you. Don't ever leave us again."

"I missed you too." I hugged Sprig, but my eyes

were latched on Ryker's.

His white eyes roamed over me, and his feet moved till they were flush with mine. His hand clutched my cheek. "You're hurt."

"I'll heal." I swallowed over the lump in my throat. Ryker dropped his arm back to his side. Seeing Ryker, feeling the warmth of his body near mine, made me want to throw my arms around him, feel his wrap around me, and never let go. But neither of us moved.

"Where have you been?" he whispered. His fingers twitched, coming back for my face, but he stopped himself, guiding them through his hair.

"Seattle." I already wanted to forget every memory of the place. But I made a promise to a girl, a girl who would think I simply up and ran, leaving her my promise behind. "It's a long story, and I will tell you everything. But the most important thing right now is I saw Garrett. He knows. He almost caught me... and he saw me jump."

Ryker shifted back, a wall falling between us. "Garrett saw you jump? If you could use the magic, why didn't you come back here sooner? How could you leave me... us like that?" Ryker motioned between him and Sprig. "*We* thought you were stranded somewhere. Hurt. Not able to get back."

"I was."

Ryker ignored me, continuing with his rant. "The only reason I didn't think you were dead was because I still didn't have my powers back. I was sure if you didn't come back, it was because you couldn't."

"I couldn't."

"I was helpless. I couldn't sense you anymore. I had no idea where you went, and I couldn't leave in case you came back here."

I smacked his chest, his mouth clicked shut, almost like I hit his reset button. "Shut up, and I will explain."

He breathed in, waiting.

"When I jumped from here, for some reason I went to Marcello's warehouse."

"He's still alive?"

"Uh... yes, but Maria is now running it. Actually, a man named Duc is." I waved my hand. "Not important right now. Maria caught me. Their underground fighting ring has expanded. I was unable to jump or glamour and was forced back in..." Ryker knew of my fame as the Avenging Angel. He seemed to understand what it meant for me to be caught by them again. "Garrett was at the fight."

Ryker lifted his finger and gently touched my broken lip, his frame protectively curved over me. Amara rustled next to me, and Ryker stepped back. I looked between them, feeling my jealousy growing. *What happened while I was gone? Did she convince him they should be together again? Did he sleep with her?* I shook my head, deposing the thoughts. This was not the time.

"Seeing him triggered me to jump again." I gulped, staring at my feet. "And there is something else you should know."

The room was silent. Sprig clung to my neck, causing sweat to build along my throat. Amara and Croygen watched me, waiting for my words. Ryker's entire physique was rigid, his jaw rolling with aggression.

I anchored myself, taking a deep breath. "I have them now."

"You have what?" Amara folded her arms.

My regard caught Ryker's, his gaze really sinking into me. I was about to change everything between us. A couple of words, and I would have my murderer standing across from me, no longer my friend.

His Adam's apple bobbed, and he let his head fall forward. "I know."

"What happened?" Amara's gaze ping-ponged between us.

"She has my powers, Mara."

"She's had your powers for months now."

"No. She has them completely. As they are no longer mine. Not unless I kill her."

"Then do it." Amara threw her arm up toward Ryker. "Because now she is killing you."

"Amara," Ryker growled.

"Kill *Bhean*?" Sprig peeled away from my neck, sitting back on my shoulder. "Are you serious? You would *never* do that, right?"

Ryker licked his lip and stared at the ground.

"He has to," I stated to Sprig, not letting myself think of or feel what it really meant.

"Well, tough imp jerky! You don't have your powers," Sprig screeched. "Deal with it."

"Sprig." I placed my hand on his paw, trying to calm him. "It's the only way to get them back. He will slowly die without them, and I already am."

I already am. The words rang in my own ears. If I were dying, why did I feel the exact opposite? I felt healthy. More alive than before. No headaches. My fingers went to my nose. It wasn't bleeding. Was that because his abilities had fully acclimated to me now? My mind reflected back to every nosebleed I'd had since obtaining his powers in Seattle.

They only came when I jumped. No other time.

What if I weren't dying, and my symptoms had more to do with my body responding to the magic?

No. I couldn't go there. It probably wasn't even true. I shoved the thought away. I didn't want to hope for something I couldn't know for sure. He had to kill me to get his powers back. The only thing making this a tad easier for him was the fact I was dying anyway.

Daniel had said seers were immune. They lost my fellow experiment brothers and sisters because we could not be saved. They had already tested Sera and me, and we hadn't responded to fae blood.

A gasp throttled my throat. *Oh no.*

"What?" Ryker moved back to me. "Are you all right?"

I nodded. "Yeah. I need to use the restroom." What I really needed was to run.

Ryker didn't believe me, but he let me go without a word. I placed Sprig on the bed and dashed for the bathroom, slamming the door.

I went to the mirror. My refection showed a girl who had been beaten a few days ago when it actually had been fifteen minutes prior. My hair was filthy, still sprinkled with glitter Maria put in it. The tips of my fingers explored my healing skin while Daniel's words came back to me.

"Going through my father's research, I learned people with the sight, seers, are those rare people who are immune to fae blood. It doesn't kill you, but you also would not benefit from it either."

I couldn't believe I didn't think of it before. *I'm so stupid!* It was right in front of my face the whole time. I fell against the door and slid to the floor.

Fae *blood.*

One word changed everything. Transferring them through blood was not how I got Ryker's powers. If it was, I probably would have been resilient to it like a normal seer, but I got his powers another way—from a current of electricity charged through Ryker's body into mine. Transferring them magically to me. Fae magic relocated them into my body, which was more powerful than anything on this Earth, including my DNA.

Deep down, I had known it. I could feel the transformation, the way my body healed like a fae, but I pushed it off with the excuse the change was only superficial. I no longer got tired like I did before I met Ryker. The migraines had lessened and even the nosebleeds were different. I did not want to believe. Everything would be easier if I were dying. *Dammit.* Even good news flipped on its head and turned on me.

If Ryker didn't kill me, he would eventually die. The only thing making it easier for either of us was if I were heading there anyway. I placed my head in my hands.

"Zoey?" A tap came on the door. "Are you okay?"

Leaning my head back on the door, I sighed. "Yeah. I. Am."

The moment I stepped out of the bathroom, the shock of my return had morphed into a strained awkwardness, an unease at us having so much to say, but no one talking. There was a line between me and the three of them now. A familiarity of being in the same room together, a subtle unsaid awareness of each other's habits I no longer was part of.

Amara's body language screamed the loudest at my intrusion. A transparent confidence in the way she moved around the room like I had come into her territory, this was her room, and I was invading. She had taken over two of my drawers and some of the closet with her new purchases, and lined the miniature refrigerator with small cartons of milk.

"Can I get you anything?" Amara smiled over sweetly, opening the fridge, offering me a beverage like I was a guest.

"No. I'm good." I couldn't fight the strain in my voice.

Her saccharine smile twisted in a smirk. "Let me know if I can."

We watched each other before she turned away, grabbed a magazine, and flopped back on the bed. "Maybe now we can get back to retrieving the stone. Actually do something."

Ryker rubbed at his head and sighed, but did not respond. I had the feeling this wasn't the first time this topic had come up.

"Did you come up with a plan while I was gone?" I asked, glancing around the room at everyone. "How will we deal with Vadik and get Regnus?"

Croygen huffed. "There hasn't been much accomplished since you left. Let me rephrase that... nothing has been done." His gaze darted over at Ryker.

"Really?" I responded.

Ryker folded his arms. "You're surprised?"

"Yeah. A little." I shrugged. Amara threw up her arms, like *See, even she thinks you should have been doing something.*

"I'm sorry I was concerned about what happened to you... finding you. Next time I won't bother." Anger laced his words.

"That's not what I meant."

"What did you mean?" he replied. "Without you it's a little hard to transfer back my powers anyway. And now what is the point? Regnus can't do anything for us. Not anymore!" He roared, causing both Croygen and Amara to slink back and stay silent.

Not me.

"You're going to leave him? Let him be tortured or killed? He can't help you so fuck him?" I marched over to Ryker. The muscles in his arms twitched as he clenched them across his body harder. "And how do you know he can't? You're giving up? Throwing yourself a pity party because you no longer have your powers?" I punched a finger into his chest, only causing it to puff out more. "Strap on a pair!"

"Excuse me?"

"Strap. On. A. Pair," I repeated, my teeth gritting together.

Fire rolled behind his eyes, his fury pushing the air from the room. We stood only inches apart, our chests heaving.

He took in a long draw through his nose, tipped back on his heels, whipped around, and stormed out of the room. The slam of the door shook the foundation.

Everyone stayed silent for a long time before Sprig's voice came from the table. "Sorry, only want to know when it's okay to talk again." My chin jerked to him. "Too soon? Okay..." He mimicked zipping his lips closed, then quickly unzipped them, shoving a mango chip in his mouth. "Soooo good. Want one?"

I placed my head in my hands, letting a strangled laugh erupt.

Ryker returned an hour later and the friction in the cramped room only continued to rise to astronomical levels. My return didn't only irritate Amara. Ryker's concern and relief at my homecoming turned quickly to animosity after our fight. Strangely, Croygen was the one who was pleasant to me, even nice, which did make me suspicious. But I wasn't about to question the only kindness coming my way. Whatever his reason was—I would take it.

To avoid the hostility from the other two, I took an extra-long hot shower, rinsing my body of filth and blood. I wanted my memories to wash away, too, but there was a girl I would not let myself forget. "I promise I will get back there for you." I failed Lexie; I would not fail Annabeth. She might hate me for a while thinking I abandoned her, but I would go back and get her, and anyone else who wanted freedom from the Scorpions.

Everyone was getting ready for bed when I came out, dropping my dirty clothes beside the overflowing laundry basket.

"These clothes stink." Ryker nudged the mound of fabric with his foot. I couldn't deny there was a sharp odor coming off them. "I can smell human blood on it."

"And probably sweat and alcohol as well." I plopped on the bed.

"Get rid of them," he ordered.

"Excuse me?" I folded a leg underneath me.

"And here I was hoping he'd get more pleasant with her back." Croygen settled on his pad on the floor.

Amara gave Croygen a dirty look and fell back on her pillow. "I already miss having the bed to myself."

And why did I want to come back here?

Sprig coiled on my pillow. He was the only one truly happy about my reappearance. He wouldn't let me out of his sight for too long. "It was torture without you, *Bhean*, and not once did we go to Izel's. I mean, come on. How cruel is that?"

I scratched behind his ear. "We'll go tomorrow for breakfast, and you can have all the honey pancakes you can eat."

His eyes went wide with adoration. "I've. Missed. You."

"Same, buddy."

Ryker huffed, redirecting my attention onto him.

"What?"

"I can't sleep with the stench of human blood and sweat in my face."

"And alcohol."

He arched one eyebrow.

"Move them then." I motioned to the clothes. What

was his problem?

Ryker's eyes narrowed on me, then he bent over, letting me get a view of my old comrade. I couldn't help sighing. *I've missed you, perky friend.*

He gathered the clothes in a ball, walked to the window, and chucked them out.

My eyebrows went up my forehead. *O-kay.*

He strode back, wiping his hands together. "They are moved." I watched him as he sat on his bed on the ground. He tugged off his boots, ripped his shirt over his head, and lay back, never once meeting my gaze.

Amara rolled onto her side, switching the table light off, plunging the room in shadows. The soft light of a streetlamp down the road shimmered through the sheer curtains.

I scanned the room. This was not how I thought my return would be. Okay, I did from Amara. Even Croygen, but Ryker? What the hell was his problem?

I flopped back on the bed, Sprig twisting around my head.

I guess I would hate someone who stole my powers and forced me to be a murderer. Still, after what I'd been through, I needed him, like the nights he had comforted me after bad dreams. Even after our fight, his arms were the only thing I craved. At our worst I still didn't want to be without him.

After fitfully trying to sleep, I picked up my head and glanced at Amara. Her chest rose and fell in slow rhythmic intervals. A slight snore came from the floor beside her. With them sound asleep, I felt braver to act.

I sat up slowly, trying not to disturb Sprig or Amara. The bed groaned softly as I rose to my feet. Ryker lay on his back, his arm slung over his face, shielding his eyes. At the sound of the squeaking bed, his head popped up. He watched me crawl down to him; he took a deep breath.

He didn't move as I curled into his side and settled my head in the crook of his shoulder. There was another beat of his heart and heat flooded my cheeks at the thought of him rejecting me. Then I felt him shift, his arm curling around me, pulling me into him. Happiness engulfed my chest when his arms closed around me.

Now I was home.

He could invoke such passionate extremes from me. One moment he calmed me, as though I finally found someone with whom I could let all my walls down, and the next moment I wanted to tear off his clothes. Both sounded nice, but tonight I needed his comfort. Simply to be wrapped in his arms was enough.

"You're okay," I whispered, one finger touching his chin. The bristles of his beard scratched my hand. His eyes narrowed at my statement. "The balam... you got away."

A cocky grin tugged the side of his mouth. "Did you even doubt?"

"No." My gaze fastened to his. Somewhere in my gut I had known he had made it out. He had to. He was the invincible Wanderer. A fae legend.

His hand slid to my face and trickled over my healing cuts. He leaned forward, his lips warm and tender on my forehead. Then he wrapped me tighter. Without a word I knew what his actions were telling me. *Sleep. You are safe now.*

My lids drifted closed, tucking my head deeper into him. Home. Safety. Happiness.

Before, I imagined those things would be objects or material items. But now all those things came in a form of a Viking.

TWENTY-THREE

A light breeze trickled across my face, stirring me out of my deep slumber. After a few nightmares of trying to save Annabeth from faceless, leering, violent men, I finally settled into Ryker's arms, letting sleep consume me. My lids struggled to open, my body and mind wanted to remain asleep.

The memory of falling asleep next to Ryker on the floor forced me out of the sweet oblivion. The night before I didn't care, but in the stark morning light, I was not prepared to have Amara awake and see us. Her threat flooded back into my conscience.

"If I see you go off with him again. Are alone with him in any way... Nothing will stop me from butchering you into tiny chunks and feeding you to your monkey. Stay away from him, human. You do not belong in our world, and I will take you out of it if you persist."

My lashes clung to each other as I tried to pry my lids open. One by one they separated, allowing my eyes to focus. A dim gray glow lighted the windows, keeping the room shadowed in a colorless portrait, like I had stepped into a black-and-white film.

I was also back on the bed. Alone. Even Sprig was gone. I lifted my head and glanced around the room.

The breeze billowed the curtains and fanned the room. The quiet disturbed me. I sat up with a huff. Loneliness crept over me, which made me angry. As strong as I pretended to be, I still got rattled. Being chained and beaten shook me, but strangely what unnerved me more was almost being caught by Garrett. I was the portal to capture Ryker. Also, I was carrying this knowledge about myself with a deep belief I could not tell Ryker. It was another weight on my chest.

Dragging myself out of bed, my toes skated on the wood floor, and I staggered to the bathroom. The girl looking back at me was almost healed. Only pink lines indicated where I had been cut or hit. I touched my skin, tugging at the old sores. How long I was asleep? I didn't hear any of them get up or feel Ryker put me back in the bed. Did I go in a coma-like state to heal like I had seen him do?

Curious as to where they went, I quickly pulled on clothes and boots. The bag strap around my shoulder felt like an old friend. It was comforting to me, my safety trigger.

Even with fae powers, I was still exhausted, muscles stiff and sore. My feet struggled to pick up and walk forward. Everything felt heavier than normal as I dragged my feet down the stairs.

A gust of cool wind hit me as I stepped outside. A storm was coming. Swollen black clouds churned angrily above my head. The smell of rain loomed in the air. The developing tempest was a perfect reflection of what I felt on the inside. I tried to push off the sensation of it being some strange omen.

"*Bhean*," a tiny voice called for me. I whirled around to see Ryker and Amara walking toward me. Sprig leaped off Ryker's shoulder. He hit the ground and scrambled up my body, and hunkered on my shoulder. "You are *finally* awake. They told me we couldn't go to Izel's till you got up. I have been waiting *forever*."

"We'll go right now." I smiled, rubbing his head. I glanced at both Ryker and Amara, trying to stuff down the growl wanting to erupt from seeing them together. Amara walked close to Ryker, her arm brushing his. They looked every bit a couple. "Where is Croygen?"

"Good question," Ryker snarled. "He was already gone when we awoke this morning. Again."

Again? I didn't get a chance to ask before a voice pierced the air behind me.

"Did you miss me? How sweet." Croygen slipped next to me. It was disturbing how he could sneak up on you out of nowhere.

"Yeah. Sweet." Ryker's muscles knotted around his neck and shoulders. "Where the fuck were you?"

"Mom? Is that you?" Croygen tilted his head to the side in question. "I don't need to tell you shit, Ryker."

One step and Ryker was nose to nose with Croygen. "I don't trust you. You would sell out your own mother for a price."

"Only for the *right* price," Croygen sneered.

"You've been disappearing a lot lately," Amara said with a slight accusatory tone.

I was only gone a week, but I felt like I missed a lot. Ryker never trusted Croygen, but whatever issue was going on between them had intensified.

"Shocked you noticed." Croygen motioned at Ryker. "Now you have your boy back, Amara, I'm surprised you were even aware I was standing next to you."

Amara glared. "Croygen."

Ryker cut off Amara. "I've known you too long, Croygen. Money is your true love. You are up to something."

"It's my business and has nothing to do with you. I know you think the whole world revolves around you, but it doesn't." Croygen shoved Ryker away from him. Ryker reared back, barreling toward the pirate with his whole body.

"Guys, stop." Amara pushed them apart. "I've had enough of this! You have been at each other all week."

The chests of both men heaved in and out; neither wanted to be the one to back down first.

"I know what will make this better," Sprig spoke, making me peer around to see if anyone outside our group was within earshot. "Pancakes!"

Ryker's eyes drifted to Sprig, then to me. His jaw clenched as he swiveled around and stomped away.

Amara ran after him. Catching up, she grabbed his arm, pulled him down to her, and whispered something in his ear. Whatever she said made him chuckle and nod. My legs moved forward, following. But the rest of me wished to go back upstairs and not have to witness this. She leaned in more, saying something else, her face bright with joy. Ryker's head went back in a laugh. Stabbing myself with a thousand daggers would have felt better.

I felt a presence move next to me, but my eyes would not leave the gorgeous couple.

"It is fun, isn't it?" Croygen strolled along next to me, observing them with the same regard as me.

"What is?"

"Watching them together." He pressed his mouth closed. There was a flicker of pain before he blinked and it was gone again. But it was too late. I had seen it.

My gaze followed Croygen's and came back to him. "*You're* in love with her."

A humorous smile wavered over his lips and he peered over at me. "And *you're* in love with him."

"I am not," I replied indignantly.

Croygen smiled smugly and winked. "Sure." A silence fell between us, and we turned back to observing them together, reminiscing and laughing. "We make a pathetic pair, human." Pained amusement danced in his eyes.

"Yes, we do, pirate."

Was Amara the reason he and Ryker didn't get along? What was their story? Something in Croygen's manner told me not to ask. Not yet.

Sprig's bouncing on my shoulder turned into full-blown jumping the closer we got to Izel's.

"In." I pointed to my bag. Sprig didn't hesitate before climbing in. "Rememb—"

"I know, I know. No talking," he chattered excitedly.

"Yeah, just like that, monkey." Croygen chuckled.

When we entered, Melosa immediately bounded for me, wrapping me in a warm hug. "Where have you been? You and your dear man have been missed," she rattled off in Spanish.

Amara's face tightened at the reference to Ryker being my man.

"Sorry, Melosa." I pulled back. "I got tied up."

Croygen snorted next to me, and I cast him a look.

Melosa halted when she took in Croygen, pursing her lips together, she mumbled something under her breath, her hand going to her cross necklace. I thought she was going to turn us out, but then she swiveled around, motioning us to a table.

"She really doesn't like you," I leaned in and muttered.

"Not many do." A naughty grin lifted his mouth. "It's a tradesman's life."

"Yo ho, yo ho, a pirate's life for me," I sang, causing him to stare at me.

"Come sit." Melosa motioned us over to a table. Two of Melosa's daughters came out of the back with trays. The oldest, Lucia, was a doppelganger of her mother—sweet, energetic, and loved everyone. The youngest girl, Raquel, was the exact opposite. She didn't bother to hide her dislike of me.

Lucia gave me a wave and continued on to her table. Raquel stopped, a snarl arching her upper lip till her eyes landed on the man next to me. Unlike her mother, her expression changed to pleasure at seeing Croygen. He was a striking man—tall, dark, and handsome. He had an abundance of charisma, which fae usually used to attract humans. Raquel's eyes widened in appreciation, looking him up and down, but narrowed when they ventured over to Amara.

Oh, good. At least I wasn't alone in Raquel's "fan" club.

Ryker sat facing the entrance. I sat across from him, my back toward the café, allowing me to feed Sprig. Amara sat next to Ryker, and Croygen slid in the chair next to me.

"Pancakes. Pancakes. Pancakes." A murmured chant came from my bag. I bonked Sprig's head to quiet him.

"If that *thing* gets us in trouble." Amara frowned into my bag.

"Hey, Medusa?" Sprig whispered low enough so only we could hear, curling his finger so she would lean in. Then he stuck his middle finger out of the bag. I couldn't stop my laugh from spurting out.

Amara glared at Sprig and me, turning to Ryker. Ryker's eyes met mine, glinting with humor. My smile widened, and under the table I held out my hand to give Sprig a high five.

Melosa came to our table. "Welcome, *friends* of Ryker and Zoey," she said in Spanish. The word *friends* coming out strained. Melosa's gaze stuttered when Amara put her hand on Ryker's shoulder, rubbing it affectionately. Her lids tapered on Amara, and her lips thinned the same way they did with Croygen. "What can I get you?"

"The usual for me, Melosa." I handed the menu to her. She smiled, winking at the little monster in my bag. Sprig was practically shaking with anticipation.

"Me too." Ryker nodded.

Amara squeezed his arm and turned to Melosa. "Make sure everything is separated. He hates his food touching."

Melosa stiffened. "I am aware of his preference." The woman looked as if someone not only insulted her cooking, but her family.

Amara smiled thinly at the woman. "I'll get the veggie omelet."

"Same. Except fill mine with only meat. Human's if you have it." Croygen winked at the woman. Melosa's hand immediately went for her cross, her body stiffening as she swung away from our table.

"Stop that!" I slapped Croygen in the arm, making him snicker. "She's a sweet woman who clearly is smarter than us. She warned us to stay away from you."

He reclined, grabbing his water glass. "That's because she remembers me from when she was a girl." He took a sip of water. "She's pissed because she's aged... I haven't."

"What?"

"I've been around this area off and on for a long time." He shrugged. "She's more aware than most humans. She sees—"

"She sees you're an asshole." Ryker stretched out his legs, pushing his chair back away from Amara, or at least that's how I wanted to perceive it. "I was thinking after breakfast we could do some training." Ryker, unmistakably changing subjects, directed his glance at me. Not one bit of emotion soaked through his expression. I could feel him putting up a fence between us. Letting me know, without having to say it, the closeness of last night would not happen again. The formality in his voice assured me we were back to being partners. Nothing more.

I stared down at Sprig, rubbing his soft fur. It comforted me. "Sure. Why?"

Ryker cleared his throat.

"Now the powers are yours, you need to learn how to use them. How to manipulate them to your advantage in a fight."

I nodded.

"If we are going to get Regnus, I want you able to handle yourself better. This won't be like collecting fae." He folded his hands over his stomach. "You need to battle with a sword. The way fae fight."

"Can we help?" Amara flipped her hair over her shoulder.

"Yeah. It would be good for all of us." Ryker adjusted in his seat. "Especially for me since I no longer have an advantage." His voice constricted on the last word.

My fault or not, the guilt of causing this pain made me shift in my seat. Rolling my shoulders, I played with my bag, not able to look at Ryker. This was so painful. With no chance to regain his powers except to kill me, I wondered if the reality was setting in.

When Melosa came back to our table with food and drinks, I kept my hand on Sprig, waiting for her to walk away. Then I ripped off a piece of crepe and shoved it into his mouth before he could utter a noise.

He mumbled something which sounded a lot like, "Crapping fae biscuits... soooo good."

The table went silent as we ate. The honey pancakes were bliss on my tongue after the chalky, tasteless food I had choked down in Seattle. I didn't realize I was famished. It was a battle to get enough food in my mouth before Sprig was tugging at the plate.

"*Bhean. Bhean,*" Sprig whispered, grabbing for my fork as I tried to finish my bite.

"Hand him to me." Ryker stretched his arms across the table to me. I slipped the bag over my head and passed it to Ryker. He settled the bag on his lap and cut off some of his own pancakes, dipping them in extra honey from my plate, before feeding Sprig. Sprig grinned widely at Ryker's speed at feeding him.

Amara looked back and forth between Ryker and me. "He can't feed himself?"

"No," both Ryker and I said at once, connecting our eyes in a recollection. Sprig could feed himself, but we would need to cover the restaurant in plastic first.

I pointed my fork at Ryker. "I still have honey in my bag from the time you let him eat in it."

Ryker snickered, nodding.

"You lied. It never washed out."

The side of Ryker's mouth hooked up, his attention on Sprig as he supplied him with more honey-covered dough.

Again Amara's head bobbed between the two of us. A nerve twitched across her forehead. She bit on a pepper and swallowed.

As I shoved more food down my throat, Sprig blinked. His eyes no longer fixed on the food or the plate. "He's goin' down." I motioned to my bag. Ryker dipped his napkin in his water and cleaned off Sprig's mouth, hands, and anywhere else the honey had dripped. Sprig's head was already tilting back and his mouth was open when Ryker tucked him inside the bag.

My stomach knotted watching Ryker take care of Sprig. I bit down on my tongue so the crazy emotions I was feeling wouldn't come to the surface.

"We ready?" Croygen threw his napkin on his plate.

Ryker looped the strap over his head and stood. "Yeah. And thanks for paying."

"What?" Croygen responded.

"Consider it rent for staying with us." Ryker slapped Croygen on the shoulder and advanced to the door.

"Tell her to add it to our tab." I patted Croygen's other shoulder and got to my feet, following Ryker.

My next visit to Seattle would entail a visit to the bank

.

TWENTY-FOUR

Rain hit the dirt in large droplets, soaking my boots with mucky water. The wind whipped at my loose, fading violet strands, flicking them into my face.

Ryker walked out to the middle of the open space. "Zoey, over here." Ryker pointed in front of him. He had taken us outside the village to a semi-flat space in a meadow where we could work without being seen by humans. He returned Sprig to the room, along with our babysitters, soap operas and honey papayas, and grabbed a few things before bringing us here.

I walked over, tying my hair in a ponytail.

"I know you can fight with your fists, but it lets your enemy too close. Today, I want you to work with a broadsword. They are the most used weapon in the fae world." Ryker withdrew a sword from his back, where his axe and other weapons were located, and held it out for me. "They are heavy, and you will have to learn to handle its weight."

When my fingers clasped the handle, taking it from Ryker, my arm dipped with the weight of the metal. No wonder fae were toned. Damn. Widening my stance and heaving up the blade, I gripped it.

A howl of laughter bellowed from Croygen. "She looks like she's ready to club someone with it, not stab."

I struck my tongue out at Croygen.

"Relax your shoulders." Ryker nodded toward them. "And loosen your grip."

"Loosen my grip?" The sword was already slipping out of my fingers.

"Your legs are too far apart." Ryker's boots nudged at mine, pushing them together. "Your hips are too far back. Now your legs are too close to each other."

I let the steel drop to the ground, and I stepped back in irritation. "Sorry. I never took sword lessons. Shooting you guys was a lot quicker."

Ryker's lids tapered and he glanced at the sky. "Amara?"

She came over as Ryker took out another sword from his halter, thinner and lighter looking. The handle was ornate and delicate. "My blade!" Amara grabbed for the weapon, a smile growing on her face. "I didn't know you still had it."

"Had it since the night—" Ryker stopped. We all knew the night he was talking about. The night when everything changed.

Amara nodded in understanding. "Thank you for keeping it with you."

Ryker gave her a brisk nod and turned back to me. "Can you show her the stance?"

Amara's face glowed with delight, rejoicing in the fact she was the one Ryker needed at the moment. She pulled her damp hair into a perfect messy bun. Her skinny black jeans were beyond tight, and a loose tank top showed off her bra every time she moved. It was like standing next to a supermodel who was trying to be grungy, but it only rendered her sexier.

She completed a plié while lifting her sword in an elegant but firm grip.

"Like her." Ryker pointed at Amara, causing her face to beam more with the praise.

I rolled my eyes but tried to copy her posture. A chuckle from Croygen told me I was still far from mimicking Amara.

"No." Ryker shook his head and moved around me. "You're still sticking out your ass." His hands came down on my hips, brushing the exposed skin between my tank top and cargo pants. I gasped, as though his fingers went straight through my body into my lungs, squeezing the air from them. Fire zipped up the nerves where he touched me. He twisted my hips, pressing himself tighter into me. "Keep them forward." His voice was hot against my neck. There was a moment I felt his fingers move below my pants line, softly brushing the skin, before he was gone. I swallowed, trying to keep at least the pretense I was listening or aware of anything other than his touch.

"Croygen, can you come on the other side and show her basic moves?"

A strange glint shown in Croygen's eyes as he moved in front of me. "Sure thing." A secretive smile tugged at the corner of his mouth.

For the next four hours, in the pouring rain, I was drilled, yelled at, and tortured. But because of all my other training through Daniel, I was actually learning things faster than I thought.

"So, when are we going to get to the part where I jump my ass home and into the bath?"

"You need to know the basics of fighting before we get to the jumping." Ryker wiped at the sweat and water on his forehead.

"And you definitely are horrendous at the fighting part." Amara frowned, stabbing her sword into the wet earth, letting it stand on its own. "I think the monkey could do better than you."

Every hair up the back of my neck felt like it was brushed the wrong way. "As bad as I am, I bet I can still kick your ass." During the years of others jeering me and trying to provoke me, I had never fallen for it. It was what made me such a great fighter. That was until I met Amara.

Her eyebrows cocked in surprise before a defiant smile curled her mouth. "I'll take that bet."

"Oh no." Ryker stepped between us. "Absolutely not."

"What's wrong, Ryker, are you afraid your *human* is going to get hurt?" Amara stepped closer. "At one time you were the one wanting to fight the humans. Even kill them. But now little Zoey has made you all fluffy inside."

His jaw clicked.

I licked at the rain falling on my lips, feeling the fire in my belly to fight. "Come on, let's see if you can back up your words, because so far I've only seen someone get the drop on you, while you cried like a little damsel, and Ryker did all the fighting."

Amara's brown eyes flared. Taking the bait, she

dislodged her blade from the dirt.

"Oh, I got Xena the Warrior Princess all flustered." I winked at her then turned to Ryker.

"Zoey, stop." Ryker grabbed my arms, pushing me back. "Both of you. Stop." When neither of us looked like we wanted to back off, Ryker yelled at Croygen. "Hey, you could help out here."

Croygen folded his arms, shaking his head. "No fucking way. This is hot."

"Let her go, Ryker. Think your human needs to be put in her place. You're not always going to be around to protect her *substantial* ass," Amara snapped.

Ryker glared at Amara over his shoulder.

"I'm shocked your boney one can hold such a massive stick up there." The fervor building in me rubbed at my muscles. My mouth salivated at the thought of my fist messing her perfect face. Something it wanted to do since the moment I saw her.

Ryker's hands clenched my wrists firmer, walking me away from Amara.

I tried to wiggle free. "Let. Go. Of. Me."

Ryker's white eyes latched on to me, watching me for a moment before he let his hands drop and stepped back.

This fight had been coming for a while. It was bound to happen at some point, and we all knew it. And we could all pretend it was about the human/fae thing, but it wasn't. Not mainly. This was about Ryker.

It stung my pride to think I could fight over such a petty thing—a man. But as a street kid, you had little, you battled for anything belonging to you, or what you wanted to belong to you. In my gut Ryker was mine.

Ownership over a person was wrong. I understood this, but it didn't take away the basic feeling.

Amara swung her sword, barely giving me a moment to respond. We circled each other and crouched low like cheetahs hunting dinner. As I blocked it, she shifted the opposite way, moving in close, and elbowing me in the face. Warm liquid slipped from my nose. The taste of tangy metal coated my mouth.

Bitch.

The anger in me was roaring. I needed to pummel her. The image of me ramming her face into the mud over and over flashed in my head.

Jump, Zoey.

I did... but not at all near her. I stood yards away on the other side of the field.

"Why the hell did you jump way over there?" Croygen hollered over.

Amara swiveled around, sneering at me. "Come on, Zoey. Are you ready to quit so soon?"

I gritted my teeth and jumped back. The sensation didn't inflict dizziness or require too much concentration like it had before. It simply happened when I wanted. When I had intent to move, the powers were completely mine. But *where* I landed seemed to be the problem. Once again I arrived yards away from my target. Out of the corner of my eye I saw Ryker pinch his nose and shake his head.

"Try again."

I jumped next to Ryker. I huffed, my nails digging into my palms. This was embarrassing.

A burst of laughter came from Amara. She bent

over, one hand holding her stomach, the other let the sword drop to her side. I didn't hesitate to take advantage. I barreled forward and slammed into her, taking her to the ground. Her sword went flying, sinking into the murk.

She got on her hands and knees, grappling for her sword. My foot squashed down on her hand before she reached it. She let out a cry and swiped for me. I moved over her, my feet straddling either side of her rib cage. Amara rotated her arm, grabbed my ankle, and tugged me down. I stumbled to the side. She rolled out from underneath me and popped up. Mud coated her from her neck down. Speckles of mud spotted her nose like freckles, but she still looked gorgeous, like a cover shoot in a jungle.

What the hell? She can't even look bad in a fight?

With a grunt, she ran for me. The force she used to collide into me sent both of us back to the sludge in the field. She climbed on me, and her fingers wrapped around my throat, squeezing down. She mumbled in my ear, "Whatever is going on between you and Ryker ends now. This is your last warning."

I grabbed her fingers, trying to bend them back. "Ditto."

Jump. This time when I opened my eyes, I was across the field but so was Amara. Her fingers still wrapped around my throat. A wicked smile coiled the corners of her mouth. "Didn't you know? If you are touching someone, they come with you."

I felt dumb because this should have been obvious. Ryker and Sprig always jumped with me, if I were touching them. But in the moment I believed I could jump away from her.

Stupid.

Embarrassment transformed into fury. The roar in me filled every place that felt pain, loneliness, and fear. The buzzing in my ears turned out to be shouting I heard beside me. The dark part of me, the one who would kill if need be, was taking over. I was sick of playing by someone else's rules.

My fist hit her nose, then her cheekbone. I could feel the crunch of my knuckles, but nothing more. She fell off me and I got to my feet, ready to pounce.

"Zoey. Stop." Ryker's voice moved in close behind me.

I lurched for the woman on the ground.

A large hand darted in, cupping my hand, before I could hit Amara again. Then my body was lifted and dragged away. The arms held me tightly. A steady heart beat against my shoulder blade.

"Calm down," Ryker whispered in my ear. His warm breath curled around my ear and down my throat. The feel of him pressed against me. All of him.

"No," I muttered. I wanted to fight against him, to protect my heart. Stop the way his heartbeat and body could still me.

He kept his arms wrapped around me, my chest heaving with hatred and adrenaline.

Croygen moved over to Amara, helping her up. Her lashes stayed low, glaring at me. Blood leaked from her mouth and her cheek swelled up, already hinting at the bruised bone underneath. Anger stiffened her frame, but she didn't move to come after me.

"Can I say how hot that was?" Croygen pointed to

both of us. "Especially the rolling on the ground in the mud."

Ryker's arms dropped, and he stepped away from me. I turned to see him and stopped in my tracks. Fury expanded over his face, his shoulders rolled up as the wrath moved down his body, reaching his clenched fists. Foreign words I didn't recognize rumbled under his breath.

Uh-oh. Viking was pissed.

He swung away, his hand rubbing his stubble.

"Why are you mad? You wanted us to fight! And I kicked her ass!" I spit mud from my mouth, laced with my own blood.

He whirled around on me. For some reason seeing him like a bull ready to charge plunked me down to earth, fast.

"Because you can't fight fae with your fists," he growled. "And you have no control over my... your powers. You will lose in a fight. And you will die."

"Then you kill me first," I screamed back. "Problem solved."

"Don't tempt me."

"Do it! Stop whining and act. End all this bullshit now."

He stared at me; fury raged behind his eyes. He let his head fall back, splatters of rain bounced off his forehead. "Fuck," he shouted into the sky. Without another word he spun around, stomping away from us.

"Ryker, wait!" Amara ran after him. I stood in place, watching them walk off together.

"You got some balls challenging him like that." Croygen sidled up to me, nodding after Ryker. "Most fae warriors I know wouldn't even do that... except you seemed to have a power over him no one else does."

"No, I don't."

He grinned, peering at me. "I'm impressed, human. You've got some moves."

I glanced over at the pirate. His black hair was slicked back, wrapped tightly in a knot, except a single strand hanging limply down his face. "If you say *for a girl*, I will pummel you."

He held up his arms in surrender. "I wasn't. You fight fair for a girl, guy, human, or fae."

I shifted back on my heel, my eyebrows furrowing. "Thank you." It came out more as a question.

"I know. I'm shocked I'm complimenting you. Believe me." He chuckled. As I walked, his footsteps joined mine. "I also can't deny seeing you kick her ass didn't bring a smile to my face."

"What?" I cringed. The adrenaline was waning, and my body was starting to feel the effects of four hours of training and the fight with Amara. "Don't you care about her? Love her?"

"Yeah." He sighed heavily. "That doesn't mean I can't see her for what she is—a self-serving uppity bitch who probably deserves to be put in her place a time or two. But all those things make me love her more. She's had a hard life and doesn't put up with crap. She'll go after what she wants and doesn't sugarcoat things. I like that. She is who she is."

"Yeah. Sure." I stared at Amara's lithe frame walking close to Ryker's.

"If it wasn't for the Wanderer, you two might see

you have more in common than you think."

"So... I'm a self-serving uppity bitch?"

"No. She's not only those things." Croygen kept his strides even with mine. "She's brave, tough, stubborn, and fierce."

"Funny, I didn't hear sweet or kind in there."

"Think we both know Amara is neither sweet nor kind," he replied, glancing over at me. "And you aren't either. Not unless you let someone in, allow them past the barrier. She's the same."

It was strange hearing about Amara from a different point of view. It wasn't pleasant to think we might have more things in common besides Ryker.

The rain let up as we continued to the room, being replaced by the wind whistling down the ravines of the mountain range into the village. Croygen stayed with me, waiting when I straggled far behind everyone else. He seemed a lot more relaxed around me, like we shared something no one else could understand and had bonded by the misery of wanting those we couldn't have.

"This is strange," Croygen mumbled.

"What?" I cringed, rubbing at my sore ribs. Amara was petite, but damn she had a bite.

"The turn of events."

"Huh?"

Croygen shook his head. "Nothing."

I was about to ask him for further explanation, but my attention was grabbed by two little girls playing kickball with some neighborhood boys in the streets.

One couldn't have been older than five, the other appeared around eight. What caught my attention wasn't that they were the only girls among the boys, but what the girls were wearing. They had on my clothes; the items Ryker had thrown out the window the night before. The white T-shirt, once covered in blood, now with pink spots stained across the front, adorned the five-year-old. The shirt fit her like a nightgown. The other girl wore the torn yoga pants. She rolled them so her bare feet could locate the ground, which kept tripping her when she ran, but she clung to the pants as if they were a prized possession. She called out to one of her teammates and giggled.

Life was tough for these people, but they lived life here simply and happily. It struck me as being both beautiful and sad. It was beautiful because they were happy with what they had, but sad because they never let themselves dream about achieving more. Most would be born here and die here; only a few going off to the big city to struggle to make a living. Most Americans, even the poor, were better off than a lot of countries. But here in their childhood innocence, it seemed most of them were happy. With no shoes, raggedy clothes, and a deflated ball in the mud, they were in heaven.

"Come on." Croygen kicked at the back of my heels, herding me into our building. Tired, wet, and muddy, I crawled up the stairs. If I had the energy to jump, I would have done it. Using magic exhausted my human body. I didn't tire out like other humans, but I still wasn't used to the powers.

When we got back to the room, Sprig was jumping on the TV. "Can we go to dinner now? Those papaya chips only lasted me ten minutes. I'm starving. Pam wants to go to Indio Feliz's for dinner. It's our anniversary... and I wanted to take her—"

"Sprig!" All four of us shouted at once. "Shut up."

He sat back on his hind legs. "Wow. A roomful of grumpy assholes. They've all turned Viking, Pam! Retreat! Retreat!" He grabbed his goat, tucking her in his arms as he jumped over to the bed, leaping between gaps in the pillows and tugging the top one over his head.

I couldn't fight the smile he put on my face. At my lowest times, Sprig was able to cheer me up. I went over to the bed and snatched the pillow off him.

Sprig took in my disheveled appearance and squeaked. "They have become rabid, Pam. Hide!" He grabbed the pillow out of my hands and tugged it back over their heads. A snort of laughter hiccupped from my chest.

"Okay, stay there till we get immunized and clean, then we'll go to dinner. Okay?"

He didn't respond.

"All right?"

"Yes. Only because I would *die* from starvation anyway," he responded.

"Yes. Positivity. Good," I quipped.

Amara was in the shower before I could even move to the dresser. Croygen quickly claimed the one down the hall, leaving Ryker and me alone.

He was back to ignoring me, staring at the trees waving outside the window. I was fine with it. I couldn't deal with his effect on me when he got too near. The best plan would be to stay away from each other completely, except the room was the size of a closet. It was hard to stay out of each other's way. And with neither of us talking, the painful silence in the room boiled under the ceiling, swelling the ever-growing awkwardness between us.

We both kept busy with our tasks: him staring out the window and me searching for a top to wear after my shower. Since I only had four, including the one I was wearing, this undertaking didn't last as long as I wanted.

I kept my back to him, his presence throbbed behind me, tickling every nerve. Coating me like a blanket till it smothered me, forcing me to move. I swallowed, my throat patchy and dry, and I moved around the bed, heading for the small fridge. At the same time he stood up from the chair.

Wham.

Our bodies collided, knocking me back. He grabbed my waist, pulling me into him as he steadied me. My hands clutched his forearms. The instant his body was against mine, all fight and stubbornness dissolved along with my willpower.

Let go and step away, I told myself, but my muscles did not listen. We stood there. His fingers rolled tightly around the top of my pants, digging into my sides. He leaned forward, and I felt his breath filter over my lips. Under my lashes I could see his lids were hooded, his lips parted.

My lungs faltered, yearning and desire overriding all thoughts. My eyes shut as his mouth grazed my ear.

Then he jerked back, my eyes burst open as he moved quickly around me. His expression stony and distant. He ripped open the dresser, grabbing clean clothes.

I couldn't help but watch him, every muscle tensed and strained his shirt.

A frustrated noise gurgled from his mouth, and he leaned over the dresser, his eyes squeezed shut. He slammed the dresser into the wall, and then pivoted on his heels and marched for the door, almost running into Croygen.

"What's your problem?" Croygen watched Ryker as he slammed past him and proceeded down the hall. Ten seconds later a door slammed so loud it shook the building. Croygen closed the room door behind him. "What did you do to him?"

"Nothing."

"That kind of nothing leads to jacking off in the shower by yourself." Croygen smirked. "Not that I would know anything about it."

"Sure," I replied while walking to the fridge. I yanked two bottles out and threw one to Croygen.

"Thanks." He twisted off the lid.

I did the same and gulped more than half before taking a breath. "I was thirsty... and now I'm hungry." I rubbed my belly.

"Yes. Food. Fantastic idea," a voice came from the bed.

Croygen set down his boots, pulling them back on his feet. "Why don't I go out and get some? We're probably all exhausted and want to stay in tonight. I'll go get us hamburgers at Pipi's. Kind of sick of Peruvian right now," he rambled, getting into his long velvet coat.

"What are you doing?" I asked. Croygen never did anything nice.

"Getting dinner." He grabbed the handle.

"You don't get dinner."

"No, but I'm not actually buying it, am I?" He winked and went out the door. I was tempted to follow him. What was he up to? *You have disappeared a lot lately.* Amara's words came back to me. I was out the door and down the stairs before I gave myself time to think. What was he doing, and where was he going when he left? He'd been too nice to me since I came back. His manner had changed toward me. The question was: why?

The breeze blasted against my face as I stepped outside, dry leaves crackled into tiny pieces, getting dust into my eyes. I glanced down the street. Croygen was nowhere in sight. Dammit. His magic of blending made it impossible to follow or spy on him.

A gust ran over me. It was a warm wind, but my arms still prickled with goose bumps. Intuition tugged at my gut. Something was off. I glanced down the street again in the direction of the restaurant where Croygen supposedly went. I wanted to go there and check for myself, but something kept my feet planted on the porch.

Between two buildings far down the walkway, the two little girls wearing my clothes from earlier were standing and talking to someone. They stood side by side, shaking their heads. The person they were conversing with was just out of my sight line, hidden by the buildings. It was mostly likely their parent or a friend, but I couldn't shake the unease running up my spine. I rubbed my arms and went back inside.

You should never doubt your instinct.

Ever.

TWENTY-FIVE

I climbed out of the shower, wrapping a towel around me. The cold water did nothing to wash away the earlier feeling of Ryker's body pressed into mine. Even the memory thumped my heart. I wanted him. Along with hot, unrelenting sex. Only a couple weeks ago he had given me an open invitation to join him in the shower, and I didn't go because I was too scared to follow him. I should have never let the opportunity go by. Fear was such a controlling emotion and held you back from doing things you really wanted. Now it was too late.

Stupid, Zoey.

Wind gushed past my ears. The room tipped.

Holy shit.

When I opened my eyes, I was in a bathroom, but no longer my own. Ryker's bare ass was pointing my way through the clear curtain. *Jump back, Zoey.* My body ignored my brain as I watched the soap glide down his back.

He stirred a hunger in me I could not deny, but one I could no longer act on. Desire overwhelmed me, gripped my muscles, and pooled below my stomach.

He turned, looking over his shoulder, and saw me

standing there. Watching him. He did not react, only stared back at me, our eyes locking. Water dripped in trails down his form, curving over every muscle before falling to the floor of the tub.

Suddenly I became aware of the small towel wrapped around my torso. It would be so easy. One tug and the towel would be on the ground... along with my resistance. Time stopped. Neither of us moved. The only sound was the infiltration of water pouring from the spout. And my heart thumping in my chest. If I moved, it would probably be to him. The fantasy of joining him in the shower, our bodies intertwined, clenched my lungs. He licked the water off his lips, his eyes not leaving mine.

"Ryker?" A knock tapped at the door, Amara's voice permeated from the other side of the door, causing me to jump. "You want me to come and join you?" Her tone was thick with innuendo. "Remember the time in Bruges when we broke the shower door?"

The stab of pain fought with the fear of her finding me in here. His eyes still drew me in, and I knew he saw the pain flash across my face before I could hide it. Emotion changed his features, but I couldn't make out what they meant.

I breathed deeply, shut my eyes, and imagined my own bathroom. The room vanished before me, then my feet were on my own tiled floor. The sink took my weight as I fell back onto it, shaking and holding my head. *Not embarrassing at all.* He probably figured I purposely went to him, hoping for a little side action. Looks like Amara had the same thought.

A few seconds later I heard the door to our room slam, and Amara stomped in, grumbling. A choked laugh hiccupped from my heart, filled with relief and sadness.

I wanted to be upset, but I couldn't. He was doing the right thing by keeping us at arm's length. He was respecting my decision. I simply didn't want him to.

From the bathroom window, a gush of air whistled through, blowing my wet hair off my shoulders. The lights overhead flickered then went out. Shadows grew around me in different variations of gray.

"Are you kidding me?" Amara spouted angrily in the next room. "Are we back in Seattle?"

"Does it look or feel like Seattle, Medusa?" Sprig replied.

"I wasn't talking to you, baboon."

"Oh, are your imaginary friends conversing with you again? I've heard crazy chicks who don't eat enough damage their brains and start hearing voices."

I sighed, knowing I should get out there before things got ugly. I got dressed and ran into the next room when I heard their voices rise higher.

"Hey," I yelled before I even got the bathroom door fully open. The sight in front of me had me biting on my lip to not laugh. Sprig stood on top of the television, stretched to his maximum height, his fists balled in the air. Amara stood in front of him, one hand on her hip; the other hand poked at his chest. They stared at me like they had been caught with their hands in the cookie jar. "Both of you stop it now."

"She started it!"

"This little shit started it!"

"Oh. My. God." I threw up my arms. "Really? How old are we?" My mother voice kicked in. "Sprig, you go out and see if you can find Croygen. He's supposed to be getting us dinner."

"But... but why do I have to go? It's yucky out there," Sprig whined. "She was the one—"

"Sprig! Now!" I pointed to the window.

He folded his arms, stuck his tongue out at me. "Fine," he snapped and hopped out the window, disappearing into the darkening evening. The open window blew the curtains toward the ceiling. I lowered them enough to break the wind, but still allow Sprig through.

"That thing is not natural." Amara shook her head. I peered over my shoulder at her, my lids half-mast in a glare. "What? It isn't."

I took in a deep breath, trying to keep myself from throwing her out the window after Sprig. I went over to the drawer I knew held candles, remembering the previous time the lights went out. It was the last time Ryker and I were together. Scenes of raw, passionate sex on the table, against the dresser, and on the bed came into my head. I instantly shoved them back and grabbed the last two candles, lighting them.

The room felt suffocating. I was about to lose it being in the room alone with Ryker's girlfriend, where I had done things with him I had never imagined possible. Ryker's entrance into the room only caused more tension to constrict my shoulders. Amara brightened, forgetting her agitation with Sprig and me. The candlelight turned her smile into a sexy expression as she watched him move across the room, putting his dirty clothes in our laundry bag.

Please, Sprig, Croygen, come back. The three of us

in a room together was torture.

"Croygen went out to get dinner," I spurted out, wanting to fill the empty gap in the conversation.

Ryker's eyebrows went up. "Croygen went to get dinner?"

"Yeah." Neither of us could look at the other. "About an hour ago."

Ryker snorted, then his jaw crunched together. "Like I trust..." Ryker's words tapered off as the door swung open, and Croygen walked in with an armful of takeaway boxes. Sprig rode on his shoulder, chirping excitedly.

"Dinner by candlelight. How romantic." He strolled into the room.

Holy shit. He really did get us food.

Ryker stood there with a bewildered expression on his face, which didn't go unnoticed by Croygen. "What? You didn't think I was coming back, did you?"

"Not with food." Ryker's voice held an icy tone.

"Where's the trust?"

"Not with you."

The moment Croygen set the bag down, Sprig's head was inside, grabbing for the closest item.

"Hold on." I pulled him back, but he batted at my hands.

"Need. Food. *Bhean*. Now." He wiggled, and I had to grab him with two hands.

Ryker stepped up, taking my place in handing out the burgers.

"Ryker..." I sighed and re-gripped the squirmy

monkey.

Without another word, Ryker handed me a couple of fries, which I immediately stuffed into Sprig's mouth. His struggles died away, his muscles relaxing under my hand. His eyes rolled back as he chewed on the fries. After handing everyone their containers of food, Ryker grabbed the bear full of honey and squirted a glob inside the top lid of my container, then divided my fries between the sides. I plopped Sprig on the table, near his share of the food.

He moved to scoop the honey with his hands. "No." I pointed at the fries. "You use those to dip in the honey, not your fingers."

"But *Bhean...*"

I tilted my head. He immediately picked up a fry and gingerly dipped it in the honey, watching me the whole time. I knew as soon as I turned my back he would go back in with his hands.

Ryker grabbed Sprig's wrist with his two fingers and pushed the monkey's hand into the puddle of sticky concoction. My mouth fell open, and I slowly turned my head toward Ryker. The corner of his mouth hitched in a grin. "You knew it was going to happen anyway."

"Yeah." I shrugged out a small chuckle, facing Sprig again. His face was pure bliss between licking his sugarcoated hand and eating a fry with the other.

Ryker still watched me out of the corner of his eye. Something flittered across his face but vanished as quickly as it came. Then his attitude flipped. Straightening his back, he cleared his throat and turned away from me, heading for the farthest point in the room.

It wasn't only me who felt the ice wall come down between us. Croygen's eyes darted back and forth between us, a slight crease between his eyebrows. Embarrassment and anger devoured me. My stomach told me it was starving, but I didn't taste anything as it was shoved in.

"Training didn't go as well as I wanted today, but we can't wait anymore." Ryker leaned against the wall. "It's time to plan and act."

"About fucking time," Croygen mumbled between bites.

"Seriously," Amara replied.

Even I agreed with them. I was tired of waiting. Good or bad, it was time to act.

Ryker scowled over at Amara and Croygen. "Zoey and I will go get the stone."

"What?" Amara stood up from the bed. "No. No way. We all go together!" she exclaimed, then sat back on her heels, taking a breath. I understood why Ryker wanted to separate us so we could pretend we were going after the stone, even though we didn't need to go anywhere. After all this time, he didn't trust them enough to tell the truth.

"We are still going to do this my way." Ryker tossed the empty food container onto the dresser. "It's safer for us to meet you two back here."

"Goddammit, Ryker!" Amara wailed. "When did you turn into this man? You used to go after what you wanted... nothing and no one held you back. You acted! You were ruthless... the fierce Wanderer. People feared you. Now all you do is sit and ponder. Talk about safety and danger. You've been here for months and done nothing. Where is the fae warrior I knew? Did he disappear along with your powers? Did she cut off your balls too?"

"Whoa." I stood up.

"Plus, I have been with you since the beginning of this, and *she* gets to go?" Amara put her hands on her hips.

"Zoey has to go; I can't jump anymore," Ryker growled. "I really don't want *anyone* to go."

Though our travel was only pretend, the dig still stung. Between the hurt and anger, I knew if I didn't get out of the room, I was going to snap. Fists were going to fly. Mine.

Amara's continued rants turned to background noise in my head, all I could hear was my own breath pumping in and out. My gaze locked on the flame of a candle, and I watched it sputter and fizzle out, leaving a single candle in the room.

Without a word I grabbed the flashlight off the table and was out of the room before anyone could react.

Would it be bad if I jumped? Leave this place and never came back? Find a new home?

That was the problem.

The only place that felt like home was where Ryker and Sprig were.

TWENTY-SIX

My footsteps reverberated as I crossed the dim, empty hallway. The howling wind tore through the mountains and wailed through any crack in the windows it could find.

The closet filled with candles, blankets, toilet paper, and other hospitality supplies was straight across from our room. I stepped into the walk-in storage room, the flashlight bouncing off the products on the shelves. For several minutes I scanned the shelves, searching for the candles, then I heard a slam of a door. Our door.

A deep huff came from the hallway, and I knew it was Ryker. Like me, he probably needed to flee Amara before he exploded.

Footsteps fell, echoing down the corridor.

Turning to the back wall, I focused on searching for the candles. My irritation still rode across my neck. The door clicked shut behind me, and I craned my head over my shoulder.

Ryker's outline filled the space. His white eyes glittering under the weak light. I exhaled and turned back around. "What do you want?" No response. "I think I can find candles by myself."

348

Again, he didn't say anything, but I heard him move to me, his boots hitting the wood floor. I stiffened as I felt his body behind mine.

I wanted to ask what he was doing. To tell him he better leave, but nothing came out of my throat. His hand grasped my elbow, sending electric shocks through me, and grabbed the flashlight from my hand, switching it off. The room went pitch black. The clank of the flashlight being placed on the shelf by my head rang in my ears.

"What are you doing?" I rasped out.

"Ruthlessly going after what I want," he whispered and moved in closer. My back still toward him, I sucked in a jagged gulp of air. We weren't touching, but his heat and energy felt like a thousand tiny fingers pressed against my skin. Without sight, my other senses fired up. My skin became extremely sensitive, feeling every molecule of him.

We stood there, tension crackling between us. He trailed his fingers along the backs of my arms. I squeezed my lids together. Even a slight touch from him shook my knees. Amara was right across the hall. Her warning earlier was not an empty threat. She would come after me.

"Stop. Someone might hear." My voice was barely above a whisper.

He responded by stepping flush with me, his body heat engulfing my back. I could no longer think straight, his alluring smell filling my nose and thoughts.

"Please." If he didn't stop touching me, I was going to be a puddle on the floor.

Ryker ignored my hollow pleas. The tips of his

fingers skimmed the tops of my shoulders before wrapping around my hair, brushing the loose strands over to one side of my neck, causing my heart to thump wildly in my chest. He leaned down, his lips grazing the back of my neck and kissing the sensitive area behind my ear. A soft whimper escaped my lips. He moved me to the wall, pressing me into the wood paneling, trapping me. His hands went to my thighs, skating up them and under my cotton shorts. His mouth barely touched as he skimmed over my shoulders and the base of my neck.

I could no longer fight him or try to be good. There was a strange feeling of being completely in the dark. Like it was safe. What happened here wasn't actually real.

My head went back, leaning into him. His breath trickled my neck as his hands roamed over my hips and back down my legs. I could feel him pressed against me. Hard and wanting.

The desire for him spun my head. I craved him. Inside.

I went to reach for him, but he stopped my hands. Twining our fingers together, he placed them on the wall in front of me. Without a word I knew he wanted me to keep them there. His fingers left mine and moved slowly over my body. My muscles shook as he traced every inch of my skin, moving beneath my clothes. The overabundance of yearning for him was hitting the point of no return, where he only had to touch me, and I would explode.

"Ryker," I whispered his name.

One hand trailed between my breasts as the other

found its way down my shorts. His fingers nudged at my underwear, pushing away the fabric. Air rushed through my teeth. Both his arms came around my waist, pulling my weight back into him. He prodded my legs to open more as his fingers found their way inside.

I moaned, and he nipped at my ear, hushing me. It was like a game—how quiet I could stay.

He gripped me harder as my knees almost gave out. His fingers found the spot and my teeth dove into my bottom lip, trying to prevent any noise from escaping.

My breath hitched as he moved quicker, building the friction. He took on my full weight, my muscles no longer able to hold me. I felt it coming, and I couldn't stop the low groan pumping out of my lungs. He vigorously moved inside me, his thumb working at the sensitive part. As I began to climax, he nipped his teeth into the curve of my shoulder, inflicting an exhilarating pain, heightening the peak. Everything shattered. His hand covered my mouth as a deep wail burst from me.

Holy shit.

Sex had always been my thing, not bothering too much with the foreplay. I knew guys wanted to get to it, and I let myself believe I did too.

Ryker changed that. He was mind-blowing. Not solely at sex, but all the before and after stuff. He had me all twisted up and turned my entire world around. In every aspect.

His chest went up and down in frantic gulps as if we had marathon sex. My back curved into his stomach, feeling him still hard against me. Sweat caused our shirts to cling together. I steadied my legs underneath me. He took a step back. The absence of him was instantaneous. I went to turn around, and he clutched my shoulders, pointing them back to the wall. In the dark I felt his lips on the base of my neck, between my shoulders, before he spun and walked out.

The moment he shut the door behind him, I fell against the wall, trying to regain myself.

What the hell just happened?

That was another thing I wasn't used to. Someone who wasn't about only getting himself off. He could have easily had sex with me and left. I would have done it willingly, but he didn't.

My hands covered my face as I tapped my forehead against the wall. *Well, that was hot as hell.* In the dark I could almost pretend it didn't really happen. A dream. I straightened my clothes, sucked in a deep breath, pushed back my shoulders, and went back to the room.

Ryker sat at the table and glanced at me as I entered. He quickly went back to eating with Sprig, acting like nothing happened.

Amara sat on the bed, and Croygen leaned against the far wall by the dresser, a strange gleam in his eyes. I dropped my gaze from him, feeling for some reason he could see right through me.

"So where are the candles?" Croygen's eyebrow quirked up.

My mouth dipped open. Fuck.

"You didn't get them?" Amara shook her head. "What the hell were you doing then?"

Uh...

"Really, Zoey. We send you to get *one* thing, and you get distracted." It was slight, but I saw Ryker's lips twitch with amusement as he shoved in another fry.

Meticulously licking his fingers.

Hell. The shit was taunting me.

"I apologize." My lids narrowed in on him. *Oh, it's on.*

"Think it will be faster if I go get them." Ryker stood, his shoulder brushing past me. My skin immediately reacted to his nearness. I was thinking of ideas of how I could leave without it being obvious, when Ryker turned. "Stay here."

"Where were we going to go? You won't let us go or do anything." Amara raised her arms.

It was meant for me. Damn.

Ryker shut the door. The candle flickered from the slight breeze.

"You all right, *Bhean*?" Sprig burped, rubbing his tummy. "You look twitchy."

"Funny." Croygen strolled across the room. "I thought she looked relaxed. Like someone who recently had sex."

My head jerked to Croygen. He winked.

Amara groaned, leaning back against the bedframe, oblivious to Croygen's underlying meaning. "Please don't talk about sex right now. It's been way too long." Amara's glare turned on me.

I excused myself and stomped to the bathroom, needing to hide from the room for a moment. When I returned Ryker was still gone, and Croygen was no longer in the room.

"Where did Croygen go?"

Amara glanced up from the magazine she was reading and shrugged. "He disappears all the time."

"Where does he go?"

"Why would I know?"

"You never followed him?"

She shook her head. "It's his business, not mine."

"Even if he's up to something? What if he's selling Ryker out? Don't think I haven't wondered how those jaguar shifters found us. Ryker doesn't trust him."

"Ryker doesn't trust anyone."

He trusts me, I wanted to blurt out. I was the only one in the room who knew the true whereabouts of the stone. It was hard not to shove this fact in Amara's face, but it was a secret I could not tell, especially out of petty jealousy.

"Sprig?" I turned to the furball on the table, surprised he was still vertical. "You want to come with me?"

"Where are you going?" Amara sat up.

"I am going to try and find him. If he's about to fuck us over, I want to know." I pulled a black long-sleeved shirt over my white tank and slipped into my boots.

"You really think you can find him?" Amara stood up, tailing me. "He can vanish in front of our faces, and you think you can track him?"

"I'm going to try." I could still see fae auras. I'd gotten lazy, grown so used to seeing them, I barely even noticed them anymore. I was cross with myself. Just because I was comfortable with fae, didn't mean I should let my skills go soft. Of all the people in here, I was the one who should see Croygen come and go. He was planning something. I could feel it in my gut, but my indolence let us be sitting ducks.

"You ready?" I asked Sprig.

"Aye, matty." He jumped on my shoulder. "Let's go capture a pirate."

"It's matey." I rubbed my head. "Never mind." He was never going to get it.

Amara sprang for me, grabbing my arm. "You are being a fool."

"Sounds about right." I tugged away from her and seized the doorknob. Did I think I would merely go outside and find Croygen? Not really, but if there was a chance, I would take it. I would protect what was mine. "And why would you care what I do?"

"I don't." Her nose wrinkled. "But you know Ryker would not want you to go."

"You going to tattle on me?"

Spitefulness curled her mouth.

I mirrored her grin. "Have fun finding me." I jumped from my spot and reappeared in the alley where Ryker and I made out.

"I think I'm gonna be sick." Sprig clung to my neck.

"Sorry." I hadn't planned to jump. For a long time I either couldn't control it or I limited my use of the magic, so I kept forgetting it was another available travel option.

I slunk to the opening of the passageway. The streets were mostly empty; only a few hard-core people ventured to and fro. Electricity was out through the village, and most shops and cafés had closed early. The wind howled down the dark street, whipping at the telephone wires, swinging them like giant jump ropes.

Sprig huddled close into my neck, hiding from the onslaught of air blowing my hair around. My skin prickled with apprehension as I slipped through the dark town. The same feeling from earlier was growing, unsettling me, my attention on alert to everything moving or tumbling down the streets.

Sprig kept quiet but clicked his tongue continuously. If his nails clinging to my neck or the fact he hadn't mentioned food once were any indication, he felt the same unnerving energy mounting. With the storm brewing around me, it took me back to the night in Seattle when all our lives changed forever. The same niggling swirled in my gut. Had I listened to it then, Daniel might still be alive.

This reasoning should have turned my ass right around, but it didn't. Curiosity compelled me past reason or welfare. I wouldn't confront Croygen; I wasn't *that* stupid. *I only want to see what he is doing then jump back and tell Ryker*, I reasoned, knowing I would never have turned around, no matter what I had told myself.

The silence in the village only swelled the flourish of nerves bundling in my stomach. My boots cautiously stepped forward, keeping to the darkest shadows. Far at the edge of town, my eyes caught a glow. Several different fae auras circled the edge of the forest. Fae were everywhere around here, but instinct told me not all were trolls or water fairies.

Croygen was one of them.

I edged down, slinking along a fence, trying to get closer to see the group better.

Baaamm!

Something hit the fence where I crouched, and a choked cry stuck in my throat. A low-pitched shrieking of a cat made me leap from my hiding place. I vaulted away as claws swiped at the animal on my shoulder.

"Holy dingleberry nuggets!" Sprig moved in closer to me, his free hand batting back at the feline. Sprig was three times smaller than the normal monkeys around here. More like a mouse, or maybe a rat. He would make a perfect meal for a cat. "Stay back, you Chinese takeout dish."

I clutched my chest, regaining my breath. Then I glanced over my shoulder, searching the location for where the fae had gathered. The spot was empty.

"Dammit," I muttered.

Sprig hissed back at the growling cat. I kicked the fence, sending the tabby running.

"Yeah, run like a pussy," Sprig called after the animal. "Scaredy cat!"

"Sprig!"

"What? Come on. That was funny. I can tell you want to laugh." He poked at the side of my mouth, trying to raise my lip. After a while I couldn't help but smile. "See? I knew it. What would you do without me?"

"I don't know." I honestly didn't anymore. Life without Sprig was inconceivable. He had weaseled into my heart and become my buddy. My best friend. I rubbed his head and turned around to head back home.

My curiosity had ended at the edge of town. The fae controlled the forests at night; things were out there I probably never heard of. I wasn't going to let my snooping convert me into a blatant idiot. Too many things out there would look at *me* like Chinese takeaway.

Hoping to spot Croygen again, I didn't jump, but

wandered back through town. As I drifted across the bridge, the unsettled feeling didn't ebb, sparking at the hairs at the back of my neck. Sprig stirred under my hair.

"You feel it too?"

"Yeah, *Bhean*. There's a lot of magic out here tonight."

Two streets away from our building I spotted a cluster of glowing auras. Warning bells shrilled inside my head. This was double the group I saw at the edge of town.

"What?" Sprig must have sensed the tension tighten my body.

"The group there. They are all fae."

"Can you see who they are?"

"No. Not this far away," I whispered back and pointed. "I'm going to get a little closer by jumping to the alley over there, okay?"

Sprig wrapped his arms around my neck in response.

I closed my eyes and jumped. We slammed into a garbage can and tumbled to the ground, splaying across the lane. The shrill sound of metal clanging echoed down the alleyway.

Fuck!

I scrambled back up. The instinct to jump home before we were caught took hold, but I stopped myself.

Sprig!

I scanned fervently for the little sprite. My eyes latched on to a lump of fur at the entrance of the alley. He was out cold. The shock of our landing probably kicked in his condition. My feet leaped over a crate, heading for my friend. I reached down to grab Sprig, but another pair of hands snatched him first.

My head jerked up, eyes landing on a beautiful fair-haired fae. His eyes glinted as they looked back into mine.

It felt like my chest collapsed, sending an avalanche into my legs.

"You should keep your pets on a leash." He held Sprig by the neck. "So they can't get away from you."

"Maxen," I uttered his name, more in trying to believe he was in front of me than confirming who he was.

"You remember me?" Maxen grinned. "But really, *I am* hard to forget."

Maxen's presence meant Garrett was here too, and they all led back to Vadik. I wanted to jump, to get away from Maxen, to warn Ryker. But I couldn't leave Sprig. They would not hesitate to kill him. To most fae he was unnatural and wrong. My presence kept him alive, and I could never abandon him. He was my family.

"You killed my partner." My teeth clenched together.

"Right." He nodded, his eyes sparking with pleasure. "Good times." He took a step, his finger pressing on Sprig's throat. "How about we keep up the tradition."

"Stop!" I yelled. "Don't hurt him. You want me. Take me, but leave him out of this."

"See, that's the thing. We don't really want you either. You are merely leverage." Maxen shook Sprig. His little body swung limply. "Just like this thing."

A noise came from the far end of the opposite alley

entrance, and I swung around to see more fae blocking my way. One pushed his way in front and strolled down the alley to me. His red hair and beard shone bright enough to make out in the darkness. A large dark-haired fae walked next to him, his gun pointed at my head. I recognized him from the night of the storm. The one who grabbed Amara.

"Zoey. May I call you that?" Garrett feigned politeness. His man came beside me and pressed the weapon to my temple. "I feel a bond with you now. Like a long-lost *sister*."

It was how he had searched for me in Seattle. Showing people my picture and telling them I was his sister. Using his Irish charm and fae glamour, he seduced people into telling him anything they knew. I was almost caught the night at the Red Cross by this tactic.

"This is how you treat a sister?" I lifted my eyes to the gun.

Garrett shrugged. "I'm an only child."

"And I killed *my* brothers," said the fae holding the gun to my head.

"Yes, Cadoc dispatched his siblings. Guess we're not good with family relations." Garrett walked around me. "Now tell me, *Zoey*. Where is the Wanderer?"

I pressed my lips together, folding my arms in defiance.

"You really want to play it this way?" Garrett got within an inch of my face. "We will find him no matter what, especially when he hears your screams. It's up to you if you want to be tortured first."

The threat of being beaten did not affect me like it

would others. Besides street fighting, I had experienced my fair share of being tied and beaten by a few foster parents. Getting hit was not enough to scare me into leaving Sprig or caving in about Ryker's whereabouts.

I gave Garrett a slow sneer.

I was ready for the hit and about to jump a couple feet back. I wasn't going to leave Sprig, but I also wasn't going to make it easy for Garrett. He was a slight man, and only a few inches taller than me. The other fae were his muscle, but Garrett was the brains, the leader. Before I could move, his hand cracked across my face. His speed shocked me and so did the intensity of the blow.

I flew into Cadoc, the barrel of his gun slipping and ramming into my eye. Cadoc pushed me off him with disgust and clubbed the back of my head with the pistol, taking me to my knees with a grunt. I could feel warm blood seep along the back of my neck.

My brain scrambled as I tried to get myself to concentrate. "Keep a hand on her at all times in case she tries to jump," Garrett said to Cadoc. One hand landed on my neck as a fist collided with my face with such force I went flying again. I could tell this time the punches were packed with magic. The impact seeped into my skin, slicing through my muscles, creating a burning pain deep in my tissues, causing every nerve to spasm. Logic and focus dashed away under the dizziness of the agony. My head was yanked by my hair. My eyesight went spotty.

"I don't like hitting girls, Zoey, but I've seen you fight. I know your kind. This is the only way you know how to communicate, to understand I mean business." Garrett's green eyes flamed with anger. His voice sounded like he was in a well... or I was. "I am tired of playing these games with you and Ryker. I am getting what I came for this time."

I didn't feel him hit me again, but I felt the back of my head hit the pavement before I blacked out.

TWENTY-SEVEN

"Ryker! Come out. We got your human."

I lifted my aching neck as consciousness slowly seeped back to me. I felt two pairs of hands clutching my sides, holding me upright. Throbbing pain in my face and the back of my head cracked my lids open. We now stood in the middle of the unlit main drag. The glow from the moon from behind the clouds casted a silvery gleam. Garrett's arms were out as he circled, his thick Irish accent rolled out into the wind. I struggled trying to understand what was going on. Garrett's dozen men filled the street, all armed with swords and knives. I shifted my gaze to my left then right. Cadoc was on one side of me, and another huge fae on the other. Maxen and Sprig were not in my line of sight. My worry for Sprig overrode my desire to getaway. Not that I really could. With fae hands on me, there was no point in jumping, they would only come with me.

"Come on, Wanderer. You spineless motherfucker!" Garrett yelled. "You want your human to take your punishment for you? I shouldn't be surprised. You did with Amara. What kind of man does that make you?"

Not one person looked out of their windows at the commotion occurring in the street. Either they were extremely afraid, or Garrett was glamouring us from human eyes, the latter being the most likely. It seemed strange this could be happening right in front of humans and they would have no idea.

"I know you hear me," Garrett bellowed, walking backward to me. "If you don't come out now, I will start cutting." Garrett drew out a long, scary-ass dagger. The metal had a greenish tinge, which made my belly tighten. Seers could tell the difference between an earth-made weapon and a fae one. Their weapons had auras. The green tint told me it was the highest of fae-metal. Goblin made. Goblin metal was the most powerful and the most poisonous if it got into your system. The pointy end would kill a human, but the toxic metal was what destroyed fae. I was both. "I'll start with little slices along her wrists, next her neck, then maybe I'll take an ear or finger."

"If. You. Touch. Her. I will gut you and hang you by your intestines." A deep voice came out of the dark, and the enormous outline of a man stepped from the shadows with a battle axe in hand.

Even I sucked in a breath seeing Ryker standing there. I had seen him angry before, even livid. Here he was way beyond both. His form seemed double the size, wrath swelling his chest and shoulders. His white-blue eyes were so bright, the blaze reflected on his cheeks. He took a step, vibrating the ground.

"Ever hear of the Nordic Blood Eagle, Garrett? If you lay a hand on her, I will rip out your lungs and throw them over your shoulder. You can watch your lungs take their last breath."

Garrett didn't flinch as Ryker approached, though some of Garrett's men did. I'd grown accustomed to Ryker. But this fae, the true Wanderer who stood in front of us? *Holy. Shit.* He was frightening. Even when he hated me, he never showed this side. I would have peed my pants, huddled in a ball, and cried. If I'd known he could be like this, I wouldn't have taunted and messed with him as much as I did.

"Back down, Wanderer. You might be able to kill us, but not before I could slice her head off. Let's keep your temper in check." Garrett inched the blade up my neck.

Ryker blinked; his eyes locked on the knife. Then slowly his gaze moved to me, taking in my bruised and puffy face. His jaw twitched as his teeth ground together.

"I'm fine," I said softly. I didn't know if it was the truth, but in my gut I knew he needed to hear me say it. He was only seeing red, and the bloodshed would be bad if he made a move. I didn't doubt Garrett would make a point and take my head off if Ryker made a move.

"Throw your axe down." Garrett nodded to Ryker's hands. Ryker rolled his jaw, gripping the handle harder.

"Do it, Ryker." Amara stepped out, touching Ryker's arm. He jerked, almost like he was going to swing it at her but caught himself.

Garrett shook his head and snorted at seeing Amara walk up. "Oh, Amara, I've missed you. Been lonely at the house without you."

She glared at Garrett. "No one else to harass?"

His green eyes sparked. "Not one I enjoyed as much

as you." There was a strange tone to his words, like there was a hidden meaning only they understood.

A low growl emanated from Ryker.

Amara pushed at Ryker's hand, lowering the axe. "Just do what he says." Amara directed her head to me, implying without words whose life was being threatened.

"Let me give you some motivation." Garrett moved the tip of the blade over my chest. Blood gathered along the thin line he cut. Goblin metal felt like a thousand hot coals being shoved inside your wound. I groaned in pain and sucked in at the sharp sting, my eyes watering as I held my tongue.

Ryker's axe hit the ground, ringing on the brick-lined road.

"That's better. Now I feel we can have a civilized conversation." Garrett's knife moved to my neck.

"You don't think I couldn't kill you with my bare hands?" Ryker rolled his fingers into balls.

"You're right." Garrett nodded and men from all directions lunged at Ryker. He reacted, his fist knocking back the first two men.

"Ryker, stop!" Amara screamed as a few fae grabbed her, pulling her back. Ryker ignored her, continuing to fight the throng of men. A few got close enough to carve at his arms with their knives. He roared as the goblin knives sliced his skin.

Pain exploded at the side of my neck, and I screamed out involuntarily.

Ryker froze.

"I will cut the artery next if you don't behave. Your actions will be what kills her."

Ryker snarled but didn't move. Eight men with fae-welded blades surrounded him, pushing him to his knees.

"Good work, Garrett," a low voice cut through the air, stopping everyone. A tall, broad-shouldered man stepped from the darkness. Every inch of him screamed cold, powerful, and commanding. There was something about him I instantly feared, but it was the man's aura that iced the blood in my veins.

He was a demon.

There were as many types of demons as there were fae, most exceedingly unpleasant. The most dangerous types of demons were the ones with yellow eyes. He was not one of those. Thank goodness. From his aura I couldn't tell what type he was.

He was striking. Handsome, intriguing, and intimidating with his sharp, chiseled features. He appeared to be in his early forties, but was probably centuries old. Dressed in a dark suit, the man's hair was so blond it almost was white. The sides were cut short and the top was smoothed back. His eyes were so dark navy blue they almost appeared black, blending in with his pupils.

Vadik. I somehow knew it without needing any confirmation. When he glanced at me chills ran up my arms. I could sense the ruthlessness in him. There was something cruel and calculating in his eyes.

Ryker stared at him; his fury replaced with apprehension. This was bad. Very, very bad.

"Sir." Garrett gave Vadik a nod. Vadik strolled casually by Ryker, Amara, and me.

"What is that?" Vadik pointed behind me. Maxen walked into my peripheral, a sleeping monkey hanging from his hands. Sprig. Seeing his chest rising and falling sent relief through me. He was still alive.

"It's their *pet*." Maxen snarled at the unconscious monkey.

"Oh, right. The manufactured creature." Vadik lip rose in disgust. "Kill it."

"No!" I screamed, pulling against my capturer's hold.

Vadik tilted his head, finally really taking me in. "I thought your kind hated fae. Wanted us all dead or a lab experiment like this thing."

"Don't hurt him."

Vadik shoved one of his hands into his slacks, the other one rubbing at his chin. "Much has changed for you, hasn't it, Collector?" He was letting me know he had done his research. He knew who I was.

"Clever to dye your hair. From afar, you'd confuse and dissuade your enemy from engaging you, believing the rumors they heard were false." Vadik walked to me, taking the tips of my hair between his fingers. "Unfortunately, this disguise would only work on the incredibly inane."

There was no doubt he was the most dangerous fae here. Power and magic oozed off him. I wanted to get us out of here, to jump to Ryker and Sprig, but the fae's hands on my arms kept me in place.

The feel of Ryker's gaze focused my sight on him. The nod of his head to the side was so slight I almost missed it, but I couldn't mistake the way his eyes drilled into me, screaming, *Don't do anything stupid.*

Vadik's large frame moved gracefully toward Ryker. "Give me the stone."

Ryker sneered while his eyes flashed. "I don't have it."

"You might fool others, but I know you. Better than you think. I've studied you for years. It was the reason I hired you." Vadik's studying gaze drifted over the Viking. "But I am far smarter than you, Wanderer. And there is a reason people fear me. I always get what I want. You can choose how this happens and how painfully."

Ryker kept his face unreadable.

Vadik nodded to Garrett and his blade cut across my chest again. My legs gave out as the agony from the blade seared my skin. A cry sprang from my lips.

"Stop!" Ryker shouted. "Deal with me. Leave her out of this."

"I will deal with you, but I never said the pain would be yours." Vadik curved around, taking in the figure being held next to Ryker. He smirked and sauntered over to Amara, gripping her face between his fingers. "I will make those you care about pay for your obstinacy." His words were meant for Ryker, but his attention was completely on Amara.

"Let me go," Amara seethed at Vadik. There was no fear in her eyes, only irritation.

"Why?" Vadik pinched her chin firmer. "I am not pleased with you at all right now."

Amara's lids tapered with annoyance, but she didn't pull from his grip.

"You kept a lot from me, Amara." He pulled her face closer to him. "You really thought going against me was a wise decision?"

"I didn't go against you."

"You left. Destroyed my compound. Killed some of my men in the process."

"So I'm being punished?" She tore her face from his hand.

"Yes. No one goes against me, *including* you."

"You wouldn't listen to me. I did what I had to do." Indignation flamed her brown eyes. "If you let me do it the way I wanted from the beginning, you would have had it by now."

Like fog rolling over a mountain, realization of the scene taking place crept over me, sinking to the pit of my stomach.

Vadik moved close to her. "I think we both should admit I sent in the wrong girl." Amara flinched at his words. "I think this *human* would have done a better job in her sleep."

"No! She wouldn't have." Amara pulled against the men holding her. "Taking me hostage last time was your mistake. You thought it would invoke him to act. I told you it wouldn't, but you didn't listen to me. Don't turn this around on me now. By the time I came back, this human had burrowed in. It was going to take time to regain his trust again."

"Well, I've grown impatient waiting."

"You've been waiting for thousands of years. What were a few more months?"

"What. Is. Going. On. Amara?" Ryker's voice was low and rough, his gaze slicing between them.

Her gaze fluttered over to Ryker, then reverted to Vadik. "Let. Me. Go. Now."

Vadik sighed then nodded to the men behind her who released her arms from their hold.

She rubbed at her biceps with irritation. "Was that necessary?"

Vadik seized her neck. "I thought you liked it rough?" He pulled her in, aligning their bodies, his gaze becoming primal. Amara's lips frowned, but a glint of excitement and desire flickered in her eyes.

Bile slithered up my esophagus. There was obviously more than employee/employer relationship here. I felt sick.

Ryker was like a statue as he watched the woman he thought cared about him flirting with his enemy. I couldn't imagine the betrayal he felt. "How long?" he asked.

Vadik moved away from Amara, strolling over to Ryker. "From the beginning. She was always mine. *I* sent her to seduce you, to learn you... find where you hid the stone after you vanished with it. From the moment you met her in Romania, she was playing you."

Did Vadik let his lover fuck someone else because his desire for the stone was greater than her? And she willingly did it? Something about the way Garrett shifted next to me with irritation also told me there was a lot more going on there. Was she with him too?

The relationship fae had toward sex was different from what humans thought of it, but still... It felt wrong in many ways. And mainly because she had messed with Ryker.

"It was all a lie? Your escape? Is Croygen in on this also?" Ryker's asked.

Amara brushed her hair out of her face. "The best lies are rooted in truth. Everything I told you about my breakout was technically true. Two things made Croygen the perfect person: his unwavering love for me and his connection to you. I knew he was probably the only person in the world who would be able to find you because of his link to you.

"We made sure Croygen heard about my capture, and as I knew he would, he came running. I couldn't make it too easy for him or his crew to get me out, but there was no question he was going to. He bought the lie as easily as you did."

"You told him our whereabouts?" Ryker's said through his teeth. "Why did you wait till now?"

"Amara didn't tell me." Vadik shot her a look before his attention came over to me. "It was your human who led us here."

"What?" Ryker and I said at the same time.

"Your appearance in Seattle. Face splashed all over town on underground fighting posters, gave us an exact date and time. You provided the perfect opportunity."

Ryker's eyes flashed to me.

"But I-I got away. You didn't get anything from me."

Maxen snickered.

Vadik faced me with a gratified grin. "You may have gotten away unscathed, but your clothes didn't. Maxen was able to plant a tracking sticker on your top before you disappeared."

"A what?" My stomach sank at the memory of Maxen's hand pressing onto my shoulder before I slipped into the crowd and disappeared.

"A minuscule, clear sticker you would never notice unless you were looking for it." Vadik folded his arms over his barreled chest. The earlier scene clicked in my head: the two little girls conversing with someone I couldn't see; one of Vadik's men trying to find the true owner of the clothing. "And you also provided the truth to the rumors I heard but were not confirmed." Vadik frowned at Amara. She looked at the ground, dodging his accusatory stares. As an employee and mistress, she still had kept a lot from him. "A *human* procuring a fae's powers from them... instinct wants me to kill you right here."

Ryker leaned forward, dragging some of his captors with him. Vadik's hand halted the Viking, his attention still on me. "Your very existence is a threat to fae. Not only are you a seer who worked for DMG, but you should not be alive or able to contain a fae's powers. It's unnatural, and you should be terminated." Vadik stepped within an inch of me, leaning into my face. "I would love for your blood to water the earth under my feet. But you are more valuable alive than dead. For the moment anyway." His voice went to a low threatening whisper. "If you even think about jumping, I *will* slice both your lover's and your pet's throats before you can even close your eyes."

Maxen held up Sprig. The monkey was awake, his claws scratching at Maxen's fingers as the fae pinched down on Sprig's neck.

"Stop it!" I jerked forward, feeling the knife dig into my skin. "Leave him alone."

Maxen loosened his grip. The sound of Sprig choking and gasping for air tore me in half as a small whimper hummed from my chest.

"Then I would do the wise thing and keep still. Even with powers you are still a human to me and easily disregarded. Garrett is exceptionally quick with a blade." For emphasis Garrett pressed the sharp metal into my throat. Blood slipped over the metal down to my top. My stomach already coiled with nausea. The toxins slowing down my system made me feel feverish and weak. The two men on either side of me gripped me tighter as the contaminants seeped into my blood stream. "I am curious to see how quickly the goblin magic will affect you and how slow and agonizing your death will be."

A loud snarl came from Ryker. His neck muscles vibrated with tension. "If you want me to do anything, you will let her go." Vadik stepped away from me, a gratified smirk on his mouth. "Like you said, she is human and has nothing you need. Let her go first, and then we can talk."

What the hell was he thinking? Once again, Ryker was putting up the stone for me?

Vadik arched his frame toward Ryker. "I knew I picked the wrong girl. Who would have ever thought a human girl would captivate you so much?" The way Vadik's top lip curved over his white teeth was more threatening than the knife in my throat. "I guess I should not be surprised with your upbringing you would have a weakness for humans."

"This is between us. She has nothing to do with this."

Vadik sauntered over to Ryker's kneeling form. "The human might have no value *to me*, but she stays where she is."

No value? Ouch.

"Then you will *never* get the stone." Spit flew out of Ryker's mouth.

Vadik nodded at Garrett. His hand crushed down on my throat, the knife nicking at my vocals, forcing a gasp out of me. Ryker lunged forward, bellowing with anger. The men around him sliced their knives into his arms and neck in shallow cuts. Veins in Ryker's neck pushed against the skin. His lids inched down as his system took in more poison.

"No. Stop." I shook my head, requesting him to end his struggle. If either one of us were doused with any more, we would be useless. I knew from my years of being a Collector how much goblin metal a fae could handle before going into a coma-like state. Ryker's neck, shoulders, and arms were already dripping with blood from the blade wounds. I would be affected even faster.

Our fight was over. We lost.

We stared across the dark space at each other, the wind howling around us. Defeat shown in our eyes as we stared at each other. For one moment it was simply him and me. It was then I realized I did love him— hopelessly.

For so long, I didn't want to, thinking I was betraying Daniel. He was gone, and I knew Daniel would want me happy. No matter who it was. Fae or human.

My love for Daniel was the past. Ryker was who I wanted in my future, except we would probably never have one.

"I respect your tenacity. But I told you, I get what I

want in the end." Vadik studied Ryker with an intent interest. "And whatever leverage I have to use, I will." He clicked his tongue. "Believe me, you will wish I simply killed your human right here. She will too. Because there are far bigger plans destined for her."

Bigger plans?

"What are you talking about?" Ryker's eyes flashed with fury.

Vadik smiled and flicked his arm, motioning to Garrett once again. Cadoc and the other fae holding me up pushed into me, seizing me tighter so I couldn't even wiggle.

"This is the part I've been waiting for all day. The irony shouldn't be lost on you," Garrett whispered into my ear. Ryker thrashed against his captives' holds as he watched Garrett move something toward me.

A cloth came over my face. A slightly sweet but sharp smell clogged my nose.

Chloroform.

Hell.

The exact compound we used on fae when we collected them for DMG.

I twisted my head, but Garrett smashed the fabric into my face, covering my nose and mouth. The substance trickled down my throat as I gasped for air.

I wiggled free of Garrett's hand, my blurring vision finding Ryker. "Promise me." The drug already slurred my words.

Ryker's eyes widened, understanding my meaning. "No."

"*Promise* me."

"Promise her what?" Vadik glanced between us.

Ryker and I ignored him. Our eyes fastened on each other. Finally he nodded, keeping his expression guarded. "I promise."

His words hit me like a weight, crushing me.

"Shut up." Garrett's rag found my mouth again, the chemical scratching my throat and watering my eyes as it moved down into my lungs.

My neck fell to the side, no longer able to hold my head up. Muscles bent under the influence of the drug. My eyes rolled past the men standing to my one side, landing on a murky alley behind them. Two dark eyes sparkled through the blackness, spearing me. I blinked, trying to stay focused on the shape. I was the only one who noticed him. Lightness captured my mind, making it harder to know what was real and what wasn't. The figure took a step, his sharp features and almond-shaped eyes becoming clearer through the shadows.

Croygen.

Our eyes latched on to each other before he gave me a slight nod and drifted farther into the shadows, vanishing from sight and becoming a part of his surroundings.

Croygen. My mouth tried to call for him, but nothing came out.

Of course he would leave us. He was a pirate. Only out for himself.

Yo-ho...

Darkness seeped into my sight, my body no longer able to fight, the tune humming in my mind drifted me toward my own Neverland.

"Zoey!" Ryker cried out for me, sounding far away,

almost like I was being called from a different time and space.

I tried to turn my head, to look over at him, but each eyelash weighted my lids down. My legs bowed as lethargy ripped me quickly from the world. Arms encircled me, holding my body up.

Don't fall asleep. I thrashed my head back and forth, fighting the inevitable. I struggled to keep simple thoughts from muddling my mind. My body no longer could support me and went limp. Cadoc's arms turned into a dark twisted spirit in my mind, pulling me under the soil, dragging me to the obscure depths of the earth.

No.

Inside my head I grasped frantically for something to hold on to, to keep conscious. But everything I struggled for turned to smoke, evaporating in my mind.

Noooooooooooo. I felt myself fall, slipping away into the void.

TWENTY-EIGHT

The deep, murky black swirled, lighting into gray overcast. My limbs and mind were weighed down, forcing me to struggle through the sludge, hauling myself into consciousness. A rhythmic beep continuously broke into my peace, dragging me out of nothingness, and away from the place where nothing hurt and nothing was wrong.

Beep... Beep.

The sound rubbed at my eardrum, grating on my nerves. I felt my forehead pinch in irritation. A stab of pain darted between my eyes, and an involuntary groan fell from my mouth, startling me out of my slumber. My lids blinked, immediately blinded by light. Another moan came out from my throat as I pried my eyes open again. Slowly, my sight adjusted to the brightness, taking in the off-white paneled ceiling. A zigzag pattern displayed on the heart monitor next to my head. The smell of rubbing alcohol and chemicals saturated the inside on my nose, coating my throat.

I know this place... but my mind felt too jumbled to make sense of the warning flickering through me.

Beep. Beep. Beep.

Memories seeped into my mind, recalling my situation before the drug had stolen my consciousness. Vadik. Amara. Garrett. Sprig...

Ryker! The Viking slammed into my head, and I tried to sit up, but my body disregarded the impulse. *Where was he? Was he safe?*

Was I?

Anxiety pulsed into my veins, pumping my heart faster.

Beepbeepbeepbeep.

A hand came up and flicked off the monitor. Peaceful silence. "You are awake." A figure moved in front of the light above my head, the outline of a man. I squinted, blinking until familiar blue eyes peered down at me.

No. This can't be happening.

Dr. Boris Rapava nodded his head; his face held no warmth or friendliness. "Welcome *home*, Zoey." His eyes held a glimmer of excitement I had seen in him when we brought in unique specimens. "You've been out for weeks. There is much to catch up on."

Panic choked off my air.

Home? Weeks?

Not home! I wasn't *home*. But I *was* back in the place where I was created.

With the man who gave me life...

And could take it away.

Thank you to all my readers. Your opinion really matters to me and helps others decide if they want to purchase my book. If you enjoyed this book, please consider leaving an honest review on the site where you purchased it. Thank you.

Want to find out about my next book? Sign up on my website and keep updated on the latest news.

www.staceymariebrown.com

Across the Divide (Collectors Series #3)

The Avenging Angel has fallen...

Waking up inside DMG, Zoey is no longer an employee, but a prisoner. A testing subject to Dr. Rapava's sick experiments and torture, forced to play the brainwashed, fae-hating collector to survive.

Deep inside the labs, she finds more secrets and horrors of Dr. Rapava's depravity, only enduring because of her honey-addicted buddy, Sprig, and the sexy pirate, Croygen.

Ryker has been taken by Vadik, locked up, and tortured for one of the most powerful objects in the world—the Stone of Fál. An object that wants to find its way back to Zoey as much as Ryker does.

Both don't want to just find her. They want to kill her.

Turning himself over to Dr. Rapava to get closer to her, Ryker fights the impulse to both protect and destroy her at every turn.

Though, it is Zoey who is forced into the cruelest sacrifice—killing someone she loves to keep another alive.

But it might be her life that is taken in the end.

BOOK 3 AVAILABLE NOW!

Acknowledgements

I can't believe how lucky I am to do what I love for a living. I feel so blessed and I couldn't do it without some amazing people.

To Rachel at Mark My Words P.R.: So lucky to have you. Could not do this without you!

To Jordan: Your developmental help and editing are crucial to me. Your insights have made me a better writer. Thank you!

To Hollie: How I adore you...let me count the ways! You are incredible. Told you once you there is no getting rid of me now! http://www.hollietheeditor.com/.

To Judi at www.formatting4u.com/: Thank you! You have made the stress of getting my books out on time so much easier.

To all the bloggers who have supported me: My gratitude is for all you do and how much you help indie authors out of the pure love of reading. I bow down. You all are amazing! My Street Team for being awesome and so supportive, thank you.

To all the indie/hybrid authors out there who inspire, challenge, support, and push me to be better: I love you!

And to anyone who has picked up an indie book and given an unknown author a chance. THANK YOU!

About The Author

Stacey Marie Brown is a lover of hot fictional bad boys and sarcastic heroines who kick butt. She also enjoys books, travel, TV shows, hiking, writing, design, and archery. Stacey swears she is part gypsy, being lucky enough to live and travel all over the world.

She grew up in Northern California, where she ran around on her family's farm, raising animals, riding horses, playing flashlight tag, and turning hay bales into cool forts. She volunteers helping animals and is Eco-friendly. She feels all animals, people, and environment should be treated kindly.

To learn more about Stacey or her books, visit her at:

Author website & Newsletter:
www.staceymariebrown.com

Facebook Author page:
www.facebook.com/SMBauthorpage

Pinterest: www.pinterest.com/s.mariebrown

Instagram: www.instagram.com/staceymariebrown/

TikTok:
https://www.tiktok.com/@staceymariebrown

Amazon page: www.amazon.com/Stacey-Marie-Brown/e/B00BFWHB9U

Goodreads:
www.goodreads.com/author/show/6938728.Stacey_Marie_Brown

Her Facebook group:
www.facebook.com/groups/1648368945376239/

Bookbub: www.bookbub.com/authors/stacey-marie-brown